HAIL MARY

HOPE ANIKA

978-1-7362553-0-8
Copyright © 2020 by Hope McKenzie

All rights reserved.

No part of this book may be reproduced in any form or by any electronic or mechanical means, including information storage and retrieval systems, without written permission from the author, except for the use of brief quotations in a book review.

Even cowards can endure hardship; only the brave can endure suspense.

> MIGNON MCLAUGHLIN

>

PROLOGUE

IN THE BEGINNING, the dream is always good.

Her hand gripping his; her scent filling his head. Her smile. Anticipation and joy for the night to come.

Them, together.

As it should have always been.

The evening is balmy; humid and fragrant. The electric pulse of club music ripples toward them on a salty breeze. To the west, the sun is sinking in a ball of fiery orange-red, streaked by brilliant strands of pink and gold. Palm fronds dance where the pavement gives way to pale white sand, whispering as the wind strokes through them.

He can taste chocolate and hops; his belly is full, his wife is laughing, and life...

Life is fucking good.

The tingle whispers across his nape as they cross the street; slight, probably nothing. He ignores the flash of awareness that immediately follows.

Because no one would dare take him. Not here.

Not now.

The Jeep's door sticks when he opens it for her.

Unusual but not surprising; it's an old Jeep. A creak as he closes it, and he makes a mental note to oil the hinges.

Seagulls watch as he circles the front of the Jeep, and the tingle hardens to a bristle; the fine hair that covers his frame stands abruptly to attention. He hesitates. And then his wife smiles at him through the glass, and he discounts the flicker of unease, intent on the invitation she emanates.

Arrogant and thoughtless and fucking stupid. So many signs—

He smiles back, and the dream tears like a worn piece of paper; he shimmers into ghostly being, a handful of feet from his fate. Even knowing the words are futile, he begins to scream.

Stop. Stop! Get her out. Don't go forward—go back.

Go the hell back!

It's wrong—all wrong—you saw the signs, pay attention, know—KNOW—don't open that goddamn door—

The Jeep's handle is warm from the fading sun; he thinks nothing of taking it in hand. Of pulling open the door of the vehicle that will take him home, where he will pull his lovely wife beneath him and—

Click.

The explosion is instant, ignition so quick there is nothing but sound—a deafening blast and a shock wave so violent it shatters bone. His eardrums perforate; her scream is soundless as he is launched like a rocket across space and time only to crash abruptly back to earth, his body bouncing over the unforgiving concrete like a stone skipping across water. His ears ring; his head throbs. Blood fills his mouth.

Debris pelts him as he skids to a stop; smoke clogs his throat. Her face is burned into his mind's eye; that brief, horrific instant of realization. And then...*flames*. Eating her up.

He rolls over, his heart ready to burst, adrenaline like acid in his blood. Ready to leap into action, to *save* her... only to realize there is nothing left of his right leg but jagged bone and charred flesh connected by only the tiniest sliver of tendon. For a moment, he feels nothing, as if his mangled femur and disintegrated kneecap belong to another; as if the blood spilling out around him is being pumped from someone else's veins.

But he tries.

To roll onto his good leg, to get it beneath him, *to fucking stand up*. But his brain is churning in his skull, and his arms are numb, and his good leg—the only one left— won't work. He fights to drag himself to her, but nothing is cooperating, and he can only lie there and watch her burn, smoke acrid on his tongue, his blood a thick, deep, pool in which he hopes he will drown.

God willing.

Because the Jeep is black smoke and hungry white flame, and he can't see her, he can't hear her, but he knows —he knows—she is in there—just as he knows this is *his* fault.

His arrogance. His stupidity. The unforgivable certainty of his ability to keep her safe, protected from the realities of his existence.

She is burning because of *him*.

The pool of blood grows deeper, but it isn't enough. He has no desire to survive this atrocity. He is prepared to go— has always been prepared to go—but she isn't like him. She is good and strong and true; she brings hope and light and love.

While he brings only death.

She has saved him a million times. From war; from

apathy. From himself. Tempted him into trying. Enticed him into believing.

Seduced him into living. To live...as she burns.

Murdered right in fucking front of him.

As he imagined taking her home to bed, someone watched and waited, breathless with anticipation. He knows; he can feel them. Still watching. Still breathless.

Hungry for his pain.

He should want revenge; to survive so he can peel away their skin and splinter their bones; make their world bleed red. *Burn it to fucking ash.*

As his now is.

But he doesn't care. There is no part of him that would sacrifice death for life in search of vengeance. To avenge her means he must survive. *Without her.* And that is not something he is prepared to do.

The river of blood that streams away from him is a relief.

Be with her.

There is no other option: he will not survive without her.

Fate could not be so cruel.

Could it?

A thought he cannot bear; he turns it aside, tells himself, *soon.*

Soon.

The Jeep burns. *She burns.*

And he watches.

CHAPTER 1

I'M BEING WATCHED.

Wynn Owens did her best to ignore the heavy weight of the stare that tracked her as she made her way through the collection of booths that lined the Superior County fair building. Her neck prickled as she surveyed the goods for sale: Mr. Glenn's raw honey, Mrs. Baker's ceramic pigs, and old Hanley Jenkins' homemade salsa. Organic herbs, fresh cheese, free-range eggs. A collection of fruits, and berries, and homegrown vegetables. There was even a booth with fresh fish and an earthy array of wild mushrooms.

The sight gave her a pang.

"Next year," she consoled herself.

Because *stupid birds*.

Greedy and voracious, the raucous black starlings had decimated her yield. Her apples, and cherries, and sweet, crisp pears. *Heartless vultures*. It wasn't like there wasn't enough to go around, or that she begrudged them an easy meal.

But *come on*.

Then, unexpectedly, a red-tailed hawk had appeared.

Two days later, its mate had arrived—and together, they'd made a meal of the starlings.

"Circle of life," she'd told the pile of feathers left behind.

She hadn't exactly celebrated—death always made her sad—but she had taken heart that her fruit might make it to, well, fruition. And beyond that, the hawks' presence was evidence that—*finally*—the land was beginning to heal.

Nine long years of fighting blight and pests and leaching toxins out of the soil; of composting and growing field cover and coaxing life from the earth had finally begun to pay off. This year, there would be plenty of food, and, if she was very lucky, some to sell as well.

Her heart fluttered at the thought.

Not just because it meant extra money—which was always welcome—but because it meant *success*.

The farm had recovered. Without fertilizer; without pesticide; without eradicating wildlife.

It could be done. Sustained. And profited from.

"Shove it up your arses, Superior County Farming Association." She punched the air. "You can suck it!"

Because she'd done what every farmer in the valley had told her was impossible: she'd turned a barren, overworked, and lifeless patch of ground into a thriving, diverse ecosystem that maintained and enriched the food she grew. The soil was rich and black; the trees were thriving; the wildlife had started to return. And while she'd had to ride out a long transition—one that tested the limits of both her patience and her hope—the wait had been worth it. Watching the land reawaken had been a profound experience, one that mended places inside of her she hadn't known were broken.

It also provided a much-needed stock of food that was

growing more bountiful every year. And the purpose and joy it gave her elderly tenants...well.

"Priceless," she declared and turned down the next long row of booths, acutely aware she was still being watched. The gaze that followed her was unwavering and intent.

But Wynn refused to look.

Don't do it.

No matter the temptation.

She passed fresh pastries and jams but stopped to consider a collection of delicate handmade chocolates.

They looked...like celebration.

And didn't she deserve some festivity? Not just her—everyone who lived at the Owens Boarding House had worked tirelessly to make the farm a success. Even Jenna, her fourteen-year-old sister, had given up afternoons with friends and after-school events to shovel manure and dig planting beds. This victory belonged to them all.

"Thank you, Fran," Wynn whispered, a deep and painful ache in her chest.

If only you'd lived to see it.

Life was nothing if not a consistent kick to the face. That her aunt had not survived to witness the germination of the seeds she'd planted so long ago was profoundly unfair.

Fran hadn't gotten the chance to taste the fruit or harvest the corn; she'd never had the pleasure of thrusting her hands into that rich, silky soil. She'd never—

"Don't ruin it," Wynn scolded herself.

But old hurts died hard deaths. Many years had come and gone since her jagged, dark and—*let's face it*—fucked up childhood, and yet still, there were nights when she awoke cold with sweat, her heart a drum in her chest, certain she had to run.

Run!

Even though those days were long gone.

Missing Fran was like that—no matter the bounty, all Wynn felt was loss. And that made her angry. *So angry*. That the beauty and richness of today could be soured and undone by the ugliness of yesterday was infuriating.

"Looking back just points you in the wrong direction," she reminded herself.

And then snorted, because *motivational poster, much?*

That Fran had suffered so badly before she'd died—so much so that she'd chosen to pass before her time—didn't help the healing. Or the forgetting. Or the moving forward.

Not that Wynn could blame her. There was mercy in letting go.

Even if it hurt like hell.

"Stop it," she ordered.

Because her grief would change nothing; it would just undermine her joy in this accomplishment. And she deserved a little joy.

"A butt load of joy," she decided.

Abandoning the chocolates, she moved on.

The gaze watching her refused to waver, like a fiery beam of x-ray vision burning a hole into the back of her head. But she resisted the urge to look. Instead, she turned down the next row of booths.

Hand-painted scarves...homemade lotions...stamped leather bags...*there*.

Buck Ferris and his impressive collection of Damascus steel.

The best bladesmith in Superior County, no one could match the quality of Buck's work. Everything from hatchets and short swords to daggers and the finest kitchen knives decorated his booth, but Wynn was in search of more delicate fare.

She had two of his pieces: a sweet, serrated hunting knife, and a tactical edge he'd given to her when she turned sixteen, the latter of which she was never without.

Another remnant of her childhood: her love of steel.

Or maybe just her love of survival.

"Wynn? Is that you?"

Aw, crap on a cracker!

Which was not, Wynn knew, the response the man who suddenly stood behind her was going for. A fact he'd made clear—more than once.

Crap!

She had zero desire to deal with him. All of those fragile male feelings took too much stinking effort; men were *exhausting*. But blatantly ignoring him would be inexcusably rude—even for her. So she made herself turn and look at him.

"Hey," Eric Henry said and smiled.

It was a nice smile, friendly and warm; it really shouldn't have annoyed her.

"Hey," she replied reluctantly.

Then she continued toward Buck.

Maybe Eric wouldn't—

He followed. Tall and broad, with coal-dark hair and glinting blue eyes, he was handsome, she supposed. If you went for that sort of thing.

She didn't.

"It's been a while," he said.

Not really. Less than a year, since she'd walked into the Department of Natural Resources office where he worked and picked up a firewood permit. He knew that; he'd issued it to her. Along with an invitation to dinner, which she'd politely declined.

Eric was a decent human being. She'd had biology with him in ninth grade, and he hadn't wanted to dissect a frog any more than she had. But that didn't mean she cared to date him.

She didn't care to date anyone.

"How's everything going?" he asked.

She stopped in front of Buck's stand. "Fine."

"So what have you been up to?"

A sigh escaped her. She shrugged. Buck approached, his long red beard filled with silver beaded braids, his thick fingers smudged with black.

"Winifred," he said with his customary lack of inflection.

"Buck," she replied.

He spared Eric a glance and then ignored him. "What do you need?"

"A filet knife." She looked down at the array of finely honed blades spread across the counter of his booth. They were beautiful, dazzling, and deadly. "But I need something with a wider handle. It's for Earl, and his grip isn't what it used to be."

"I can make you one if none of these work," Buck said.

"His birthday is next week."

Buck only folded his arms across his chest and shrugged. He was a giant of a man, with a thick neck and arms heavy with muscle. His red hair was cropped short; a fine spray of freckles covered his alabaster skin. Clad in a Packers sweatshirt and a matching beanie, his coveralls were scuffed and stained. There was nothing soft in him. His manner was gruff, his pale green eyes were hard, and he seemed much happier in the company of his forge than people.

But Wynn had known him a long time. Buck's mother had been Fran's best friend, and he knew far more about Wynn than she liked anyone knowing. Which would have annoyed her if he was normal. But he wasn't. Like her, he was an odd duck in a pond full of swans. Which made her far more tolerant—and besides, Buck never trespassed. He didn't gossip or prod or poke his nose where it didn't belong.

And they'd always been—if not friends—friendly.

"I can do something with a wide walnut handle," he said. "You want the blade a little wider, too?"

"No, just the handle." Wynn eyed him. "How much?"

Another shrug. "We can trade."

"Sweet." Because the barter system was much kinder to poor folk—of which she was one—than the financial system was. She could almost always find something to trade; she couldn't always find cash. "Thanks."

"What kind of trade?" Eric wanted to know.

They both ignored him.

"I'll get to work on it in the morning," Buck told her. "I'll bring it by when it's ready."

"Perfect," she said and smiled. "I really appreciate it."

He only nodded curtly. Then he gave Eric a black look and turned away.

Which cracked Wynn up. Buck knew she was never unarmed; he'd made the blade she carried. Still, she appreciated the thought.

It was nice to know someone cared.

"What kind of trade?" Eric repeated, his tone hardening.

Annoying. And presumptuous. And why he was always a pain in her rear end.

She sighed and made herself look at him. *Again.* "See you around, Eric."

Then she moved to step around him.

He planted himself in her path like a stubborn weed. "Why do you always blow me off?"

Because, no.

Surely it was obvious? She was nothing if not obvious.

Still, she strove for patience. The hair at her nape was bristling beneath the force of the unrelenting stare that remained locked on her.

So intense and resolute.

Determined. She had to kind of admire that.

No, you don't.

"I'm not going out with you," she said bluntly.

Eric blinked and looked annoyed. "I didn't ask."

"You want to. I can tell. But I'm not..." She waved a vague hand. "I'm not *her*."

"Her who?"

"*Her.* The one you date. The one you marry. Babies and birthdays and...and all that gobbldeygook."

He stared at her for a long, silent moment. Then a slow smile spread across his face and alarmed her.

"So it isn't because you don't like me?" he asked.

"I don't like anyone," she told him honestly.

The smile grew. "I'll have to see what I can do about that."

Balls! Why did words never work with him?

She looked him up and down; a good looking guy with decent taste in clothes and—she had to admit—a fantastic smile. "What's wrong with you?"

His brows rose. "What do you mean?"

"Look at you." She waved another hand. "Why aren't you taken? The girls in town aren't exactly picky. No offense, but if you were a keeper, one of them would have sealed the deal *long* before now."

For another drawn moment, he only stared at her. Then he began to laugh. It was a pleasant laugh, husky, and deep. Inviting. And he smelled like pinecones.

Still. *Because, no.*

"I have a cow to milk," she told him. "Later."

Then she walked around him before he could protest.

"Wynn," he said.

She ignored him.

"I *will* see you later," he called.

She didn't reply. Instead, she strode toward the door, hyper-aware of the eyes searing into her.

She could feel them.

No.

Don't even think about it.

Past the organic peanut butter, the fresh arugula, and spring peas. Past the sweet corn and dark red cherries.

You can't afford him. You know better.

One hundred percent fact. Unarguable.

So you just keep walking.

And then he made a sound—a soft, forlorn wail that pierced the deepest part of her.

Maybe he needs you.

Maybe you need him.

Maybe—

"Oh, for the love of Pete!" She slapped a hand against her forehead and halted. "You're an idiot."

Another unarguable fact.

Still, she felt herself bending. And it felt good to bend.

To reach back.

She sighed. Unable to help herself, she turned back toward him.

Idiot, she thought again. But as she grew closer, the gaze boring a hole into her widened. Grew hopeful.

Desperate.

And Wynn knew desperation; it had been her sole companion for years.

Another sigh. She stopped in front of a booth filled with homemade rag dolls. An old cardboard box sat on the counter of the booth, surrounded by handmade Raggedy Anns. From within the box, a tail began to thump. The eyes watching her grew almost feverish.

"How much?" she asked, pointing at the box.

The girl who stood in the booth shrugged. "Free."

"Why?"

"He's the runt. Nobody wants him."

Human nature never failed to dishearten. The assumption that people were somehow superior to the millions of other species on the planet was profoundly stupid, and yet it seemed like a belief most of the population ascribed to, no matter the evidence to the contrary.

"I'll take him," Wynn said.

"Go for it," the girl replied, looking bored.

More thumping tail. The dog stood up in the box, wobbly and malnourished. His coat was dull and thin, his spine a stark ridge of bony beads pressing against his skin. An odd mixture of German shepherd and something else, something with spindly legs and a weird little tail. But those amber eyes...

They glowed.

Wynn lifted him out of the box.

Too light; skin and bones in her hands. A wild, ecstatic heartbeat and a wet tongue. And...*phew*. Stinky.

But that was easy enough to fix.

Another mouth to feed.

But the farm needed a new sheepdog; it had been almost six months since Jesse died of old age. If this little guy got tall enough, he would fit the bill. And if he didn't—

Well, he was hers now.

Just freaking brilliant.

But she wasn't sorry.

So what if her biggest weakness was that she couldn't pass by something in need? That no matter how abrasive her edges, inside she was soft, gooey mush?

Let someone call her on it. She'd kick their stinking ass.

The pup licked her cheek. Whined in her ear. Made her eyes burn with his stench.

Now, this is a celebration.

She turned and took him home.

CHAPTER 2

SHERIFF BEAU GREYSTONE stared at his computer screen, the peppermint mocha latte he'd had an hour earlier souring in his stomach.

Stupid coffee wannabe.

Not something he would have ever ordered, nor something he would have ever consumed, had it not been brought to him by his Aunt Velma, a willful and wily woman with whom one did not argue.

But now he regretted it because his belly was churning. Or maybe that was just the scene playing out before him.

Goddamn bank robbery.

What the hell had he been thinking, agreeing to come back to this town? To sign on to Velma's crazy write-in campaign for Sheriff?

Because the worse he would have to deal with was missing livestock and the occasional drunk?

You're an idiot.

It was no less than he deserved.

His life had effectively ended three years ago. Taking this job had been a futile attempt at purpose. Going through the motions to pacify family who were scared shitless he was going to wake up one morning and decide to eat the end of his Glock.

Not that he hadn't considered it.

Every single fucking day.

But breathing was penance, and no matter how it grated, it would never be enough to earn him absolution. He deserved every painful moment of his existence. And if he'd thought purpose might yet be possible...well. All he'd done was saddle himself with duties and responsibilities and accountability he didn't particularly want.

But the people of Superior County deserved more from their new Sheriff than apathy.

No matter how much of a pain in the ass it was.

A goddamn bank robbery!

The figure on screen, who held an ancient .45 in a grip besieged by violent tremors, was stooped, stick-thin, and moved at a rate of speed easily overtaken by a herd of turtles. When the bank teller asked him if he wanted her rolls of quarters, too, he'd had to cup his ear and yell, "What's that?" three times before he'd heard her.

He wore a long black Dover, cowboy boots, a wide-brimmed straw cowboy hat, and a red and black bandanna that covered everything but his eyes.

"Shit," Beau muttered and rubbed a hand down his face.

Eight grand and some change. Hardly worth ending up in the pen.

What the hell was the old fool thinking?

Earl Randall Barry, age seventy-three. Vietnam vet and former Army sniper. He'd spent his time after the war working a mixture of odd jobs: used car salesman, fishing guide, cattle wrangler. He had one arrest for public intoxication and thirteen speeding tickets under his belt. And last year, he'd taken out the Blossom Hills Post Office sign after having his eyes dilated.

There was nothing on the screen to give Earl away—other than his obvious lack of youth. No, the old man had managed to drop his grocery card on the floor of the bank—the one that had his name and address on it, which he used for discounts at Eckhart's Grocery—and if that wasn't enough to tie him directly to the crime, there was all the blood he'd left behind.

A trail of bright red drops that led from the teller's booth right out the front door, where they abruptly stopped. Beau didn't know why Earl was bleeding, but he was pretty sure—if he got a court order for the old fart's blood—it would match.

Cows and drunks.

Sure.

By all rights, he should just go arrest Earl Barry and get it over with. But...well, *shit*.

What the hell was the old rascal doing?

Because it made no damn sense, and it was up to Beau to get answers. He had a job to do, one that required more than just a cursory nod at enforcing the law. The people who'd elected him deserved better than a checked-out Sheriff who didn't give a damn about their town.

Even if that pretty much summed him up.

But he'd never done anything by half-measures. He wouldn't start now.

It wasn't their fault he'd never expected to win the election. That he hadn't even bothered to protest when Velma brought it up because he'd been certain he had a snowball's chance in hell of walking away the winner.

But he'd severely underestimated Velma's determination and astute political acumen. And the price for that had been success.

Jesus Christ.

Beau sat back in his chair and rubbed his aching thigh. It hurt like hell. The explosion that had killed both his wife and his desire to keep breathing had also ended his days as a fully functioning human being. Between the surgeries to put him back together, the skin grafts, the steel rods, the pins, and screws and titanium plates, there wasn't much left of his leg but a long, twisted length of scar tissue—tissue that ached and throbbed and burned every moment of every day.

He couldn't run; he couldn't jump. Some days, he could barely walk.

More penance.

Permanent disfigurement and chronic pain.

Again, no less than he deserved.

He'd hoped leaving behind the humidity of Miami would lessen the pain, but the weather everywhere had gone to hell in a handbasket, and there was so much moisture currently in the air that storms churned over the Blossom Hills valley in a never-ending cycle, a constant, extreme fluctuation in barometer that only inflamed his leg.

Not that it mattered. Staying in Florida had never been an option.

He'd spilled far too much blood.

And even though much of it had never been tied to him, both those he'd hunted, and his former employer, knew full well who was dropping cartel boogeymen like flies.

They'd feared him. And for a while, it'd been enough. Bloody hands and an empty soul; hunting purely for the kill.

Drowning in death had felt *good*.

But then—

You dishonor yourself—and her memory—by painting it in blood. Do you even realize that?

He hadn't.

Not until the cousin he'd grown up with, probably the only person left in the universe Beau trusted other than Velma, had been brave enough—or maybe stupid enough—to point it out.

She wouldn't want this, Beau.

The words had cleaved him in two.

Marie, sweet, gentle, loving Marie would've been sickened by the blood he'd shed to avenge her death. In the beginning, he hadn't wanted revenge; he'd wanted death. But fate had cheated him, and when faced with waking anew each day to a life he didn't want, he'd turned to the only other path that remained: making someone pay.

So they'd paid. Not like he had, and not nearly enough, but they weren't walking around breathing anymore.

And sometimes a man had to take what he could get.

Beau would've gone on killing everyone involved in turning his life to ash—happily, without remorse, deadened to everything and everyone else—if Tristan hadn't appeared on his doorstep one day and beaten the homicidal asshole out of him.

Logic and reason hadn't done it; nor had threats. No, it had taken fists, he and Tristan going at it no holds barred like the wild, stupid kids they'd once been. They'd trashed his apartment, destroyed his furniture, and both broken bones. But in the end, Beau had acknowledged that his cousin was right.

Marie's memory deserved better. And delivering death was no way to live.

So he'd reluctantly agreed to return to Blossom Hills,

the small town in which he'd spent the latter half of his childhood, up until he joined the service at eighteen.

He was going to make a fresh start.

God help him.

And now he found himself with a badge on his belt—again—and the problems of many now solely his.

First and foremost, Earl Randall Barry, Blossom Hills bank robber.

Edward Duggar, the man who owned the bank Earl had robbed, was biting at the bit for an arrest. Even though it was a measly eight grand, and even though he was fully insured. But Edward Duggar, Beau had decided, was a dickhead.

He'd met with Duggar immediately after the robbery, and Duggar's insistence that he "get the job done" hadn't gone over well with Beau, who'd never had a problem getting any job done. And it had only served to feed Beau's reluctance to simply slap the cuffs on Earl Barry and process him without first figuring out what the hell was going on.

He might be a brooding, moody bastard, but he still, apparently, had a heart and a goddamn sense of decency, and he had no particular desire to see an old man go to federal prison for stealing what amounted to—in bank robbery terms—chump change.

The mystery of it intrigued him, and Beau hadn't been intrigued by anything for a long, long time. In the years he'd spent with the DEA in Miami, the cases had all been clear-cut, no puzzles to solve, no agendas to uncover. Every crime had been about profit, nothing more.

But this...*what was this about?*

He rubbed at his head, which was beginning to ache.

He looked down at the address he'd scribbled onto a piece of scrap paper and sighed.

Owens Boarding House, 785 Chokecherry Lane.

He could take a drive out there. Talk to Earl. See if maybe he couldn't get a confession. At least then he might be able to work something out with the DA, some kind of plea deal that would keep the old guy from having to spend what was left of his life in the state penitentiary.

It would be better than just showing up and cuffing him.

Trying. It would be trying.

And that was something he didn't do much of anymore—another thing that would have to change with his new occupation. Because he still had some fucking standards.

Doing the right thing had to be one of them, no matter how much it burned his ass.

For years, Marie had been his moral compass, especially after Iraq and Afghanistan, when he'd come home and not given a damn about much of anything.

She'd dragged him into the light. But then she'd gone, and the darkness had returned.

Now, if he wanted the light, he had to step into it.

Freely.

A far more fitting memory than blood, and death, and dishonor.

"Shit," he said again, defeated by his own damn head.

He grabbed Earl's address, stared at it.

Then he pushed painfully to his feet and went to do the right thing.

CHAPTER 3

"Winifred, dear? There's a man on the front porch. Perhaps you should comb your hair."

Since she needed a man like she needed a hole in the head, Wynn ignored that rather pointed observation. Never mind that she was trapped beneath the kitchen sink, wrestling with a crescent wrench, which made grooming impossible—and completely useless.

Stupid crescent wrench.

What she needed was a proper pipe wrench. But she didn't have a proper pipe wrench, and she didn't have the money to purchase a proper pipe wrench.

The crescent should work. *Please?*

"Wynn?"

Crap!

"I'm in the kitchen," she yelled. "Deal with it."

"Should I let him in?"

"I don't care!"

"Are you sure? He appears quite...potent."

Wynn fought with the wrench.

"I really think you should—"

"Esmeralda!" *For the love of Pete.* "He's probably here for the room." She braced herself against the interior wall of the cabinet and cranked on the wrench. "Just let him in."

"If you say so, dear. I daresay you'll be sorry."

The wrench moved—a quarter of an inch. The musty scent of mildew filled Wynn's senses and tickled her throat; sweat poured down her back. The tight space made it impossible to get any leverage, and the sad truth of it was, she was getting nowhere fast.

Pipe 1, Wynn 0.

So it was only fitting that her new tenant would show up a day early. Before the room was ready. While she was ankle-deep in a DIY plumbing project at which she was failing miserably. When she looked like she'd just crawled out of a city sewer.

Which, really, was just par for the course.

Welcome! Are you comfortable with disaster and chaos? Can you deal with nosy, forgetful, meddling housemates who rarely turn off lights and sometimes set fires?

She pulled desperately on the wrench. *Please come off, you stinking thing.*

Because she couldn't afford to hire someone to take it off. Even with a new tenant and the extra cash the farm was producing, it was going to be tight this month. Scraping by...*also par for the course.*

But it wasn't anyone's fault. Certainly not poor Mr. Sanders, who obviously hadn't meant to die. He'd passed peacefully in his sleep over a month ago, and she could hardly blame him for having done so, no matter the financial hole it left her in. That his death made her sad, and she mourned him, wasn't something she much focused on.

There was always too much else to do.

She sighed and swiped her hand across her brow,

leaving a streak of grime and several strands of sherry colored hair plastered to her forehead. Beowulf the Runt watched curiously from where he sat beside her, his head tilted in question.

"I've got this," she told him. "Really."

She knew what she was doing; she had a plan. She just needed to get the dumb thing apart—

"...a beautiful day, don't you think? Winifred is just through here...I'm afraid we're having some trouble with the pipes. But Winifred is *very* handy...and really, quite lovely. Don't let those manly overalls fool you."

Wynn gripped the wrench, gritted her teeth, and pulled.

"Winifred?"

Her hands slipped off the wrench and it gave, releasing from the pipe. It bounced off her ribcage and slid down to clatter against the floor of the cabinet. "*Aw, crap!*"

Beowulf barked in agreement.

"He's...it's the Sheriff, dear."

Wynn sat up automatically; her head slammed into the bottom of the porcelain sink, and she snarled.

"Winifred?"

The Sheriff!

The beer-bellied, tin-star wearing, evil incarnate bastard who'd killed her mother over a decade ago.

Here, now.

Her heart stopped, and for a long, motionless moment, she didn't move.

Couldn't move.

"Did you hear me, dear?"

"I heard," she whispered.

She picked up the crescent wrench and stared at it. Her

heart burst to life and began a too-fast, too-hard tattoo; blood roared in her skull. She felt sick.

"Are you coming out, dear?"

It wasn't a good idea.

Because what was to stop her from beating the Sheriff to death with a crescent wrench?

Nothing. Nothing at all.

She fought the surge of adrenaline that poured through her.

No. It's over.

Done.

You need to let it go.

But she never had and never would, no matter the futility of holding on.

Justice, Wynn had learned, was for the wealthy. Not for people like her, or her mother, whose life had been erased with the stroke of an official pen.

Seeking it now would only destroy all that she'd built. All that she'd sacrificed for.

All that Fran had sacrificed for.

So she counted slowly to ten. And prayed a little.

Beowulf whined softly as if sensing her chaos.

You're grown now. He can't hurt you anymore.

But it wasn't herself with which she was concerned.

"Winifred?" Esme sounded worried. "Are you alright?"

No. But she had responsibilities. People who relied on her not to murder the local sheriff and end up on death row.

So she would have to deal.

Forward, not back.

"Stupid," she muttered and forced herself to wiggle out of the cabinet, wrench in hand. She told herself to put it down, but the child who'd watched her mother die refused to let go.

"Ms. Owens?"

The unknown voice made her blink, and she looked up, startled to find a stranger standing next to Esme.

This was not the Sheriff.

The man who towered over her bore no resemblance whatsoever to Jasper Hatfield. He wore no uniform, carried no obvious weapon, and sported no tin star. Just worn jeans, cowboy boots, and an obnoxiously bright Hawaiian print shirt that was so busy, she felt dizzy looking at it.

So she just sat there for a minute, staring at him.

"Are you Winifred Owens?" he demanded and stared back at her.

He looked...angry. Dark and stormy and dangerous; the walking antithesis of his cheesy, cheerful shirt.

"Who wants to know?" she retorted, eyeballing him.

Her hand flexed around the wrench, and his gaze—which was startling, brilliant lime green—caught the movement and narrowed.

"Beau Greystone," he replied, his voice rough and deep and unmistakably grim. "Sheriff of Superior County."

Wynn could only arch a brow. "Congratulations?"

He frowned, and it made him look even more sinister. Which was kind of a shame. Because he was beautiful in a rough, scary kind of way. Like a mountain was beautiful. Or a storm.

Or a lightning bolt that shot from the sky and cooked you to a crisp.

Beowulf growled softly, his amber gaze narrow on the giant who hovered over them. Wynn stroked a hand over his bony back.

Good boy.

"Winifred," Esme admonished, her Mississippi accent

gently scolding and ice sharp in a manner only Southerners ever accomplished. "Don't be rude, dear."

"Where's Hatfield?" Wynn demanded, ignoring her.

The new Sheriff of Superior County had cold eyes, a hard mouth, and lines etched deep into the carved planes of his face. He shifted as he stood there, the muscle that lined his jaw taut, and she realized abruptly that he was in pain. Oh, you couldn't see it, not unless you knew what it looked like. But Wynn knew. She'd lived with people in some form of pain her whole life.

Sympathy should have stirred, but didn't. Probably because he was looking at her like she'd crawled out from under a rock.

"Jasper Hatfield is dead," the new Sheriff said.

Again, she blinked. A wild, chaotic mass of emotion burst within her, and she laughed.

"Oh, dear," Esme said and shook her head.

"Dead," Wynn repeated, smiling broadly. She couldn't help it. *Hatfield was dead and gone. RIP—not.* "Hot damn!"

Beowulf's odd little tail thumped against the linoleum.

The new Sheriff leaned down over her. He looked like he ate nails for breakfast. "Sheriff Hatfield died in the line of duty."

Good.

It almost escaped. But a set of dog tags suddenly tumbled from the neckline of the new Sheriff's horrific day wear and prevented the word. The tags were dented and scarred, and he looked annoyed as he tucked them back into his shirt.

A soldier—then or now, didn't much matter. Wynn had been around veterans her whole life, too, and she respected them. Hatfield's death in the line of duty would mean something far different to him than it did to her. And he clearly had no clue about her history with the former Sheriff—which was how it would stay.

So she stuffed her euphoria and rage and grief away, and said only, "What can I do for you, new Sheriff?"

He stared down at her. So she stared back. Tension rose and crackled between them. Heat flared through her—anger, annoyance, what the *hell* was he wearing?—and she did her best to ignore how directly he looked at her.

As if none of her barriers would stop him.

Esme cleared her throat delicately. "Well." She moved toward the coffee pot with purpose. "You're Velma Greystone's nephew, aren't you?"

The new Sheriff scowled faintly. "Yes, Ma'am."

"You knew about him?" Wynn cut in, annoyed.

"Of course, dear," Esme replied. "I am an unashamed connoisseur of local gossip."

"And you said nothing?"

A shrug. "I saw no need to upset you. After all, I didn't expect him to show up on our doorstep." She turned and looked at the new Sheriff. "You came from Milwaukee, didn't you?"

He spared her a glance. "Miami."

Well, that explained the shirt.

"What brought you to Wisconsin?"

The new Sheriff said nothing.

Esme only eyed him speculatively, unfazed by his rudeness. She filled the coffee maker with water and coffee and turned it on. "Are you married, Sheriff?"

If he'd been grave before, now he turned to stone. "No, ma'am."

"I have pipes to wrestle," Wynn told them impatiently. "What do you want, new Sheriff?"

Esme made a sound of censure, but again, Wynn ignored her.

"I need to speak with Winifred alone," the new Sheriff said.

An order, not a request. A ripple of unease whispered down Wynn's spine. She held that brilliant, lime green gaze and tried to pretend dread wasn't spilling through her chest.

What could he possibly want? She hadn't broken any laws—at least, not lately—and she went out of her way to stay under the radar.

So what was going on?

Esme's silver brows rose. Her gaze moved between them. "I don't imagine I'd win an argument to stay?"

"No," said the new Sheriff coldly, "I don't imagine you would."

And Wynn considered smacking him with the wrench.

"Well, it's been a pleasure." Esme smiled, the picture of southern graciousness. "I must say I've heard quite a lot about you."

"I'm sure." A small, dark, and wholly unexpected smile touched his mouth. "Please don't believe any of it."

"You have a nice smile, Sheriff," Esme told him. "You should share it more often."

Red flushed his cheeks, and Wynn bit back a snicker.

"Ma'am," he said and nodded.

Definitely a soldier.

Esme sent Wynn a sharp look—*behave yourself, young lady*—and sauntered out.

"Now that you've run her off, can we cut to the chase?" Wynn asked him.

For a long moment, the new Sheriff was silent. Studying her with that intent, probing gaze she didn't at all appreciate.

"What?" she demanded, exasperated.

He looked at the wrench she held. "That's the wrong tool for the job."

A fact to which my ribs can attest. Thanks for nothing.

"What do you want?" she asked flatly.

He looked at Beowulf. "Who's this?"

Beowulf growled at him.

Good boy.

"Beowulf the Runt." She ran another hand down his back. "Future sheepherder."

The new Sheriff eyed him dubiously. His gaze moved to her, and for a long moment, he simply studied her. But then he straightened, took a small step back, and grimaced. "We can do this at the table."

He offered her his hand. A strong, scarred hand, tanned and capable.

One she wasn't touching with a ten-foot pole.

"I'm good," she said and ignored the offering. "But you're welcome to sit."

The scowl returned. "Ms. Owens—"

"Wynn," she corrected.

"We need to talk, Wynn."

His face was dark, his expression grim, but beyond that, she couldn't read him worth a damn.

He'd come here, looking for her. Demanding to speak with her *alone*.

Nothing good was going to come of this.

She sighed and then pushed herself to her feet. She set aside the wrench—but kept it within reach, just in case—and pulled two old coffee mugs from the cupboard. Beowulf accompanied her, making sure he kept his scrawny little form between her and the new Sheriff.

Really, really good boy.

"Do you take milk or sugar, new Sheriff?" she asked.

"Black," he replied tersely.

"Shocking," she muttered. She poured him a cup and made herself one as well—with plenty of milk and sugar—and set his down on the kitchen table.

He hadn't moved; he still stood in front of the sink, watching her.

"Sit." She waved a hand at him. "Let's get this show on the road. I've got stuff."

He went to the table where she'd set his coffee and slowly lowered himself into one of the old wooden chairs.

Definitely in pain. Had he been to war? He had the look. Or was there an accident? Maybe—

Shut it down, woman. Who cares? Not your problem.

But he *was* her problem. Clearly. *Crap.*

She leaned back against the counter and sighed.

The chair that sat across from the one he occupied was suddenly pushed out from beneath the table by his booted foot. It slid smoothly across the worn linoleum floor in front of her. "Sit with me."

That bright green gaze double-dog-dared her.

"I'm good," she made herself say again.

"Sit," he said softly.

She looked at the wrench.

"Don't," he warned.

"Stand down," she told him. "I'm just fantasizing."

One of his brows rose, and something sparked in his brilliant gaze and then was gone. "Sit down, Wynn."

She didn't want to. But the longer she argued, the longer he would remain. So she sat down in the chair and drank her coffee and waited.

Beowulf took up residence beside her, his gaze alert on the new Sheriff.

Suspicious, she thought.

Smart dog.

"What happened between you and Hatfield?" the new Sheriff asked.

"Ancient history." She waved a hand. "Why are you here?"

He reached into his breast pocket and pulled out a small notepad and slender silver pen. "This is your residence?"

"Do I look like I fix other people's pipes for fun?"

That earned her a dark look. "This is a boarding house?"

"That's what the sign says."

His jaw hardened. "How many residents?"

Wynn leaned toward him and said nothing until his gaze met hers. "What do you want, new Sheriff?"

He surveyed her, silent. Her unruly hair and filthy face; her stained overalls and worn t-shirt. She felt like showing him her battered combat boots but the temptation to kick him might prove too much.

So she just let him look.

"There's a vacancy sign in your window," he said.

"Looking for a room?" She arched a disbelieving brow. "A man of your overwhelming charm and sweet disposition?"

That spark lit his eyes again and was gone. "How many tenants do you currently have?"

She said nothing, watching him. Alarm was worming its way through her.

What was he getting at?

"I can always talk to them instead," he said.

"You leave them alone," she warned. "They've been through enough."

"The woman who answered the door—Esme—said you'd lost one recently?"

A sudden, unexpected swell of emotion thickened her throat. *Damn it, Esme.* Always gossiping. The woman simply couldn't help herself. "Mr. Sanders."

In the hallway, the clock began to chime.

"I'm sorry," the new Sheriff said quietly.

Wynn only blinked at him.

He folded his arms on the table. The muscle that roped his forearms shifted and flexed and an awareness she didn't at all appreciate flared deep within her. *Stupid man.* Like a mountain, alright. Dwarfing her kitchen and sucking out all of the oxygen.

"How many tenants, Wynn?"

She regretted telling him to call her that. She should have left it at Ms. Owens. Because who was Ms. Owens? No one she knew. "Five."

"And Esme mentioned your sister, Jenna?"

The dread turned to sharp, piercing fear. "Spit it out, new Sheriff."

"It seems like a lot of responsibility," he continued. "A younger sister, half a dozen elderly tenants. Leaking pipes. Livestock. A farm is a lot of work. Running this place can't be easy."

Again, Wynn said nothing and stared at him.

He looked around the kitchen, taking in its battered white cupboards and scarred linoleum floor, the ancient appliances, and ugly florescent lights. He lingered on the cheerful, sunflower-strewn curtains—courtesy of seamstress Esme—and the pot of stew simmering on the stove before moving his gaze to the small disaster under the sink. "Money must be tight."

She didn't like the opaque surface of his gaze; the cold

expression on his face; the indecipherable, unspoken question he was asking.

"You have a tenant named Earl Barry," he said. "Is Earl here?"

She sipped her coffee with false calm. "Why? Did he hit the Post Office sign again?"

"No." The new Sheriff scrawled something unknown into his notebook, his mouth a hard line, and she wanted to grab him by his ugly shirt and shake the stiff out of him.

What the hell was going on?

"You're certain you don't know where Mr. Barry is?" he asked again, that brilliant gaze clashing with hers.

Wynn said nothing. Of course, she knew where Earl was; her boarders weren't just tenants, they were family. They didn't go anywhere without telling her. But she would eat her left boot before she spilled those beans.

The back door suddenly flew open and smacked the wall. Jenna breezed into the kitchen, clad in her soccer gear. She stopped short when she caught sight of the new Sheriff.

"Holy shiny shirt," she said. "Who are you?"

He pushed himself to his feet, shifting his weight carefully, and Wynn found herself watching him closely. Wondering what had happened. How.

Silly goose; he's the enemy.

"This is the new Sheriff," she told her sister. "He was just leaving."

"The new Sheriff?" Jenna eyed his shirt dubiously. "Are you sure?"

Wynn only arched a brow. The new Sheriff gave her a dark look and lifted the tail of his shirt; a shiny silver badge and a large black Glock decorated the belt he wore.

"I'm looking for Earl," he told Jenna shortly.

"Earl's gone," she replied. She bent down and rubbed

Beowulf's head; his tail wiggled in delight. *Thump, thump, thump.* "He went fishing up in Canada."

Wynn was surprised by the sardonic look the new Sheriff shot her. *So a human being lurked in there, after all.*

"Canada," she said. "Huh. Who knew?"

"When did he leave?" the new Sheriff wanted to know.

Jenna shrugged. "Monday, I think. He said he'd be back Thursday. Griff went with him."

"You're not respecting our tenant's privacy," Wynn chided.

Another dark look.

"Did he hit the Post Office sign again?" Jenna demanded. "Why do you want to talk to him?"

"Yes, new Sheriff," Wynn added. "Why *do* you want to talk to him?"

"That's Earl's business," was the new Sheriff's brusque reply.

Jenna frowned. With her sleek, corn silk blonde hair, slender build, and refined features she was the mirror image of their mother. Sometimes the resemblance was so close it hurt to look at her. "Did you tell him?"

Wynn blinked. "Tell who what?"

Jenna rolled her eyes toward the new Sheriff. "You know what."

Uncertainty flickered across her face, and Wynn realized abruptly what she was talking about.

"No," Wynn said.

The new Sheriff looked up to pin her with that glinting green gaze. "Tell me what?"

"Nothing you need to worry your big, surly self about, new Sheriff." She gave him a wide, phony, prom queen smile. "I'll tell Earl you came by."

"You're sure?" Jenna asked doubtfully.

Wynn shot her sister a quelling glance. "Tell the new Sheriff goodbye, Jen."

He turned and set his gaze on Jenna. "Tell me what?"

But Jenna just sighed. "Nothing."

"Buh-bye, new Sheriff," Wynn said. "It's been real."

Real crappy.

He made a sound like a growl. Then he turned and looked at her.

She only lifted a hand and waved. "Thanks for coming by."

He leaned toward her, and her kitchen table suddenly felt like a school desk. He was far too big. Far too intense. And he smelled like...fresh-cut cedar?

His gaze crashed into hers. For a long moment, they just stared at each other. Then he leaned closer and snarled, "*Wynn.*"

Beowulf made a surprisingly sinister sound in response, and something foreign and thrilling and terrifying rippled down Wynn's spine.

This man was dangerous.

In more ways than one. She wanted him out of her house.

Now.

Jenna's phone rang; she pulled it from her pocket and answered it. A moment later, she was gone.

But the new Sheriff didn't move.

"You need to tell me what that was about," he ordered softly, his gaze like green fire.

Wynn had assumed it was anger that he stirred; annoyance, fear, the history she couldn't seem to bury. But something deep within her shivered beneath that look, and it had nothing to do with anything other than the agitated, electric current that crackled between them. Which was a shocking and unnerving revelation; one she didn't at all welcome.

It just made her want him even more gone.

"I need a lot of things," she told him. "An oil change. A pipe wrench. A rebuilt roof. But the new Sheriff sticking his big, fat nose into my business isn't one of them."

For an intractable moment, they stared at one another. And then, abruptly, he straightened. He shoved his notebook into his pocket and pulled out a business card, which he held out to her.

"For Earl," he said.

"I'll pass it along." Wynn reached out and took the card. But as she moved to pull it away, he held on, until her gaze lifted to meet his.

"You do that," he said.

Something unspoken smashed into the space between them, and awareness licked through her, as hot and searing as any flame.

His lashes flickered, as if he felt it, too.

"I'll be back," he warned.

She pulled the card from him and crushed it in her palm. "I'll be waiting."

CHAPTER 4

"She didn't threaten to shoot you?"

Beau flicked a glance at his Deputy Sheriff, Harry Baker, who stood leaning against the water cooler in the corner of Beau's office. "No."

"Huh." Harry blinked. "Last time I was out there, she threatened to put buckshot in my backside. I guess she's mellowed some."

Remembering Wynn Owen's witchy gray eyes, sharp tongue, and her big crescent wrench, Beau would have to disagree. "What were you doing there?"

"One of her tenants set Mr. Humphries' pigs free."

Beau's brows rose.

"The old gal was going through an eco-warrior phase." Harry shook his head. "She was freeing them into the wild."

It just gets better and better. "What happened between Wynn and Hatfield?"

Harry grimaced. He was younger than Beau, but as far as Beau could tell, good at his job. Handsome and charismatic; people liked him. A plus, since Beau had neither of those traits. Harry was also a walking directory for every person who lived in Blossom Hills.

"Well, now, that was a bad deal," he replied in a subdued tone.

Beau's gaze narrowed on him. "She laughed when I told her he was dead."

"Can't say I'm surprised."

Hot damn, she'd crowed. And those dark gray eyes had glittered, and that smile had been downright *joyful*—

"Get me the file," Beau told him.

"If you're looking for answers, you won't find them in the file."

He sank behind his desk and rubbed his throbbing leg, thoroughly annoyed. By the fact that Jasper Hatfield was quickly turning into a grade-A piece of shit. And by the fact that Hatfield had a history with Wynn Owens that Beau hadn't known about.

"What happened?" he asked brusquely, not at all surprised that Hatfield's files were worthless. The mess Beau had discovered in Hatfield's wake—in the computer system and filing room, not to mention the evidence locker—told him all he needed to know about the former Sheriff.

Harry rubbed the back of his neck and stared for a moment at the cheap wood paneling that lined the office. "It's been a long time. Over a decade."

Time does not heal all wounds. Something to which Beau could personally attest.

"And?" he prodded.

"Hatfield...well, he killed Wynn's mother."

Beau froze. He'd expected...well, hell, he didn't know what he'd expected.

But not that.

"Explain," he demanded sharply.

His deputy flinched, and he bit back an irritated sigh. Beau knew he was a brusque bastard at least eighty percent of the time, but he'd been a soldier too long to temper himself. When you ran a unit of Army Rangers, you had to be the loudest, harshest, rudest asshole in the crowd—and old habits died a hard death. The DEA had been no different. And that didn't even touch what Marie's death had done to him.

The endless, relentless pain didn't help any, either.

"I'd been on the job less than a week when it happened. Talk about trial by fire." Harry shook his head. "I haven't seen anything like it since. I hope I never do."

Impatience speared through Beau. "Harry."

"There were rumors they were involved—Jasper and Wynn's ma, Lara. I don't know if it was true. But Hatfield was a powerful man. Folks didn't cross him or question him. He got away with a lot."

"Like killing an innocent woman?"

"He claimed self-defense." Harry shrugged. "The coroner said there was enough crystal meth in Lara to take out an entire SEAL team."

Beau gave him a flat look. "Unlikely."

Harry flushed. "I'm just repeating what I was told. Hatfield claimed she drew a gun on him, and he fired in self-defense."

"Witnesses?"

"Just Wynn and Fran."

"Fran," Beau repeated.

"Fran Owens, Wynn and Jenna's aunt. Lara's sister. She took Wynn and Jenna in after it happened; they've lived out there ever since. Fran died a couple of years back. MS."

Which meant it was all Wynn. Running the boardinghouse and the farm; caring for her sister. Her tenants. A hell of a lot of work and responsibility—not easy and not cheap.

"What did the witness statements say?" Beau asked.

"There weren't any."

"No one bothered to investigate?"

"People took the Sheriff at his word. Like I said, he had power, even upstream. And Lara...Lara was trouble. Always had been."

"So he got away with fucking murder?" Beau ground out, appalled.

"I don't know," Harry admitted. "Maybe. You have to understand, Fran was really sick. And Wynn was just a kid. Jenna was four, maybe five. And there wasn't anyone else who cared. Lara had a reputation; she'd burned a lot of bridges in town. She'd been in and out of jail and halfway houses and rehab since she was sixteen. Frankly, I wouldn't be surprised if she *was* involved with Hatfield. She liked fire. It's no surprise she finally got burned."

"So no one cared when he gunned her down in cold blood?" Beau pushed himself to his feet, agitated as hell. "Jesus H. Christ."

No wonder Wynn Owens had smiled at the news of Hatfield's death.

What the hell happened that night?

Just what he needed. Another goddamn question to eat at him.

He limped over to the window, which revealed the tidy, manicured landscape of the town square, and stared out at the large oak tree that dominated the space. A fat gray squirrel was descending its thick trunk, cheeks fat with acorns. Beyond the oak's lush green foliage, dark blue-gray storm clouds roiled, as if boiling in a giant, heavenly pot.

It had begun as a gorgeous, bluebird day, but the

moment Beau had headed toward the Owens' place, the clouds had started to gather, violet smudges on the horizon, the smell of rain so strong and thick he could feel it leaking from his pores. The robins were fluttering along the grass, clearly excited at the coming downpour, and across the street, the hardware store owner was moving the flowers he had for sale beneath his awning.

Blossom Hills was a quiet town. Unlike Miami, there were no screaming sirens and honking horns, no throbbing bass, and squealing tires; no deafening, dangerous clashes of humanity. It was, Beau thought, a place one should be able to find a little goddamn peace and quiet.

But this morning he'd come face to face with a woman who'd just as soon brain him with a crescent wrench as look at him. And now he was presented with the likelihood that his predecessor hadn't just done his job badly—he'd done it corruptly. He hadn't been incompetent; he'd been a criminal.

And, from the sound of it, a murderer as well.

Fan-fucking-tastic.

"She didn't know Hatfield was dead," Beau said, staring out the window. "How is that possible?"

"Guess she's been busy."

"It was all over the web."

Another shrug. "She pretty much runs an old folks' home. I imagine they take up a lot of her time."

"She had no idea I was the new Sheriff," Beau bit out. "The whole damn town knows I got elected—they wrote me in. She must not vote, either."

The censure in his voice vibrated through the air.

"The only government Wynn has ever known shot and killed her mother right in front of her when she was just a kid," Harry said quietly. "It's no surprise she wouldn't vote."

"Goddamn it. It would've been helpful to have known all this *before* I went out there."

Harry only blinked. "You were already gone when I got here."

Beau rubbed a hand down his face.

"Did you talk to Earl?" Harry asked.

"No. Barry is up in Canada, fishing." Allegedly anyway, although Beau had his doubts. Not because he thought Jenna Owens lied to him, but because he suspected Earl had lied to *her*.

Earl was in a boatload of trouble.

"You really think he had something to do with that robbery?" Harry was clearly skeptical. "I mean, he's pretty old."

Beau had seen kids as young as eight commit felonies. Earl wouldn't be the first seventy-six-year-old who'd decided to take up bank robbing in his golden years.

Still. It begged the question *why*.

A question Beau wanted to answer.

He wouldn't have much time; the feds wouldn't be long. The only reason the FBI hadn't yet descended was that they were dealing with a rash of domestic security threats, and the robbery of a small-town bank wasn't a high priority. But they *would* come, and he wouldn't be able to do a damn thing to help the old man once they got here.

He'd mistakenly assumed getting answers would be easy. Just drive out to the Owens' place and talk to Earl; find out what he was thinking and what the hell had possessed him to rob a damn bank. Give him a chance to confess, to see if they couldn't find an out for the old guy that didn't include the federal penitentiary. Do a good deed and his job all in one, maybe start to earn the badge he now wore.

And then he'd found himself staring into the dark,

stormy gaze of Wynn Owens, facing down her smart mouth, mocking smile, and battered crescent wrench.

None of which he'd been prepared for.

Stand down. I'm just fantasizing.

Goddamn her. She'd been talking about hitting him with that bloody wrench when what had flashed through *his* mind's eye was—

Well.

It hadn't had anything to do with assaulting an officer. At least, not with a hand tool.

Jesus Christ.

He'd been dead inside for a good, long while. *And that was how it would remain.*

He had no desire to feel anything ever again.

It was wrong—a profound and devastating betrayal of the woman he'd vowed always to love. In the years since Marie's death, he hadn't even thought about sex, let alone felt that exhilarating rush of blood into his—

"Boss?" Harry prodded, staring at him.

Beau pinched the bridge of his nose and told his body to calm the hell down. What the fuck was this?

Wynn Owens had been covered in sweat and grime. She'd been wearing paint-spattered overalls and a stained men's undershirt. *She'd had on combat boots.*

But she'd smelled like sunshine and apple pie. She'd had a wide, full mouth that was quite pretty when it wasn't mocking him, and those eyes...dark, turbulent gray, churning like a storm over the Atlantic.

Too smart for her own good.

Looking for a room? A man of your overwhelming charm and sweet disposition?

Hell, he'd almost smiled at that.

And then he'd looked around her aging home and

thought about how far eight grand would go. No matter how clean and well cared for—or how delicious the meal on the stove smelled—the place was coming apart at the seams, warped siding badly in need of paint, a sagging front porch, a roof ready to cave in.

Eight grand wouldn't even put a dent in it.

"Earl Barry is our prime suspect," he said flatly. "The evidence is there."

"It's circumstantial," Harry pointed out.

"For now," Beau agreed grimly.

The blood would change that. DNA was even more definitive than a fingerprint; Earl had no chance of outwitting conclusive physical evidence linking him to the scene of the crime.

It was a done deal.

Canada. Huh. Who knew?

Wynn Owens had lied to him; she'd known exactly where Earl was.

But did she know what he'd done?

Another question chewing on Beau with sharp, persistent teeth. When he should be far more concerned with where Earl was and what the hell he was doing. Spending that money, no doubt.

But chasing the old guy across the border would just make a bigger mess, so Beau would have to sit back and wait patiently and hope the feds didn't show up first.

Patience and hope. Two things at which he sucked.

"Maybe it was some asshole looking for drug money," Harry suggested. "I like that answer a heck of a lot better."

So did Beau. But that was a *wish in one hand* kind of thing.

"How's the leg?" Harry asked.

Beau realized he was rubbing it and stopped. "Fine."

"Must hurt like hell some days."

All days. "Yes."

"They catch the guy?"

"He's dead," Beau said.

Another flinch. "That's good, I guess."

Beau only shook his head. There'd been nothing good about any of it.

"Yoo-hoo, anyone home?"

The bell over the front door jangled.

"Helllooo?"

Beau sighed; a headache burst into being between his brows.

He loved his Aunt Velma. She'd taken him in after the death of his parents, and a year after that, she'd taken in Tristan when his mother passed from leukemia. Velma was feisty and opinionated, and she ruled with an iron hand; she was also loving, compassionate, and unrelentingly supportive. Sometimes too supportive.

Can't never did anything for anyone, dear.

He'd missed her when he left. So much so that sometimes he was glad he'd come back.

"Oh, you *are* here." Velma swept into the office, clad in slender, fitted black trousers and a billowy blue blouse. Her shoulder-length white hair was streaked with hot pink highlights and the rhinestones inlaid into the frames of her eyeglasses twinkled in the overhead fluorescent lighting. She smiled broadly at Beau and tossed her giant purple purse into one of the chairs in front of his desk. "Hello, dear. I thought you might have been...held up at out at Wynn's."

Beau narrowed his gaze on his aunt. "How did you know I went out there?"

"Harry told me; he said you left a message that you were

on your way there." She arched a brow. "We wondered whether or not you'd come back in one piece."

Harry's cheeks went pink. "I ran into her at Sally's."

Sally's was the local coffee shop and a hotbed of town gossip; Beau went out of his way to avoid it. *You're not much of a politician,* Velma had observed after his election. She didn't approve of his refusing to mingle with his electorate over lattes and gluten-free pumpkin muffins. But Beau had taken an oath to protect them, not talk to them.

Not unless it was necessary. He was a rough, plainly spoken man who had no patience for chitchat and no talent for social niceties. He'd spent three tours in Afghanistan and five in Iraq; in the years since, he'd fought a different but no less dangerous war on the streets of Miami while working for the DEA. All three had tried to kill him. He knew intimately how fucked up the world—and many of the people in it—were, and he had no desire to put himself on display and pretend to be someone he wasn't.

Someone he never would be.

But he would get the job done. He was direct, honest, and unflinching in the face of adversity. If he'd been accused of being brutally efficient, well. Oh well.

"Did you talk to Wynn?" Velma wanted to know. She sat down in the chair across from his desk and leaned forward, her expression avid. "What did she say?"

Beau arched a brow. "Am I the only one in this town who had no clue what I was walking into?"

"Oh, I'm sure the summer people don't know." Velma smiled sweetly. "Did you like her?"

Alarm flared through him. "Was I supposed to?"

"Wynn is lovely." His aunt assumed a nonchalant expression. "I thought you might have noticed."

He blinked, suspicious. "You know her?"

"Of course. In Blossom Hills, everyone knows everyone, dear."

Another monumental problem with this place. "She expected Hatfield."

"I'm not surprised. She never comes to town."

Annoyance speared through Beau. "Because she was afraid of him?"

"For him, not of him." Velma snorted. "Wynn is no shrinking violet. But neither is she a fool."

"You like her," he said.

"I do." Velma nodded. "Very much. I've watched her grow into a strong, capable, good woman who spends much of her time devoted to others. *Some* people could learn a thing or two."

Beau ignored the dig. "She's dirt poor."

"What are you implying?"

Nothing he could share. "It was an observation, not a slur."

"You don't think—" Harry began, but Beau shot him a quelling look.

"Think what?" Velma asked.

Beau only shook his head. "What can I do for you, Velma?"

For a moment, she studied him, but the flat surface of his gaze made her sigh noisily. "I've come about the ribbon cutting."

"What ribbon cutting?"

"For the new hospital wing. I told you last week. The Board members are all out of town, so I volunteered you to do it. And you said you would."

Beau had no memory of that. "I did?"

"Well, of course, you did. Do you think I would make it up?"

He stared at her, well aware that she was very capable of a bald-faced lie if she believed it lay in his best interest.

"Besides, you could use a little good press," she added and stood. "People feel like they elected a stranger!"

"They did," he said.

Velma snorted. "There's nothing wrong with letting them get to know you, Beau. You're a fine man, and one I'm very proud of. I *like* sharing you."

Heat licked at his cheeks.

"I'll never be polished enough to shine," he told her stiffly.

"Sweetheart, you don't need any polish. You aren't silver. You're steel." She turned and smiled at Harry. "Deputy Baker."

Harry nodded. "Ma'am."

She paused at the door. "I'll see you later then, Beau?"

He sighed.

"Dare I hope you will dress appropriately?" She eyed his bright Hawaiian print shirt. "Surely you have a uniform."

Not one that fit. Besides, he liked his shirt. Marie had bought it for him. "Harry has a uniform."

Velma scowled. "You will never get re-elected at this rate."

He could only hope.

"Four-thirty," she told him. "And not a minute later!"

"Ma'am," he said.

She shook her head, sighed noisily once more, and took her leave.

"Family," Harry said.

Beau only grunted.

"You don't really think...you don't think Wynn had something to do with that robbery, do you?"

Maybe. Maybe not.

What Beau knew about Wynn Owens wouldn't fill a thimble. And he didn't trust anything he'd felt in her presence. That unexpected, powerful, visceral physical reaction was meaningless. *Biology.* It signified nothing.

Even if a traitorous part of him wanted to rejoice: *he was alive again.* Finally.

When he shouldn't give a goddamn about his cock getting hard.

Fuck.

"I think anything is possible," he said bluntly.

Harry rubbed a hand down his face. "Shit."

Beau couldn't have said it better himself.

CHAPTER 5

"He's the most beautiful thing I've ever seen."

Wynn grinned. "Isn't he though?"

Sasha leaned down and canoodled with Beowulf the Runt. "He's perfect. Who needs a man when you can have a dog?"

Wynn's sentiments exactly.

"He's no Dean Winchester," Jenna said with a snort. She pointed at the TV, where brothers Dean and Sam were battling a crossroads demon in all of their *Supernatural* glory, and said, "I'd take Dean over a Doberman any day."

"Dean's too alpha." Sasha shook her head. "He'd be all up in your business. Now Sam...he's sensitive. He'd give you some space."

"Sam." Another snort. "Sam is just eye candy. Dean is the Dom."

Wynn blinked at her sister. "Jenna."

She only shrugged. "Seems pretty obvious to me."

Beside her, her friend Penny Harkins giggled. They were having a Supernatural Sleep Over, which Wynn wouldn't have normally allowed on a weeknight, but

Penny's dad was out of town, and she needed a place to stay. Since Earl and Griffin were still in Canada, there was plenty of room, and it was bingo night, so Ethel and Eloise were in town. Esme sat on the couch, watching the show avidly.

"I'm no expert," she put in, "but I'm afraid I have to agree with Jenna. Dean is the show-stopper."

Sasha rolled her eyes. "Too much work."

Now it was Wynn who snorted. "Like you'd know."

Sasha snorted back. "Like you'd know."

Jenna snickered.

Wynn went into the kitchen; Beowulf and Sasha followed. Two large pizzas sat in the center of the kitchen table.

"You went all out." Sasha flipped one of the boxes open. "You shouldn't have."

"It's not every day my best friend passes the bar," Wynn told her. "You deserve only the best."

Sasha grinned and helped herself to a piece of pepperoni. "I expected PB&J."

"Har," Wynn told her. "I'm not that poor."

"Don't tell it to the bank."

"Hmph," was her unenthusiastic response. She looked at the lopsided pile of papers that sat on the counter. It wasn't much of a business plan—what in Hades did she know about business plans?—but the bank wouldn't loan her a penny to expand the farm's orchards without one, so even though she suspected it would all be for naught, she'd given it her best go—with Sasha's help. Sasha was highly intelligent, financially savvy, and one of the only people in the world Wynn trusted without question.

A true friend, through the dark and the light; everything they never spoke of, but couldn't forget.

"I think it's freaking impossible," she admitted. "And we've wasted our time."

"Positive thinker."

"I mean it. This place isn't worth a hill of beans, and it's the only collateral I've got. Even if they loan me the money, if I can't pay it back, I'll lose the farm." Wynn shook her head. "It seems foolish and stupid to even try."

"No risk, no reward."

Well, that wasn't helpful.

"I have to tell you something," she confessed.

"What?"

"I met the new sheriff today."

"There's a new sheriff?"

"Apparently, so. Hatfield's dead." Something that filled her with both elation and fury, a paradox with which she was still struggling. "Killed in the line of duty."

According to Google, the former Sheriff had been plugged by a .38 during a domestic dispute over in Angel Falls—a twofer, since the man who'd been busy beating the tar out of his wife had also taken a round to the chest and died on the way to the hospital.

Two assholes in one fell swoop. Sometimes life was good.

Sasha eyed her with concern. "I didn't know that."

Which wasn't a surprise since Sasha lived over in Bentwood, which was outside of Superior County. But Wynn only smiled broadly. "Me neither."

"A new sheriff," Sasha murmured. "Does that mean we can close the chapter on the old one?"

It wasn't an unreasonable request. But neither was it one Wynn could honor. She would never forget or forgive Jasper Hatfield.

Ever.

"The new sheriff is Beau Greystone," she said bluntly.

Sasha froze. Her cheeks went bright red with angry color. For a long moment, she said nothing.

"I'm sorry," Wynn added hurriedly. "The band-aid method seemed best."

Sasha said nothing. Then, "It's been a decade." She shook her head. "It shouldn't matter."

But it did. For whatever reason, it still very much did.

The summer after graduation, Sasha had fallen madly, passionately in love with Beau's cousin Tristan; their affair had been searing and intense and all-consuming. Wynn hadn't understood love could be like that until she'd witnessed it. But at the end of that summer, something had happened—something that separated them instantly and permanently—something Sasha had never spoken of.

Not even once.

Too bad for words, Wynn thought. She'd known moments like that. So she didn't push.

But Sasha's experience with Tristan had closed a door that remained unopened. She was a stunning woman: raven-haired, blue-eyed, with lovely, delicate features and the kind of smile that stopped people in their tracks. She was a spectacular human being, giving, loving, compassionate, and empathetic; she deserved to find happiness. Instead, she'd just...quit.

It made Wynn angry and sad.

If that's true love, I'd rather have cheesecake.

"I always liked Beau," Sasha said finally. "He was rough around the edges, but he was honest, and when you needed him, he was there. What's he like now?"

Remembering that piercing, intelligent green gaze, and the sheer, annoying force of his presence, Wynn said, "Intense."

"You're blushing."

She scowled. "So?"

An unexpected laugh broke from Sasha. "You liked him."

No. Well, maybe. A tiny bit. He was...compelling. And beautiful. But that was just hormones. She wasn't *dead*. "He's a curmudgeon."

"Well, he was always a little brusque."

"Like the night is a little black. Besides, he has a stinking badge."

"Not every man in law enforcement is Jasper Hatfield."

Wynn wasn't willing to bet on that. "He limps." *And he's in pain.*

"He was an Army Ranger. He probably saw combat."

"How do you know that?"

"Velma. I ran into her a few years back. She felt the need to fill me in on the numerous and glorious accomplishments of both of her nephews."

"She had high hopes for you and Tristan."

Sasha waved that away with a sigh. "What did he want?"

"Earl." Which worried Wynn. There had been nothing friendly or neighborly in the new Sheriff's visit. And Earl was more than capable of getting himself into some kind of ridiculous pickle. "He wouldn't tell me why."

"The Post Office sign again?"

"No." Remembering the opaque surface of Beau Greystone's eyes and the flat tone of his deep voice made the unease within her churn. "Whatever it is, it's worse."

And she was very afraid it might have something to do with what Jenna had discovered out in the pasture behind the house.

Because what were the odds?

"So you'll see him again?" Sasha asked innocently.

Another thing Wynn didn't want to think about. Because the idea of seeing the new Sheriff again should have filled her with angst, not anticipation.

Crap!

"Whatever he wants with Earl, it isn't good," she said, because of that, she was certain.

"Well, maybe some good can come of it."

Wynn gave her a disbelieving look. "How's that?"

"You need to deal with your cop hang-up. Exorcise that shit."

"Oh, just put a cork in it."

"Why not?"

"Stop talking."

"Seriously—I think Beau's the perfect badge for the job. If I remember correctly, when he was on it, he was *on it*. I mean, like—"

"For the love of Pete!"

"Okay. Your loss. Maybe I should give him a call?"

"Be my guest," Wynn told her stiffly.

And Sasha laughed again. "Oh, it's so on. Finally. I've been waiting for this day."

"We're done talking about this."

For a long moment, Sasha was silent. Then, "Didn't watching Fran teach you anything? She never stopped living. Not ever. Hell, she met old Jake Perkins out at his hunting cabin every chance she got. She took her pleasure where she found it, and let it be enough."

"He wanted to marry her. She turned him down. Said she didn't want to saddle him with her disease."

"Then more fool her." A flicker crossed Sasha's face. "She should have taken all that she could."

Wynn didn't know what to say to that, so she said nothing. Instead, she looked around the kitchen, with its chipped linoleum and crooked cupboards and sighed.

Pain. Life was pain.

For everyone.

"Did you get a new tenant yet?" Sasha asked and finished off her pizza.

"No." The young man she'd mistaken the new Sheriff for had failed to show. "I'm still looking."

"I'll spread the word."

"Thanks."

The sound of a vehicle pulling into the long drive drifted in through the open windows, and they listened as it parked and the engine was cut. A squeak as the doors to the old Buick were pushed open; the crash of them slamming shut. Then, "Be careful, Ethel. I told you not to have that glass of beer."

"It was bubbly. I liked it."

"Well, you're not having it again. You can hardly walk."

"That's because my shoes are too tight."

"I told you not to buy them. You look ridiculous."

"Mr. Harcourt liked them."

"Mr. Harcourt is a charlatan."

Wynn grinned. Eloise and Ethel had been tenants since she was fifteen. The sisters were in their late seventies; Eloise had spent most of her life watching over her twin, Ethel, who'd suffered brain damage as a child. Ethel was innocent and mischievous and—oftentimes—hilarious. But she wasn't capable. Eloise was the one who carried the load, making certain Ethel was dressed and fed and not getting into trouble—something else at which Ethel was proficient. Eloise was stoic and unbending and never far from her Bible, but she loved her sister and did right by her. Which Wynn admired and respected, but it hadn't escaped her, how Eloise sometimes looked out the window as if she dreamed of another life entirely.

Wynn had looked out that window, too. Because sometimes you did the best you could with what you were given—and you were grateful for it—but that didn't stop you from dreaming.

Eloise and Ethel shuffled into the entryway, then down the hall between the kitchen and living room. Jenna had turned down the TV, and their argument regarding the length of Bernadette William's skirt floated into the kitchen.

"It was too short for Bingo," Eloise muttered.

"I thought it was pretty," Ethel argued.

"The fabric was pretty—her bare behind wasn't!"

Sasha snorted out a laugh.

"Maybe she was airing herself out," Ethel replied. "Sometimes I like to—"

"Ethel, enough. It's time for *Jeopardy*."

"But I want to watch *Wheel of Fortune*."

They ascended the stairs, still arguing.

"You should think about it," Sasha said. "Beau, I mean. Seriously."

Wynn shook her head and ignored the wild rush that arrowed through her. "That's trouble I don't need."

"If you say so."

"I do."

"Well, the seed has been planted." Sasha pushed to her feet. "Thanks for the pizza. Now I think I'll go home and air myself out."

CHAPTER 6

THE DIRT and gravel driveway that led to the Owens Boardinghouse was severely rutted and marked with deep, muddy potholes. As Beau steered his truck around the worst of them, he thought *one more thing that needs work.*

The house, while large and gabled and lined by a broad front porch, looked timeworn and haggard; the paint was peeling and faded from the sun. The old barn behind it drooped. A metal building sat off to one side, the steel rusting and dented, the door crooked on its frame. Behind the collection of buildings, the farm was lush with fruit trees, planting beds, and a healthy pasture filled with frisky black sheep. A dairy cow and two gray donkeys grazed with the sheep; in the middle of the pasture, a huge oak tree unfurled toward the sky, its limbs swaying in the growing wind.

The place was half promise, half disaster.

Wynn Owens, he thought, was swimming upstream. Whether she realized it—or admitted it—or not.

Which may or may not have been motive enough for bank robbery.

Goddamn it.

He pulled the truck to a halt next to an aging orange Volkswagen van and parked. Lightning flashed, illuminating the storm rolling across the valley. It also illuminated Wynn Owens, who stood on the roof of the house, her slender form outlined against the dark, churning mass of clouds.

Beau stared at her, and his hands tightened on the steering wheel until it groaned.

A bright yellow slicker swallowed her; in one hand, she held a hammer. Far below, standing next to an ancient extension ladder that had been propped against the side of the house, stood an old man.

One who wasn't Earl Barry.

Wynn yelled something down at the man; he yelled back.

Goddamn it.

Fucking insanity. What was it with this woman?

Beau climbed out of his truck, anger licking through him.

He stalked toward the old man, his leg throbbing, his heart pounding with painful intensity.

"Evenin'," the old man said and nodded. He was tall and lean and gaunt, his bones pressed against his skin as if they were trying to escape. A pair of thick, black-framed eyeglasses dominated his face, making his faded blue eyes huge. He, too, wore a yellow slicker and black mud boots. An old red knit cap covered his head.

"Sheriff Beau Greystone," Beau said brusquely. "And you are?"

The man's bushy brows rose. "Griff."

Beau looked up the fully extended ladder and felt his chest tighten. "What the hell is she doing up there, Griff?"

Thirty feet from the ground.

Where he couldn't follow. Because he couldn't trust his leg on solid ground, let alone on a ladder rung.

Goddamn it.

Griff shrugged. "Fixin' the roof."

"And you let her go up there?"

Again, those wild brows rose. "Have you met her?"

A growl rumbled in Beau's chest. "This couldn't wait for a nicer day?"

Griff shrugged a second time. "Guess not."

Beau felt his skin prickle. "She needs to come down. Now."

"I expect she'll come down when she's done."

Beau only shook his head. This was nuts. Dangerous as hell; *stupid*.

He went to the ladder and gripped it.

"Careful," Griff said. "Ladder's missin' a step."

Jesus Christ. The woman needed a keeper.

Beau took a deep breath. Would his leg even work? Because it didn't always, and a ladder would be pushing it. But the fear suddenly winding around his throat had nothing to do with his leg.

What the hell was she thinking?

So he began to climb, one painful step at a time. Griff steadied the ladder, but it still wobbled, and the missing step was a pain in the ass that tested the limits of his good leg. By the time Beau finally crested the roof, his whole body hurt, and the fury simmering within him was at full boil.

Wynn didn't even notice him. She was on her knees, pounding nails into an asphalt shingle.

"What the hell are you doing?" Beau snarled at her.

She straightened, turned, and looked at him over her

shoulder. She had three nails between her teeth and a smudge of black on her cheek.

"Earl's down at AA," she replied around the nails. "Come back after six."

Then she turned around and began hammering another shingle into place.

"Goddamn it," he hissed. He looked at the slope of the roof and felt a fine tremor shake his knees.

Fucking useless.

If he was whole, he'd just climb up there and haul her ass down. End of story.

Instead, all he could do was stare at her in muted fury, his hands digging into the ladder. Furious with her, his own demoralizing lack of mobility, and the fear that was turning his blood cold.

If she fell—

"Wynn," he grated. "It isn't safe up here. You need to come down."

She sent an annoyed look his way. "When I'm done."

"*Right now*," he snapped coldly. A harsh, blunt order, bellowed from him in the same tone that had made the Army Rangers he'd led snap to attention.

"Go away, new Sheriff," she said without turning around.

Beau ground his teeth together. The wind gusted, making the ladder sway and the trees whistle. The rain grew heavier.

"Don't make me come and get you," he warned, even knowing he couldn't carry out the threat.

"Oh, just cool your tits," she retorted. "There's only a few more."

"They can wait."

"No, they can't." She sent another nail home with a

violent slam of the hammer. "Another week until we see the sun; I can't wait that long."

"Then fucking hire someone," he growled.

"I fucking can't!" she yelled back, and Beau belatedly realized she was just as angry as he was.

"I can," he said calmly. "I'll help you get it fixed. Just come down."

Another whack of the hammer. "I don't need your help."

The hell she didn't.

"Wynn," he said harshly.

She ignored him.

"I'm going to paddle your ass," he hissed, his blood so hot, he was certain he must be steaming.

"You and what army?" A shingle flew past him, down to the ground. "Go away, Greystone. This isn't your problem."

She was right. This wasn't his problem. *She was not his problem.* And he didn't want a damn thing to do with her. She was *no one*.

He stared at her, utterly infuriated. With her; with himself. Lightning flashed, thunder cracked, and the fear within him tightened like a chokehold.

"Wynn," he ground out, another tremor shaking his leg, "please come down."

"One more."

He *was* going to paddle her ass.

"Storm's gettin' worse," Griff yelled from the ground. "Best be gettin' down now."

"Bossy," Wynn muttered. "Knew I should've done this by myself."

Beau waited with gritted teeth as she put the last shingle into place and hammered it home. Then she pushed to her feet and walked toward him carefully, hammer in one hand, a bag of worn, recycled nails in the other.

She was soaked through, her slicker hanging open, rain rolling down her cheeks. A long, dark red rope of hair flowed over her shoulder to caress the tip of her left breast.

White heat bolted through him at the sight.

"You're in the way," she said, staring at him.

Defiance shimmered in her gaze, but it was ruined by the exhaustion he could see. Dark smudges beneath her eyes, her skin pale, her pulse a wild beat in the hollow of her throat.

She didn't want to be up here, either.

She just didn't have any other choice.

Was that why Earl had robbed the Dorchester National Bank? Because this place was on its last legs?

"Did you get them all?" he asked.

"For now." She moved to the edge of the roof and tossed down the hammer and nails. "The rest can wait until tomorrow."

Tomorrow. When she would be back up here in the goddamn pouring rain, a human lightning rod, hammering away.

Fuck that. That was not happening.

Beau climbed down the ladder, his leg pulsing with pain, his gut churning.

He couldn't have it both ways.

He either gave a damn, or he didn't.

He'd assumed penance would be, if not easy, at least predictable; not caring was his way. It had been for a long time, and returning to that state had felt completely natural, as if he was simply embracing what he was always meant to be.

But if he thought he'd never give a damn about anything ever again, he'd been wrong.

So wrong.

Was it wrong to be wrong?

Goddamn it.

He nodded at Griff, who stood holding the ladder and hit the ground. His legs wobbled beneath him, and for a moment, he just stood there, regaining his balance. He became aware that Wynn was on the ladder above him, waiting, but she just watched in silent patience, and he realized with an unpleasant jolt that she was aware of his pain.

He stepped back, out of the way, annoyed. Angry. And not at all happy with the realization that penance wasn't turning sightlessly away from the woman in front of him; it was turning away in spite of what he saw.

That was his punishment. Not a half-life dominated by mourning and pain, but one spent denying himself the temptation of more.

It shouldn't have been hard. He didn't deserve more.

He didn't deserve a fucking thing.

"You're not getting up there again," he said tersely.

Wynn lifted the ladder from the house and shook it; the extended length slid down and slammed into the ground. "Not your call, new Sheriff."

Beau reached out and gripped the ladder, forcing her to look at him.

"It isn't safe," he said, doing his damnedest to be reasonable. "If you fall, what happens to Jenna?" He nodded toward Griff. "Or to him?"

She stared at him for a long, silent moment. "I have life insurance."

"Goddamn, it woman." Frustration lit through him. "You're going to break your fool neck."

"Which is not your problem," she replied shortly. "Buttinski."

She turned and walked toward the front porch.

"She's been getting' up there since she was sixteen," Griff said from behind Beau. "Good luck stoppin' that train." He paused. "I know a guy who can probably do the work."

"Call him."

"You sure?"

"Call him," Beau repeated.

Then he followed Wynn.

He didn't bother to knock on the screen door, he simply stepped onto the porch and moved toward the front door, which he walked through without hesitation. He knew Wynn had come this way; she'd left a trail of water and tiny black asphalt shavings behind her.

The house was old, probably built in the early 1900s, with tall ceilings and thick wooden trim. The walls were pale beige, the plaster patched in many places, the wooden floors scuffed and scarred and faded from use. But it was clean and dry, and the scent of baking bread made his mouth suddenly water.

He walked down the hall and halted in the doorway to the kitchen.

Wynn stood at the sink, looking out the window. She'd shed her slicker, and the t-shirt she wore clung to her wetly.

His leg throbbed as he stood there, staring at her back. "I can wait in the truck."

She said nothing.

"Wynn," he said, annoyed.

"What did Earl do?" she asked quietly.

"I need to talk to him first. Then I can talk to you."

She sighed. "Coffee?"

"Yes," he said, relieved she wasn't kicking him to the curb.

He entered the room, painfully aware of his heavy limp. *Goddamn ladder.* A kettle of potatoes simmered on the stove, and a fat, glazed ham sat on a platter on the counter, waiting to be carved. His stomach rumbled in interest.

Wynn waved a hand at the table. "*Mi casa es su casa.* I guess."

He removed his coat and sank onto one of the hard oak chairs, trying not to groan in relief.

"I have pie," she said. "You want pie?"

Again, his belly signaled interest. "No."

"How about a shot of whiskey?"

"No."

"A smoke?"

"No," he growled.

"Just the coffee, then?"

He looked up and stared at her.

"You sure are a ray of sunshine," she told him. "Must be hard to shine so bright all the time."

He ground his teeth together. Few would dare to give him the shit she did. Velma, maybe. Tristan. A handful of his fellow Rangers. But no one else.

"This isn't a social visit," he replied brusquely. "I'm here to talk to Earl and, believe it or not, to help."

She went to the coffee pot, grabbed a mug, and filled it. "Are you?"

"Black," he reminded her.

"Like your heart," she replied easily and turned to put the mug in front of him. "I remember."

"I can wait in the truck," he repeated.

His blood was a dull roar in his head, and suddenly he was furious again. With her; with himself.

He shouldn't want to be here.

But part of him did. Part of him very much did.

"Such a prickly little pear," she murmured and poured a second cup of coffee. "For a man who likes to dish it, you sure don't take it very well."

It was an astute observation, and one Beau didn't appreciate.

"Miss Owens?"

They both turned to look at the man who stood in the kitchen doorway. He was tall, broad, clad in conservative khakis and a button-down oxford shirt; round silver spectacles perched on his nose. He held a book in his hands.

Rough hands, Beau noted. Tanned skin, sun-bleached hair, a nose that had been broken. Twice.

"Come in, Sean." Wynn smiled warmly, and Beau's gaze narrowed.

She didn't smile at him like that.

"I'm sorry to interrupt," the man said apologetically. "I was wondering what time dinner will be?"

"Seven sharp," Wynn replied. "But if you're hungry, I can feed you now."

He flicked a glance at Beau. "That's alright. I'll wait."

"Beau Greystone," Beau said abruptly and pushed himself to his feet. He ignored the pain and moved toward the man. "Sheriff of Superior County."

"Dr. Sean Evers," the man said, and they shook hands; the doctor's grip was firm, his palm callused.

"What kind of doctor?" Beau asked.

"I have a doctoral degree in biology."

"Here for fieldwork?"

"Yes. I'm studying the northern leopard frog."

If the man standing in front of him studied frogs for a

living, Beau would dance a jig all the way back to Miami.

"Where are you from?"

"Texas."

"Married?"

"I'm afraid not."

"What—"

"New Sheriff," Wynn said pointedly. "Please stop interrogating my new tenant."

"I just arrived this morning," Evers put in.

Beau shot Wynn a dark look. "Did you check his references?"

She only arched a mocking brow.

"He's a stranger," Beau told her.

"You're a stranger," she retorted.

Another jolt went through him, and he wanted to argue. But she was right. It wasn't his place to vet her boarders; who she rented to was none of his business.

A realization that in no way pacified him.

"You have to be careful," he said shortly. "You can't let just anyone in."

"Obviously."

"I'll come back at seven," Evers said and escaped.

Beau watched him go. "How long is he staying?"

"As long as he wants," Wynn said.

Beau turned and looked at her.

She leaned back against the counter and sipped her coffee. Smirked at him.

Which just rubbed him the wrong way. He could still see her on the goddamn roof, her slender form outlined by the coming storm. *Going to break her fool neck.* Jesus. She took care of everyone.

Did no one take care of her?

"You have questions for Earl, ask them," she invited. "But you leave everyone else in this house alone."

He found himself stalking toward her, even knowing he shouldn't. But at that moment, he didn't give a damn. And he didn't stop until he was close enough to smell the coffee she held, to feel the warmth she emitted. Her t-shirt was damp, clinging to her breasts, and his fingers twitched, despite the angst welling within him.

"You shouldn't take in people you don't know," he said, his voice hard. "It isn't safe."

"Don't be ignorant," she scoffed.

The words stopped him.

He leaned down over her, acutely aware of their difference in size. Of her scent; her heat. How intense the pull toward her was becoming. "Ignorant?"

"Do I appear to have the resources of someone who has the luxury of turning people away?"

The pipes chose that moment to rattle. Loudly.

Beau told himself to back off. He was standing too close. But those stormy eyes were glinting at him, her smile hard with an edge that he wanted to wipe away. "Better poor than dead."

"Says the rich man," she muttered.

"I'm not rich."

She looked pointedly at the watch he wore. "If you say so."

His gaze followed hers, to the gold Rolex on his wrist, a gift from Marie.

Marie.

The reminder punched through him. But still, he didn't move.

"It was a gift," he replied coldly. "From my dead wife."

Wynn blinked. Then flushed bright red.

"I'm sorry," she murmured. "I shouldn't have said that."

Again, not pacified.

"No," he agreed. "You shouldn't have."

Her eyes sparked, but before she could respond, the front door opened and closed. Then, "I'm home!"

A *woof* sounded. *Me, too!*

"Earl," she said.

Beau stared at her, unmoving. *Too close.*

But not close enough.

His heart was beating too hard; his skin was tight, his blood thick. And his body was primed. No matter his guilt, the crushing sense of betrayal, the relentless need to punish himself.

"I hear you're lookin' for me?"

The man he'd been trying to pin down for three days appeared in the doorway, accompanied by Beowulf the Runt, future sheep-herder. For a long moment, Beau didn't respond.

Because they weren't done yet.

Off the fucking rails, he thought. What the hell was wrong with him?

He forced himself to turn away from Wynn. "Earl Barry?"

"Yes, sir," the man said. His slender, slightly hunched form was swallowed by a pair of overalls and a plaid flannel shirt; a faded John Deere baseball hat covered his head, and a corn cob pipe sat in the corner of his mouth.

"Reportin' for duty," he added, somewhat defiantly, and reached down to pat Beowulf on the head. The pup stood beside him, a decidedly suspicious look on his face as he surveyed Beau.

"Mr. Barry." Beau moved toward the old man. "Beau Greystone, Sheriff of Superior County."

He held his hand out; Earl squinted at him. "Mr. Barry was my father. I'm just Earl."

A weathered, thin-skinned hand slid into Beau's, and he was struck by how fragile the man's grip was. "We need to talk, Earl."

Earl sat down at the table; Wynn served him a cup of coffee.

"Thanks, Chickpea," he said and winked at her.

"Welcome," she replied. Then she resumed her spot leaning against the counter and took another sip of her coffee. Beowulf went to her side and collapsed against the linoleum at her feet with a sigh.

"Well, I haven't damaged any property owned by the U.S. government lately," Earl declared, blinking. "So what is this is all about?"

CHAPTER 7

BEAU SAT down across from Earl, his face tight and hard.

Wynn watched him, her heart beating like a drum in her throat.

What was his problem? The way he'd looked at her—

Well. What did she know about men?

She might as well try to figure out quantum physics.

"Well?" Earl demanded, chewing on his pipe stem—a sure sign he was nervous. "What's the word, tin man?"

Beau's hard jaw pulsed, but he didn't rise to the bait. Instead, he pulled out his little notebook and removed a pen from the front pocket of his shirt, which was a wild mix of greens, from bright, neon lime to the darkest forest, a pattern of leaves and lush jungle undergrowth.

Wynn didn't get it. He was abrupt and gruff; unsmiling and unbending. What was he doing wrapped in such vivid, mind-bending color? A veritable celebration of life?

Who in Hades shopped for him?

And then she thought *oh*.

No doubt the same woman who'd bought him his gold watch.

His dead wife.

A woman he grieved deeply. Those words had slapped her, the pain in them so sharp and piercing, she could have reached out and touched it.

You're a jerk. Even though she hadn't meant to wound him.

But how was she to know? It wasn't like he wore a ring.

"Have you heard about the bank robbery down in Dorchester, Earl?" he asked.

Bank robbery?

Wynn straightened and set her cup down on the counter.

"Sure." Earl shrugged. "It's been all over the news."

"Can you tell me where you were on Monday morning at eleven a.m.?"

Earl folded his arms on the table.

"You bet," he said conversationally. "I was down at the flea market, lookin' for fly rods. The old ones are worth somethin', you know. Every once in a while I stumble across one."

Which was true. She was constantly tripping over the long, slender rods when she made Earl's bed.

But why was Beau asking Earl about a bank robbery? *A frigging bank robbery?*

Her heart fluttered painfully. Because Earl didn't seem at all surprised.

And he should have been.

"The flea market down in Dorchester?" Beau clarified, scribbling into his notebook.

"The one over in Violetta is too small. Full of junk. The one in Dorchester is on a circuit. Better stuff."

"Were you by yourself?"

"Nope. Everybody except the Sisters went down to the market that day."

"The Sisters?"

"Eloise and Ethel," Wynn said.

"Did you buy anything?" Beau asked.

"Nah." Earl blinked. "I didn't find no rods."

Beau sat back in his chair and stared at him. Earl stared back.

And Wynn began to feel a little sick. It wasn't like Earl to take an interrogation lying down. When he'd run over the sign at the Post Office, Hatfield had been forced to chase him through the streets of Blossom Hills on foot. People still talked about it.

"What makes you think I'd have anything to do with a bank robbery?" he asked finally. "I'm just an old man."

Wynn snorted.

"What happened to your hand?" Beau looked pointedly at the collection of Hello Kitty band-aids that covered the back of Earl's left hand. "Looks like it hurt."

"I'm an old man," Earl repeated and shrugged. "I fall down."

Another short stare-down ensued.

"You can't be serious," Wynn said to Beau because *come on*. "He's a suspect?"

"I found something that belongs to you, Earl," Beau said, ignoring her. "And I'm having a hard time understanding how it could have ended up at the scene of a federal crime."

She watched Earl's Adam's apple bob. And thought: *aw, crap.*

"You don't say?" Earl's brows rose. "Huh. What was it?"

"Your senior discount card for Eckhart's Grocery. Strangely enough, it was on the floor of the Dorchester

National Bank, right in front of the teller's booth where the bank robber stood."

Wynn stared at Beau's flinty expression and felt her coffee sour in her stomach. She was afraid to look at Earl.

"When was this?" Earl wanted to know.

Beau's brilliant green gaze was cold. "Monday afternoon."

"Hell, I lost my wallet more than two weeks ago," Earl told him, shaking his head. "Down at the mall in Edgerton."

Wynn tried not to stare at him. *The liar*.

"Did you report it?" Beau asked.

"Nah. Didn't have nothin' worthwhile in it—just my grocery card and a few scraps of paper."

"Hard to shop with an empty wallet."

"I wasn't shoppin'!" Earl snapped. "I was escortin' the ladies. Some of those young punks who hang out down there give 'em a hard time."

They'd all gone to the mall; they went to the mall once a month. But there'd been no missing wallet. Earl would have had kittens if he'd lost his wallet. He would have launched his own personal investigation and taken out a full-page ad in the Blossom Hills Gazette.

Liar.

"I figured I must've left it someplace, but if my grocery card turned up at the bank, it must've been stolen." Earl nodded as if it all made perfect sense. "Huh. Small world."

Wynn resisted the urge to slap her forehead. *For the love of Pete.*

Earl had *not* robbed a bank.

Had he?

"That's your story?" Beau asked, his voice like frost.

"It ain't a story, it's the truth!"

Beau looked at Wynn, who could only shrug helplessly.

"What about your trip to Canada?" Beau wanted to know. "Where did you go?"

Earl leaned back in his chair and crossed his arms over his chest. "Up to Sault Ste. Marie. Me and Griff, we like to go up and fish for northern."

Beau lifted a brow. "Pretty far to go for northern."

Earl shrugged. "Sometimes we like to give Wynn a break."

Wynn watched him chew on the end of his pipe; she was tempted to resolve the entire issue by strangling him.

Bank robbery. Had he lost his mind?

Did this have anything to do with what Jenna had found in the pasture?

"So you went to the flea market Monday morning," Beau clarified, "and then headed up to Ste. Marie right after?"

"Yep, we did."

"Where in Sault Ste. Marie did you stay?"

"Same place we always stay. The Ste. Marie Inn, right on the water."

Beau wrote everything down. Meticulously. And he wasn't happy.

Not by a long shot.

"Hello, Sheriff Beau."

They looked up to see Ethel in the doorway, an orange and green afghan she was crocheting in one hand, the TV remote in the other. She smiled at Beau, a beautiful, radiant, worshipful smile that immediately set off alarm bells in Wynn's head.

"Hello," Beau said politely.

"We're busy, Ethel," Earl told her.

Ethel ignored him. She moved into the kitchen, the afghan she held trailing against the floor. Her eyes were locked on Beau's wide form. "You saved her," she said. "You saved Clementine."

"Damn fey woman," Earl muttered.

"She's my friend, and you helped her." Ethel stopped next to Beau and showed him the afghan. "I'm making this for you. Do you like it?"

Beau blinked at the afghan. For the first time since Wynn had met him, he looked uncertain.

"You sweet-talked her right out of that dumb old tree." Ethel smiled at him. "Everyone at the library saw. It was the best Storytime hour *ever*."

Earl snorted.

"It isn't finished yet," she continued, returning her focus to the afghan. "But I'm working hard on it."

"It's beautiful," Beau said stiffly. "But I don't need an afghan."

Wynn couldn't help it. She laughed.

"Oh, it's not an afghan," Ethel told him. "It's a cape."

He blinked. "A cape?"

"When I saw you save Clementine," she said, "I knew you were the one."

"The one?" he repeated.

Ethel looked at Wynn. "He's going to save us."

Suspicion lined Beau's face. "What the hell is she talking about?"

Wynn just gave him another shrug. With Ethel, who knew? Clementine, the old tabby cat that lived next door to the Blossom Hills Public Library, was infamous for finding trouble. People were always saving her.

Wynn didn't know why Ethel would single Beau out. But...well.

It was hard to hate a man who could sweet-talk a cat out of a tree.

"He's the one," Ethel said softly, staring at him.

Annoyance flashed across his face. But whatever he was going to say was interrupted by the ring of a cell phone. He fished it from his pocket and answered it shortly, "Greystone."

And Wynn watched him go from irritated to dangerous in a heartbeat. His expression closed; his eyes turned to ice. He looked up at her, and a sudden, chilling wave of goosebumps washed across her skin.

"I'm on my way," he said flatly. He slid his phone back into his pocket and pushed to his feet. "I have to go."

Beowulf growled softly.

And Wynn understood why—the look on his face was scary as hell.

"I'll be back." He slid on his coat and looked at Earl. "I'd suggest you think long and hard before we meet again."

Then he turned to Wynn.

"Walk me out," he ordered.

She was tempted to wave at him like Miss America, but the look on his face stopped her. Something had happened.

Something bad.

"What?" she demanded as they made their way toward the front porch.

"Nothing that concerns you," he said. They stepped out onto the front porch, and he halted. "Did he tell you he'd lost his wallet?"

Wynn said nothing. She wasn't admitting to anything until she talked to Earl.

"Goddamn it." Beau ran a hand through his hair, which was dry now, the color of rich, dark chocolate. "The feds won't care that he's old."

Fear shot through her.

Earl couldn't have robbed a bank.

But she knew just from his laissez-faire response to Beau's interrogation, that he wasn't innocent. At least, not entirely. And Beau was right—if Earl *was* guilty, they would put him away. It wouldn't matter how old he was or why he'd done it—

Why had he done it?

"You think he's guilty," she said, her stomach filled with lead.

"He did it." Beau shook his head. "There's more than just the grocery card."

More. Like what?

"They're coming," he warned softly. "I can't stop them."

Wynn only stared at him, silent.

"Talk to him," Beau said.

Then he turned and disappeared into the night.

CHAPTER 8

SHE'D BEEN LEFT in a cornfield.

Her arms and legs were outstretched, tied with coarse, rough rope to thick steel railroad spikes driven into the ground. Vacant brown eyes stared up into the darkness; her mouth was open as if she'd died mid-scream, and blood was dark, viscous pool beneath her. Her hair was pale white-blond, stained with red, and she was just a kid, no more than fourteen. Her wrists and ankles were black with bruises, and every naked inch of her was covered in fine, short cuts and deep punctures. The wounds painted all of her: her face, her hands, and feet, everything in between. It was sickening and gruesome, and it made Beau want to puke.

He'd seen a lot of death. But he'd never seen anything like this.

"Emma Farley," Harry said tightly. His eyes were wet; his hands were shaking. "She disappeared two months ago from up in Stockton."

Beau stared down at her, ice in his blood.

A few drunks and loose stock. Right.

"It looks..." Harry faltered. "It looks like him."

Beau knelt carefully beside Emma Farley's horrifically abused body and forced himself to study her. "Him who?"

"The Stick Man."

He went still. "This has happened before?"

"Yes," Harry whispered.

Beau looked up at him. "Like this?"

"Yes."

"How do you know?"

"The cuts. He did that before. They're all little stick men."

Beau focused on the fine lines and deep holes covering every inch of the girl's skin. When the pattern suddenly materialized in front of his eyes, bile nipped at the back of his throat. "A serial killer?"

Harry cleared his throat. "Back in '09 a girl from Badger Creek disappeared on her way home from school; they found her six weeks later, cut up like this. Then about two months later, there was another one. She had the same wounds. The press took to calling him the Stick Man."

"How many victims total?"

"Just those two, I think. That they found, anyway."

"No one was ever caught?"

"Not as far as I know. FBI came in, and there was a suspect, some guy from Dorchester, but they ended up cutting him loose. I don't know why." Harry looked down at Emma and blinked rapidly. "I've never seen anything like this."

"Call Lancaster," Beau told him. "I want him to take a look at her before we get forensics in here. Don't touch anything."

"You want me to call her folks?"

Harry's voice wavered, and Beau's respect for him grew

a notch. The last thing anyone wanted to do was tell someone their child was dead. But having to tell them she'd been murdered by some sick fuck whose identity and whereabouts were completely unknown was a special kind of hell.

"No, I'll do it," Beau said.

Harry nodded and headed back toward his truck. "I'll call Lancaster."

Thunder rolled in the distance, but the rain had stopped. The field was soft but not muddy, covered in the short, tough bristle of old corn stalks. It was nearly full dark, the moon lost to the clouds, and they were going to have to get some light if they wanted to process the scene before the rain washed their evidence away.

If there was any evidence.

Beau felt the cold in his veins sink into his bones. He rubbed his leg absently, his eyes locked on the patterns sliced into Emma Farley's skin. Judging by the look of her, she hadn't been here long. Rigor mortis hadn't set in, and there were no signs that animals had gotten to her. An hour or two. Three, tops.

The owner of the field had found her. Fred Bigsby had gone out looking for a stray heifer and stumbled across her instead.

Christ.

Beau pushed himself to his feet. He pulled out his notebook and pen and circled Emma's body. He sketched a copy of the pattern that decorated her skin, his stomach churning. He still wanted to puke. But more, he wanted to kill.

No judge, no jury. Just death.

An instinct at odds with his newly minted position as the man who enforced the law, not the one who broke it.

He wondered grimly which would win.

"Lancaster's on his way," Harry said from behind him. "Shouldn't be long. He was down at the Legion playing cards."

"What did you tell him?"

"Just that he was needed and where."

"Good. We keep this need to know only." Beau turned away and looked out at the field. "We're going to need lights and tarps."

"We've got portable LED spotlights and a couple of framed canopies in the storage unit."

"Go get them."

"You sure? I mean..." Harry looked around. "He might still be out here."

A cold smile curved Beau's mouth. "One can only hope."

His deputy looked down at Emma and swallowed hard.

"She's just a fucking kid," he said, his voice raw. "Who does something like this?"

Beau had no answer. "Grab coffee, too. We're going to need it."

Harry tore his gaze away. "I'll be back as soon as I can."

"Not a word to anyone."

"No, sir."

Rain began to patter down, and Beau moved his truck, parking so the headlights lit the scene. He could see tracks—tire and foot—but some of those were his and Harry's, and some belonged to Fred Bigsby, and the rain was working against them.

As was history. If Emma Farley's death was a new chapter in an old crime, odds were long against finding anything so obvious as tire tracks and footprints. If this bastard had been murdering girls for the last decade—

without getting caught—chances were, he'd gotten damned good at it.

Clearly, he was patient. The intricacy of the cuts had taken time and patience and—sickening as it was—skill. There was nothing hurried or impulsive about this crime. Whoever had done this had planned it, probably down to the last detail.

And he'd enjoyed it.

Headlights bounced across the field, and Beau looked up to see the county Coroner, Elliot Lancaster, pulling in, his dark blue station wagon swaying as it covered the uneven pasture. Old school, Beau thought. *Christ.*

Elliot parked and climbed out of his Griswold-era car, clad in a hooded, bright yellow slicker and red mud boots. He removed a large black medical bag from the passenger side and slowly made his way over to where Beau stood.

"Must be bad," he said as he halted next to Beau. "Harry didn't sound good. That boy is not cut out for—"

His words cut off abruptly as he focused on the motionless form of Emma Farley.

"Oh no," he murmured. "Not again."

And Beau thought: *fuck.*

"Again," he repeated.

"The Stick Man," Elliot said softly.

"We need to be sure," Beau told him.

The older man nodded and moved toward Emma's body. He looked down at her for an eternal moment before carefully kneeling beside her. Then he removed a small tape measure from his medical bag and used it to measure the length of the cuts that covered her. Beau watched, his heart a hollow thud in his throat, adrenaline spiking in his blood.

A fucking serial killer. Perfect.

Elliot moved on, testing the depth of the puncture wounds. He moved slowly, methodically, and it seemed to take forever before he sat back and said, "It's him."

"How do you know?" Beau asked.

"The cuts. They're identical in length and depth to the ones that covered the victims back in '05. Then again in '09."

"'05 and '09?" Beau repeated sharply. "Harry only mentioned two in '09."

"He was just a teenager in '05. He probably doesn't remember." Elliot sighed. "But the four in '05 were the first, right after I was elected. Not nearly so neat as this, mind you. Not as precise or as calculated, but I'd bet my bottom dollar, done by the same hand."

"Why?"

"Because the length and depth of the cuts were never reported. A copycat might get the pattern right, but not the depth. And the instrument used to make the cuts is the same—too jagged to be a scalpel, too precise to be a knife. I never could figure out what it was. It's definitely him." Elliot stretched a hand toward Beau. "Help an old man up."

Beau took his hand and hauled him to his feet.

"Well." Elliot blinked at him. "You might be slow, but you're strong as an ox."

Annoyed, Beau said, "'05 and '09. So this is the third time."

"Afraid so. The four back in '05 were all high school girls. Went missing from all different parts. Found 'em scattered like old bones—in fields, state parks, reservoirs. Like I said, they weren't done the same as this poor girl. He was just getting the hang of it back then. But it's close enough, I know it's him."

Beau stared down at Emma's pale, vacant gaze. "And the two in '09 were him, too? You're sure?"

"Yes. I remember being surprised there were only two. Not sure why; usually these kinds of things escalate."

Only two.

"Maybe the rest weren't found," Beau muttered.

"I doubt it. He likes to make sure someone finds them. That's why he goes to such trouble to display them. He wants people to see what he's done. Like he's showing a piece of fine art."

Going to snap his fucking spine.

Beau took a deep breath. "What about sexual assault?"

"No; never. Apparently, that isn't in his wheelhouse. He just...carves them up."

"Post-mortem?"

"Oh, no, they're alive for it."

"And the pattern? Any significance?"

"The stick figures are primitive, almost juvenile, but there's nothing overtly symbolic about them that I could figure. I would imagine they must mean something—but what, well, only he knows."

"What makes you sure it's a 'he'?"

"Well, statistically, the odds are likely. Less than fifteen percent of serial killers are women, and they tend to kill men, although there is always an exception to the rule. And by and large, their crimes tend to be more low-profile. They aren't interested in making a statement so much as not getting caught. So, yes, I'm fairly certain. Still, anything is possible."

"What about suspects?"

"Nothing in '05 that I know of. But back in '09, they looked at a young man from Dorchester. The Sheriff had to let him go due to lack of evidence."

"Hatfield?"

"The one and only." Elliot shook his head. "He went through the motions, called in the feds, said all the right words, but I don't think he gave a damn about those dead girls."

No, all Jasper Hatfield had given a damn about was himself.

"Goddamn it," Beau said harshly.

"Amen to that." Elliot looked around. "Rain's gonna make it hard to find anything."

"Tents are coming. I've got a tarp in my truck; I'll cover her." Hot, molten rage pulsed in Beau's chest. "Call forensics; oversee the process. You know this bastard. They don't."

"Of course." Elliot hesitated. "He never leaves anything."

"He will. No one is one hundred percent all of the time."

"I hope you're right."

He was. The only question was how many would die first.

"Cause of death?" he asked grimly.

"If she's like the others—and judging by the state of the body, I'd say she is—then it was the blood loss that killed her. I daresay they bleed out as he works on them."

Jesus Christ.

"I knew she'd gone missing," Elliot continued, "but I thought...I don't know. That she'd run off with a boy, I suppose. I hoped never to see this again." He looked at Beau. "Have you thought about what you'll tell the press?"

He hadn't. Mostly because all Beau could picture was pure fucking chaos. But the public had the right to know. And every minute of his tenure as Sheriff would be shaped by the decisions he made in this case; he was painfully aware of that. But it wasn't a burden with which he was unfamiliar. When you led men into war, you had to make impossible choices and stand behind them.

This was just a different kind of war.

"We process the scene and notify her family," he said. "Then I'll decide what and when to tell the press."

Elliot nodded. "I don't imagine this is what you anticipated when you threw your hat into the ring for Sheriff."

"No," Beau said.

"I wasn't a fan of Jasper Hatfield."

Beau slanted him a look. "I haven't met anyone who was."

"He was a mean, arrogant, careless man I despised. Both times this demon rose, he escaped because Jasper couldn't be bothered to do his job. But you're different." Elliot looked at Emma Farley; deep lines wreathed his face. "This time we might actually catch the son of a bitch."

"Oh, we're going to catch him," Beau said softly. "And he's going to wish he was never fucking born."

CHAPTER 9

"Hold it right there, mister!"

Earl froze, one foot out the door. "I got me an appointment."

"For what?" Wynn leaned against the kitchen counter and folded her arms across her chest. "A mani-pedi?"

He shot her a confused look. "What the hell is that?"

She only shook her head. The old dog was trying to sneak out, but she'd been listening, knowing he couldn't hide forever. The thud of his bedroom door—it tended to stick in the humidity—the squeal of hinges that needed to be oiled, the creak of the wooden floor as he crossed it—by the time he was opening the back door and preparing his escape, she was right behind him.

"We need to talk." She pointed at one of the kitchen chairs. "Sit."

His chin lifted. "I gotta go."

"Now."

"There's nothin' to talk about," he said, unmoving.

She only stared at him, equally unmoving.

Sunlight slanted through the window, turning his white

hair to gold. He looked old. When had that happened? He'd always been gray and grizzled, a man who'd led a hard life long before she'd met him. But now he looked...tired.

Frail.

Like Mr. Sanders had. Mr. Sanders, who'd been such a kind man.

She missed him. There'd been nothing to indicate he was ill; no signs of decline, no change in his schedule or personality, nothing that warned his death was imminent. Not like with Fran, who'd gone downhill at a steady, rapid rate that'd been impossible to stop. Infuriating to watch; impossible to process.

"That new Sheriff doesn't know what the hell he's talkin' about," Earl told her. "He's just tryin' to stir up trouble."

Wynn arched a brow. "To what end?"

"How would I know?"

"You lied about losing your wallet."

He blinked innocently. "Did I not mention that?"

Ever since Beau Greystone had darkened her door in search of Earl, Wynn had been worried. Worried for Earl; worried that whatever he might have done would have severe consequences; worried that she couldn't save him. That the peaceful, if chaotic, life they'd finally managed to achieve was about to blow up in her face—*again*.

But now, looking into Earl's shifty, anxious gaze, anger shoved aside the worry. Because she took good care of him—of *all of* them. She fed them; cleaned up after them; drove them anywhere they needed to go. She entertained them and kept them company and always—*always*—put their needs before hers. She made sure they were up in the morning and safe in their beds at night; she ensured they had their meds and access to whatever they might need; she badgered and nagged and annoyed their families into visiting.

And she never, ever lied to them.

"You're going tell me what's going on right now," she told him.

He thrust out his jaw. "Better you don't know."

Aw, crap. "What did you do?"

He looked away, swallowed. "It ain't got nothin' to do with you."

"Earl."

"No," he said.

They stared at one another.

"Did you do it?" she asked bluntly, her insides churning.

"What you don't know can't hurt you," he insisted.

"The hell it can't!" she yelled. Then she took a deep breath. *Do not strangle him.* "They could take Jenna away from me, Earl."

Color flooded his cheeks. "I wouldn't let that happen."

"You'd have no control over it!" Fear and fury flooded through her; *what had he done?* "She can't live under the same roof as a bank robber!"

"Now, just calm down." Earl raised his hands as if she'd drawn on him. "I ain't no bank robber. I told you: that new Sheriff is just tryin' to make trouble."

But Wynn knew better. She'd known him too long; she could see the truth. *He'd robbed a frigging bank.*

And he was going to get caught.

"Why?" she demanded, incredulous. "Why would you do something so stupid and reckless?"

"Reckless!" he spat. "You don't know the half of it. You wait until you're where I'm at—and then you'll see!"

"See what? I don't understand."

"And you don't need to!"

She could only stare at him, stunned. "Why are you doing this?"

"Because I ain't got no damn choice!" he bellowed. "Not in anything, not anymore. I'm just an old man nobody wants!"

The rage and pain in him hammered at her. She took another deep breath, struggling for calm. "Beau *knows* you did it. He has evidence. You have to come clean. You have to confess."

"The hell I will!"

"Jenna found a *gun* in the pasture," she snarled, her voice rising. "Was it yours? Did you use it to rob that damn bank and then leave it there for her to find?"

"It wasn't mine!"

"Covered in blood! And you, with half a dozen Hello Kitty band-aids on your hand. Coincidence? I think not!"

"Don't you get smart with me, missy!"

Infuriated and sick inside, she told him, "If you make me chose, you'll lose."

He blinked, and all of his bluster and rage seemed to wilt away. He sighed heavily. "You do what you gotta do, Chickpea. I'll understand."

Then he turned and walked out the door, and Wynn watched him go, her heart beating so hard she thought she might be sick. She wanted to grab him and shake him and make him confess.

Because what she'd told him was the truth: if he made her choose, she would choose Jenna.

Every time.

Fuck!

She turned and kicked the stove. Tears burned her eyes; her chest was tight, and for one brief moment, panic threatened to steal everything she was. As if she would simply disintegrate into ash, leaving only grief and terror and paralyzing uncertainty behind.

In the aftermath of her mother's death, that uncertainty had frozen her into place. She'd spent months locked in a disassociated state of disbelief and terror that even Fran hadn't been able to touch. Watching what Hatfield had done—

Well. Some moments changed you into something you hadn't imagined you could become.

Even after all that life with her mother had been— sleeping in drug houses and eating from dumpsters and stealing anything she could get her hands on so that Jenna would have something to eat, to drink, to wear...nothing had prepared Wynn for what transpired the night her mother died.

That Lara's life had ended in violence was no surprise; she'd lived the same way, driven solely by two states of being: rage or rapture. Hungry or high, both equally dangerous. She'd dragged her children behind her like an afterthought, using them when it worked to her advantage, abandoning them when it didn't.

Wynn didn't know the identity of her father. Or Jenna's. Or who her mother had been before the addiction had leached away anything good. Maybe she'd been someone worth knowing. And maybe not. All Wynn remembered was the frenzy...the hunger or the high. The rage or the rapture.

Eat, sleep, survive, repeat.

She'd done her best to give Jenna a good life. But her own childhood had been steeped in darkness and desperation and death, so she wasn't sure she'd succeeded. How could you give someone something you'd never had?

Fran had helped. Strong, salty Fran, who the Universe had stolen far too young. All of those fools plunging poison into their veins, embracing the same death she'd fought with every breath.

Life made no sense.

And now this...

Fuck.

They'd come so far.

They'd survived Lara; they'd buried Fran. They'd built a home.

Wynn had worked her butt off, ringing up groceries and pumping gas. She'd scooped ice cream and flipped burgers; she'd even spent two summers mucking stalls and baling hay. Anything and everything she could to hold on to the farm. She'd worked the land and planted the fields; she'd learned everything she could about horticulture and permaculture and how to turn manure into nutrient-rich fertilizer. And she'd done all of it for Jenna, so her sister would grow up in a place where she was safe and loved.

There were few sacrifices Wynn wouldn't make for the people she cared about—and she cared about her tenants. Every last one of them. And they cared for her in return, had supported her relentlessly—through the ugly and crazy with her mother, through Fran's disease and painful, endless death, through every dark time and difficult day— they were *family*.

But this...

There was a line. And this was it.

A robbery. A gun... *That stinking gun.* Battered and old, its finish dull, its hammer rusty, its trigger sticky. Tossed into the back pasture for Jenna to accidentally stumble across... even unloaded, that was wholly unacceptable.

It wasn't mine!

The hell it wasn't. It had to be his. Because who else would abandon a weapon on her property?

She was going to have to act. She couldn't just sit on her hands and stew; she had to do something—before something was done to her.

Balls! Because that meant only one thing.

Only one person.

Sheriff Beau Greystone.

Surly and impatient and grieving. Worse: a man with a badge.

Terse and impatient and obstinate—but, at least, real. Abrasive and generally unfriendly, he was who he was, and if you didn't like it, that was your problem.

Not unlike herself. *Not normal.*

Another odd duck.

Which should have mollified her, but in reality just served to annoy the crap out of her.

Because it was so much easier to focus on their differences.

But if Beau had the evidence he'd claimed—irrefutable proof that Earl had robbed the Dorchester National Bank— he could've just arrested Earl and been done with it. Instead, he'd made an effort to allow Earl to come clean.

Before it was taken out of his hands.

They're coming. I can't stop them.

A warning he'd hadn't had to deliver. Maybe he was trying to help.

And *let's face it*: her only stinking hope. If he failed her...well.

A lot of people had failed her.

She would still have Sasha, who had a newly minted license to practice law in the state of Wisconsin. Something, at least.

The front door creaked, and she took a deep, calming breath.

Time to roll the dice. Swallow her not inconsequential pride and ask Beau for help. If he screwed her over—

Well. Lesson learned.

Jenna appeared in the doorway then, her face pale and strained in a way that made all the anxiety Wynn had just managed to smother flare to life.

"What?" She stepped toward her sister, her heart in her throat. "What is it?"

Jenna dropped her backpack to the floor and stared at it. "They found her."

"Found who?"

"Emma. They found Emma."

No. No more.

Not today.

"He killed her," she said dully. "She's dead."

Wynn's heart skipped a beat. She reached out and wrapped her sister in a tight embrace. "I'm sorry."

"He just left her there," Jenna whispered. "All cut up. Why would he do that?"

Memory bled through her; old, remembered fear shivered into being, and her blood turned to ice. "Who left her there?"

"The Stick Man. He's back."

CHAPTER 10

CASE NOTES, the Stick Man
  September 17, 2009
  FBI Special Agent Kyle Miller

After reviewing the case files from 2005—of which there are few, due to the bodies' improper handling and loss of forensic evidence, as well as local law enforcement's decision to withhold the deaths from the Bureau until the last victim was found—I have very little to composite an accurate profile of the killer behind the "Stick Man" murders.

The victims were all female, between 13 to 15 years of age. Their physical appearances were similar: blond, athletic, attractive. Their socio-economic backgrounds varied, as did their academic performances. Two were taken from Beaver County; one from Lewiston County; and thus far three from Superior County. Based on an examination of the victims' social media accounts, there was no direct interaction between them, other than shared school events: football games, soccer matches, etc. I have found no obvious connection between them other than the commonality of their age and appearance.

The first victim, Bridget Long, was taken from Camp Blossom Hills, a summer camp located in northern Superior County, on the night of June 3, 2005. Her body was found three weeks later in Blossom Hill's City Park playground. She had been staked to the ground with aluminum metal tent stakes, her body left in purposeful display. She had numerous cuts and punctures, as documented by photographs taken by the ME, but none as calculated or precise as what would be done to the second, third, and fourth victims in 2005. With every successive victim, the cuts and punctures became more detailed and exact—in both length and depth—until they covered every square inch of the victim's skin.

Certainly, there is some type of symbolism in the design of the cuts; the work is complex and meticulous, despite its simple design. Stick figures, historically, do not denote any specific mystical or religious meaning; with such limited information, one can only guess at what our killer is trying to say.

None of the victims displayed any signs of sexual assault, which is a rare occurrence among serial murders, and one that makes the compilation of the Stick Man's profile even more problematic. It may be that—

The phone sitting on the table beside Beau began to ring. He sighed, rubbed a hand down his face, and picked it up. "Greystone."

"Sheriff," Harry said. "Edward Duggar called again. What should I tell him?"

That I have a fucking serial killer to catch.

"That we have bigger problems than his goddamn

bank," Beau replied bluntly. "The feds arrive tomorrow. They'll deal with his robbery."

And Earl Barry would go to prison.

"He's pretty pissed off. Says he's going to call a Council meeting and talk about a recall election."

"Good for him. Did you get the toxicology back yet?"

"Not yet. Lancaster said the state office is working on it."

"Call me as soon as it's in."

"Will do. You find anything?"

He had, but nothing he wanted to share. Not yet.

"No," he said shortly. "Go home. Tomorrow will be another long day."

"Yes, sir. Night, sir."

Rain pelted the window beside him as he tossed his phone down. The fire in the woodstove across from him was nothing more than coals, and his belly was empty. His head was throbbing, his leg ached from spending the day running all over hell's half-acre, and he couldn't get the look on Emma Farley's face out of his head. Or the look on her parents' faces when he'd told them she was dead.

He'd spent years hip-deep in sand and blood and death. He hadn't thought it could be worse.

But this was just a different kind of hell.

Miami had taught him that the same brutality and apathy toward life that existed on the battlefield was alive and well stateside. What happened to Marie, to him, had made him understand that no place was safe. No one, not ever, not anywhere. And yet, he'd made the unforgivably stupid mistake of thinking that this place would be different. Simple. Easy. *Benign*.

As if the ugliness of human nature would somehow stop at the county line.

Stupid fool.

That's what Velma would say. And Beau could only agree: *I'm a fucking idiot.*

Because now he had a dead child. A serial killer. And a town on the verge of cracking.

It hadn't taken long to decide the course. People might panic; they might do stupid things and that stupidity would cause problems, but the thought of anyone walking around blind to who was hunting them was unacceptable to Beau. People deserved to know they had a monster in their midst.

So he'd notified the press.

Curfews had been implemented, the schools were on lockdown, and the state was sending in Troopers to help patrol the outer reaches of the county. The feds that were arriving tomorrow would split their time between the bank robbery and pursuing the Stick Man.

Beau was going to do everything in his power to make it impossible for the killer to strike again. And then he was going to catch the murderous SOB and rip his fucking head off.

The mayor didn't have to like it. The feds didn't have to like it. Hell, his own men didn't have to like it. Beau didn't give a shit. He was arming people the best way he knew how: with knowledge.

Not that he was going to win any medals for it. Velma was right: he was never going to get reelected.

And he was okay with that. A politician, he wasn't.

But a politician wasn't going to get it done. A politician didn't know the first thing about hunting a man.

Beau did.

It was some kind of sick, that for the first time since being sworn in as Sheriff, he felt alive again. Useful. He'd always been a weapon aimed at a target. At terrorists; at cartels. At tyrants and despots and genocidal fucks. It had been too long since he'd been fired.

He was primed and ready.

Even broken.

Something to which he was still struggling to grow accustomed. In his head, he was still *then*. Healthy and whole; so fit few could keep up. No matter the constant, unending grind of pain and the darkness that came with it; the lack of patience and lack of hope; the unrelenting reality that he was *changed*. No, in his mind's eye, *he was still the same*. When nothing was further from the truth. A fantasy, that one day he would simply awaken, whole and restored. And yet, somehow that was easier to believe than the pain that never ebbed.

But broken or not, he was going to end the Stick Man's reign.

Emma Farley had disappeared from Stockton, but she was one of Blossom Hill's own. And the fact that she'd disappeared months before his election didn't change the fact that she was his, now. When he'd been sworn in and briefed on the handful of ongoing cases, Emma's had been relegated to runaway status, and truthfully—shamefully— Beau hadn't thought much about it.

Stupid, self-absorbed asshole.

And now it was too late to save her, to do anything other than catch the bastard who'd taken her from them.

So that's what he would do.

The fucking least he could do.

The case files hadn't offered much. They were mostly a chronology of events and a list of facts; everything else was just speculation. Highly educated speculation, but speculation nonetheless. And the files Hatfield had compiled were nothing short of horseshit. A few photos, a handful of medical documents. The small number of interviews done had been conducted by an inexperienced deputy who—while seeming to be the sole person who gave a damn about the case—had taken only cursory notes.

Hatfield had either been asleep at the wheel or actively working against the case. Beau couldn't tell which.

His stomach growled again as the rain turned to hail. He set aside the file and pushed to his feet, hissing as needles of pain speared through his ankle and knee, down his shin, and up his thigh. He made himself add a few logs to the fire and then headed toward his kitchen.

The cabin he occupied had once belonged to Velma; it was small, only two bedrooms, but cozy and warm and recently renovated. It met his needs, and more, it was private and quiet.

Just as he liked it—

A fist pounded on his front door.

"Goddamn it," he muttered.

He abandoned the kitchen, limped to the door, and wrenched it open.

Wynn Owens stood there, soaked to the bone.

Anticipation crashed through him. Followed by something hot and luscious and infinitely dangerous.

He pulled open the door. "What's wrong?"

Her eyes were as dark as the sky behind her. "Can we talk?"

His skin tightened. He held open the door, and she stepped inside, the green windbreaker she wore stuck to her skin. Her jeans were faded, her feet covered in those scuffed combat boots, and her hair was a long, dark fall of blood-red down her back. Rain slid down her cheeks and kissed her chin. She smelled like the wind and the rain and the forest, and for a moment, he was gripped by the intense need to see if she tasted the same.

Goddamn it.

"What do you need?" he asked brusquely, closing the door behind her.

She stalked over to the woodstove and thrust her hands toward it. "Help."

He stilled. "What kind of help?"

She said nothing.

"Wynn."

"I don't trust you," she muttered. "Or your shiny badge."

Annoyance flared. "Then why are you here?"

"Because I don't have a stinking choice."

"There's always a choice."

She snorted.

"Make it," he told her.

For a long moment, those dark, stormy eyes glared at him; she wanted to turn tail and run. He could see it. But if she thought he was going to let her go after she'd come to him for help, she had another thing coming.

Let her try.

His heart pounded hard at the thought.

"You're right," she said abruptly. "He did it."

Surprised by the admission, Beau quirked a brow. "Alone?"

She froze. "What do you mean 'alone'?"

"I mean I don't think he did it by himself."

She just stared at him. Then she lifted her foot and kicked his woodstove. Hard. "Fuck."

Which was how he'd been feeling for the last twenty-seven hours.

"Take off your coat," he said.

She gave him a long, narrow look. "Will you help him?"

"Take off your coat," he said again, in spite of himself.

Because he shouldn't invite her in; he shouldn't want her to stay.

She shook her head. "I just want to know if you'll help him."

"I don't say things I don't mean," he said, annoyed all over again.

Another snort. "You'd be the first."

His gaze narrowed on her. "Yes."

Color flared in her cheeks. "How do I keep him out of jail?"

He turned away. "Are you hungry?"

More words he shouldn't have spoken. Like he wanted her to stay. When he didn't.

He didn't.

Goddamn it.

"I brought you some chili. It's in the van."

He halted and turned to look at her.

She'd brought him dinner.

"Don't get your knickers in a twist." She held up a hand. "It was leftover, and I figured you could use it."

"Thank you," he said, staring at her.

She blinked. The heat in her cheeks spread into a flush. "I'll go get it."

Before he could protest, she was gone. She returned a minute later with a large white bowl covered in cling wrap and a loaf of crusty bread.

"Bread," he murmured.

She shoved it at him. "I had an extra loaf."

"Thank you," he repeated and took the bread. He stared

down at it, something unknown, prickling and painful and unnerving, moving through him.

It's just fucking bread.

"Come," he said and turned to lead her into the kitchen.

"You've very bossy," she said conversationally. "Has anyone told you?"

He halted so abruptly, she almost ran into him.

"I am who I am," he said flatly.

She nodded. "Bossy."

Goaded, he bit out, "Would you like to have dinner with me?"

"I didn't mean it like that." The color in her cheeks deepened. "I was just giving you a hard time. I enjoy it."

He was beginning to realize he enjoyed it, too. "Have you eaten?"

"No."

"Then you should eat."

"Well," she said, "you tried to ask nicely."

"I can do a lot of things nicely."

Jesus Christ.

What the hell was wrong with him?

But she only snorted again. "That's just inappropriate."

A rare smile pulled at his mouth. "My specialty. Just ask Velma."

He turned and resumed his slow gait to the kitchen. "Would you like to take off your coat?"

She followed him into the kitchen. "You learn quick."

Yes.

She set the chili down on the counter and slid off her windbreaker, hanging it on one of the stools that lined the large butcher block island. "It's still warm. Bowls?"

He pointed to the cupboard next to the stove and retrieved the butter dish, utensils, and two large glasses.

Dinner.

It meant nothing.

"I have beer and beer," he said, looking in his cavernous and mostly empty fridge. "Or would you like beer?"

Her gray eyes were like pewter when she looked at him. A dimple winked at him from her left cheek. "He can be funny. Someone call Guinness."

She was beautiful.

Tempting.

But he had no desire to be tempted. To step from the shadows he'd lived within for the past three years. He liked the shadows.

And they liked him.

"Just water," she said. "Thank you."

Anger rippled through him. What the hell was he doing?

Being near her was a slippery slope; she was nothing but trouble. Disrupting the uneasy peace he'd finally made, prodding him back to life when all he wanted was to stay dead.

He poured her water.

"White chili with chicken, garlic, onion, green chilies, and northern beans. I like it hot." She pulled the cling wrap from the bowl. "But if you can't hack the heat, the bread will help."

Aware that he was again being given shit, Beau shook his head. "You poke the bear at your own risk."

"Every bear needs a good poke."

"That's how people get eaten."

She snickered, and he found himself smiling at her. Again.

"Esme's right, you know," she said, sobering. "You should smile more often."

He looked away. He got the unnerving feeling that she saw everything. His pain, his frustration. The confusing, exciting, arousing lust she stirred.

His fury and fear and hollow self-loathing.

"It's getting cold," she said into his silence.

Then she shoved a bowl at him and sat down on the stool that held her coat. Beau sliced up the bread and offered her a buttered piece. Then he sat down—next to her, because goddamn it, he couldn't help himself—and ate the dinner she'd brought him.

It was good. Really good. Spicy and rich, thick with cream and tender chicken. The bread was fresh, soft, and yeasty; he could've eaten the whole loaf.

"I heard about Emma," she said when she was done.

Beau nodded.

"The Stick Man is back."

Don't worry, I'm going to kill him soon.

He bit back the words. "Did you know her?"

"Yes." The word wobbled, and he looked at her sharply. "Jenna played soccer with her. She was a sweet girl. I keep thinking about her lying there and..." She shook her head. "I want him *dead*."

He will be. Again, words Beau swallowed. "Were you here the first time?"

"No. But we were here the last time. Fran wouldn't let us step foot outside for six months. It was like...like the whole town froze in wait." She turned and looked at him. "Why stick figures, do you think? What do they signify? Did you know the first illustrated use of them was for the 1964 Tokyo Olympics?"

Bemused, Beau blinked at her. "No."

"They're prehistoric. It has to mean something, doesn't it?"

"To him, yes."

"They're universal symbols, you know. And the first thing any kid learns to draw."

"Well," he said. "Good luck with that puzzle. Let me know when you figure it out."

"That's not very investigative of you."

He helped himself to more chili and another slice of bread. "Nope."

"Maybe I'll solve it."

"Please do."

"I might, you know."

Another smile tugged at his mouth. "Thanks."

She snorted. Silence fell.

Then, "You'll really help?"

"Yes," he told her. "But the feds are due tomorrow, and Edward Duggar wants someone's head. Getting Earl out of this mess won't be easy."

"But it might be possible?"

Her gaze was so guarded, Beau wondered what had happened to her.

Besides Jasper Hatfield.

"Maybe," he said because he wouldn't lie. "But he has to come clean. Confess his sins. And he'd better have a damn good reason *why*. He turns himself in, returns the money, tells the feds why he did it, they might be lenient. That doesn't mean Duggar will be."

"Edward Duggar is a douche canoe," she retorted.

"That's not a crime."

She rolled her eyes. "A third of the world would be in prison."

Wasn't that the truth.

Beau swallowed the last bite of his chili and thought carefully about his next question.

She wouldn't like it. But he wanted to know.

"What happened to your mother?" he asked quietly.

She turned and looked at him. He waited.

If she chose not to reply, he would respect that. No matter how much it might irritate the hell out of him.

"I read the file," he added. "It sounded like a bunch of shit."

She stared at him, silent.

"I'd like to know the truth," he told her.

"Why?"

"Because..." Goddamn it. "The truth matters."

You matter.

He couldn't say it. Even if he feared it might be true.

Wynn only blinked at him. Silence stretched between them, and his jaw hardened. If she didn't want to tell him—

"My mother," she said with a sigh, "was an addict. And not a nice person. Maybe the drugs did that, maybe not." She shrugged. "I was fourteen when she dumped us on Fran."

"Your aunt," Beau said, remembering.

"Yes. A superb human being. I miss her."

Her grief was palpable. Beau could relate. "I'm sorry."

When she said nothing more, he pushed harder. "What happened that night?"

She looked at him, her eyes roiling like a storm.

"Tell me," he said. "Share it." He paused. "Please."

For a moment, he didn't think she would. But then she pushed her bowl away and sighed again. "When my mother dumped us at Fran's and drove away, I was relieved. Anything was better than her. But two days later, she was back. Hatfield had stopped her on her way out of town and they'd...hit it off. Birds of a feather, I guess. I don't know. All I know is that a month later, she showed up, high as a kite. Higher. She was hysterical, screaming that he was going to kill her. That he was going to kill us all. She grabbed Jenna and threw her in the car, and I couldn't let her take Jenna without me. So I got in, too."

She fell silent. Rubbed her finger along the grain of the butcher-block countertop.

"Fran let her take you?" he prodded.

A cold smile, one he didn't particularly like. "Fran was no match for her. Violence was my mother's weapon of choice, and she used it often and well."

"On you?"

He tried to stem the rage that bled through him. Because he already knew the answer.

He could see it.

"Sometimes." Wynn shrugged. "Fran called 911. Hatfield must have been close because he was there in five minutes. When he showed up, my mother went bonkers. Complete and total meltdown." Her gaze met his. "It terrified me. I'd seen her take on dealers, junkies—gang bangers and barely bat an eye. But when Hatfield showed up, she lost her ever-loving mind. That's when I knew he'd done something to her."

"He was a corrupt piece of shit."

"He was a murderous bastard."

Thunder drummed overhead, a loud, startling clap that made Wynn start violently beside him.

He wanted to touch her. She was pale; all of that lovely color had drained away.

"And then?" he asked.

She gave him a raw, piercing look that made his chest tighten. Again, he had the uneasy sensation that she saw right through the adamantine shell he wore, right into the dark heart of him, where nothing existed but pain and rage and a bottomless well of grief.

"Tell me," he murmured.

She stroked the grain again, caressing the narrow amber lines. "Hatfield pulled her out of the car and tried to get her into his truck. She fought him like an animal. She kept screaming, 'I saw you. I saw you! I know what you did.'"

Cold slid through his veins. "Do you know what she was talking about?"

"No."

"And then?"

"She kneed him in the groin and ran. It was dark, but I saw her coming toward us. I'll never forget the look on her face. And then a shot rang out, and her chest turned red, and she fell. She was close; another step or two, and she might have made it. But she was dead by the time she hit the ground."

For a moment, there was only the sound of the rain pattering against the tin roof. Beau growled softly, rage pressing against his skin. "He shot her in the back? As she was running from him?"

"He did. And then he called it self-defense. But I saw it. Fran saw it. We knew."

"Why didn't you tell anyone?"

"Because he killed my mother right in front of us. He didn't have to make any threats; her blood staining the ground was more than enough to keep us quiet. Fran was afraid—for us, for her tenants. And she felt guilty. If she hadn't called..."

Beau's hands curled into fists. He was sorry Jasper Hatfield was dead.

"I would have enjoyed killing him," he said.

Words he didn't mean to speak.

But Wynn only looked at him and said, "Me, too."

Rain hit the metal roof in a sudden deluge, so loud it was almost deafening. A moment later, it settled into a low, steady roar.

"So." She pinned him with that dark, penetrating gaze. "I told you my deepest, darkest secret. What's yours?"

CHAPTER 11

BEAU'S FACE WENT BLANK.

"No secrets here," he muttered. He collected their bowls and limped to the sink. "I'm an open book."

"Hardy har har," Wynn retorted. "How did it happen?"

"How did what happen?"

The growl in his voice probably cowed a great many folks. She didn't happen to be one of them. Even if he was big and intense and talked about delivering death like it was the mail. "Your leg."

He didn't respond. Instead, he stood at the sink and stared out into the storm.

"Is it a state secret?" she wanted to know. "A matter of national security? An injury suffered while on a clandestine mission that you can't talk about under penalty of death? Did they make you swear on a Bible?"

"You're a piece of work," he said.

"I know." When he turned to glower at her, she smiled. "It's a gift."

His gaze fell to her mouth, and awareness speared through her, a hot, electric slide that made her cheeks burn.

He was attracted to her, the same way she was attracted to him. And he didn't like it.

Not one bit.

You and me both, bucko.

"You don't have to tell me," she told him and shrugged. "It doesn't matter."

Darkness rolled across his features. "Then why did you ask?"

She only stared at him. Beautiful, angry man. Layer upon layer of pain and grief and fury; it should have made her run for her life. Instead, she wanted to peel them away, one by one, until she reached the man underneath.

And then do what with him?

"Because I know you're in pain," she said finally. "And I know it helps to talk about it."

"It's all I fucking think about. I don't want to talk about it, too."

She held up her hands. "Fair enough."

But that response just seemed to annoy him further.

"Every minute of every day, and people wonder why I don't smile and laugh; why I can't take a fucking joke." He leaned back against the counter and glared at her. She wondered if he realized his nostrils were flaring, that every line of his body was tense and his hands had curled into tight fists. There was no obnoxiously bright shirt tonight. Instead, he wore a pair of worn jeans and a plain black t-shirt that fit him like a glove. Muscle padded his chest; his arms were sinewy and roped with strength. And his forearms...

Good gravy.

The heat that was coursing through her was a freaking revelation. Pheromones, she told herself. Nothing more than a simple chemical reaction.

But damn. *Damn*.

Beautiful, angry man. "What happened to you, Beau?"

He only looked at her, his brilliant green eyes hard.

"Was it a King James Bible?" she asked and wiggled her eyebrows at him.

"Fuck," he said and wiped a hand down his face. "Someone really needs to paddle your ass."

A fiery wash of heat pulsed through her. And she thought: *aw, crap*.

Because what was wrong with her, that those words were...exciting?

Idiot.

Still. "Them and what army?"

His gaze narrowed. Fell to her mouth again. "I don't need an army."

White heat flooded her belly. That look...it felt like a touch. "Are you threatening to spank me, Sheriff?"

He stared at her, and the air between them almost crackled. Her skin prickled; her knees went weak. A flutter rose deep within her.

"It was a car bomb," he said, the words falling like a hammer. "A drug runner I'd been hunting for the DEA attached a block of C-4 to the frame of my Jeep and rigged it to blow when I opened the door. My wife was already inside. She died instantly."

Wynn sat back, silenced.

His grief and fury were living, breathing things, spilling into the room around them. Seething with violence, so tangible they stole her breath.

He turned and began to pace in front of the sink, his gait uneven, his hands clenching, unclenching. Clenching, unclenching. Wynn watched him, regret welling inside of her.

She hadn't meant to hurt him. *Again*.

"I'm sorry," she said.

"I was thrown clear, but my leg was hanging by a thread. Just a piece of useless, mangled meat. I couldn't get up, I couldn't walk, I couldn't even fucking crawl. I just laid there and watched her burn."

Her heart hurt. She'd just had to push.

Jerk.

"And the man who did it?" she asked quietly.

"Dead," he hissed.

"Did it make you feel better?"

That bright green gaze crashed into hers, churning and dark. "No."

She nodded. She understood completely.

Finally.

Just a little too late. Jerk!

"I didn't mean to make it worse," she told him.

He shook his head. Continued to pace. The lines in his face deepened. "It was my fault. Arrogant and fucking stupid, and she paid for it with her life."

There was nothing to say to that, so Wynn said nothing.

"I should have been the one to die," he continued raggedly. "Me. Not her. It makes me want to take the world apart, piece by goddamn piece."

Tears massed without warning in her chest. His torment and grief hurt. So much pain, bleeding from him like an open wound.

He couldn't forgive himself. And likely never would.

And you had no clue. You idiot.

She'd ripped open the scar and could only sit there, watching it bleed.

"So I came *here*," he snarled and turned again to pace. "I

let Velma talk me into coming back, into running for goddamn Sheriff, and now I have a dead fourteen-year-old girl and a fucking serial killer. I want to tear him limb from limb. I don't want to wait for a judge or a jury; I just want him *dead*."

A shiver moved through her. The Stick Man finally had a worthy adversary. "Good."

He halted. Lifted his head and speared her with his gaze.

"Put him down," she added, so there was no misunderstanding.

Because she wanted him dead, too.

Emma Farley had been Jenna's friend; she'd slept under Wynn's roof, eaten at her table. *She could have been Jenna*. And that knowledge sat like a hard stone in Wynn's stomach.

She wanted the Stick Man *gone*.

A harsh laugh broke from Beau. He shook his head. "So fucking tempting."

She didn't know what that meant, but he turned and resumed his pacing. Wynn watched him, her heart beating too hard. She couldn't imagine being responsible for an entire community of people when there was a serial killer on the loose.

And he was a soldier. He wouldn't sit on the sidelines and watch.

He would hunt the SOB down himself.

"You need to be careful," she told him. "The Stick Man is a crazy bastard."

But Beau only smiled, a grim, chilling curve that spoke of blood and death and made another, deeper shiver move through her. "I'm dangerous, too."

An understatement, she thought.

"I'm sorry," he said and halted abruptly. "I didn't mean to..."

"To what? Tell me the truth? That's what I asked for."

"And now that you have it?"

He was watching her with narrow eyes, his hands still fisted. As if he expected judgment.

"Now I get it," she replied.

His brows rose. "Get what?"

"Why you act like a pissed-off badger most of the time."

For a second, she thought she'd gone too far. Again. But a harsh laugh broke from him, and the sound stroked over her like a warm, rough hand.

"Thank you," he said.

"For what?"

He shrugged and looked distinctly uncomfortable. "For listening."

She only shrugged. "I'm all ears."

He turned away and stared out at the storm again.

So alone, she thought. She understood that, too.

"So," she said and sighed. "Earl."

"Earl," he agreed without turning.

She took a deep, bracing breath. "Why do you think he had help?"

"Because someone distracted the security guard by throwing a handful of pebbles at the bank window. And because CCTV tracks him until he runs around the northwest corner of the building, and then he just disappears. No one saw him drive away. No one saw anything. I'm certain it wasn't just him."

No. What he was saying...it wasn't possible.

Was it?

Esme and Griff...the Sisters...they wouldn't have signed onto this madness.

Would they?

Wynn stared at him, and the dread she'd tried to keep silent and contained spilled through her like wet cement. *Had they helped him? Were they all in on it? Why? Why would they be so reckless and foolish? Risking everything they had—everything she had—and for what?*

It was painful and overwhelming; *impossible to comprehend.* But she was going to have to get to the bottom of it. Root out the truth and then figure out what in Hades to do with it.

"There's something else," she said reluctantly.

Because if the man in front of her was an angry badger under the best of circumstances, the confession she was about to make would turn him into a pissed off grizzly.

"You're going to get mad," she added.

He turned from the window and leaned against the counter. He folded his arms across his chest and focused intently on her. "Tell me."

Back to ordering her around, because he was used to being obeyed.

Boy, was he barking up the wrong tree.

Nonetheless, she said, "The morning after the robbery, Jenna found something in our pasture."

His gaze bored into her. "That's what she was talking about the first time I came by."

"Yes."

She fell silent. He waited.

"Wynn," he growled, his voice low and rough, and a tremor skittered down her spine.

But not out of fear.

Why him?

The only man she'd ever met who pushed her every

button without even trying; a man her deepest instincts told her to reach toward when he would never reach back.

Because you don't have enough problems?

She sighed, reached into the pocket of her windbreaker, and pulled out the gun she'd placed carefully into a Ziploc bag. "Earl said it wasn't his." She held it out to him. "But I know that was a lie."

Beau's face closed. He took the gun. "Jenna found it?"

"She was crossing the field, coming from Amy Morgan's place. Her parents live next door."

He turned the weapon over, studying it through the bag. "There's blood."

Wynn tried to ignore the growing darkness she could see in him. "There is."

He stared at it, his jaw like granite.

"I thought maybe it was just kids," she said, defensive. "Look at it; it's older than dirt. And I didn't know what he'd done. I didn't think it might be connected to something...real."

"You didn't think," he repeated softly, and her hackles rose.

"Don't," she told him.

"Don't tell you how stupid and irresponsible it was to keep this from me?"

"Just cool your tits." She held up a hand. "I'm telling you now."

"I'm the goddamn *law*."

"Another man with a badge and a gun and the impunity to hurt whoever he wants." She snorted. "I'm familiar."

He growled at her. "Not with me, you aren't. You withheld evidence."

"I didn't know it was evidence!" she yelled.

"I won't help you if you lie to me." His voice was so cold, it only inflamed her more.

"I came here to roll over on a man I *love* because I believed you when you said you wanted to help him," she snarled.

"I do," he snarled back. "But you have to fucking trust me."

Her mouth snapped shut. She didn't want to trust him; she didn't want to trust anyone.

Problem was, she was pretty sure she already did.

Or she never would have told him about her mother.

Crap.

"I brought it to you," she pointed out, exasperated. "Didn't I?"

He looked down at it. "You did."

She stared at him, her heart rattling around in her chest. Good grief, the man got her blood up. Half the time she wanted to strangle him.

"Earl used it in the robbery," he said grimly. "The blood on it is his. We found it at the scene, too."

A sudden, furious rush of emotion filled her throat. "What the hell was he thinking?"

"I don't know."

Tears burned her eyes, which just infuriated her more. "He's risking all of us."

"Then he must be desperate."

The words were like a blow; they made her reel. Because he was right. Earl was many things, but stupid wasn't among them. Or selfish or thoughtless or cruel. If he was stealing...

It was because he had to.

You are a moron.

"I have to go," she said and slid from the stool.

"Not yet." Beau shook his head. "We aren't done."

She pulled on her coat. "I'm done."

"Wynn."

"Bossy," she told him. "I'm going."

"No."

"I need to know why he did it," she said, exasperated again. "So I'm going to go find out."

Beau stared at her, his brilliant eyes glinting. She couldn't tell what he was thinking, but he had that dark, obstinate look on his face that spelled trouble.

"I'm going," she insisted and held up a hand. "Just swallow that down, because it's happening."

"This isn't finished," he warned softly, and something she didn't want to name flooded through her.

Something hot and wild and stupid.

"I'll let you know what I find out," she said and turned away.

"Stop." His voice was sharp, a bark he probably used in the military.

Wynn only rolled her eyes. *Bossy*. Like he could argue.

"From now on, you don't go anywhere alone," he declared. "It's isn't safe."

"Nothing is safe," she said.

But he wasn't wrong. She kept remembering about Emma, and each time it felt like a dagger stabbing into her heart. Sickening and infuriating and terrifying. Emma had been *hers*.

It wasn't fair. And it wasn't over.

"I'll follow you home," he said.

"No worries." She picked up the chili bowl, found enough for another meal, and re-covered it in cling wrap. She shoved it into the refrigerator, along with the leftover bread. "I'll be fine."

He didn't argue. He just walked over to the coat rack beside the back door and grabbed his coat. "Let's go."

"I'm a grown-up," she pointed out, annoyed. *And armed.*

With both her knife and Fran's old .45. But the .45 wasn't registered, and he probably wouldn't approve.

"Jenna fits his profile," he growled.

"I know," she growled back.

"Good." He nodded. "Then you know to be careful. I don't want to worry about you."

Which just offended her. "We can take care of ourselves."

He only stared at her and waited.

"Bossy," she muttered.

See also: *brooding, arrogant, and stubborn as a damn mule.*

Which just made her a big dummy.

Because she was kind of starting to like him.

CHAPTER 12

"I'm sorry, Sheriff, but that kind of request is going to require a warrant. We have a duty to protect our campers' privacy."

Beau bit back an impatient snort. *This* was the problem with not being a politician. Sometimes it wasn't the badge that got things done. It was the ability to talk your way around people. "And your campers' lives, Ms. Jenkins? Do you have a duty to protect those?"

Lillian Jenkins sighed in his ear. "Of course we do. But this request—I can't just provide those records to you, not without—at the very least—the permission of our ED, Mr. Duggar."

Beau stilled. "Edward Duggar is the camp's Executive Director?"

"Yes, since the camp was built back in 2001. He owns the land the camp occupies and kindly allows the nonprofit to lease it for a minimal cost."

What a deal. "How long have you worked for the organization, Lillian?"

"Oh, well." She softened slightly at the use of her first

name. "Since before the camp was built. I used to do the fundraising, but all of the social media changed things so much, I moved over to the administrative side of things. I do all of the accounting and record-keeping, now."

"Did you happen to know Bridget Long?" He paused. "She was the first victim."

Lillian was silent. Then, "I knew her."

"And Mary Barnes?"

"Yes. She was in my daughter's Girl Scout troop."

"And Sarah Bancroft?"

"I don't understand. Why are you doing this?"

Because I want those records. "Just between you and me?"

She hesitated. "Okay, yes."

"I have a theory, Lillian."

"Lily," she corrected. "My friends call me Lily."

So apparently they'd graduated to friends. *I can still be charming.* Who knew?

"What's your theory?" she asked, her curiosity palpable.

"I think that every girl he's killed has been up to the camp at some point or another."

"No. That's not...I would know if that were true."

No, Lily, you wouldn't. "Well, now, that's why I'd like to get a look at those records. I just want to cross-check some names. I'd also like a list of the employees for each year, anyone and everyone who was at the camp, and what their purpose for being there was."

"Goodness, that's a tall order. Some of those things I have, but the others...I'd have to put those together."

She was weakening. "I'd sure appreciate it, Lily. A warrant takes time, and the clock is ticking."

"Well, I...I really should call Mr. Duggar."

Who would no doubt demand a search warrant.

"I won't show them to anyone," Beau promised softly. "And if I find anything, I'll get that warrant, and we'll go through the proper channels."

"But Mr. Duggar..." She laughed uneasily. "He's quite the stickler."

That was one word for him.

"Is there someone else I can talk to?" Beau asked. "Someone else who might know about—"

"I'm the record keeper," Lily said quickly. "I'm in charge of all the files."

"Well, then. Looks like I'm talking to the right lady."

"Yes. I just..."

"I know it's unorthodox," Beau conceded in an easy tone. "And I can appreciate your reluctance to break the rules. But I'm trying to find a killer, Lily. A man who cuts up little girls and leaves them on display. Little girls you've known personally. Not just pictures on the news, but real people. And I thought that maybe since you're so close to the case and all, you might be willing to help me out with this. Like I said, just between us."

She fell silent. Beau only waited. There wasn't much else he could do. He'd played his hand.

"Can I...can I scan and email them to you?"

The line of tension digging into the back of his skull eased. "I'd appreciate that. And I'll give you my private email, which uses an encrypted server, so there's no chance of anyone else setting eyes on them."

A sigh rushed from her. "Okay, that sounds good. And you won't tell anyone?"

"You have my word, Lily."

"Okay. Then I can send you the list of campers and employees right now. But it might take me a few days to put together the list of people who came and went—we have a sign-in station, but not everyone follows that particular rule, and we have a lot of volunteers who come in and give classes, and you're asking for over a decade's worth of records—but I'll see what I can do. Is that okay?"

"That's better than okay," Beau told her honestly. "Thank you, Lily."

"You're welcome, Sheriff." She hesitated. "Will you promise me something?"

"Anything."

"I want you to get that murdering son of a bitch."

Startled by the harsh order, Beau said, "Count on it."

He gave her his email and hung up. Then he sat back in the driver's seat of his truck, somewhat amazed that he'd managed to talk her into it. And damn glad, because he had a strong feeling that Camp Blossom Hills might just be the key.

It had been the scene of the first crime: Bridget Long's kidnapping. And although there'd been nothing in the files to connect the other victims to the camp, last night, while reading the police report filed by the Farleys, Beau had realized that Emma's stepmother Lois worked at the camp cleaning cabins.

A connection. Tenuous and unlikely; he was probably grasping at straws. But it was something.

As opposed to nothing.

Hopefully the records Lily had agreed to provide would help him figure out if he was chasing his tail or actually onto something. He figured even if the victims hadn't attended the camp, they may have visited or had family who worked out there.

Hell, the girls who had died might have used that land as their own personal playground, unbeknownst to anyone else. Kids had secrets.

He had.

Unfortunately, other than his gut's insistence that the camp was part of it, Beau didn't have anything else to go on. The toxicology had come back clean, and forensics hadn't found anything. No blood or skin or hair. Nothing to point toward a location, or a method of transportation; no clues as to who'd killed Emma Farley or why.

He had nothing but a town filled with terrified people and the killer who was hunting them.

The Universe, he thought, had a shit sense of humor. But then, maybe this was just all part of his penance. For all of the lives he'd taken; for Marie. For being him.

Maybe this was the only way he could put a dent in any of it.

Is it a state secret? A matter of national security? An injury suffered while on a clandestine mission that you can't talk about under penalty of death? Did they make you swear on a Bible?

Not doubt Wynn Owens was part of his penance.

Smart, beautiful. Snarky as hell.

And unafraid to take him on.

The threat he'd made to paddle her ass for that smart mouth had backfired spectacularly, breathing life into the very thing he'd been trying to diffuse. And when he'd realized that, he'd thrown the truth between them like a bomb. But in his hurry to push her back, *away*, he'd ended up telling her things he'd never told anyone. Private thoughts and personal torments; the rage and chaos and grief that lived ever-present within him; the entirety of his self-loathing laid out before her like a hot buffet.

Christ.

And she'd just looked at him in perfect understanding, unsurprised, without judgment or opinion.

Now I know why you act like a pissed-off badger most of the time.

Jesus. What was wrong with him, that he'd wanted to kiss her for that?

He knew Marie wouldn't have wanted him to quit living; she'd been a generous and loving woman. Everything he wasn't. That had been part of the attraction. She was kind; he wasn't. She felt things like happiness and hope and belief; he didn't. She was always certain that good would win the day; he knew better. Maybe he'd thought some of that would rub off, but it never much did.

She wouldn't want her memory used as an excuse. Not for any reason.

But he'd made a vow: *never again.*

And he had no desire to break that vow. He didn't want anything, not from anyone.

Not ever.

He deserved nothing.

He'd killed the man who'd strapped that C4 to his Jeep, slowly and without compunction. It had been worth the career he'd lost, and he'd enjoyed every minute of it. But it hadn't been enough. He'd hungered for more; a sea of red in which he might finally be able to drown.

He'd had nothing left to lose—they'd destroyed the only thing that made him human.

And he was good at killing. War had taken the strong, naïve and stupidly brave kid he'd been and turned him into a killer. A great killer, but a killer nonetheless, and no matter what outfit he donned, he would always be a man who sought justice from blood.

Bad enough. But worse, he was a broken killer. Hurting and hating and half of a man. Hell, he could barely get himself out of bed. He couldn't walk further than half a mile without the pain being so bad, he was half-temped to take a hacksaw to himself. He couldn't run. And while he could still fight, if he went down—

He'd be fucked.

Everything he'd ever been was tied to his physical self. His stamina, his strength, his endurance. A definition he'd never questioned; a safety net he'd always taken for granted.

Gone, now. Never to return.

Three years, and every day that realization—and its acceptance—was a struggle. To let go of *what was* and swallow down *what is*. It seemed impossible, and Beau didn't see that changing.

Ever.

So even if he broke his own goddamn vow, and let himself want something—anything—he had no intention of tying a woman to that. To his pain, his disability, his own fucked up thoughts. He was impatient and cold, and when he was really hurting, downright mean.

He wouldn't put that on anyone.

Especially a woman he barely knew.

"So why the hell are you thinking about her?" he muttered and wiped a hand down his face. He was tired. Another bonus of chronic pain: he didn't sleep worth a shit.

He hadn't even gotten out of his driveway yet.

But he hadn't wanted to call Lily from his office. Because while he knew he should trust Harry and his part-time deputy Cam, he didn't. Well, not that he *didn't*, he just worked best alone. The DEA had taught him to keep his cards close, and the habit had served him well.

He had no intention of stopping now.

The open page of his notebook stared up at him from the passenger seat; the cheery, smiling stick man grinned at him.

They're universal symbols, you know. And the first thing any kid learns to draw.

She wasn't wrong. But hell if Beau knew what it meant.

His cell phone rang, and he sighed.

Harry.

"Hey, Sheriff. Are you on your way in? Anna Barnes returned your call. I don't think she was happy about it, but she said you could call her back at work."

"Good," Beau said. "Hatfield's head deputy, Winston Reynolds. Where can I find him?"

"Reynolds? Why do you want to talk to him?"

Because he'd been the only one of Hatfield's men to actually look for the Stick Man. The only one who interviewed witnesses and took notes—even if they sucked—and the only one who appeared to give a damn that four young girls had been brutally murdered while on his watch. Add to that the fact that Hatfield had fired him for insubordination—well.

Winston Reynolds would be worth buying a cup of coffee.

"Is he local?" Beau asked.

"I think he still lives out on Red Hill Drive, over by the cheese factory. Why?"

Because obviously, I have some questions for him. "Get me an address and send it to my phone."

"Okay. But..."

"But what?"

"I hear he's pretty much pickled himself."

Beau rubbed his face again. "Just send me the address."

"Will do, Sheriff. Oh, and somebody named Garrett Morrison called."

Fanfuckingtastic.

Special Agent Garrett Morrison, FBI. Who could only

be calling because he'd been tasked with solving a bank robbery.

And finding a serial killer.

Beau had known the feds were coming, he just hadn't known who they would send. Garrett was a surprise. He'd known Morrison since his DEA days. It wasn't often the agencies mingled, but occasionally, they'd crossed paths. Garrett was the last agent Beau would have expected the Bureau to send. The last he'd heard, Garrett was at Quantico, moving up the FBI ladder at the speed of light.

What the hell had he done to get sent into the backwoods of Wisconsin?

Shit. This was not good news. Stalling an FBI agent Beau didn't know would've been a hell of a lot easier than bullshitting one he did.

Because Garrett Morrison was a crack agent.

Goddamn it.

"Send his number, too," Beau muttered.

"Ten-four. Anything else? Cam is on his way in, and HP is out patrolling, so I can do some interviews if you want. I know you haven't gotten around to—"

"Just man the phones and hold down the fort," Beau told him. "I'll be there soon."

"I'm a good deputy, sir," Harry said quietly. "So is Cam. We can help you."

Beau didn't doubt it. That didn't mean he wanted his deputies conducting interviews without him. "I hear you. But for now, I just need you to hold the damn place together. Can you do that?"

"Yes, sir."

"Then do it."

CHAPTER 13

"Ethel? Come see what I found."

Sometimes, Wynn thought, you had to do what you had to do.

The tiny white kitten she held purred loudly, the small rumble loud in the quiet kitchen. She'd found him hunting mice in the hay shed that morning; she had no idea where he'd come from. The valley was filled with feral barn cats. Sickly, too thin, haggard from hunger.

But like Beowulf, this little guy had a fierce will to live.

"I'm coming!" Ethel cried from the living room, where she was working diligently on Beau's cape. "I'm coming! What is it? Is it a pony?"

The kitten kneaded Wynn's sweatshirt; he was skin and bones; she'd have to worm him and get him neutered. But he was a lover, nudging her chin, flexing his tiny paws against her. Thanking her profusely for saving him.

Sweetness, she thought and rubbed her nose between his ragged ears.

"Oooooo!" Ethel squealed as she halted in the doorway and saw the kitten. "Can we keep him, Wynnie? Can we?"

"Yes. If you sit down, I'll let you hold him. But you have to be very, very careful."

Ethel moved toward the kitchen table, her faded gaze locked on the kitten. She wore a pair of purple polyester pants and an orange sweater covered in tiny snowmen. Pink socks, several strands of gold Mardi Gras beads, and big green foam curlers completed her ensemble. "I know. I'll be careful. Oh, he's so beautiful!"

Ethel sat down, and Wynn carefully handed her the filthy ball of white fur.

She was not being purely altruistic; she had a motive.

Whether anyone realized it or not, Ethel knew most of what went down at the Owens Boarding House. They assumed that because she was child-like, she didn't grasp what went on around her, but Wynn remembered being a child who heard and saw everything, and she knew from experience that Ethel was far more aware than those around her would ever recognize.

If Earl and Esme and Griff had lost their minds and committed armed robbery, Ethel would likely know. Even if she didn't realize what it was she knew.

So Wynn had sent Eloise off to the grocery store along with Esme, despite Eloise's protests. Wynn knew no matter how she much grumbled, she'd be glad for the break. Sean Evers had disappeared at dawn, presumably frog hunting, and Griff and Earl had escaped soon after to go fishing. Jenna was with Sasha shopping for school clothes (because, according to them, Wynn had the fashion sense of a scarecrow), so now was the perfect time to corner Ethel and do some digging.

"Oh, he's wonderful," Ethel cooed. "What's his name?"

Wynn sat down beside her. "He doesn't have one yet."

"We should call him White!"

"Bo-ring," Wynn said. "What else you got?"

Ethel scrunched her face in thought. Then she smiled. "How about Winter? Because winter is white!"

"I think that's perfect." The kitten blinked at her, his gold-green eyes glinting in the light. "Sweet Winter storm."

"Oh, he's purring!"

Wynn grinned. Ethel was like the kitten: pure, undiluted joy. She didn't stay angry or hold grudges; she was never mean or bad-tempered. And every experience was new and wonderful, full of magic and opportunity. No one saw a better world than Ethel.

Wynn tried hard to take that lesson and learn from it.

"Can he sleep with me?" Ethel wanted to know. She leaned over and kissed Winter gently on the top of his head. "He can lay on my pillow and purr in my ear."

"Eloise would just love that," Wynn said wryly. "I think he'd better stay with me at night."

She expected a protest, but Ethel only looked at her, her expression oddly serious. "He can keep you company."

A painful flutter whispered in her chest. "Yes."

"But he can sit with me during the day, right?"

"He sure can." Winter mewed softly, and Wynn reached out to pet him. "Ethel, can I ask you a question?"

"Mmm-hmmm." Ethel kissed his head again.

"Is there something going on that I should know about?"

Her smile faded. She looked down and shrugged. "I don't know."

Translation: *yes. Yes, there is.*

"Because I think someone is keeping secrets from me," Wynn continued, "and I don't know why."

Bright pink flooded Ethel's cheeks. "Sometimes secrets are necessary."

Aw, crap. "Who told you that?"

Another shrug.

"Ethel, do you remember when the Sheriff came by?"

"I remember." Ethel hugged Winter gently. "Sheriff Beau is my friend."

Well, Wynn thought, Beau Greystone could definitely use a friend. Or two. And while she wasn't certain they'd entered friend territory, their unexpected, mutual exchange of history had left her with less of a desire to bash him in the face with a crescent wrench.

So, there was that.

"He came here looking for Earl," she continued, determined not to get sidetracked. "Do you know why?"

"No!"

Ethel looked defiant but panicked.

"Ethel," Wynn said quietly. "I need to know what's going on."

"I don't know!" she cried loudly and buried her face in Winter's fur. "I don't know what's going on!"

"Yes, you do," Wynn said. "Can't I count on you, Ethel?"

It was blatant manipulation, but Wynn didn't care. Getting to the truth was all she cared about.

"You can count on me, Wynnie!" Ethel stared at her, a stricken look on her face. "I promise."

"Not if you're going to lie to me."

She reached for Winter, and Ethel made a sound of distress.

"Please don't take him away," she whispered.

You are going to burn in hell. But sometimes, being a hard-ass was the only option. "If I can't trust you—"

"She said you would throw us out if I told!" Ethel began to cry. "I don't want you to throw us out!"

The anger that had been simmering within Wynn for

days threatened to boil over because, in that instant, she was certain: *they were all in on it.*

Beau was right.

"I would never, ever throw you out," she said quietly. She stroked Winter's back but didn't move to take him away. "Cross my heart, Ethel."

Tears slid down Ethel's cheeks. "She said you would."

She. Eloise. "She's wrong."

"I'm sorry," Ethel said and hiccupped. "I'm not supposed to tell. I promised. And I c-can't break a promise."

She would spill her guts in a heartbeat if Wynn threatened to take Winter away again, but Wynn was pretty sure she didn't have it in her to do it a second time. Once had been worth a try, but twice would just be cruel. Like something her own mother would have done.

And wasn't that just an awesome realization?

"Okay," she said. "If you can't tell me, can you show me?"

Ethel's gaze flew to hers and widened. "She didn't say I couldn't show you!"

Thank freaking God. "Then please show me."

Ethel stood up, clutching Winter tightly. "She didn't say *anything* about not showing you. Come on!"

A mixture of relief and apprehension speared through Wynn. She followed Ethel out of the kitchen, through the living room, down the narrow hallway that led to Earl, Griffin, and Sean Evers' rooms, past the laundry and the broom closet, until finally, they reached the small, warped wooden door that sat at the end of the hall.

Wynn stared at it blankly.

"I don't understand," she said.

Ethel put her finger to her lips. "Shhhhh." She pointed at the door and stared expectantly at Wynn.

Great.

Because the damp, dark, musty basement was just where Wynn wanted to visit. Sighing, she pulled open the door and turned on the light.

The smell of mildew assailed her.

So awesome.

Never mind what it probably housed. Or the sense of claustrophobia that immediately filled her chest as she stared down at the steep, narrow wooden steps. The spiders and mice and—likely—snakes that lay in wait.

"Are you sure?" she asked.

Ethel nodded vigorously. Pointed.

Crap!

Wynn sighed. She took a deep breath, gripped the wobbly railing, and carefully descended the stairs. *Because if she fell she'd break her stupid neck.*

Half-way down, the damp dissipated. The smell of something earthy and green—*lavender?*—filled her nostrils, and the sound of a soft fan whirling filled the air. And was that...music?

She halted at the foot of the stairs and stared in disbelief. A big, round dingy blue carpet covered the cracked concrete floor. Atop the carpet was an equally large round folding table, the surface of which was covered by a delicately crocheted green tablecloth and a vase filled with fresh lavender and cedar boughs. Five white plastic chairs surrounded the table, underneath which a small electric heater sat on a chunk of wood, spitting warm air into the space. A row of shelves lined the wall next to the table; a small FM radio occupied the top shelf. The soft murmur of Patsy Cline filled the air.

Crazy...

Above the shelves, a large, square drawing of the

Dorchester National Bank had been duct-taped to the wall. The entire footprint of the bank was there, entrances, exits, cameras, and teller booths. A collection of Xs and stars decorated the drawing, and below the crude plans, sat a line, interspersed with small dots.

A timeline.

Wynn could only stand there and gape, trying to wrap her brain around it. *This was their lair, where they'd masterminded the whole thing.* And seeing this left no doubt that *every single one of them* was involved.

Even Eloise.

Who carried a pocket King James in her dress. Who wore a big wooden cross and prayed loudly—and at great length—before every meal. Who rode Wynn about her penchant for the word *crap* and told Earl he was going to hell on a monthly basis.

Robbing a goddamn bank. And they'd planned it here, in her basement.

"Do you see?" Ethel yelled down from the top of the stairs.

"I see," Wynn snarled.

"Are you mad?"

She was *furious*.

"Are you gonna...are you gonna throw us out?"

A tremor moved through her. She felt sick. They had jeopardized *everything*. Their home and hers. *Jenna.* They'd jeopardized Jenna.

Why? Why had they done this?

"No," she said.

But it might have been a lie. Oh, she wouldn't make Ethel go, but the others... The others were going to go to jail.

Had they even thought about that?

Bile nipped at her throat. She remembered the grim

darkness in Beau's gaze; the harsh truth in his words—*They're coming. I can't stop them*—and tears massed in her throat, so thick she could barely breathe.

There had to be a reason, she thought dimly. And it had to be bad. Because they weren't these people...were they?

"Wynnie...are you okay?"

No. She was pretty sure she'd never be okay again.

CHAPTER 14

"Get off my land—and tell that son of a bitch you work for, if he's got somethin' to say to me, he can come here and say it his goddamn self!"

Beau stood beside his truck, his hand on his Glock. The sun was hot on the back of his neck, and his leg hurt like hell; it was only nine-thirty in the morning, and he was already out of patience.

"Hatfield is dead," he yelled back, annoyed.

The man who stood in the doorway of the ancient yellow mobile home—presumably, Winston Reynolds, Jasper Hatfield's former deputy—squinted at him. His hold on the .22 rifle didn't falter. "Bullshit!"

Beau glared at him. "Read a damn newspaper once in a while! I was elected in April. My name is Beau Greystone. I want to talk to you about the Stick Man."

Winston didn't move. He was somewhere in his fifties, with a head of wild gray hair that stood up in frizzy tufts over a face weathered by time. A tall, thin man with knobby knees and sharp elbows—as revealed by the worn green t-shirt and orange boxers he was wearing. Sagging socks covered his feet.

"Prove it!" he shouted.

Beau gritted his teeth, dug out his badge, and held it up.

"You don't look like a lawman," Winston said in a milder tone, eyeing Beau's bright orange and red shirt.

"Neither do you," Beau retorted.

For a long moment, Winston just stared at him: a hard, direct, unflinching look Beau recognized. So Beau stared back.

"Dead, huh?" Winston lowered his rifle. "Too bad. I'd have liked to put him in the ground myself."

Then he turned and disappeared into the mobile home.

Beau didn't move.

Winston's gray head poked out of the doorway. "You comin' or what?"

Beau put his badge away. His hand continued to hover over his Glock as he approached the rusting trailer. It was sinking on the back end, and two of the windows were broken. Plastic covered the holes, wind-torn, and white from the sun. The roof looked ready to cave in.

Nevertheless, he climbed up the rickety wooden stairs that led to the narrow front door and cautiously stepped through. Behind him, clouds rolled over the valley, dark violet and sapphire blue, churning closer.

Even the damn weather wouldn't give him a break.

"The Stick Man," Winston said as Beau pulled the door shut behind him. "That motherfucker's back?"

"Yes." The interior of the trailer was surprisingly neat, the kitchen old but clean, the small living area uncluttered. A chair, a couch, an aging wooden coffee table upon which sat an overflowing ashtray and a half-empty bottle of Crown Royale. A handful of paintings covered the walls—simple landscapes, but originals—and an ancient television sat on a small table next to the broken windows. "Two nights ago Emma Farley's body was found in a field owned by Fred Bigsby. She bore the Stick Man's marks."

Winston stood in the middle of his tiny kitchen and rubbed a hand over his wild hair. "Fuck."

Pretty much, yes.

"I've read your notes," Beau continued. "I wanted to ask you some questions about them."

Winston nodded. "Just let me put on some joe."

Beau moved toward the chair that sat beside the table. "Mind if I sit?"

"Suit yourself."

Beau sat down and rubbed his leg. Outside, thunder rumbled heavily, shaking the trailer around them.

"Crazy weather," Winston muttered. "Just keeps gettin' worse."

"Things are changing," Beau said. "From what I could gather, you were the primary on the case in both '05 and '09?"

"I don't know if I'd use the word 'primary.'"

"You were the only one who investigated the killings," Beau noted, still disgusted by that fact.

"Yeah." Winston snorted. "Hatfield had other things to do."

"Like what?"

A shrug. "He was in bed with every dirty fucker in town. Drugs, guns, women. Take your pick."

"There's evidence missing from the evidence locker," Beau said, watching him.

"Let me guess: money and meth." Winston shook his head and stared at his brewing coffee. "He was an evil asshole."

"What happened between you two?"

Winston looked up, his gaze flat and hard. "I know what they say about me; what they all think. But I was the only one. The only fucking one. And they know it."

"The only one to what?"

He shook his head. "I joined the sheriff's department after I came back from the Gulf. I needed the outlet, you know?"

Beau knew.

"It wasn't bad at first. Hatfield kept his shit to himself. But then those girls started dyin' and he...he just didn't give a shit. Was like they inconvenienced the fucker, dyin' like that. And then the feds showed up." Winston laughed a hollow and angry sound. "I thought maybe we'd start doin' our job then, but they kicked our ass down the road. Took it all over—even our offices—and ended up with jack shit, not even one damn suspect. Then things got quiet, and they went away again."

"But it wasn't over."

"No." Winston rubbed his head again. "It wasn't over."

"It still isn't."

Winston poured a cup of coffee. "You want some?"

It looked like mud. "No, thanks." Beau watched him grab the bottle of whiskey and add a generous dollop to his coffee. "What happened in '09?"

"Same shit, different dead girls. We hadn't come anywhere near to catchin' him the first time; even the feds gave up. And then there he was again. The fucker."

"And Hatfield?"

"It was just a pain in his ass. He didn't care about those girls; hell, he didn't even care that he was supposed to care. I wondered more than once if he wasn't in on it."

Beau's gaze narrowed. "What made you think that?"

Winston shrugged and took a healthy swallow of his coffee. "I'd come up with leads, and he'd refuse to let me follow them. Wouldn't let me interview certain people."

"People like who?"

"Edward Duggar."

"Why did you want to interview Duggar?"

"Rumor was, he had a thing for high school girls." Winston shrugged. "I wanted to let him know what my fists thought about pedophiles."

Beau was beginning to like Winston Reynolds. "Hatfield nixed the interview?"

"Every interview. He told me it wasn't my job to investigate, to leave it to the feds. But the feds were fuckin' useless; none of them wanted the job any more than he did. The whole thing was a goddamn travesty."

"I found a connection between the victims," Beau said.

Winston's gaze met his. "The camp?"

Cold condensed inside of him. "You knew?"

"Sure. It was in my notes. I guess that didn't make it into the file?"

"No," Beau grated. "It didn't."

"Hatfield cleaned up a lot of messes. Could be this was one of them."

The words were mild, but Beau could see the rage that simmered in Winston's flat, dark brown gaze. "Edward Duggar owns the land the camp sits on."

Winston's brows rose. "That I didn't know."

The link made adrenaline spear through Beau.

"What about the stick figures?" he asked. "You ever figure out any meaning behind them?"

"Nah." Winston shrugged. "I just figured he was batshit crazy."

Beau stared at him for a long, silent moment.

"What?" Winston demanded.

"Your file says you were let go for insubordination." An idea had just slapped him in the face, and Beau wasn't sure if it was because it was a good idea or just because he was pissed. "What happened?"

"I didn't get fired." Winston shook his head. "I quit."

"That's not how Harry tells it."

"Harry doesn't know his ass from a hole in the ground."

Which or may not have been true.

"What happened?" Beau asked again.

Winston poured another shot into his coffee. "I was the one who found the Morris girl. She'd gone missing three weeks before, and someone called in a tip, thought they'd seen her out at White Pine lake. So I drove out there. Found her tied to a picnic table, all cut up like he does. She'd been dead for days. So I called it in. Hatfield said he wasn't comin' to the scene; said he was too *busy*. I lost my shit." Winston shrugged and took another drink of his coffee. "Drove into town, found him over at Harley's bar, and kicked the shit out of him. He didn't like that."

"And then?"

"Then he fired me."

"And you just left?" Beau arched a brow. "All meek and quiet-like?"

A slashing smile turned Winston's mouth. "Not exactly." The smile faded. "But nothin' would stick to that fucker. Not even the truth. Eventually, I stopped tryin'. I liked breathin'."

"That bad?"

"Worse."

Silence fell. Rain pattered the top of the trailer, loud in the small space.

"What about the tip?" Beau asked.

Winston shrugged. "Called in from a phone booth in Madison. No CCTV back then, no way to ID the caller. Could've been the man himself for all we knew."

Goddamn it. Not only had Hatfield been a dirty cop and a murderer—he'd been a potential co-conspirator of a serial killer, as well. A man who'd had access to all of the evidence and everyone investigating it. Who'd had ample opportunity to cover his tracks and discredit anyone who questioned him. "What about the kid they arrested and cut loose? The one from Dorchester?"

Winston gave him an ironic look. "The son of Remy Filkins, who'd just announced his run against Hatfield for Sheriff?"

"Jesus Christ." Beau rubbed a hand down his face. "It's like a bad movie."

Winston laughed and drank his coffee.

Beau sat back and sighed. For a long, quiet moment, rain filled the silence between them.

"You gonna get this son of a bitch?" Winston asked, an edge to his voice.

"I am," Beau said.

"You sound confident."

"I'm not worried about catching him," Beau retorted. "I'm worried about not beating him to death by my bare hands."

Surprise shone in Winston's gaze. "Most wouldn't admit that."

"I'm not most," Beau replied grimly. A factor that both helped him and hurt him in equal measure.

"Glad to hear it," Winston said.

Beau's phone vibrated in his pocket. He ignored it. "I've got funding for another deputy. Pay sucks, but I might be able to get you the head of a serial killer."

Winston stared at him.

"You'd have to be sober," he added. "You show up sauced—even once—and you're done."

"Why?" Winston looked stunned. And angry. "Why would you do that? You don't know shit about me!"

Which was true, and something of which Beau was keenly aware. He didn't know this man. In spite of what his gut was telling him, he could be wrong. God knew he'd been wrong before.

But he was running on empty. Harry and Cam were smart, dedicated, and well-intentioned, and someday—if he did his job right—they'd be damn good deputies. But right now they were too eager, too green, and too goddamn young. He needed someone with some kind of experience, in life as well as law enforcement. More, he needed someone who gave a damn.

"Do you want to get him?" Beau asked softly.

Winston's gaze met his, glittering, and hard. "I fuckin' dream about it."

Beau pushed to his feet. "Then you'd better drink another cup of coffee."

Winston looked down at his cup. "They won't like it. Not any of 'em."

"Then they can fire me." Beau shrugged. "The job kind of sucks anyway."

A laugh rasped from Winston. He looked at Beau for a long, quiet moment. Then, "I want to take his head clean off."

"Get in line," Beau told him. "The Feds will be here at three. Can I count on you?"

Winston stared at him; his knuckles were white around his coffee cup.

"Either way," Beau said. "You're welcome to join us."

He pulled out his phone and checked it.

Harry.

Jenna Owens is in your office.

Alarm speared through him.

"Goddamn it," he said and turned toward the door.

"Trouble?" Winston asked, his gaze narrow.

"Never-ending," Beau muttered. He pulled open the door, looked at Winston. "Three sharp."

Then he left.

CHAPTER 15

"You have some explaining to do."

Four pairs of eyes avoided her. Earl was looking out the window; Griffin's long face stared at the floor. Esme was studying her nails, and Eloise was examining the ceiling.

Only Beowulf was looking at her, his gaze worried as he watched her pace.

It would have been funny if she wasn't so angry. But Wynn had promised herself she would be calm. Reasonable. *Rational*.

Because someone had to be.

"I found your lair; I know what you've done," she continued evenly. "But I don't know why. So let's start there."

No one said a word.

"I could lose everything," she told them darkly. "I deserve to know why."

"You?" Esme blinked. "Why would you lose anything, dear?"

"How do you think social services is going to react to the

news that my ward is living under the same roof as a bunch of bank robbers?"

Esme blinked and said, "Oh."

Griff shook his head. Earl chewed on his pipe stem.

"I warned them," Eloise sniffed. "I told them they were going to hell."

"But that didn't stop you from participating. Did it?"

She gripped the wooden cross she wore. "We had no choice."

Wynn took a deep breath. *Calm. Rational.* "Tell me everything."

The clock in the hall chimed. Dr. Evers was still out amphibian hunting, but Jenna would be home any minute. Of course, there was going to be no keeping this craziness from her.

By the time this was over, the whole stinking town would know.

"Winifred," Esme said quietly. "Do you know why Mr. Sanders died?"

"Because his heart stopped beating." Wynn frowned. "Why? What does that have to do with anything?"

"Do you know why his heart stopped beating?"

Confused, she blinked. "Because it was his time to go?"

"Bullshit!" Earl muttered.

"What's that supposed to mean?" she demanded.

"It means his death wasn't natural. It means he didn't die because he was old, and his heart was tired." Esme sat back and folded her hands in her lap. "He died because he ran out of his medication—the medication that kept his heart beating."

Wynn went still. "What do you mean?"

"I mean that he couldn't afford them!" Esme snapped.

"He was cutting the stupid things in half, and then, finally, he ran out. Two days later he was dead."

Understanding was like a sharp, brutal slap. Stunned, Wynn turned and looked at Earl. "Why didn't you tell me? I could have helped him. I could have—"

"Could have what?" Earl demanded. "Paid for 'em? You got an extra four hundred dollars lyin' around?"

"Four hundred dollars?" she echoed, appalled. "You're not serious?"

"Medication is expensive," Esme said coolly.

Wynn stared at them. They stared back. She realized then that what she'd read as defiance and self-righteousness was just plain old fear.

And rage.

"Fuck," she said.

No one argued.

Emotion welled inside of her, a great, painful wave that almost choked her. Fury and grief and the same infuriating helplessness that had gripped her in the wake of Fran's death.

She didn't have to die. There were treatments. Hope.

But only if you could afford them.

This was why they had taken such desperate measures— why there was no too much.

Only not enough.

Fran had missed endless opportunities at experimental treatments because her insurance company wouldn't pay for them. She'd had to ration her meds and skip doctor appointments to put food on the table. And she'd deeded her property to Wynn long before she died so they wouldn't be able to take it after she was gone.

"We did what we had to do to stay alive!" Earl slammed

a fist against the arm of the chair he occupied and Beowulf yelped. "And we'd do it again—in a heartbeat!"

Silence fell. Wynn didn't know what to say.

"Fuck," she said, for lack of anything better.

"It was our hail Mary pass," Griff said quietly. "We were desperate."

"What other choice did we have?" Esme demanded.

Wynn stared at them, reeling. Horrified.

And terrified.

Because they couldn't go to prison. It would kill them.

"Is there anything left?" she asked, remembering Beau's words. *He turns himself in, returns the money, tells the feds why he did it, they might be lenient.*

"Hell, no. We got three months of stuff for everybody: my insulin, Esme's heart packets, Eloise's pain patches, Ethel's crazy pills, and Griff's Parkinson's goop, and that was it. Every penny spent."

Awesome. Wait—

"Parkinson's?" she repeated. She looked at Griff. "You have Parkinson's?"

His face tightened. "Doc confirmed it last week."

The pressure welled, pressing painfully against her spine. *Parkinson's.* Almost as much fun as MS. And something only manageable through medication.

What next? A meteor? The plague?

"I'm sorry," she said, knowing it was inadequate.

Griff nodded. "Me, too."

Outside, the wind blew, making the entire house whistle.

"Can you return the unopened medication?" she asked.

Earl blinked. "Why the hell would we do that?"

"So I can keep your butts out of jail, that's why."

"Then what?" he demanded. "We're free, but we drop like flies because we ain't got the meds we need?"

He wasn't being contrary. He was furious and scared, and Wynn couldn't blame him.

"We will find another way," she told him.

"You gonna start playin' the lotto?" he asked sarcastically.

"Stop it," Esme admonished. "She's just trying to help."

"She can't help. No one can help. We're just a bunch of old farts no one cares about!"

"Have I ever abandoned you?" Wynn demanded, her voice hard.

"No." Earl looked down at his boots and sighed. "I'm just upset."

Join the frigging club.

The truth—finally. And so much worse than she'd imagined.

"We will figure something out," she said calmly. "But we have to get as much of the money back as we can."

"Not possible." Earl shook his head. "We got the stuff in Canada. They ain't gonna take it back once it's crossed the border."

"They don't know it crossed the border," Griff said. "Customs never even knew it was there."

For the love of Pete.

"I don't wanna take it back!" Earl protested. "I did the crime, I'll do the time. Meanwhile, at least you got what you need. For a time, anyway."

"We will figure something out," Wynn repeated.

"You keep sayin' that. And don't get me wrong, Chickpea, I appreciate it. I really do. But there's no way outta this. I'm okay with that. I done made my peace. I'm ready for your new Sheriff to come and take me to the big house."

"He isn't my new Sheriff," she retorted, her cheeks warming.

Good grief!

So maybe she was attracted to Beau—*big hairy deal.* And maybe last night, she'd finally begun to understand him. And maybe she'd even started to like him—a little.

But that didn't mean anything.

Because if Beau belonged to anyone, it was to his dead wife.

"We need to explain this to him," she said tightly. "Because he might be able to help."

Earl snorted. "He ain't gonna help me!"

"He hasn't arrested you, in spite of all the evidence you left behind. Why do you think that is?"

"'Cause he likes you."

Her heart leaped. "No. This isn't about—"

"She can't see it," Esme murmured. "She's too busy smarting off."

"And pushing buttons," Griff added.

"Every man likes his buttons pushed," Earl told her. "Even if he pretends otherwise."

Wynn closed her eyes and counted to ten.

"Well, it's true," Esme said.

They had lost their minds.

"I'm going to go talk to him," Wynn replied calmly. "And then we're going to make a plan. Okay?"

Earl only snorted again, but Esme and Griff nodded in agreement. Eloise surprised her by reaching out and gently touching her hand.

"I am sorry," she said. "We never meant for this to touch you."

Wynn shook her head. "I just wish you'd come to me for help."

Why hadn't they?

"You already do too much," Griff said gruffly. "We didn't want to burden you with this, too. You've been through enough."

Every difficult day.

Through the darkness and the light; all of the gray in between. Tears massed with sudden, unexpected force in her throat.

"You're my family," she whispered and swiped a hand across her burning eyes. Other than Jenna, they were all she had. "Don't you understand I would do anything for you?"

"Ah, hell, Chickpea, we know that."

"Of course, dear," Esme added softly. "We just didn't want to ask it."

Wynn glowered at her. "That's what family is for, isn't it?"

"I reckon so," Griff said.

Silence fell; rain began to drum down on the roof.

"Speaking of family..." Esme cleared her throat. "The Stick Man is back."

A chill moved through Wynn. *Like she could forget.* "I know."

"We need to keep an eye on her," Eloise said starkly. "She fits his profile."

"I know," Wynn said.

Because after Emma—

Well. They had to be vigilant. Careful.

And prepared.

"Least your new Sheriff ain't nothing like Hatfield," Earl muttered. "He's a different breed. He just might hunt that son of a bitch down."

"He will," Wynn said.

"And I bet he won't stop, not 'til the bastard's dead."

"He's not judge, jury, and executioner," Eloise protested.

"You can tell him that," Griff invited.

Which made Wynn smile, in spite of herself.

In spite of everything.

She glanced at the clock. If she left now, she might still catch Beau at his office.

A thought that electrified. And dismayed.

Because she didn't want to feel anything, especially when it came to a man who was trying hard to bury himself beside his dead wife.

Nope, she thought.

Just nope.

But this wasn't about her.

So she would have to put on her big-girl panties and face the music. Go to Beau, spill the beans.

And see what he did with them.

CHAPTER 16

"Don't blame me." Harry held up his hands. "She planted herself in there and refused to leave until she'd seen you."

"Some badass deputy you are," Beau told him.

"She's an Owens," Harry replied. "They fight dirty."

Since Beau figured that was probably true, he didn't argue. Instead, he poured himself a cup of coffee and walked into his office. Jenna Owens occupied one of the battered chairs that faced his desk. Several shopping bags sat on the floor beside her; she wore torn jeans, a Brewers t-shirt, and a pair of brand new, bright blue tennis shoes.

She was a pretty girl, with fine, delicate features and pale hair. Her eyes were a lighter gray than Wynn's, but no less shrewd.

"Jenna," he said and pulled the door shut behind him. "What can I do for you?"

She watched him walk slowly to his desk. "We need to talk."

Shades of her sister echoed in her tone. She watched him closely, her gaze assessing.

Fantastic.

"My time is limited," he told her brusquely as he sat down. "Today is not a good day."

She shrugged. "It was good for me."

Definitely Wynn's sister. "What do you want?"

"I need to tell you something, but you have to promise not to arrest anybody."

The same alarm that had clanged in his head when he'd received Harry's text sounded again. "I can't make that promise."

Another shrug. "Okay." She grabbed her shopping bags and stood up. "Never mind."

Goddamn it.

"Jenna," he said, reaching for patience. "I don't have time for games."

She stilled. "I know. He's back."

Beau's skin tightened. "Yes."

She sat back down. "You can't arrest her."

"Who?"

"She wasn't trying to do anything bad. She just...has issues with authority figures."

Wynn. He only arched a brow. "Why are you here, Jenna?"

She stared at him, silent, her light gray gaze annoyingly perceptive. Outside his office, the phones continued to ring, a freaked out public seeking constant reassurance. The sky was grumbling again, and it was half-past five, and the feds had yet to show.

Nor had Winston Reynolds made an appearance.

"I found something in our pasture," she said finally, reluctantly. "I was going to bring it to you, but now...now it's gone. I think Wynn did something with it."

The gun. Relief prickled through him. "She did. She brought it to me."

Jenna blinked. "She did?"

"Yes. You don't have to worry. I didn't arrest her."

That gray gaze narrowed. "You like her."

Annoyed by the heat that suddenly crept up his neck, Beau scowled. "I'll tell you the same thing I told her: withholding evidence is a crime. You should have brought it to me as soon as you found it."

"Mmm-hmmm," she said. "She must like you, too."

He tried hard to ignore that. But then, "Why do you say that?"

"Because she trusted you."

Something inside of him went taut. "She doesn't trust many people?"

A snort. "What do you think?"

A slender, insidious thread of heat wound through him. *Wynn trusted him.*

"Whose is it?" Jenna wanted to know.

"Whose is what?"

"The gun," she said. *Duh.* "Whose is it?"

And Beau realized she had no idea what was going on with Earl. "We're working to determine that."

"Mmm-hmmm," she said again. "Is it his?"

"Whose?"

"The Stick Man's."

Beau shook his head sharply. "No."

"Are you sure?"

Her open skepticism grated. "Yes. Is there anything else?"

She stared at him.

"Jenna." He sighed impatiently. "Is that all?"

"She said you were a prickly little pear. She was right."

Goddamn it.

These women were going to be the end of him.

"There is one more thing," Jenna said. She sat back, folded her arms over her chest, and fixed him with a hard look. "I want you to get him."

"Get who?"

"I want you to make him pay." Fury vibrated through her voice. And grief. "I want you to make sure he never hurts anyone else ever again."

"I'm sorry," Beau told her quietly. "I know Emma was your friend."

"I *loved* her. And he doesn't get to just take someone I love. He needs to pay."

"He will."

"He'd better. Because she's me. She's all of us. Everyone is scared. Do you know what that's like? To be scared of everything?"

He'd had his moments. "You need to be careful."

"I know that," she retorted. "That's not the point: *you* need to take care of him so we don't *have* to be scared. That's your job, isn't it?"

"It is."

"Good. Then do it."

Christ. And here he'd thought he had his hands full with Wynn. "I'm working on it."

"Work faster." Her chin jutted out. Wobbled. "It isn't fair."

"No," he agreed softly.

"She didn't do anything wrong."

"No, she didn't."

"I hate him. I want him dead."

He will be.

Beau supposed there should really be more of a struggle

going on inside of him, a quandary as to the question of what his job truly was—justice on a human level? Or on a cosmic one?

But he already knew exactly what he *should* do. And he knew exactly what he *would* do.

"If he comes for me," Jenna said, "he'll be sorry."

Something in her voice made Beau straighten. "You leave him to me."

"I'm not stupid," she scoffed. "But I won't be his victim, either."

Strong. This girl was strong. Like her sister.

Still. "I hear you. But for now, I need you to just sit tight and let me do my job. Keep your head down and stay under the radar." He held her gaze and willed her to listen. "I promise you, he won't get away with it."

She didn't move, her eyes searching his.

A mistake, he thought, to make promises, but beyond her bravery and bravado lay a terrified and desperate kid, and he would be damned if he was going to send her away without something to hold onto.

Finally, she nodded.

"Okay," she said and stood. Gathered her bags. "My keeper thinks I'm at Bernice's trying on Homecoming dresses. So, I'd better go."

"Your keeper?"

Harry chose that moment to burst through the door. "Sheriff!"

Beau rubbed a weary hand down his face. "What now?"

"We've got trouble, sir. The feds just rolled in, there's smoke coming out of Eckhart's Grocery, and Jack Farley's got a group of armed men headed down Main street, right for us."

Perfect.

"I'll get the riot gear!" Harry turned and ran.

Jenna took a step, but Beau gave her a black look.

"Sit," he ordered. "Stay."

Then he pushed to his feet and left his office before she could protest. He walked through the small main entryway and stepped out the front door. To his right, a collection of gleaming black SUVs were pulling up and parking along the road.

The Feds.

To his left, Emma Farley's father Jack led a ragtag collection of men toward him, all armed to the teeth and loaded for bear.

And across the street, smoke poured from the roof of Eckhart's Grocery store. A small crowd had gathered out front to gawk at it.

A few drunks and some loose cows.

Maybe on his best day.

If he was lucky.

CHAPTER 17

WYNN PARKED the van in front of the library and stared at the chaos that was Main Street.

Smoke was pouring from the roof of Eckhart's Grocery. A line of black SUVs was parked along the road; suited men and women spilled from them like shiny coins being spat from a slot machine. And Emma Farley's father Jack was marching down the street with a band of what appeared to be very angry and heavily armed men.

Beau stood on the sidewalk in front of the Sheriff's Office, watching them approach with that tight, cold, impatient look on his face. He wore a bright red and orange shirt, but it did nothing to lighten his grim expression. Above him, clouds churned in a giant, billowing mass of violet.

Maybe I'll come back tomorrow.

Or never.

And then Jenna appeared behind him, her hands filled with shopping bags.

Crap!

Wynn climbed from the van and hurried toward the scene, wondering where in Hades Sasha was and why

Jenna was standing outside the Sheriff's office with her new school clothes in hand.

Halfway to Jenna, Wynn's neck prickled. She turned to see Sean Evers across the street, eating an ice cream cone. He was leaning against the rough brick of Langley's Pharmacy, watching her.

She lifted a hand, and he nodded.

He'd turned out to be a great tenant. Respectful, friendly, helpful. Unobtrusive and courteous. He enjoyed talking about frog anatomy a little too much, but Wynn liked him, and he'd paid her for the next month in advance.

At least one thing was going right.

He would probably turn out to be the Stick Man.

"Don't borrow trouble," she told herself, exasperated.

Even though he *had* shown up right before the notorious serial killer's reappearance, something that hadn't escaped her notice. And which probably meant nothing, but had to be noted.

Vigilance.

There was no other choice.

"Mr. Farley." Beau's voice rang out, strong and deep as Wynn got closer. "I'd suggest you turn around and take your friends home."

Jack Farley halted in front of him. His face was lined with sorrow and fury, unshaven, and flushed. He was the same height as Beau, but heavier, thicker in girth, and compact with muscle. He held a shotgun in one hand; the other was a tight fist at his side. The men behind him fanned out and stared at Beau with distrust.

"If you aren't going to do your job, *Sheriff*," Jack said loudly, "then we will."

Beau only arched a brow. The crowd watching smoke billow from Eckhart's Grocery turned and stared at him instead. The suited men and women hovered off to the side, watching intently.

The FBI, Wynn realized abruptly.

Panic raced through her. She strode up to Jenna and hissed, "Let's go."

"Not yet," Jenna hissed back.

Beau didn't notice either one of them.

"And how will you do that, Mr. Farley?" His voice was mild. "Go door to door and ask if the Stick Man is home?"

Jack took a step forward, snarling. "It's better than what you're doing!"

"You don't know what I'm doing," Beau pointed out calmly. "But if you'd like to come into my office, I'll tell you."

Jack only shook his head. Sweat beaded his brow; in his throat, his heartbeat was a furious pulse. His eyes were wild, turbulent with grief. Watching him made Wynn's chest suddenly tighten.

So much pain and fury.

She couldn't even begin to imagine—and she'd felt plenty of pain and fury.

"I'm not going to sit around and do nothing!" Jack shouted.

The men behind him nodded, and Beau sighed and rubbed a hand down his face. He stepped closer to Jack.

"Don't do this," he said, his voice low. "You aren't helping her."

"I'm not helping her? *You're not helping her!* Sitting around on your ass like that piece of shit Hatfield!"

Jack lifted the shotgun, but Harry was suddenly beside him. The deputy wore shiny black body armor and an unbuckled helmet.

"Don't," he said, his hand on his weapon.

"Stand down," Beau told him.

He opened his mouth to protest.

"Now," Beau added, his voice like a whip.

Harry scowled and stepped back, but his hand remained on his weapon.

"Go home," Beau told Jack. "Or I'll arrest the lot of you, and your women and children can spend the night without you."

A ripple went through the crowd of men. They looked at each other.

"Go to hell," Jack said harshly. He lifted the shotgun and aimed it at Beau. "I'm done being told what to do."

"Goddamn it," Beau growled.

Wynn's heart lurched in her chest; Harry took a step forward. The crowd gaped, and the FBI agents froze, but before anyone could move, Beau grabbed the barrel of the shotgun, let loose a brutal punch that put Jack on his knees, and unloaded the chamber of the shotgun onto the street. Two fat red shells rolled away.

"You're giving him what he wants." Beau reached down and hauled Jack to his feet, his jaw like granite, his eyes flinching as his leg faltered. He put his hand on Jack's shoulder and steadied them both. "I will bring you his head on a platter if you just let me do my damn job."

"She's gone," Jack said starkly. Blood leaked from his nose. "She's just fucking *gone*."

Beau squeezed his shoulder. "I know."

Wynn's throat thickened.

"Gone," Jack said again. He looked like someone had hit him in the face with a baseball bat. "Just gone."

"I'm sorry," Beau said quietly.

"You have to find him." Jack reached up and gripped Beau's shirt and shook him. "You have to."

"I will," Beau said, his voice hard.

Jack stared at him for a long, motionless moment. The crowd watched, frozen, tension and fear and grief stretching between them like an invisible web.

"C'mon, buddy." One of the men behind Jack stepped forward and took Jack's arm. "Let's go."

"You promise me," Jack whispered, his eyes searching Beau's face. His desperation made Wynn want to sit on the sidewalk and weep, but Beau only nodded once, curtly.

"I promise," he said.

Jack stepped back. He released Beau's shirt, and Beau handed him the shotgun. Then Jack turned and walked away. His men followed. One of them stopped to scoop up the shells and put them in his pocket. Then they were gone.

Beau turned to the FBI agents and said, "Inside."

He looked at the crowd in front of Eckhart's and asked, "Did everyone get out?"

"Yes, sir," Mr. Eckhart said.

"You're sure?"

"Yes, sir."

"Then call the damn fire department."

Then he turned around and saw Wynn and Jenna. Darkness rolled like a storm across his face.

"What the hell are you doing here?" he snarled.

"It's a public sidewalk," Wynn retorted, stung.

Something fierce and oddly wild glittered in his eyes. "I don't have time for you."

She recoiled, her heart beating too hard.

Because, *ow*.

"I was just watching the show," she told him, striving for cool indifference. "When's the next episode?"

He stepped toward her, his voice harsh. "I have to deal with this."

She stared at him, her blood a dull roar. Everything she didn't want to feel burned like wildfire in her chest.

He isn't your friend. He isn't anything.

"You do that," she told him, her voice like frost.

She turned to walk away, but he reached out and caught her arm, halting her.

Awareness jolted through her, which only served to infuriate her.

Stupid, beautiful, angry man. She'd had just about enough.

"Goddamn it," he said. "I can't—"

"Sheriff Greystone," interrupted another voice, and she looked up to see one of the suited FBI agents striding toward them. Tall, sleek in his expensive suit, with a head of gorgeous golden hair and piercing blue eyes. "Can I have a word?"

"They're talking," Jenna told him. "Take a number."

Wynn gave her a dark look. "We're done here."

"We're not fucking done," Beau ground out. "I'll come by when I'm finished."

Sean Evers suddenly materialized beside them. "You need some help, Wynn?"

Beau gave him a cold, flat look that made goosebumps ripple down her arms.

"Greystone," the FBI agent said again, coming closer. "We need to talk."

"Oh, just cool your tits," Jenna snapped.

For the love of Pete.

Half of the town was watching this ridiculous scene.

Wynn tugged against Beau's hold. "See you around, new Sheriff."

He only growled at her. His hand tightened.

And she thought *I should have brought my crescent wrench.*

She tugged again, desperate to escape. Part of it was Jack Farley and his utter desolation; the sudden, casual eruption of violence; the fear and frustration of the people around her. But most of it was the damaged, dangerous man before her, and her visceral, inexplicable, and monumentally stupid reaction to him.

"I'll see you later," Beau said in a hard tone.

"Not if I see you first," she told him.

Jenna snorted. "Good one."

"We should go," Sean said.

Beau stared down at her, a muscle pulsing in his jaw, his hold unyielding.

"Greystone," the FBI agent said again as he halted beside them. "We have more important matters."

"Don't be a dick," Jenna retorted. "Just wait your turn."

"Jenna," Wynn said sharply.

Her sister fell silent and glared at the agent.

"Let *go*," Wynn snarled at Beau.

He didn't want to. She could see it in that churning green gaze. But she didn't care.

"I will kick your stinking ass," she warned softly.

His eyes glinted. *Try it.*

"Beau," said the FBI agent, his voice sharp.

But Beau ignored him. Instead, he yanked Wynn close, leaned down, and pressed his mouth against her ear. "I don't like threats, sweetheart. We're going to talk about that later, too."

Then he released her.

Wynn whirled around and began to march toward the van. Her heart was beating like a hollow drum; in her stomach, a thousand butterflies had taken flight.

Jenna and Sean hurried after her.

"I think he likes you," Sean said conversationally.

"I know, right?" Jenna added.

"You two can make your own stinking dinner," Wynn told them.

CHAPTER 18

Rain fell in cold, slanting sheets as Beau climbed from his truck and headed toward the front door of the Owens Boarding House. The relentless moisture had sunk deep into his bones, and every part of him ached. The run-in with Jack Farley had tweaked his already throbbing leg, and sitting across from FBI Special Agent Garrett Morrison for two and a half hours afterward sure as hell hadn't helped any.

Where is Earl Barry now? Why isn't he in a cell? What the hell are you doing, Greystone?

Damned if he knew.

But he'd managed to sidetrack Garrett and his crew with the Stick Man paperwork. Every old file, the forensic and pathology reports, photos and interviews, and what little physical evidence existed. Ultimately, they would realize there was nothing worth a damn in the entire pile, but for now, they were busy, and he was free.

Because Beau had other plans for his evening.

I will kick your stinking ass.

Goddamn her.

Those words had lit him like a fuse. And at that moment, he'd realized how well and truly fucked he really was.

Because he welcomed the fight.

No matter the lip service he gave himself, some part of him had decided.

He wanted Wynn Owens.

And he was going to have to fight himself to walk away.

It didn't much matter that he was broken and somewhat useless, or that he would always be a moody, brooding, ornery bastard.

He just didn't give a shit.

Excuses. Marie, his penance, the relentless need to deny himself—all excuses.

Reasons to quit.

And he didn't fucking want to quit.

He was sick of punishing himself—and everyone else, too.

For too long, he'd been blind to everything but his misery. And he sure as hell hadn't bothered to think about the pain he'd caused anyone else. But today, that abdication had slammed into him like a brick wall.

Today, his words had caused pain, and for the first time in a long time, he cared about the price.

I don't have time for you.

Jesus Christ, he'd made Wynn *flinch*.

And had no excuse but his own goddamn fear.

Because Jack Farley had been a hairsbreadth from snapping, and his little army of militiamen would have followed in a goddamn heartbeat. Because it was the closest Beau had been to a battlefield since Fallujah.

Because he hadn't even realized Wynn and Jenna were standing right fucking there.

In the line of fire.

His reaction had been instant, white-hot fury. Followed by mindless, abject terror—the likes of which he'd never wanted to feel again.

So he'd punished Wynn with words, and when the bold, brave, fearless woman he knew had faltered beneath the blow, he'd felt something he hadn't experienced in a long time: shame.

The look on her face had made him go still and silent inside, paralyzed by the sudden thought that he might have made a mistake there was no coming back from.

And that abrupt, gut-wrenching insight had turned everything he thought he knew and felt and believed inside out. Because the idea that they would just be *done*...

No.

As complicated, and simple, and life-changing as that.

No.

He wasn't certain where it left him, or her, or them. But he knew he had a hell of a mess to clean up. And the thought that she might not let him...

Well. He was determined.

And to hell with the consequences.

It was just par for the course that tomorrow he and Garrett were going to arrest Earl—something about which Beau couldn't do a damn thing because this was the Fed's cluster now—and the old scoundrel's arrest was likely to make the whole goddamn thing blow up in Beau's face. Earl, the Stick Man, his own fuckery. So many odds stacked against him.

Something that would have—at one time—only made him stronger. But Beau hadn't been that man for a long time. He wasn't sure that man even still existed.

The porch light went on as he laboriously climbed the

front steps. He was surprised when Jenna swung open the door.

"You were a dick, too," she announced and leaned against the doorjamb with her arms crossed. Beowulf appeared beside her and watched him with his usual suspicion.

Beau braced himself against the railing and swiped away the rain streaming down his face. "Is she here?"

"Like she wants to see you." Jenna scowled. "How come you didn't tell me about Earl?"

"It wasn't my place to tell you."

"You're the one who's going to put him in jail. You should have told me."

He only shook his head. "Tell Wynn I'm here."

"Why? You didn't want to talk to her before. Why should she want to talk to you now?"

God help him. "Jenna."

"What? You *hurt* her."

"I know," he snarled. "But I can't make it right if you won't let me fucking talk to her."

Jenna's eyes widened. Her mouth fell open.

"Sorry," he muttered and sliced the rain from his face again. "It's been a long day."

She stared at him, silent.

"Please," he grated.

"Are you really going to arrest him?" she asked, her voice small.

"Yes."

She swallowed. "There's nothing we can do?"

"I don't know."

"Is that why the Ken doll is here?"

"The Ken doll?"

"Mr. We Have More Important Matters." She made a face. "Such a dick."

"You need to watch your language," he told her sternly, even though a smile pulled at his mouth.

The Ken doll. Garrett would lose his shit if she called him that.

"If the shoe fits." She shrugged. Hesitated. "If I tell you where she is, do you promise to apologize?"

"Yes," he said evenly.

For a long moment, she said nothing, that unnervingly perceptive gray gaze surveying him. Then, "She's in the barn. She's got a pitchfork, though, so you should be careful."

He turned and started down the steps. "Thanks for the warning."

"Beau," Jenna said.

He looked at her over his shoulder.

"Don't do it again," she said.

His gaze met hers. "I won't."

She nodded and closed the door.

More promises he shouldn't be making.

To her; to Jack Farley.

Mistakes. And here he was, about to make a few more.

He no longer cared.

The barn was lit by warm amber light as he approached, rays that spilled out and kissed the falling rain in gold. The ground was soaked, his feet sinking into several inches of water, making the uneven surface even more painful and treacherous. The large oaks that dotted the property creaked with the wind. Beyond the rain, he could hear the rushing water of a stream, and he wondered how high it was, how much danger it would present to the property if the rain continued.

One of the dusky gray donkeys greeted him as he stepped through the open door, into the blessedly dry, warm atmosphere. Wynn was on the far end, clad in worn overalls, a pair of black rubber boots, and a black tank top. She stabbed the pitchfork she held into a bale of straw and tossed the pale yellow strands into the stall next to her.

Her movements were practiced, the muscle in her arms flexing, sleek and strong, her familiarity with the chore clear. But she was definitely agitated. Stabbing the fork into the straw, tossing it into the stall.

Stab, toss. Stab, toss.

"Am I the fork or the hay?" he asked.

"You're nothing," she replied flatly.

And he didn't like that response. Not one bit.

No matter how entitled to it she was.

He limped toward her, trying to ignore the ache in his leg that had grown into searing, tearing pain. "We need to talk."

"No, you need to leave." Her voice was grim. "Or I might just stab you."

She was furious.

Heat licked along his veins.

He'd been anticipating this confrontation since she'd stormed away from him, and he was more than ready to go a few rounds. He might owe her an apology, but she owed him, too. "I warned you not to threaten me."

"Oopsie." *Stab, toss. Stab, toss.* "Was that your aorta I just perforated?"

Beau halted and tried to rein in the dangerous mix of fear and hunger and sickening desperation inside of him. He rubbed his leg and looked around; the other donkey stuck her head out of the stall next to him and neighed.

"Hey, girl," he murmured and reached out to rub her nose.

"You think I'm kidding?" *Stab, toss. Stab, toss.* "Just try me, tin man."

Wynn's open agitation smashed into his, ratcheting the tension riding him until it was taut as a well-strung bow. The anticipation and the heat and all of the hungry need he'd finally let loose inside him. *Freed.* Reaching for her now, uncaring of anything but putting them both out of their misery.

A moo sounded; the dairy cow eyeballed him from a stall opposite the donkey's. A large window filled with leaded glass sat beside the stall, open just a crack. Beneath it, on a narrow wooden shelf, sat a small silver box. It had dials and nobs and two long, slender lengths of silver wire that had been threaded through the crack in the window.

It looked like an old CB radio.

"What's this?" he asked and moved toward it.

"None of your beeswax, that's what."

A small blue notebook and pen sat beside the machine. Beau reached for it.

"It belongs to Sean," Wynn said sharply. "Leave it alone."

Sean Evers. Whose name Beau had run only to discover he was—at least seemingly—legit. A well-known, well-respected biologist at the forefront of the fight to save the rapidly dwindling population of the world's amphibians. Sought after by accredited universities and a superstar of conferences on ecosystem loss. Hell, Beau had even found a reference to a Ted Talk.

Which should have reassured him, but didn't.

And today, Evers had earned another mark against him. Beau didn't care if he was being protective. Something wasn't right about Sean Evers. Beau couldn't put his finger on it, but the man he saw, and the one portrayed on paper, weren't the same.

He picked up the pen and put it in his pocket.

"Beau."

He looked up to see Wynn watching him. A fine glisten of sweat kissed her skin; she was breathing hard, her breasts lifting and falling. Strands of that rich, sherry colored hair had escaped the messy bun on her head to cling to her flushed cheeks.

She was beautiful, like a fresh, ripe peach.

He wanted to take a bite.

But she leaned against the pitchfork and stared silently at him, her beautiful mouth an unhappy line.

I did that.

"We're going to arrest Earl tomorrow," he said.

She only stared at him, her eyes shuttered, as bright and hard as any diamond.

"I'll make sure he's well taken care of," he added.

She said nothing. And that feeling of suffocating panic, the one he'd nearly choked on earlier, flooded through him.

"Say something," he growled.

"Go home."

Not words he wanted to hear, but something at least.

He stalked toward her. "You came by to talk to me."

She watched him get closer, offering no response.

"You asked for my help," he reminded her darkly.

"That was a mistake," she said. And there was nothing at all in her voice. Not anger or pain or even annoyance. It was just...

Opaque.

Which made the simmering panic turn to a boil.

"It wasn't a fucking mistake," he snarled.

She only blinked at him, as unmoved and distant as any statue.

Fire burned through him; his heart beat like a drum. Adrenaline and fear and need twisted around him like sharp, finely barbed wire and squeezed.

He halted a handful of feet from her, just outside of pitchfork range. "Put that damn thing down."

A cold smile curved her mouth. "Afraid I'm fantasizing again?"

A jolt of pure, incendiary lust shot through him, and just like that, he was ready.

For anything.

"Put it down, Wynn," he said, his voice rough.

Her smile faded. "We're done. You should go."

Done. The word cut him.

"We haven't even started yet," he told her in a hard voice.

She stared at him. He took a step.

"Keep pushing," she said. "See where it gets you."

Oh, he would. He simply couldn't help himself. "I know you're mad."

"No." She shook her head. "I'm disappointed."

The cut deepened.

Then she turned and stabbed the pitchfork into the straw.

Stab, toss. Stab, toss.

He'd been dismissed.

Thunder boomed down; the lights flickered. The donkeys whinnied nervously.

Stab, toss. Stab, toss.

A sudden, searing bolt of pain shot from his hip to the tips of his toes, and his patience and control snapped like a twig.

He took a step, wrenched the pitchfork from her hands, and threw it to the hard-packed dirt floor. When she hissed at him, he wrapped his hands around her arms and pushed her back against the wall, closing the space between them until he was towering over her, a hairsbreadth from touching her.

The toned muscle of her arms flexed beneath his hold; she growled at him.

"Just calm the hell down," he grated, his throat thick.

Her heat and scent washed over him in a warm, seductive tide. The tensile feel of her in his hands made his cock throb. So vibrant and alive.

How had he ever thought he could resist?

"I'm perfectly calm," she snarled. Then she lifted her knee and did her damnedest to send his balls into his throat.

He managed to avoid it. Barely.

"*Knock it off.*" He pushed her against the wall and leaned into her, using his weight to still her movement; the collision of their bodies made a violent tremor move through him. Heat licked at his spine. "Let me talk to you."

"Keep your stinking words!" She slammed her palms into his chest and pushed. When that didn't work, she bucked against him, and he hardened instantly, a furious, dizzying rush that felt like live current plugged into his spine. His hands tightened on her arms. A harsh sound broke from his chest.

"Wynn." He pressed his mouth against her ear. "Stop."

She bucked again.

Jesus Christ.

He lifted her from her feet, just to stop her from doing it a third time. Because if she kept it up, he wasn't sure what he might do.

"Put me down," she ordered raggedly. Her fingers twisted in his shirt, nails digging into his skin.

Another tremor shook him. Her breasts were soft and lush against him, and he could feel the hard points of her nipples. The soft swell of her belly cradled his cock, which was throbbing, exquisite, intoxicating pulses that were scrambling his brains. He knew she could feel him, like granite against her, and he told himself to ease off.

Let go.

But he didn't. Wasn't even sure he could.

She felt so good.

"When I turned around and saw you and Jenna standing there, less than ten feet from those assholes and their guns, my fucking heart stopped." His voice was guttural. "It scared the hell out of me."

Her nails dug deeper. She was painfully tense against him. "We aren't yours to protect, Beau."

Denial surged through him. He surrendered to the hunger and nipped her earlobe with sharp teeth. "I know I hurt you. I'm sorry."

She pushed against him. "Don't."

"I'm trying to fucking apologize," he grated.

"Is that what you're doing?" Her voice was unsteady. "Because it feels like a lot more than that."

Oh, it is.

"Beau," she whispered.

And he thought: *fuck it.*

"Goddamn you." His voice was raw. He let himself sink into the cradle of her body and shuddered. "I gave up and I *liked* it. Then you came along, poking the bear, no judgment, no pity. Looking at me like you see me, accepting what I can't even fucking accept myself."

His hands skimmed down her arms, found the hollows of her overalls, and slid inside. The small of her back was bare, like silk against his rough palms. He let his hands glide down, skimming her thin cotton panties, curving possessively over her ripe, lush bottom; then he lifted her against him until his cock was pressed into the warm, welcoming notch of her thighs.

"*Oh*," Wynn said and arched sharply against him.

His fingers dug into her; he couldn't help but thrust. She made a soft, hungry sound that squeezed him like a tight fist.

"I told myself to walk away," he continued raggedly. "I'm fucking useless, a wasted limb. I know you deserve more. But I can't do it." He let his hands slide further down until he could stroke the hot, damp gusset of her panties with the tips of his fingers; she sucked in a sharp breath, and a violent tremor made his leg lock into place. "I don't want to let you go."

Her hands slid into his hair; her legs lifted to wrap his hips, and Beau thrust again, unable to stop himself.

"Please," she whispered, and her nails dug into his scalp. "Don't stop."

He couldn't have denied her, even if he tried. He thrust again. She hissed. He rubbed his bristled chin down the silken line of her throat; found that tender place where her neck and shoulder met. Bit her.

And thrust again.

"*Oh*," she said again, sharper, and ground herself against him. "More."

Beau pressed them both into the wall; his leg trembled. But he couldn't stop.

Wouldn't.

"Please," she whispered jaggedly.

So he gave her what she asked for, another hard thrust that slammed them both back into the wall.

"Holy crap," she gasped. "That's..."

His fingertips slid beneath her panties and found the dark heart of her. "Yes."

A cry broke from her when he stroked her there, gliding through the slippery, silken flesh that was weeping for him.

For him.

He lifted his head. She was panting, her skin flushed, her beautiful lips parted. When her eyes met his, they were soft and dreamy, shining like pewter. Her fingers were pulling his hair; her thighs were squeezing him tight, and she was shuddering beneath his touch; her body growing wetter, hotter, softer.

"Please," she said again.

He could smell her; it made him want to taste. He couldn't look away. She surged against him and ground against his cock, and he nearly came.

"Christ," he hissed.

"Again," she insisted and tugged at his hair.

"Kiss me," he whispered harshly. "And I'll make you come."

She trembled against him. Her dark eyes touched his mouth; she licked her lips.

"Come on, sweetheart." He pressed her into the wall. "Let me in."

For one breathless moment, he thought she would refuse. But then she tugged him toward her and pressed her lips against his.

A sweet kiss, hesitant and untried. It just about broke him.

And then she opened.

He stroked his tongue into her mouth, and he thrust again.

She moaned; the kiss deepened. Wet, hungry, sexual. He took her mouth like he wanted to take her body, and she sucked on his tongue and rode his cock while her body wept into his hands.

His spine was tingling; she was trembling.

He thrust harder and they both climbed higher.

He wanted to see her breasts. Stroke her skin; suck her nipples. Bury himself so deep, she didn't know where he ended and she began.

Need to be inside of her. Need—

"Wynn? Is everything okay? You didn't pitchfork him, did you?"

Jenna's voice sliced through him like a blade.

Wynn's thighs gripped him tighter, a raw, desperate sound broke from her. Beau wrapped his arms around her and stepped sideways, into the stall out of sight. His leg trembled beneath her weight, and the dynamic motion sent pain searing through him.

"Wynn?" Jenna repeated.

And Wynn froze.

"Jenna," he ground into her ear. His hands tightened, and for a moment, he didn't give a damn.

He wanted to finish what he'd started.

Make her come. *Make them both come.*

But she was tensing, and Jenna was getting closer, and the moment had been lost.

For now.

Wynn's thighs slid down his legs; he set her down gently, steadying them both. His hands lingered on the bare, silken strip of skin between the bottom of her shirt and the lace edge of her panties; then he slid his hands slowly from her overalls, his gaze locked on hers, enjoying the dewy flush in her skin, the soft gray of her eyes. The lush width of her mouth, swollen and red from his kiss.

Her breath was coming in unsteady spurts. She reached up and covered her cheeks.

"Holy crap," she whispered.

Her hands were shaking; Beau could relate.

He reached out, thrust his hand into her messy bun, and pulled her toward him.

"I told you," he said, his voice harsh, his hand gentle, "we're just getting started."

And then he kissed her, a hard, possessive, too-brief press of his mouth to hers, and when he pulled away, her gaze crashed into his, and suddenly they were back where they started. The air thickened; heat flared. Wynn inhaled sharply, and Beau made himself turn away.

"Go," he told her roughly.

"Winifred Louise!" Jenna yelled. "Is everything okay? I'm coming in!"

"Go," he said again. "Winifred Louise."

"I'm going to strangle her," Wynn muttered.

But she went.

CHAPTER 19

Shameless.

That's what she was.

Don't stop, she'd said. *Please. More.*

And Beau...he'd *delivered*.

Wynn stared up at the plaster ceiling above her bed and wondered why.

Why had she just...surrendered?

She'd learned not to trust at a very young age. Not her mother; not any of the people who surrounded her mother. She'd had to run from both more than once because her mother would try to barter her for the poison that ruled their lives.

Only Wynn's awareness had saved her. Her reflexes; the savagery with which she fought if anyone got too close. But most of the time, she'd run, willing to face any danger to escape the hell that chased her. She would hide until it was safe, and then, because she had no choice—Lara was still her mother, which was better than being alone on the streets—she would return.

But always wiser. More distant, her blood a little colder. Knowing that someday she wouldn't be fast enough.

When she'd found an abandoned butterfly knife in one of the drug houses her mother favored, she'd pocketed it. It was the first weapon she'd ever held, ever owned, and the glint of that steel—the smooth, sharp edge—had made her feel, for the first time in her life, powerful.

Instead of powerless.

There had never been a question of *if* she would have to use it, only when. And she'd realized then that she had to be ready to go if the opportunity presented itself. So she'd begun to stash pennies and cans of stolen food in unnoticed corners of the houses where her mother got high; behind pipes and under loose floorboards. She'd pocketed anything she could use as a weapon: an old fork, a railroad spike, a jagged piece of roofing tin. But then her mother had gotten pregnant with Jenna, and no matter the desperation she felt, Wynn couldn't bring herself to abandon her helpless baby sister.

They were all each other had.

And Wynn knew, if she left, Lara would simply sell Jenna, or give her away, or just leave her in an alley somewhere and walk away. So she'd stayed. Lara had often left Jenna unfed and unwashed, crying in a filthy blanket on a hard wooden floor while she went out in search of poison. Wynn had always known, if she ran, Jenna would die.

Or worse.

So trusting was not in Wynn's blood. It had taken a long time to let her guard down with Fran; longer still to trust Fran's tenants. Even with Sasha, it had taken years. And trusting people was something with which Wynn still struggled.

Beau Greystone couldn't possibly change that. Could he?

Bad-tempered and stubborn, with a wide strip of mean. *A lawman.*

A man who was still deeply in love with his dead wife.

Goddamn you. I gave up and I liked it. Then you came along, poking the bear, no judgment, no pity. Looking at me like you see me, accepting what I can't even fucking accept myself.

She didn't know what that meant...except that he didn't seem very happy about any of it. And even if it had been the most erotic experience of her life, Wynn wasn't happy about it, either.

Because they were headed for disaster.

Beau, she thought, was a good man. Honest, honorable, true. But he was taken. Grief owned him; rage and pain, a dark world of his own making. No one could save him from that but himself.

Least of all her.

All words she should have said—simple truths that needed pointing out.

Instead, she'd been so mad she could have spit nails. Hurt by how he'd reacted to her on the street; enraged that he'd sought her out afterward when she was still smarting. Truthfully, it was herself with whom she was the most upset.

Because she'd expected kindness from him, but that wasn't who Beau was.

Silly goose.

And true to form, he'd only been himself: brusque, impatient, and dismissive.

Really, how could she complain?

But it had *hurt*. And she hadn't hidden it well.

I know I hurt you. I'm sorry.

Damn him.

Why hadn't he just left when she told him to? Listened when she said they were done?

I told you, we're just getting started.

She didn't understand what that meant, either.

And now...

Now everything had changed.

Because he'd put his hands on her, and she'd let him.

For the love of Pete, she'd kissed him!

And if Jenna hadn't interrupted them—

Well.

It was for the best.

Because it hadn't even been the explosive sexual encounter between them that had laid her bare. It'd been Beau's raw, angry honesty.

I told myself to walk away. I'm fucking useless, a wasted limb. I know you deserve more. But I can't do it. I don't want to let you go.

She hadn't expected those words.

And when he'd lifted her from her feet and pressed himself against her, stealing her breath and smashing her willpower, she'd surrendered.

Try actively participated.

She could still feel the rasp of his skin, those rough, callused palms stroking her spine, curving down over her bottom; the deep, throbbing pulse that burst to life between her legs; the slick, wild pleasure of his fingers gliding through her—

"No," she told herself, her body stirring.

But worse was the huge, terrifying swell of something she couldn't name that filled her throat.

And the sense memory of him that tingled through her.

The fact that some part of her—some deep, intrinsic, instinctive part—clearly trusted him...well, that was just wholly terrifying.

She'd felt *free* with him, when she'd never felt free with anyone. And she'd told him things she'd never told anyone—not even Jenna.

Why? What in Hades was her problem?

"Freaking disaster in the making," she told herself.

Because she was screwed up six ways from Sunday, and he wasn't a free man, no matter what he thought, and it didn't matter what he said, or if he called her sweetheart—which had made her heart flutter and wasn't that the dumbest, most pathetic thing *ever*—and it didn't matter how it made her feel because none of it *meant anything*.

"Stop thinking and get your butt out of this bed," she ordered.

But she didn't. Instead, she stared at the cracked plaster on her ceiling, her entire being churning in uncertainty.

And arousal.

And fear.

It was too much. On top of Earl, and the robbery, and the Stick Man—

Thanks for nothing, Universe.

The sound of car doors slamming caught her attention, and she sat up and looked out the window.

Three large black SUVs were parked in front of the porch; suited men were climbing out. Beau's truck was nowhere in sight.

"Crap!"

She scrambled out of bed, pulled on her cow-print pajama pants, an old AC/DC t-shirt, and flew out of the room.

She was halfway down the stairs when a fist pounded

on the door, followed by *"FBI. Open up. We have an arrest warrant for Earl Reginald Barry."*

Ethel, who was sitting on the couch watching SpongeBob with Winter in her lap, let out a startled squeak. Eloise, seated beside her, rose to her feet and clutched her cross. Griff looked up from the piece of toast he was eating; Beowulf, who sat at his feet, stood up and growled.

Wynn had warned them Beau and the FBI were going to come for Earl, but she hadn't expected armed men on her front porch at seven in the morning, pounding on her door like it was a drug house.

That fist hammered the door again. *"FBI. Open the door, or we'll break it down."*

Beowulf sprang into action, charging the front door. Growls tore from him; Winter leaped down from Ethel's lap, ran for his life, and Ethel began to moan in distress.

Jenna marched toward the door, a black look on her face.

"Jenna, wait!" Wynn ordered, but her sister ignored the command. She just picked up Beowulf, tucked him beneath her arm, and threw open the door.

"Hello, Ken," she said to the man who stood there. "Still being a dick, I see."

The golden-haired FBI agent she'd tangled with the day before stood there, his tall, broad form clad in an expensive, custom-tailored blue suit. He gave her a narrow look and flipped open his ID, which he held up for everyone to see.

"FBI Special Agent Garrett Morrison," he said. "I have an arrest warrant for Earl Barry."

Wynn leaped down the last few stairs and hurried toward him. Morrison stepped into the living room; two other agents followed. Their hands hovered over their weapons, and anger flared inside of her.

"Where's Beau?" she demanded.

"Sheriff Greystone won't be joining us today," Morrison said flatly.

Jenna shook her head. "He's gonna be pissed at you, Ken."

The Agent scowled at her. "That's Special Agent Morrison to you."

She only laughed.

"Knock it off," Wynn told her sister. She turned to Garrett Morrison. "Beau said he would be here."

"The Sheriff has a conflict of interest when it comes to this case," the Agent said coolly.

"Does he know you're here?"

Garrett turned to the agents behind him. "Search the house."

"He's going to kick your *ass*," Jenna told him. Beowulf barked in agreement.

"You are not searching this house," Wynn snapped, stepping in between her sister and the agents. Her hands fisted at her sides. "You have no right to invade the privacy of my tenants. Earl will come quietly enough."

Garrett arched a brow. He touched the earpiece he wore and said, "Move," and Wynn heard the back door burst open, and armed men were suddenly spilling out of the kitchen, filing up the staircase and down the hallway.

Ethel started to scream. Esme ran out of her room in her flannel robe, and Earl stepped out the small half-bath that sat off the living room, clad in plaid boxers and a white t-shirt. He held a newspaper in one hand, his pipe in the other.

"Can't a man have a bowel movement in peace?" he demanded.

The agents swarmed him like a cloud of bees, pushing him

to his knees, then down to the hard floor, holding him there and cuffing him. Wynn watched in disbelief, rage bleeding through her veins; red hovered at the edges of her vision.

Ethel began to scream hysterically. Beowulf howled and snarled and nearly escaped Jenna's hold. Everyone else froze in terror.

"I give up!" Earl cried.

"You're hurting him!" Esme said furiously and moved toward him.

Every agent in the room brandished their weapon and aimed it at her. Ethel screamed louder. Jenna took an angry step, and Garrett Morrison grabbed her arm.

"Don't," he snapped at her.

Wynn felt everything within her swell. She was going to—

"Stand the fuck down!"

Beau appeared suddenly in the open doorway. His words were a sharp, enraged command that brooked no disobedience. His eyes were so bright, they glowed, and his face...

His face was terrible.

"Now, goddamn it!" he snarled.

And everything stopped.

The agents looked at Morrison; Morrison nodded. The weapons were put away, but the agents didn't move.

"You need to let us handle this," Morrison said.

"Let you handle it?" Beau stepped in and slammed the door behind him, making it shudder violently in its frame.

He met Wynn's gaze. Fury seethed just beneath the surface, so potent and tangible, had she touched him, it might have burned her. It licked at the same fire burning her veins.

Someone was going to pay for this.

"I'm sorry," he growled. "This shouldn't have happened."

"And yet it did," she growled back.

He sent Morrison a searing look. Then he went over to Ethel, who was mewling in terror and laid a gentle hand on her shoulder.

"Ethel," he murmured. "It's Sheriff Beau."

"They're gonna take Earl," she cried and shook him off. "They pushed him down and sat on him, and they're gonna shoot, Esme! I don't like you anymore!"

Another wail burst from her, and she wept, big, gusty sobs, like an inconsolable child. Eloise rocked her, murmuring softly; Wynn's chest was so tight, it hurt. Beau stepped away and moved toward the agents who held Earl down.

The old man was pale, his head pressed against the floor. They'd cuffed him; three different men detained him. His pipe lay crushed on the floor, and the broken sight of it made the fury inside of Wynn flare hotly. It was all she could do not to launch herself at them.

"Congratulations," Jenna said quietly. "You managed to terrorize a mentally disabled woman and tackle a seventy-seven-year-old man." She looked at Morrison, her gaze cutting. "The Bureau must be so proud."

He blinked at her.

"Let him up," Beau ordered, and the agents stood and pulled Earl to his feet.

"I'm sorry," Beau told him. "It shouldn't have been like this."

Earl blinked. The side of his face was beginning to bruise. "I wasn't gonna run."

"I know. I'm sorry." Beau turned to pin Morrison with his burning gaze. "I should have been here."

The Agent shook his head. "You're compromised." He looked at Wynn. "We both know why."

Wynn took a step toward him, but Beau was faster, and before she could give vent to the rage within her, he was punching Special Agent Morrison in the face. Garrett stumbled back a step, caught himself, and shook his head like a dog shedding water.

"Told you so," Jenna said.

The agents in the room froze, their hands on their guns, their gazes uncertain as they flitted between Beau and Morrison.

Garrett wiped at the blood dripping from his nose. "One is all you get," he said flatly. "The next one is assault of a federal officer."

"Don't be such a pussy," Jenna scoffed.

"Jenna!" Wynn snarled.

Garrett glared at Jenna. "You could do with a night or two in juvie."

"Bring it," she told him.

"Enough," Beau said sharply. "Jenna, sit. *Now*."

Jenna didn't even hesitate. She sat down on the couch, settled Beowulf on her lap, and gave Garrett an arch look.

"Can I get some pants?" Earl asked. "I'd rather not go to the big house in my skivvies."

Beau nodded at the agents who stood behind Earl. "Uncuff him and let him get dressed."

They led Earl out. Ethel's hiccupping sobs filled the air.

Wynn faced Morrison. "There are things you need to know." She could feel Beau's gaze but didn't look at him. "Extenuating circumstances."

"That may be," Morrison muttered. "But my hands are tied."

"I was just following orders!" Jenna mocked, and when he looked at her, she smiled sweetly.

"You," he growled, "are a brat."

She only rolled her eyes. "Sticks and stones."

"He needs a lawyer," Beau cut in. "Do you have someone you can call?"

"Yes," Wynn said.

Sasha had agreed to represent Earl pro bono, her first official client. And she was fairly confident that—so long as they could pay back the money and explain to the federal prosecutor the circumstances of the crime—she could get Earl a decent plea deal. He was old; he had no criminal record. The bank would have their money back, and Earl would promise not to do it again.

It would all be okay.

So long as Wynn could figure out how to come up with eight grand in cash.

Sure. No problem. I'll just pluck it off the money tree in the backyard...

But there was no other choice, so she would simply do whatever it took. Because letting Earl—or any of them—go to jail was a death sentence.

"Are you sure?" Beau pressed, and again, Wynn could feel his gaze. It made her skin prickle, and heat filled her cheeks as memory unexpectedly speared through her.

Not now.

For the love of Pete.

"I can take care of my own," she retorted sharply.

"Wynn," he said, and she made herself look at him, painfully aware they weren't alone.

"I've got it," she said.

He stared at her, those glinting eyes seeing far too much.

Her fury; her fear. The profound sense of betrayal she felt. Oh, she knew it wasn't fair; Morrison had obviously left Beau deliberately out of the loop.

Because of her.

So it wasn't right that she should feel betrayed. What happened between them meant *nothing*. And she didn't want to let it change her.

But it had.

He had.

And now, there was no going back.

She felt explosive and off-balance; part of her wanted to punch *him* in the face. But she also wanted to kiss him. For drawing Garrett Morrison's blood; for being kind to Ethel; for apologizing to Earl.

Even for the terrible fury she'd seen in him.

"We'll get it all worked out," he told her evenly, his gaze steady. He looked at her as if none of her barriers counted when it came to him.

As if he was already inside them.

Panic flared within her.

"Thank you, new Sheriff," she said coolly. "I feel so much better now."

His gaze narrowed. Jenna gave her a sharp look she ignored.

Earl and the agents returned then. He'd put on overalls and a blue and green flannel, his old work boots, and the red, white and blue hat Ethel had knitted for him.

"I'm ready," he said.

Beau walked over, gave the agents a dark look, and un-cuffed him.

"That's not procedure," Garrett said.

"Fuck procedure," Beau said distinctly.

He looked at Wynn and nodded, his eyes glittering with a look she recognized instantly.

Later.

Whether she liked it or not.

He led Earl out; the agents all followed. Garrett was the last, and he hesitated as he reached the door.

He looked around the room, at Griff, who stood in the doorway of the kitchen; at Esme who stood at the foot of the stairs, looking pale and distressed. At Eloise, who glared at him, and at Ethel, who was still weeping softly. Then, finally, at Wynn.

"My apologies," he said stiffly. "I didn't realize..."

"You should have," Jenna told him, her voice hard. Beowulf growled softly, showing his teeth. "You really should have."

He looked at her. "You're right." He nodded at Wynn. "I'm sorry."

Then he left.

CHAPTER 20

"You hit like a fucking brick."

Beau sipped his coffee and studied the records spread out before him on the conference room table. "Don't forget."

"I should press charges," Garrett added.

"Be my guest. And after that, we can discuss why you decided you needed half a dozen armed federal agents to apprehend a seventy-seven-year-old man."

"Christ, I didn't know it was an old folks' home." Garrett touched the darkening bruise on his jaw. "You could have told me."

Annoyance shot through Beau. "I told you two of us would be enough. You didn't listen. It serves you right for going around me."

Which he was still completely pissed about.

"You're compromised here." Garrett sat down at the table across from him. "You know that right?"

Beau gave him a cold look. "I did my job."

"Hell, man, I'm glad you're back in the saddle. It's about damned time. But whatever is between you and Wynn

Owens is a conflict, and it's my job to not let those kinds of things interfere with getting shit done."

"Keep telling yourself that, Ken."

A growl rumbled in Garrett's chest. "What the hell is with that?"

"Apparently you resemble Barbie's main squeeze."

"She's calling me a fucking *Ken doll*? She needs a good—"

"Careful," Beau warned quietly.

"Goddamn it," Garrett said. He was silent for a moment. Then, "What was Wynn talking about when she mentioned 'extenuating circumstances'?"

Beau's annoyance grew. "I don't know."

But he was certain they were the reason she'd sought him out yesterday before he'd run her off. Something she'd learned about Earl's motives.

Something they hadn't gotten a chance to discuss because he's been too busy sticking his tongue down her throat. Not that he regretted it—*not for a fucking minute*—but now he didn't know what the hell was going on, and he didn't like that.

Not at all.

And this morning, she'd looked at him with fury, and fear, and doubt, as if last night was an apparition. Or a dream.

And he didn't like that, either.

Because there was no way in hell he was going to let her pretend it didn't happen—*that they didn't happen*—no matter what kind of damage the jackass sitting across from him had done.

No matter how much of a goddamn mess things were.

"Maybe you should ask her," Garrett said. "You know, before he gets arraigned."

Beau gave him a dark look. "Mind your business."

"Look, I'm not proud of what happened. If there are extenuating circumstances, I'd like to know. Maybe I can help."

"Now you want to help?"

"It's my job," Garrett retorted. "I haven't forgotten that."

Beau rubbed a hand down his face and sighed. "If I need your help, I'll let you know."

"Fine." Garrett looked at the spread of documents. "What's this?"

"Records from Camp Blossom Hills."

"The location where the first victim was taken?"

"Yes." Beau sat back and stared at the pile. "I talked with all of the parents. Each of our victims spent time at the camp. Most of them weren't actual campers, just guests or visitors. The camp offers recreational activities and free classes that are open to the general public."

Garrett picked up one of the pages. "A link."

"Yes." And his certainty that it was *the* link was growing. There was simply no other commonality beyond the camp.

Garrett arched a brow. "They let these go without a warrant?"

"I'm a sweet talker." Beau shrugged.

"They're inadmissible, you know. If you find something—"

"I know," Beau said shortly. "But the Executive Director of the camp would have fought a warrant for weeks."

"How do you know that?"

"Because he's the same asshole who owns the bank."

"Edward Duggar?" Garrett lifted a brow. "Well, that's interesting."

"Word is, he was also in bed with the previous Sheriff."

"What were they doing?"

"I don't know." Not yet. "But Hatfield was a murderous piece of shit, so I'm thinking birds of a feather."

For a long moment, Garrett was silent. "I've looked the files over. We have no physical or forensic evidence; no witnesses. Our interviews and canvassing haven't produced shit. Our profile is supposition at best, and the timeline is all over the place." He shook his head. "We're at goddamn square one."

Beau shook his head. "He's connected to the camp. I know it. We just have to figure out how."

A knock sounded, and a young agent stuck his head in the door.

"Mahoney," Garrett said and waved him in. "What have you got?"

Mahoney was tall—so tall he had to duck to walk through the doorway—and stick thin. He wore plain, neatly pressed black pants and a white button-down shirt. His face was narrow, his dark brown hair fell into his eyes, and his skin was so pale it looked like he'd never stepped foot in the sun. He carried a sheaf of papers in one hand; the other hand opened and closed as he walked toward them, almost convulsively. When he stopped beside Garrett, he did so far out of reach.

"I found something," he said.

"Great work, my friend." Garrett leaned back in his chair. "Lay it on me."

Mahoney looked at him, then at Beau. Said nothing.

"It's okay," Garrett told him. "Beau's one of us. What did you find?"

Another uncertain glance at Beau. Then, "The composition of the soil collected from Emma Farley's fingernails contains a percentage of aluminum and silica-based clay not common to the area, particularly in the field where the body was found, the primary use of which is corn production and livestock forage."

"Clay isn't uncommon out here," Beau said. "We've got kettles and moraines all over the state where the glaciers settled and then retreated. Lots of clay in those areas."

"No," Mahoney said definitively and shook his head. "There are abnormally high concentrations of kaolinite in the sample, which contains one to one silicon to aluminum oxides."

"Okay," Garrett said patiently. "What does that mean?"

Mahoney looked at him. "Further tests are required before the hypothesis."

Garrett's eyes narrowed. "But you have a theory."

Mahoney only shook his head. "Further tests are required."

"What kind of soil would have high concentrations of kaolinite?" Beau asked.

Mahoney gave him an impatient look. "Not soil—clay."

Beau tried not to let his irritation show. "What kind of clay would have high concentrations of kaolinite?"

"The research is not yet definitive of a conclusive response," Mahoney said and looked at Garrett. "*Further tests are required.*"

Garrett signed. "Alright, do your thing. But bring me the results as soon as you have them."

Mahoney nodded and turned away.

"Wait," Beau said.

The young man halted.

Beau reached into his pocket, dug out the evidence bag that held Sean Evers's blue pen, and held it out. "Can you run this for prints?"

Mahoney looked at Garrett, who nodded.

Mahoney quickly took the pen from Beau and left the way he'd come, his hand still opening and closing at his side.

"He's on the spectrum," Garrett said before Beau could speak. "No one wanted him because he can be...challenging. But he's the smartest person I've ever met, and he does damn fine work. Whose pen?"

Beau only shook his head. "I'm thinking maybe I should take a drive out to Camp Blossom Hills and get a soil sample for comparison."

"Still a secretive bastard, aren't you?"

He shrugged.

"Getting a sample is a good idea." Garrett sighed. "I'll look through these files, see if another set of eyes can't help."

Beau nodded. He wasn't offended; he would take all the assistance he could get. Another set of eyes was important. Different people saw different patterns, picked up on different facts. He hadn't had Harry or Cam help because the records were unofficial, and he didn't want to take any chances on word of them getting back to Edward Duggar. Lillian Jenkins had done him a solid, and he had no intention of letting it come back on her.

But he knew someone else needed to comb through the information. He would've liked to have had Winston Reynolds take a look at it, but Winston was a no-show.

Beau was disappointed, but not surprised.

Another knock. Cam stuck his head in the door.

"Hey, boss," he said to Beau. "Harry said I should see if you want us to head out and do some interviews."

Cam was younger than Harry and even more eager to prove himself. Heavy-set, with bright red hair and a healthy smattering of freckles, Cam didn't have Harry's easy charisma or, being a transplant from southern Ohio, his history with the town and its people. But Cam was always smiling, happy to do whatever needed doing, and Beau appreciated his dependability.

"Not today," he said, ignoring the disappointment he saw. "I want you to check in with the Fire Chief about the Eckhart's fire, see how he's doing with determining a point of origin."

Cam perked up. "I can do that."

"Go."

Cam disappeared, and Garrett shook his head.

"You've got your hands full," he said, smiling wryly.

"They'll get there," Beau said. "Just keep those records to yourself. They don't know about them, and I plan to keep it that way."

"Worried?"

"They're young. Proving themselves matters. Might matter more than doing their jobs."

"I remember those days."

Beau did, too. "I'm going to go out to the camp."

"You should go see your girl, too," Garrett told him. "Find out what kind of extenuating circumstances she was talking about."

Beau gave him a look.

"It's good to see you back in the land of the living, you know," Garrett said. "I heard about things in Miami, bad things. I'm glad they didn't stick."

Beau shook his head. If it weren't for Tristan, he'd still be in Miami, nursing his wounds and committing cold-blooded murder, so he was pretty sure he couldn't take any credit for stepping into the light.

"I'll see you later," he said and pushed to his feet.

Another knock. Beau sighed. "Enter."

The door swung open and Winston Reynolds appeared, clad in clean jeans, a pair of scuffed work boots, and a worn *Aerosmith* t-shirt. His hair had been shorn, he'd shaved, and he looked, if not like law enforcement, at least sober. "Hey, chief, we need to talk."

CHAPTER 21

"Extenuating circumstances, or mitigating factors, are unusual or extreme facts which lead up to—or occur concurrently with—the perpetration of the offense, which, though an offense has been committed without legal justification, may mitigate or reduce the damages for or punishment of the offense by the Court."

Come again?

Wynn sighed and ate another green bean. She was supposed to be snapping them, but no one was hungry.

"It's not as complicated as it sounds," Sasha continued. "It just means that if we can prove Earl's inability to purchase his insulin was the driving factor behind the bank robbery, that fact will be taken into consideration as a mitigating factor when he's sentenced."

Wynn laid her cheek against the kitchen table. It was cool. *Nice.* "But he'll still go to jail."

"Maybe." Sasha sat back and closed her laptop. "I have an idea. I don't know if it will work, but I think it's worth trying."

Wynn shoved another green bean into her mouth. The

house was abnormally quiet. Everyone had been subdued since Earl's arrest, silently going their separate ways. Ethel was still in her room. Sean had shown up as the SUVs were driving away, and there hadn't been any way to avoid telling him what had happened. But to Wynn's surprise, he wasn't angry.

At least, not with her.

"At this rate, I'll try anything," she replied morosely.

"You need to get a grip," Sasha said, not unkindly. "This is just the beginning."

Yay.

"Do you want to hear my idea or not?" Sasha demanded, exasperated.

"Fire away," Wynn muttered.

"What is *wrong* with you? Are you giving up?"

"No." She scowled. "I'm just..." Exhausted. Scared. And filled with so much angst, she didn't know what to do with it.

She still wanted to punch Special Agent Garrett Morrison in the face.

And she wanted Earl home.

She wanted to erase every foolish, dangerous thing she felt for Beau Greystone.

And go back to being who she'd been before him.

She wanted Jenna to stop growing up.

And the Stick Man in the ground.

"Beau kissed me," she heard herself say.

"Ooooo." Sasha leaned forward. "Do tell."

"I didn't mean for it to happen. It just...did. And then the FBI came and arrested Earl, and Beau wasn't here, even though he was supposed to be, and I don't care if it wasn't his fault that he wasn't here, I feel...betrayed, even though he warned me, and I knew it was going to happen and..."

Wynn shrugged, but her throat was thick, and there was too much and nothing at all churning inside of her. "He got to me."

"Of course he did. That's what they do."

"I can't do it."

Sasha studied her. "Why not?"

But the words wouldn't put themselves together. She wasn't sure if it was Sasha she was trying to convince.

Or herself.

"Tristan," she said. "He...damaged you. And I realized this morning, Beau could do that to me." She looked at her friend. "I can't let that happen."

"Don't use me as your excuse," Sasha told her flatly.

Wynn flinched.

"I would do it all again, you know," Sasha added.

Shocked by that, Wynn blinked at her. "You would? Why?"

"Because it was the best summer of my life. It was worth every minute of the heartbreak that followed."

"That's...loco."

"Welcome to love."

"I don't love Beau!"

Panic beat like wings in her chest. *Love*. That was stupid. She hardly knew him. They'd spent what amounted to less than two hours together. Love didn't happen like that.

Did it?

"Maybe not," Sasha said. "But you could. That's why you're completely freaking out."

"It's not that simple," Wynn told her.

"Why not?"

"He was married. She...died."

"I didn't know that. I'm sorry."

"When he talked about her, it made me want to cry." Wynn shook her head. "He isn't free."

"But he kissed you."

"It didn't mean anything."

"You don't know that."

"Yes, I do."

"No, you just think you do."

Wynn glared at her.

"No risk, no reward," her friend said and shrugged.

Wynn snorted. "Says the woman who hasn't dated anyone in the last *decade*."

Color flooded Sasha's cheeks. "Touché."

The clock in the hall began to chime. Outside, the sun was trying to spear through the thick bank of clouds, and a chilled breeze ruffled the kitchen curtains. Wynn went back to snapping beans. "So what's your idea?"

Sasha looked like she wanted to protest the change in subject, but she just nodded and said, "I think we need to get the press involved."

Wynn frowned. "What do you mean?"

"Earl's story isn't uncommon. Millions of people are facing the same situation—food or meds? This is a story that will speak to the public, and if we can sway public opinion, we have a shot."

Hope stirred inside of Wynn. "You sound sure."

"I am. If we can get people to empathize, they'll act. They'll donate toward repayment of the money he took; they'll lobby the prosecutor to drop the charges. They may even pull their money out of the Dorchester National Bank."

Wynn stared at her. "You're a freaking genius."

Sasha smiled wryly. "I wouldn't go that far."

"That could work," Wynn said, amazed. "Really work."

"By now everyone knows he's been arrested. But they don't know why. The county fair opened last night. I think I can get Adam Stevens to let us set up a booth. If we can get a booth, we can tell Earl's story."

Excitement speared through Wynn. "Oh, we'll get a booth. Adam has been in love with you since Home Ec class."

"Unlikely."

She snorted. "Every time I run into him, he asks about you."

"He doesn't."

"*Always*. So he'll definitely hook us up with a booth." She paused. "But I don't have any idea where to begin."

"I do," said a voice, and she looked up to see Jenna in the doorway.

"I can totally help," she said and strode into the kitchen. Beowulf trotted in behind her. *True love*, Wynn thought.

Another thing that was working out.

"We can create a Facebook page and a Go Fund Me page," Jenna continued. "An Instagram account, Twitter. We can make a flyer and a banner; we can take donations and start a petition. We can do this."

Her eyes were glittering; energy vibrated from her. Wynn looked at her, suddenly seeing the child fade and the woman step into place. Smart, strong, willful. *Capable*. Pride and fierce, unexpected joy filled her.

I helped do that, she thought.

"I don't know," Sasha said. "I still haven't forgiven you for ditching me yesterday—

especially with a serial killer who's fond of blond teenaged girls on the loose. You scared the shit out of me."

Jenna had the grace to look shamefaced. "I'm sorry. I wanted to talk to Beau, and I wasn't sure you'd let me."

"It wasn't cool," Sasha told her grimly. "And it had better never, ever happen again."

"It won't," Jenna promised.

"I mean it. When I thought he might have you..."

"I'm sorry," Jenna said again. "I didn't mean to scare you. I didn't...I didn't think about that."

"As long as he's on the loose, it should be all you think about."

Jenna nodded, her cheeks bright with color.

"Why did you want to talk to Beau?" Wynn wanted to know.

"I decided to tell him about the gun." Jenna sat down at the table. Beowulf collapsed to the linoleum beside her. "I was going to tell you on the way home, but you were growling like an angry bear. Besides, you'd already given it to him."

"Gun?" Sasha repeated and looked at Wynn.

"You went and saw him. That's why you were standing there." Wynn glowered at her sister. "Why would you do that?"

"Because I thought he should know."

More betrayal. Wynn scowled. "Which is why I gave it to him."

"Yes, I know. I'm proud of you. I know you have issues with people in roles of authority."

Sasha smothered a smile. "What gun?"

"Earl's gun." Wynn went back to snapping beans. "He threw it in the pasture after the robbery. Jenna found it, and I took it to Beau, who immediately knew it was the weapon used to rob the bank. Because there's security footage. And Earl's blood, which was all over the gun *and* the crime scene, because he'd cut himself. And he left behind his grocery card, too—I guess it fell out of his wallet

—but he claimed that it had been stolen. The wallet, I mean."

"You couldn't open with all of this?" Sasha shook her head. "I need to get down to the Sheriff's Office and make sure he's okay with me representing him. Then I need to file an Entry of Appearance because if they have blood, they're going to get a Court Order for DNA. I need to do this today."

"Do you think the plan will be enough?" Wynn asked her.

"No." Sasha shook her head. "We need bigger guns. National news. Major media outlets and big-name talking heads."

"How do we manage that?" Jenna asked.

Sasha's expression turned grim. "We put our personal feelings aside, put on our big-girl panties, and ask for help."

The look on her face made anxiety spear through Wynn. "Help from who?"

"Who else? The *Washington Times'* Pulitzer-Prize winning war correspondent." Sasha smiled, hard and sharp. "Tristan James."

CHAPTER 22

Two wide tire tracks led through the dense hardwood undergrowth.

"That's how they're coming and going," Winston said. "They circle back behind the buildings, unload, and leave without anyone at the camp knowing the difference."

Beau stared at the overgrown but well-used road. It sat on the perimeter of the Camp Blossom Hill property, which was nearly fifty acres in size and heavily wooded. The road was wide enough for large box trucks and enclosed trailers and was separately accessible to the main highway via a narrow strip of asphalt. "What are they unloading?"

Winston slid him a look.

"I know you checked it out," Beau told him.

He'd known Winston was a wild card; that was part of the former deputy's appeal. And he should've realized that just because Winston hadn't shown up at the office, hat in hand, didn't mean he wasn't back in the saddle. That Winston would instead focus on things he'd been dialed into years before should have occurred to Beau.

It's what he would have done.

"Heroin," Winston said. "That's new. Used to be meth."

"Where is it headed?" Beau asked grimly.

"Don't know. Madison, maybe. Big Pharma got everyone hooked on oxy and then took it away. Heroin is a lot easier to get—and it's cheaper. It's a big market."

Which wasn't news. Beau knew from his time with the DEA that heroin was flooding the heartland. Overdoses from opiates made front-page news; heroin addicts died quietly, without fanfare.

Except for the families.

Beau had fought his doctors when they'd tried to give him opiates. He knew intimately the dangers; he'd lived surrounded by the fall out for too many years.

"Shit," he said.

Winston watched him, waiting.

"Anyone see you out here?" Beau asked. His soil sample was in his pocket. It seemed unlikely that such a thing would lead anywhere, but he wasn't turning any possibility aside. Mahoney had obviously thought what he'd found was unusual and worth following up on; that was good enough for Beau.

"Nope," Winston said.

"You're sure?"

"Yep. You gonna get a search warrant?"

Beau turned and headed back toward his truck. "I need probable cause for a search warrant."

"Well, I reckon if one of those trucks was to get stopped and searched, we'd have plenty of probable cause."

"We still need probable cause to stop and search the truck," Beau pointed out.

"Isn't a serial killer on the loose reason enough?"

Beau halted and rubbed his leg. Thought about it. "We could set up a checkpoint; no one would argue.

Bring in a canine unit and hope like hell they find something."

Winston grinned. "Either way, it'll piss Duggar off. And make him nervous. Nervous men make mistakes."

They did. Sometimes fatal ones.

Beau had parked off of the rough dirt road, tucking his truck into the thick green undergrowth, and climbing into it was a pain in the ass. But he hadn't wanted anyone to spot it.

"What next?" Winston asked, climbing in beside him.

"I'll see about a checkpoint. In the meanwhile, I have a set of records from the camp that I'd like you to look at."

"Records?"

"Attendance, payroll, HR, visitors, guests, all of it."

Winston whistled. "Impressive. Duggar parted with all of that?"

"Duggar had nothing to do with it, so keep your trap shut," Beau told him. "Just look through them and let me know if you find anything. Every victim spent time out here. And something—at least one significant thing—has to connect them. We need to find that one thing."

Winston nodded. "I'll take my time."

"Do that," Beau told him.

*****

The sun was reluctantly poking through the clouds as Beau turned into Wynn's driveway. He'd had Harry set up a checkpoint just a few miles north of the camp; the northern highway led directly to the interstate, which made it a reasonable location. He'd had Cam set up one on the southern end of the valley, just along the edge of the river, because he didn't want to give anyone the heads up that he was, in actuality, targeting the camp. He'd asked several of the State Troopers who were patrolling the area to help out, one of whom had a canine unit.

Now he would just wait and see what they found, if anything.

Garrett was busy interviewing the parents of the Stick Man's previous victims; Winston was tucked away in his trailer pouring over the documents provided by Lily. And Earl Barry had officially been charged with armed robbery. There hadn't been much Beau could do about that, but Garrett had okayed keeping Earl in the holding cell at the station, rather than shipping him off to the county jail, so that was something.

Beau needed to get his soil sample to Mahoney, and it wouldn't be long before Edward Duggar showed up demanding Earl's head on a platter, but for now, Beau had a few minutes.

The passing storms had turned the driveway into a muddy, rutted mess, necessitating four-wheel drive. When Beowulf the Runt suddenly appeared and darted in front of him, Beau hit the brakes and the truck's back end careened sideways while the front end dived into a large, watery hole. The files beside him slid to the floor, his coffee spilled, and the small ceramic pig Harry had stuck atop the dash—a gift for luck from his mother—flew headfirst into the back seat.

Goddamn it.

It took Beau almost five minutes to get the truck out, and by the time he pulled up to the house, he was irritated as hell. And then he saw Wynn.

On top of the roof. *Again.*

She was talking to a man Beau didn't recognize, who

was also on the roof. Griff stood next to the extension ladder on the ground, looking up at them.

Beau climbed out of the truck, his leg throbbing, his blood hot. He walked over to Griff who nodded and said, "Afternoon, new Sheriff."

"What the hell is she doing back up there?" he demanded.

"Talkin' to the roofer." Griff leaned toward him. "She's a little miffed about that."

"Miffed?"

In that instant, Wynn glanced down and saw him.

"You!" she stormed. "You did this!"

Beau folded his arms across his chest. "Did what?"

She waved a hand at the man who stood next to her. He wore battered painter pants and an old flannel. His red baseball hat said *Red's Roofing*.

He didn't look as if he was enjoying his day.

"This," Wynn said. "You sent him."

"No, I didn't," Beau said.

She snorted. "Liar! I know you had Griff call him."

Beau looked at Griff, who shrugged.

"So what if I did?" He was ten seconds from climbing up the ladder and hauling her down. "Come down, and we can talk about it."

"You had no right," Wynn told him, her dark eyes flashing. "This is not your business."

She wasn't wrong. Beau didn't care.

"Come down," he repeated, trying to sound calm.

She snarled at him. The man beside her rubbed the back of his neck, clearly uncomfortable.

"Might as well let him do the job," Griff put in. "He came all the way from Beaverton."

Another snort. "Traitor."

"I like bein' dry. What's wrong with that?"

She gave him a dark look. "You should have asked me."

"You would've said no."

Beau bit back a smile. "Let the man do his job, sweetheart. You can consider it a loan."

She stared down at him, her eyes turbulent.

"Come down," he said again.

A growl escaped her. She gave the roofer an unhappy look.

"Just do what's necessary," she told him. "And please don't fall through."

Then she headed for the ladder. Beau held one side and Griff held the other while she climbed down.

"Jerks," she muttered when she got to the bottom. Her hair was contained in a long, braided rope, her t-shirt said *Dirt Worshiper*, and her jeans were nearly worn-through. She gave Griff a scowl as she jumped down. "Thanks for nothing."

He only shrugged. "It'll get done proper."

"I do it proper," she protested.

He only blinked at her, silent.

"Oh, stuff a sock in it," she told him.

Then she turned and stomped away. Beau handed Griff one of his cards. "Have him bill me."

Griff took the card. "Will do, new Sheriff."

Beau shook his head and strode after Wynn, his leg protesting the pace. He snagged one of her belt loops and caught her just as she was going to climb the front steps. She jerked to a halt.

"I don't want your help," she said sharply.

He tried not to take that personally and failed. "I don't care."

"Why are you doing this?" she demanded and glared at him. "You don't even know me!"

Annoyed, he pulled her toward him. "I know you."

"You don't know diddly!" She tried to squirm away. "We're strangers."

"We're not fucking strangers." He hauled her toward him, and she slapped her hands against his chest. "If Jenna hadn't interrupted us, I would have been inside you last night."

Color burst in her cheeks like a firework detonating. "That was a mistake."

Anger surged through him. He wound a strong arm around her and plucked her off her feet. Her body slapped his, and they both shuddered. "Like hell it was."

"It's *not* happening again," she added, pushing against him.

His other arm wrapped around her. "Like hell, it's not."

"No," she said. "Just...no."

Beau stared at her, his heart beating too hard. He'd finally accepted this thing—whatever the hell it was—between them, and she was telling him *no*?

Before he could respond, a big, black Jeep pulled up and parked next to his truck. A giant of a man climbed out, clad in stained overalls and a Packers beanie. He was freckled and pale, his expression like flint. In his hand, he held a slender wooden box.

"Aw, crap," Wynn said.

She wiggled and tried to escape Beau's hold; for a long moment, he refused to release her. Even though she was stronger than she looked, and it hurt like hell to fight her.

"Let go," she hissed.

He didn't want to. But whatever was between them was

personal, and he wasn't ready to share it with a stranger. So, reluctantly, he set her down.

She stumbled back a step, shot him a dark look, and then turned to watch the giant approach.

"Winifred," said the man, his voice a rumble of sound. He nodded at Beau. "New Sheriff."

Finally, someone who knew who the hell he was.

"Hey, Buck." Wynn rubbed her forehead and frowned. "I'm sorry, I forgot to call you."

"Trouble?" he asked.

"You have no idea." She turned back toward the porch. "Come on, I'll fill you in. Maybe you can help."

Help?

Beau blinked, irritated as hell.

When she'd just torn a strip off of him for trying?

He growled softly. Buck looked at him with cold, pale eyes.

"You want pie?" Wynn asked over her shoulder. "I've got pecan or apple."

"Apples from your trees?" Buck asked, staring at Beau.

"Yep."

"I'm in," he said.

Then he followed her. Beau watched them, his irritation morphing into something darker. More primal. Which he knew he had no right to. He and Wynn weren't...

The hell we aren't.

Something he needed to make clear.

He followed them into the house. The living room was empty, the TV off. A faint murmur drifted down the stairs—someone was listening to music, something wistful and bluesy—and Beowulf appeared to growl at him as he approached the kitchen.

"I'm not the enemy, you know," he told the pup, who

watched him with serious, suspicious amber eyes. But that odd, stubby little tail wagged hesitantly. So Beau forced himself to lean down and offer his hand.

The pup stepped forward gingerly and sniffed.

"See?" Beau let him take a good, long whiff.

Beowulf tilted his head. Yipped softly.

"You and me, we're going to be good friends," Beau told him softly.

"Lies," Wynn said, and Beau looked up to see her watching him, her stormy eyes solemn. "It's all lies, Beo. Don't listen to a word of it."

Again, he tried not to take that personally. And, again, he failed.

"I'm sorry about this morning," he told her abruptly. "That wasn't my call."

She only shrugged. "I should've expected it."

He scowled blackly. "From me?"

"From life."

She turned and walked into the kitchen. Beau stared after her, his hands curling into fists. She had every right to be upset. There was no excuse for what had transpired that morning. He'd meant what he'd said: it never should have happened. Jesus, he'd almost burst a vein when he realized what Garrett had done. And then to walk in and find what he had—

Well. He supposed he was lucky she was even speaking to him.

Beowulf yipped again, and they walked into the kitchen to find Buck seated at the table devouring a large slice of apple pie. The slender wooden box he'd carried inside sat on the table beside him.

"Why is he here?" Buck asked around a bite of pie.

"Because he's a pain in my arse," Wynn retorted. Color flushed her cheeks.

Beau halted in the doorway, his gaze narrow on her.

"You're just biased," Buck told her and swallowed.

She made a face at him.

"You know it's true." He took another bite. "Whole town knows it."

She rolled her eyes. "Whatever." She paused. "Earl robbed the Dorchester bank."

Buck stopped chewing and stared at her.

Beau stepped into the kitchen, pulled out a chair at the table and sank into it. "You said something about extenuating circumstances?"

She ignored him. "He can't afford his meds," she told Buck. "None of them can. They said Mr. Sanders died because he was cutting his heart pills in half."

Beau stilled. Her words were hard with angry grief. Beowulf whined softly and sat at her feet. She leaned down to stroke his head.

"They robbed the bank so they could get a stash of what they needed, at least for a little while," she continued. "But Earl dropped his grocery card in front of the teller's booth. And he bled everywhere. And he used a gun, and there's security footage, so he's probably going to jail."

"That's why they went up to Canada." Beau ran a hand down his face. "For the meds."

Fuck.

Not a motive that would've occurred to him.

"That's messed up," Buck said.

"Yep," Wynn agreed. She sighed. "Sasha has a plan to get him off. I can only pray it works."

"Sasha," Beau repeated, memory stirring. "Sasha Conner?"

"The one and only." Wynn looked at Buck. "She just passed the bar."

"The bar?" Beau repeated. "She's a lawyer? Wasn't she supposed to go to Julliard?"

Wynn only shook her head.

"What can I do?" Buck asked.

"We're going to work a booth at the fair tonight, get the word out. Try to drum up some support and money for defense costs. You can hand out flyers if you want."

Buck nodded. "I'll be there."

"Awesome." Wynn smiled at him, that dimple winking. "Your mama did good."

And Beau realized the relationship he was witnessing was one of friendship. Almost like…siblings. Relief flooded through him.

"You still want the knife?" Buck asked and nudged the wooden box.

"Of course." Wynn picked up the box and flipped it open. Inside sat a broad-handled filet knife, its blade slender and gently curved. The handle was made out of a dark, rich wood the color of chocolate, inlaid with a narrow stripe of pale green turquoise. "It's beautiful, Buck. Thank you."

He just shrugged and finished his pie.

"What do you want in trade?" she asked, putting the knife away.

He squinted at her. "You still got that old John Deere?"

"Sure. It's all yours." She snickered. "Good luck getting it out of the back forty."

"Not a problem."

"What are you going to do with it?"

Buck stared at her, his face like granite. "Tractor race."

She grinned. Beau stared at her, unable to look away.

Buck stood. "I'll see you later."

He nodded at Beau and then left as abruptly as he'd come.

Silence followed him; somewhere in the house, a clock struck the hour. Wynn picked up Buck's plate and put it in the sink. Beau watched her, thinking that he liked sitting there, in her kitchen, the scent of fresh bread and apple pie surrounding him. It was...peaceful.

Like home.

"You should go, too," she said. "I have stuff."

Poking the bear. "We're not done."

She turned and gave him an opaque look.

"I want to talk about last night," he told her.

That lovely color rushed back into her cheeks.

"I know you're upset about this morning," he continued, "but that doesn't have shit to do with what happened between us last night."

"Don't you have a serial killer to catch?"

"You don't get to run away just because I scare you."

"That's not fair," she growled.

"Life's not fair." He stared at her. "I want this to be very clear: we are not a fucking mistake."

Her pulse fluttered wildly in her throat. "There is no 'we.'"

"Just keep pushing." Anger flooded him. "See where it gets you."

"You don't get to decide."

That brought him out of his chair. "Try me."

Her eyes widened, but she held her ground. "You're in no position to be giving ultimatums."

Heat burst in his belly and slid through his veins. "The hell I'm not."

She stared at him for a long, silent moment. Then, "You aren't free, Beau."

He didn't understand what that meant. "I have no ties."

Dark, stormy eyes met his. "You wear her, every day."

He stilled.

"I understand why. And I don't hold it against you. But this..." A sharp, painful laugh. "This can't happen."

She turned away, to look out the window at the clouds billowing on the horizon, smudges of dark blue and vibrant violet. Rain spattered against the pane, fat, loud drops that made the glass shudder.

Regret and rage and despair suddenly welled within him. "Wynn."

She only shook her head, silent.

Goddamn it.

He had the sense of falling, as if he'd just parachuted from a C-16 into enemy territory. Only he wasn't sure which way was up. Or down. Or how close he was to the damn ground.

His phone chose that moment to ring. He swore and pulled it from his pocket.

Harry. "What?"

"We found something at the northern checkpoint, Sheriff."

"What?"

"A truck full of heroin. And meth. And..."

"And what?"

"And people."

Beau swore. "I'm on my way."

He slid his phone back into his pocket. Wynn ignored him, her shoulders set, the line of her spine so tense, he ached with it.

Fuck.

"I have to go," he said.

"Be careful."

He took that and held onto it. "I'll be back."
"Don't," she said quietly. "We're done here."
Not by a long shot, sweetheart.
"I'll see you later," he told her shortly.
Then he left.

CHAPTER 23

"I TOLD YOU—EARL's not alone. And the size of this crowd just proves it."

Wynn couldn't disagree. People from all walks of life were responding to his story.

The fair booth Adam had managed to secure for them had been busy since the moment they'd set up, and the crowd showed no signs of dispersing. A small write-up in the local online *Blossom Hills Crier*—thank you, Sasha—had helped to spread the word, and the news that Earl had been arrested for the robbery—and why—was spreading like wildfire.

The midway was full of folks despite the curfew Beau had set. Rides were running, games were being played, and the band in the beer tent was offering a salute to eighties hair bands. The scent of fried foods and roasted corn wafted on the breeze, and the sound of happy children filled the air. So far, the storms had held off, and the town of Blossom Hills was kicking up its heels and indulging in some good, clean fun.

No one, it appeared, was going to let the Stick Man ruin the best weekend of the summer.

And if Wynn had often felt ostracized and judged by the people of Blossom Hills—especially in the wake of her mother's death—the outpouring of support for Earl humbled her deeply. Having spent most of her life on the fringe, it was startling to find herself suddenly, enthusiastically, embraced by her community.

Donations were pouring in; people were signing the petition and taking flyers to hang in their businesses, and more than a few said they would threaten to close their accounts at the Dorchester National Bank if the bank pressed charges.

The people of Blossom Hills had turned out in huge numbers to help Earl.

To help *her*.

And there was a powerful ache in Wynn's chest as she stood there, talking to people, thanking them, appreciating them in a way she never before had.

"I need a corndog," Jenna said from beside her.

"I'll come with you." Sasha slung an arm around Jenna's shoulders. "A deep-fried Twinkie is calling my name."

"Ew," Wynn put in.

"Don't knock it 'til you try it," Sasha retorted.

"I don't need a babysitter, you know," Jenna told them.

"You do until the Stick Man is behind bars," Sasha said.

"Or better yet, underground," Wynn muttered.

"Amen, sister. You want anything?"

"Something to drink. I've never talked to so many people in my life."

"It's good for you," Jenna informed her. "Broadens your horizons."

Wynn shook her head and watched them walk away.

Except for her run-in with Beau—and the FBI raiding her home like freaking Stormtroopers—the day had been downright hopeful.

Because she was beginning to think Sasha was right —*this just might work.*

They were already halfway toward their mark on donations, and public sentiment was unarguably in their favor. If Velma could get Tristan on board, and they got some national coverage—

Well. Anything was possible.

So things weren't all bad.

She just needed to keep moving ahead. She'd done what needed to be done; said what needed to be said. Now she just had to put one foot in front of the other, and not dwell.

Fat chance, woman.

She sighed.

"You did the right thing," she told herself.

Of that, she had no doubt. But it sure hurt.

Which was just reassurance that she *had* done the right thing. Even if the look on Beau's face continued to burn through her. He'd understood perfectly what she'd said to him.

Her words had caused him pain, which she hadn't expected and hadn't intended.

But it was only the truth, and there was no escaping the truth. Wynn had learned that lesson long ago.

She just had to figure out how to pay him back for the damn roof, and they could conclude their business, and everything would be fine.

Just fine.

"How the hell did you do it?" demanded a gruff voice.

Wynn looked up to see Melvin Fields, President of the

Superior County Farming Association standing in front of her, a scowl on his rough face.

"Do what?" she asked politely.

"Turn that land green." An ancient straw hat covered his salt and pepper hair, and his canvas overalls were brand new. The blue and white cotton shirt he wore looked freshly pressed. He shook his head. "I've been farming my whole life, and I've never seen anything like it. That place was dead."

She stared at him, an ache suddenly pulsing in her chest.

He blinked. "Well?"

"I went back to basics," she told him simply. "I diversified my crops, added field cover, utilized compost, and did my best to use the natural systems to regain equilibrium."

Another blink. "What's that mean?"

"It means the Earth gives us everything we need. We just have to play by her rules, instead of trying to make her play by ours."

He squinted at her. "No pesticides?"

"Nope."

"No fertilizer?"

"Only from the compost."

"How much diversity?"

"Five kinds of fruit; five kinds of berries. Grapes and kiwi. A mixture of vegetables and spices. The field cover feeds the sheep, and with the compost, it helps build more soil. And I planted with an eye toward permaculture. That made a difference, too."

"What about the birds?"

"The hawks are helping. And the falcons. But I had to get the land healthy enough for them to come back. It took a long time."

"What about the bugs?"

"The chickens and ducks eat most of them."

"What about the coons and coyotes?"

"The donkeys help, and I have a sheepdog in training. And a rifle, if it comes to it. I try to live with them, not against them."

He studied her for a long, silent moment. "You think I could come by, and you could walk me through it?"

She blinked at him, flabbergasted.

Was the sky falling?

She looked up, just to make sure.

"If it's too much trouble—"

"No trouble at all," she said hurriedly. "Come by whenever you like."

Melvin nodded. He looked down at the flyers that decorated the table in front of her. "Bad business, this."

"Yes."

"You have my support," he said.

"Thank you," she told him sincerely.

He nodded once more, then turned and walked away. Wynn stared after him, stunned.

Did that really just happen?

The head of the Farming Association had asked for her *advice*.

Holy crap. Holy crap! *Holy crap.*

Fran, she thought. Somewhere Fran was grinning from ear to ear.

Tears massed abruptly in the back of her throat, and for a long moment, Wynn clung to her composure, very aware of the people milling around her.

Too much, she thought. Earl, the FBI. The Stick Man.

Beau.

And now this—

"How dare you!"

A furious Edward Duggar suddenly landed before her. He wore his customary pinstriped suit and shiny black loafers; a burgundy tie with tiny black polka dots matched the handkerchief that stuck from his front pocket. His graying hair stood on end as if he'd been running his hands through it, and his glasses were slightly crooked.

He was a good-looking man, for a banker. In his mid-fifties, fit and tall, with features inherited from his Italian father and Greek mother. But anything pleasant about Edward Duggar ended there.

Wynn didn't know him well, but she knew enough.

"Earl Barry is a thief!" he snarled. "How dare you act as though he's the victim in this. I'm the victim here—he took *my* money, and I'm going to make sure he never sees the light of day again!"

Around them, people stilled.

Wynn grabbed onto her temper and held tight.

Just stand down. He's a jackass.

"How compassionate of you," she told him shortly.

"This is a farce!" He flung out a hand. "Selling people this ridiculous lie! Taking their hard-earned money to defend a man who is a *criminal!* Do they know you're *involved* with the new Sheriff? That this atrocity was cooked up by the two of you to steal from people and make me look bad?"

Fury rippled through her. Her hands curled into fists; heat filled her cheeks. Words crowded the back of her throat and burned.

But she just stared at him, silent.

"You won't get away with it," he ranted. "I *run* this town. People do what *I* say. I'm going to have the FBI arrest you as an accessory, and I'm going to have Beau Greystone recalled and run out of this town like the crippled coward he is!"

A ripple went through the crowd around them.

Her heart was beating too hard. Every emotion she'd never given vent to—and there were many—churned within her, dredged from the still, silent place where she kept them. Every word she'd never said; every instance of grief and rage and helplessness; every paralyzing fear.

All of the tears she'd never shed.

A giant, swelling wave rising within her, ready to crash ashore.

But then she would drown.

So, no.

She had to be untouchable. Impregnable. It was imperative.

So, don't. Just don't.

But it was so tempting.

"You should go now," she told him.

Cold words filled with contempt, but they felt...surreal. Disconnected. Like she'd been in the wake of her mother's death. And she realized how easy it would be, to return to that place, that time, as if she'd never left that dark, hollow place; how simple it would be to let all of the pain wall her off from the rest of the world and its infernal endless suffering. Because the chaos inside of her was like a storm. Earl and Beau and Emma and poor Mr. Sanders—

"Tell me!" Duggar yelled and slapped his palms down on the table; spittle sprayed across the flyers. His eyes were wild. "Do they know you're his *whore*?"

The gasp from the crowd was audible, but all Wynn could hear was the roar of her own blood. She blinked, and something inside of her cracked.

Just a fissure; a thin, hairline break.

For a moment, she thought it would be okay.

But then—

"Like mother like daughter!"

She didn't remember moving. But suddenly she was on top of the table, her hand gripping in Duggar's fancy tie, her fist arcing toward his nose. Someone screamed; someone cheered. Someone said her name, but she didn't care.

She didn't fucking care.

She wasn't going to take it. Not his judgment or his condemnation; his ignorance or his hate. She wasn't going to let him hurt Earl; she wasn't going to let him—

A hard, strong, unyielding arm wrapped itself around her middle and caught her, right before her knuckles could plow into Duggar's face. It dragged her from the table and turned her away, and she fought furiously to wiggle free.

"Wynn." Beau's voice filled her ear; his breath was hot on her cheek. His body was like tensile steel at her back, too warm, too intense. Way too strong, subduing her. "He's not worth it."

She knew that. She didn't care.

"*Wynn.*" His other arm wrapped her and squeezed, and for a moment, she fought with all she had. But then he took a lurching, unsteady step back, and she remembered his leg, and all of her rage turned to pain.

It massed in her chest and filled her eyes. She wanted to scream into the heavens and weep into the earth; to let it all out.

Just once.

Beau's mouth touched her ear. "Calm down. Please."

A tear slid down her cheek, hot, angry. She forced herself to still.

"I'm pressing charges!" Edward Duggar spat. "She attacked me! You all saw it—"

"I didn't see a thing," retorted a new voice. Wynn turned her head to see Special Agent Garrett Morrison walking toward them. "If I were you, Ed, I'd be more worried about my own skin."

Duggar glared at him. "I want her in custody. She's an accessory! I know she was in on it. *I know it!*"

"Edward Duggar, you are under arrest for suspicion of drug and human trafficking, kidnapping, rape, and possession with intent to distribute." Garrett nodded at the agent who stood behind him, a tall, slender African American woman who was eyeballing Duggar like she was starving and he was lunch. "Mirandize him and take him in. I'll be right behind you."

"Under arrest?" Edward echoed. Some of the outrage bled from his features. "What are you talking about?"

Garrett leaned toward him, his expression so cold, he could have been carved from stone. "We found that little operation you've been running, Ed. Heroin, meth, young immigrant women. I'm going to annihilate you."

"I-you..." Edward looked around at the crowd, who watched the unfolding drama avidly. "It isn't true! I've been set up." He began to back away. "I want my lawyer! Do you hear me? I want my lawyer."

The female agent grabbed him, whipped him around, and when he struggled, kicked the back of his knee and put him on the ground. Then she cuffed him and dragged him to his feet. Her gaze met Wynn's, and she nodded.

"Nice," said Jenna, who suddenly stood beside Wynn. "Less Ken, more Thor. I like."

Garrett looked at Beau. "I'll see you at the station."

He turned and strode away. The female agent and a still-protesting Edward Duggar followed.

Wynn squirmed in Beau's hold. "Let me go."

For a moment, he didn't move, and she was painfully aware of the eyes on them. But then his arms fell away, and she was free.

"Beau Greystone, as I live and breath." Sasha appeared and stepped between them; Wynn could have kissed her. "The new Sheriff of Superior County! Congratulations."

He nodded. "Sasha."

"I stopped by your office to talk to you about our mutual friend Mr. Barry, but you were out," she continued smoothly. "Do you have a few minutes now?"

He looked annoyed. "No."

Wynn walked away. She moved past the crowd and turned into the narrow walkway between the booths. Her heart was beating too hard; her mouth was watering. Adrenaline and fury and grief was a churning mass in her chest, and she wished her fist had connected with Edward Duggar's nose.

Because that would have felt *fantastic*. Even if—

"Hey, Wynn." Eric Henry suddenly materialized in her path, his handsome features drawn. "I saw what happened. Are you okay?"

She halted. Fisted her hands to stop from pushing him out of the way.

So not the time, Eric.

"I'm fine." She moved to go around him.

He stepped in front of her. She halted again.

"Is it true?" he wanted to know.

"Is what true?" she growled.

He blinked. "Are you involved with the new Sheriff?"

Wynn stared at him. *Maybe she was going to get to punch someone, after all.*

"No," she told him, annoyed. He wore his DNR uniform, and for a brief moment, she wondered what was wrong with her. Here was a seemingly decent human being who appeared to give a crap about her.

So what was her problem? Why not Eric?

Why someone who belonged to another?

"Please get out of my way," she said, "or I might have to punch you."

Another blink. "He shouldn't have said that about your mom. It wasn't fair."

And just like that, the storm in her chest threatened to unleash. Tears blurred her vision; her throat filled.

"It's what everyone thinks," she said tightly.

"Not everyone," Eric said quietly. "Not me."

Sincerity glinted in his gaze, which just made the emotion churning within her worsen.

"Thanks," she muttered and wiped at her eyes.

He took a step toward her. "Is there anything I can do for Earl?"

"Sign the petition." She shrugged. "Donate."

Pray.

"I can do that."

"Great," she said and stared at him.

"You don't have to do everything alone, you know." He took another step closer. "People in this town know you aren't your mother. They've watched you grow up; they saw how you took care of Fran, they know what a great job you've done with Jenna. They'll help you, Wynn, if you just ask them."

She couldn't argue. Tonight she'd realized she'd judged the people of Blossom Hills far more harshly than they'd ever judged her. She'd equated the entire town with one rotten man: Jasper Hatfield. And in the last three hours, they'd proven every one of her beliefs about them wrong.

She'd been wrong. So wrong. About any number of things.

It was a painful lump to swallow, but if she couldn't own her mistakes, she'd just spend the rest of her life repeating them.

"I know," she admitted.

Eric lifted his hand, and she froze as he tucked an errant strand of hair behind her ear. "I can help, too, you know."

Why not him?

Because standing in front of him was like standing in front of a fence post.

Life was so not fair.

"Look," she began. "I'm not—"

And then her neck began to prickle, and a shiver moved down her spine, and she knew without a shadow of a doubt that Beau was behind her. A look over her shoulder found him moving toward them, his face as dark as the thunderheads gathering on the horizon.

The churning turmoil within her grew closer to the surface.

She didn't want another confrontation with him; she couldn't take it. She'd had enough pain and chaos and uncertainty for one day.

Go away. Just go away.

Before she could say the words, Eric planted himself between them.

"Sheriff," he said abruptly.

Beau stepped toward him. "Who are you?"

"Eric Henry." He nodded. "A friend of Wynn's."

Beau's glinting green gaze crashed into hers. She only blinked at him.

"We need to talk," he said.

"No," she replied.

"Wynn."

She shook her head. Eric folded his arms across his chest.

"See where it gets you," Beau warned softly, and a ripple of awareness skittered down her spine.

Even handicapped with a bad leg, he could break Eric in two. Any contest between the two men would end very badly.

For Eric.

"Just settle down," she told him.

He only stared at her, waiting.

Crap.

She looked at Eric. "I'll see you later."

Which might have been a lie, but Eric only shook his head stubbornly.

"I'll stay," he insisted.

"No, you won't." Beau took another step and towered over him. "Go. *Now*."

To Eric's credit, he held his ground, which both impressed and dismayed Wynn. But she saw the same awareness wash over him, the realization that he was courting a confrontation he was unlikely to win.

"Eric," she said softly. "Go."

Beau watched him like a big cat watched a small bird.

"You sure?" Eric's voice wavered. "I can stay."

Beau growled and stepped closer to him. Eric took a step back.

"I'm sure." Wynn walked over and nudged his arm. "Go."

"Good advice," Beau said. "You should take it."

Wynn shook her head. Nudged Eric again. "Please."

"Fine, I'll go." He backed away slowly. "I'll see you later."

Beau took a step, and Wynn cut him off.

"Later," she agreed, not particularly excited at the prospect.

But better that than Eric tar-tar all over the ground.

He nodded and walked away, but not without several lingering glances over his shoulder as he disappeared.

"Who the hell is he?" Beau demanded.

"My ninth-grade biology partner," she retorted. "What's your stinking problem?"

He stepped toward her, invading her personal space as if he belonged there. "Are you okay?"

"I'm right as rain," she lied.

"Sweetheart, I saw your face when you crossed that table. You're not right as anything."

Damn him. "Don't call me that."

"You wanted to beat Edward Duggar's ass into tomorrow," he continued as if she hadn't spoken. "And you would have if I hadn't stopped you."

"Yeah." She gave him a big, fake smile. "Thanks for that."

"Wynn," he said softly.

"What?" she wanted to know. "What do you want? What is it you think you have the right to demand?"

His face drew into harsh lines.

Why couldn't he just go away?

"You should hear yourself talk about her," she said. "It breaks my heart."

He jerked back as if she'd slapped him. "I can't forget. I won't."

"Of course not. But you still belong to her. So this—this —whatever it is—isn't going to happen!"

He leaned down over her, too close, too intense. Far too real. "What happened to Marie was my fault, and I will never forgive myself for it. But I'm fucking sick of sleepwalking through my life. You poked the bear and woke him up—you did that, not her. And if you think I'm going to let you use her as an excuse to run, you have another thing coming. She's *gone*. Dead and buried. But I'm still right here."

Wynn stared at him; her heart felt like it was going to burst. His heat kissed her skin; his scent filled her senses, and the power of his presence was palpable, pressing against her pores, a temptation, and torment in one.

"This scares the hell out of me," she whispered.

That burning green gaze softened. "I know."

"I didn't want any of this, either," she said, so he understood. "You're stubborn and surly and bossy. You carry a stinking *badge*. I don't want to like you. Or trust you. Or want you."

"But you do." His hands closed on her hips. "Don't you?"

Wynn only blinked at him; she'd already said too much.

But he scowled and jerked her toward him, and when she smacked into him, the collision was like a lightning bolt jolting through every nerve, white fire forking into every vein. He made a sound low in his throat; his fingers dug into her. The heat and tensile strength of him stole her breath.

His cock was like stone, digging into her belly, and that steady, hungry pulse he'd given life to in the barn burst into being between her thighs. She remembered the intense pleasure of his touch; what it felt like to grind herself against him in mindless need, and she wanted him inside of her.

And to Hades with anything else.

"I can see it," he rasped and ducked his head to nip at the line of her throat. "I can feel it."

She shuddered, her fingers curling into his ridiculous orange and green shirt.

"You're nothing like her, you know." Lips brushed her ear. "She was quiet, easy. Peaceful. Not like you. Always challenging me, chewing me up with that smart mouth." Sharp teeth sank into the sensitive place where her neck and shoulder met, and a spear of piercing desire stabbed through her. "I needed easy when I met her; I was too fucked up for hard. But not now. Now I need a kick in the ass. Now I need you."

The words were beguiling, even more dangerous than the hands that gripped her with such unarguable strength. "Please don't."

"Don't what?" he demanded roughly. "Don't speak the truth?" He pressed hard into her belly, his gaze direct, his hunger raw. "That's for you, sweetheart. Only for you."

A violent tremor moved through her. The pulse pounding at the juncture of her thighs deepened.

"I thought it was about penance," he said. "But penance isn't quitting; it's enduring. And you make me want to endure, Wynn."

She sucked in a sharp breath. "Beau—"

"Stop fucking arguing," he said and kissed her.

His mouth covered hers; his tongue stroked into her mouth. He kissed her deeply, a wet, hungry, openly sexual kiss that devoured her. One hand slid up her back and wound into her hair; then he tilted her head and plundered.

Need and yearning burned through her. Wynn wrapped her arms around his neck and kissed him back.

He made a ragged sound, and the kiss turned rough; his fingers twisted in her hair, the pulse between her legs grew stronger. She wanted—

"Sheriff!"

Wynn started violently; she tore herself away, but Beau's hand was wrapped in her hair, and there was no escape.

"Easy, sweetheart." He untangled himself and smoothed her hair with both hands, a tender motion that made an odd flutter whisper through her. "Goddamn it. We never catch a break."

"Sheriff!"

Beau ignored the summons. Instead, he stared down at her, his green eyes like brilliant jewels, his mouth a serious line that made her heart hurt.

"I want you," he told her quietly. "Only you."

And then he kissed her again, a sweet, gentle press of his mouth to hers, and the chaos inside of her throbbed.

"*Sheriff!*"

"Goddamn it," he snarled.

They turned to see Harry standing at the opening between the booths. He stood tensely, his hands fisted at his sides. Cheeks pale, eyes dark.

"We've got another one," he said.

CHAPTER 24

"I TOLD her not to go anywhere. *I told her.*"

Beau bit back the words damming in his throat. The woman before him didn't deserve them. Kids were kids. They were arrogant and thoughtless and invincible. The idea that a monster would come for them never entered their heads.

"I'm a single mom," Brenda Ripley continued haggardly. "I can't be here all the time; I have to work. She knew she wasn't supposed to go out. She wanted to go to the fair, but I said no. I told her I would take her when I got home. But she didn't listen." Her gaze lifted to Beau's, stricken with guilt and sheer, unadulterated terror. "And now..."

Now he has her.

There was no evidence the Stick Man had taken Maddie Ripley.

But he had. Beau was certain.

The girl had been to the fair; she and her friends had ridden the Ferris Wheel and played the ring toss. She'd left an hour later, at approximately seven-thirty. From the fairgrounds, she'd walked the railroad tracks as far as Elkhorn Drive—a utility worker had seen her crossing the street—and then cut through the dog park, where she'd stopped to pet a golden retriever owned by the local librarian. But after the park, she'd disappeared.

Gone.

"He's going to kill her," Brenda said dully. "He's going to cut my baby up, and it's my fault. I should have made her listen. I should have..." Sobs shook her shoulders, and Beau handed her another Kleenex.

It was the least he could do. He had little else to offer.

No leads. No fucking hope.

Going to rip his spine from his body and snap it in front of him.

But the fury surging through him was useless. A waste of energy. He needed to focus; he had all the clues he needed.

He was certain of that, too.

Somewhere in the pile of documents Lily Jenkins had given to him was the answer.

He just had to find it. *Before Maddie Ripley died.*

"Was Maddie ever out at Camp Blossom Hills?" he asked quietly.

Brenda looked up at him and blinked. "The camp? Why?"

"I'm just curious," Beau told her. "Was she ever out there?"

"Um...yeah, yeah, she was. She took a tour they offered to the middle school kids before school ended. She wanted to take some kind of art class, but I couldn't afford it. Why? Do you think—"

"I was just curious," he reiterated.

A shaky sigh escaped her. "There's no hope, is there?"

"There's always hope. Half of the county is out there looking for her." A fact that made him oddly proud, which was misplaced and stupid, considering how reluctant he'd been to be a part of the community to begin with. But the town of Blossom Hills had come together. For Earl. And now for Maddie.

It was more than he deserved, he thought.

"I want to help." Brenda stood, her hands fisted, and looked around blankly. "I just need my keys—"

"You need to stay here in case she comes home or calls," Beau told her. "I know it's hard to sit and wait, but that's exactly what I want you to do."

She closed her eyes. "I can't do nothing."

"Then don't. Call her friends. Call your friends. Reach out and spread the word. The more people looking for her, the better."

"I've already called all of her friends." Brenda shook her head. "And I...I don't have any friends. We've only been here since January."

She began to weep in earnest, and Beau put a gentle hand on her shoulder.

"We're going to find her," he said. *Alive*.

And hoped like hell it wasn't a lie.

The front door opened, and Velma walked in. The tiny, three-room abode was hardly bigger than Winston's trailer, but it was clean and homey, filled with handmade quilts and knick-knacks.

"I'll sit with her," his aunt said, and Beau suddenly saw her age, the vibrancy that normally camouflaged her years dimmed beneath the strain of anger and fear. "Until there's news."

"You don't have to do that," Brenda protested thickly.

"Oh, yes, I do," Velma said briskly. "I've brought my

computer so we can create a flyer. Then we're going to make sure everyone in the county gets a copy. After that, we're going to make some calls. But first, coffee." She produced a cup of steaming, fragrant coffee and handed it to Brenda, then looked at Beau. "You can go now, dear. You have work to do."

"Thank you," he said, his chest unexpectedly tight.

Family. Community. Both things he'd fled and rejected; both of which had stretched across space and time to embrace him. *To save him.*

Things of which he was now a part. And if those bindings had chafed at first, now he was growing accustomed to being connected.

Now he was starting to reach back.

"Anytime," Velma said simply. She sat down beside Brenda and put her arm around the younger woman. "It's going to be okay, Brenda. My nephew is going to catch that bastard and bring your baby back to you."

And then she looked up at him, her gaze steely.

No pressure there.

But Beau only nodded shortly and walked out. Harry was going over the grid with the canine units, and Garrett was talking to a group of FBI agents who'd driven up from Madison to join the hunt. Cam was on crowd control, sending well-wishers and gawkers on their way, and Jack Farley stood off to the side with his bloodhound Lucy. When he saw Beau, he walked over.

"Can I help?" he asked, his face lined with exhaustion.

"If you're up for it," Beau said.

"I can't sit this out," Jack replied quietly. "She won't let me."

She. *Emma.*

Beau knew the feeling.

"Harry can assign you an area," Beau told him.

Jack nodded and headed toward Harry. Winston materialized next to Beau a moment later.

"That fucker," he said through his teeth.

"One down, one to go," Beau told him. "You find anything in the records?"

"Nothing obvious—because it couldn't be that fucking easy. I put 'em back in your truck."

Beau ran a weary hand down his face. His head hurt; his leg was throbbing. And he was so angry, he could spit nails. All he could do was hope they found something—tire tracks, footprints. A goddamn gum wrapper. Anything to give him a lead.

"Daylight's burning," Winston said with a look at the dimming sky.

Rain scented the air, but had yet to fall, which Beau could only hope would continue.

"There are people all over town looking for her," Winston added.

Beau knew. He'd seen them. "I told them to stay out of the perimeter."

Because the last thing they needed was the public stomping all over any potential evidence.

"What the hell is he doing here?"

Harry suddenly stood a handful of feet away, staring at Winston.

Who just lifted his shirt and flashed his badge with a grin.

Harry looked at Beau. "Seriously?"

"All hands on deck," Beau replied brusquely. "He's worked the case before."

"He's a drunk!"

"Hey, now," Winston said. "That's hurtful."

"You can't do this," Harry insisted. "It's not fair."

"Life's not fair," Beau retorted shortly, in no mood. "He's in."

For a moment, his deputy only stared at him. "Cam and I aren't good enough?"

"This isn't a democracy," Beau told him. "And we need all the goddamn help we can get."

Harry blinked. He looked at Winston, then back at Beau.

"This is a mistake," he said.

"One that's mine to make," Beau snapped, annoyed. "I'm giving you this scene. Can you handle it?"

Harry stilled. "You're leaving?"

"I'm needed elsewhere."

"But...you want me in charge? Like, of the search?"

"While I'm gone, yes."

Some of the rancor left the younger man's expression. "Where are you going?"

"Out to the camp."

"Oh." He nodded thoughtfully. "That's a good idea. We don't know what else Duggar was doing out there."

No shit. But that wasn't the reason Beau was going to tear Camp Blossom Hills apart.

"Okay." Harry stood a little straighter. He avoided looking at Winston. "I'll take care of things here, then, sir."

"Good." Beau paused. "Thank you. Let me know if you find anything."

"Yes, sir." Harry nodded once more, then turned and walked away.

"Just one big happy family," Winston murmured, watching him.

Beau gave him a dark look and rubbed his aching leg. "Play nice."

He went over to the makeshift search station that had been put together and looked down at the GPS grid. The surrounding woods had been carved into neat, half-mile sections and assigned to both the searchers and the canine units, most of whom stood waiting, along with several locals and their hunting dogs. Jack Farley was among them. They all looked at Beau expectantly.

"Deputy Baker is in charge," he told them. "You have your assigned sections. Do your section and only your section. If you finish, come back and get another one. And if you find anything—and I do mean anything—you preserve it and take it to Deputy Baker, first. Got it?"

Heads bobbed.

"There's not much light left," he continued. "Do what you can, while you can. The rain is coming, and it's going to wipe out anything that's out there to find. So do your best. And thank you."

More nods.

"We're gonna get him this time, Sheriff," someone said.

"That bastard's ticket is up," added another.

"For Emma," Jack said.

Beau met his gaze. "For Emma."

They dispersed.

"Should I go with them?" Winston asked.

"No. You're with me." Beau caught Garrett's eye and nodded. "The Judge signed the search warrant for the camp an hour ago."

"You think we'll find anything?"

"I think it's damn sure worth looking."

Thunder rumbled and the wind lifted, and somewhere, a barn owl hooted. The temperature was dropping, and a chill was settling in, summer giving way to fall.

Garrett made his way over, trailed by the agents he'd assembled.

"Sheriff," he said. "What can we do?"

"Half of you can hit the fairgrounds," Beau replied. "I've got a lot of boots on the ground, but none of them are trained in canvassing like you are. We need to know if anyone saw Maddie Ripley, if she was alone or with someone, anything that might help."

Garrett nodded. "And the rest?"

"We're going to search the camp. The warrant was served on Duggar in his cell."

A grim smile turned the Agent's mouth. "To be a fly on the wall."

"It's on video," Beau told him. "You can watch it later."

Garrett only shook his head and turned to look at the collection of men and women gathered around him. "Ray, Bixby, and Allen, you're with me. The rest of you head to the fairgrounds and see what you can learn."

"Thank you," Beau added, aware many of them were on their own time. "We appreciate the help."

They split up; Garrett, Beau, Winston and the three agents headed toward Beau's truck, while the others dispersed to their waiting SUVs. Garrett turned and looked at him. "He's never taken another one so soon."

"I know," Beau said shortly.

"Is it him or us?"

Beau just shook his head.

"She doesn't have much time," he added.

You think I don't fucking know that?

Beau bit back the words. Tension lined his frame, and his heart was thudding, heavy, painful beats; in his mind's eye, the image of Emma Farley's abused body burned brightly.

Goddamn it.

"Did you send your girls home?" Garrett halted beside the truck. "Jenna fits his profile."

"I know."

Get Jenna and Sasha; go home and stay there, he'd told Wynn. And then he'd had to leave her because he had another missing girl and a faceless fucking murderer to hunt down.

Christ, he hoped she listened.

He thought he might have finally broken through that jagged wall of fear and anger and distrust that stood between them, but he couldn't be sure. The words she'd thrown at him still rang in his ears, powerful and haunting, no matter how he'd tried to defuse them.

Like hot coals, burning through him. He hadn't realized she would even think about Marie. Let alone...

You still belong to her.

She wasn't wrong. He wore his dead wife on his sleeve—quite fucking literally. Why would she think he was ready to move on?

"Goddamn it," he said and rubbed his face.

No time for that now.

He needed to focus.

Because if he didn't find Maddie Ripley and put the fucking Stick Man in the ground, nothing else would matter.

He had work to do.

"Let's go," he said.

CHAPTER 25

"Do you think they found her?"

Wynn looked up to see Jenna standing in the doorway, her face pale and drawn in the misty afternoon light. "I don't know."

But she didn't have much hope.

She'd gone to town this morning to drop off Esme at the fair—she was on booth duty until later when Wynn and Sasha would take over—and when she'd given into the ridiculous impulse to drive past the Sheriff's office, Beau's truck was nowhere to be found. According to Mrs. Fernando, who worked at the deli on Main Street, the search teams had looked for Maddie Ripley until just after midnight, right up until the rain had started, and then they'd regrouped and started again first thing that morning.

Which meant they were likely still looking.

The knowledge hurt. Wynn couldn't stop thinking about Emma. About Maddie Ripley, and Maddie's family; about Jack Farley and everyone who was out there looking.

Beau.

Jenna walked into the kitchen and hopped up onto the counter to watch Wynn knead bread dough. Truthfully, she was beating the crap out of it, which would probably ruin the bread, but it felt so good, Wynn didn't care.

She needed the outlet.

Her encounter with Beau had left her in a chaotic quandary, heavy with a choice she wasn't sure she was ready to make.

"What if he gets away with it?" Jenna asked quietly, staring down at the floor. "Again."

A question Wynn had been asking herself since the day the Stick Man had returned, and one for which she had no good answer. He'd come and gone twice before; there was nothing to say this time would be any different—Beau or no Beau. And as sickening and infuriating as that was—well, that was life.

Sometimes the bad guys won.

"I don't know," Wynn said again.

"I want him dead."

A common sentiment.

"Do you think Beau will get him?" Jenna persisted. "The Stick Man...he seems invincible."

"No one is invincible," Wynn told her quietly. "And Beau has been to war. I doubt very much the Stick Man is the first monster he's hunted."

"You're mad at him, aren't you?"

Wynn glanced at her. "Who? Beau?"

"He likes you, you know. *Really* likes you."

Wynn tried to shrug, aware that her cheeks were on fire. She smacked the dough against the counter and scowled.

"What's your problem?" Jenna demanded. "He's a good catch."

Wynn blinked at her sister. "And you think I should keep him?"

"Heck, yeah. You could do a lot worse."

Bemused by that, Wynn said nothing.

"I mean it," Jenna insisted. "I'm not..."

She trailed off and looked out the window.

Wynn frowned. "You're not what?"

Jenna looked at her. "I'm not going to be here forever."

Wynn stopped kneading. "What does that mean?"

"This place...it's home. The only home I've ever known. But it isn't...it isn't my future."

Wynn could only stare at her, her heart suddenly beating with painful intensity. "What are you saying?"

"I work hard in school, and I do that for one reason: it's my ticket out."

Grief welled with sudden, breath-stealing intensity inside of her. "You want to leave?"

"I want to *live*." Jenna's hands fisted; her pale grey eyes glittered. "I want to see the world. Eat its food, meet its people, dance to its music. I'm not you."

Wynn wiped her hands on a towel, her stomach churning. "I'm sorry if I haven't been the role model you needed."

"Don't," Jenna told her. She reached out and gripped Wynn's arm when she would have turned away. "You're the best sister in the whole fucking world. Do you think I don't know that? You always put me first—always. This place, it wasn't your choice, but you did it for me. For us. *She was never there*. Not even when she was. But you always were. I'm smart and strong, and I know I can do anything, and that's because of you. *I love you, Wynn*. But I want more than what this place can give me. When I graduate, I'm gone. And I need you to be okay with that. I want you better than okay. I want you to be happy."

Tears filled Wynn's throat and burned her eyes. For a long moment, she couldn't speak. She wasn't surprised; she'd always known Jenna would spread her wings and fly. She was everything Wynn wasn't: gregarious and fearless and open. *So open*. While Wynn had spent most of her life sealed tightly shut. Sequestered and insulated; protected from hurt.

Even though the hurt had still found her.

Her self-imposed isolation had been an illusion; a fruitless attempt to control the chaos that was life. And there was no controlling the chaos.

There was only surviving it.

"It's okay," she said dully. "I knew you would go."

"That's not the point." Jenna's grip on her arm tightened. "I want you to be happy, Wynn. And I think Beau could make you happy."

Beau. Wynn's heart squeezed.

I want you. Only you.

Words she yearned to believe. But there were no guarantees, just a leap of faith.

One she wasn't certain was in her to make.

"This isn't about Beau," Wynn told her sister quietly. "Beau or no Beau, I will be happy. No, I didn't choose this place: it chose me. But I've poured myself into it, and watching it come back to life has given me purpose. It's as alive as you and I, and that...connection, it gives me something I can't articulate. It's beyond happiness. So don't you worry about me. Okay?"

Jenna stared at her, her gaze pensive. "Are you sure?"

"Yes." *No*. The last thing Wynn wanted was to watch her sister leave. But it wasn't about what she wanted. And she would never, ever hold Jenna back. "As long as you come home once in a while."

"You know I will." Jenna leaned over and hugged Wynn suddenly, tightly. "I love you, Wynnie. Thank you for everything you did for me."

More tears clogged Wynn's throat. They trickled down her cheeks and slid into her hair. "I love you, too, Jen. I'm so proud of you."

"Everything's going to be okay," Jenna whispered. "Earl, the Stick Man...you and Beau. I know it."

Well, at least someone did.

Wynn nodded. "Okay."

Jenna squeezed her hard and then released her. "I'm thinking about Oxford."

Wynn stared at her blankly. "As in the UK?"

"Yep. I've got my eye on an overseas scholarship they offer. But the competition is fierce."

England. Not just out of Blossom Hills, but out of the country.

To a different continent entirely.

The grief in Wynn turned heavy. Not just away, but far, far away.

"Wynn," Jenna said.

"I'm fine," Wynn said and wiped her eyes. "It's fine."

But it wasn't. It really wasn't.

"I have to," Jenna said somberly.

And Wynn met her gaze and saw that it was true. So she nodded and stuffed her fear and pain away. "And I support you."

"Am I interrupting?"

They both started. Sean stood in the doorway.

"I'm off to check my frogs," he said. "Want to keep me company?"

"Bread," Wynn said and slapped the dough against the counter.

"I'll come," Jenna said and hopped down.

But Wynn gripped her hand and stopped her. "I think you should stay here."

She felt Sean's gaze, and her cheeks burned. It wasn't that she really thought he might be a serial killer, but it felt wrong to take any chances.

Any at all.

"C'mon, Wynn," Jenna protested. "I'm going crazy all locked up."

"She'll be safe," Sean added, a quiet, intense promise that made Wynn look at him.

He knew what she was thinking.

Her cheeks burned brighter. But she couldn't be sorry. He was a great tenant, and she liked him very much, but they didn't *know* him. And with the Stick Man out there—

"I'll come, too," said another voice, and she looked up to see Griff's tall form behind Sean. He met her gaze and nodded. "I need to look for some St. John's Wort. The Interweb says it can help with my Parkinson's."

"The interweb." Jenna snickered. "You're hilarious."

"Okay," Wynn said, holding Griff's gaze. "You can go. As long as you stay with Griff."

He nodded again. Sean's gaze hardened, but he said nothing.

Jenna hooted. "Thank freaking God! Freedom!" She turned and hugged Wynn again, briefly. "Thanks, Wynn."

"Be careful." Wynn hugged her back. "And be sure to take your present from Buck with you."

Jenna smiled wryly. "Just in case those frogs are out for blood."

After they'd gone, Wynn went back to kneading her bread. The sun was trying to break through the endless line of clouds on the horizon, and the house was quiet. Eloise and Ethel were at church; Esme was still at the fair, and Earl was in jail. It was just her and Beowulf and sweet little Winter, who was curled up on one of the kitchen chairs, watching her sleepily. He and Beowulf had become fast friends, much to Wynn's amusement—and relief.

"You are pure love," she told them, her throat still thick, her chest still aching at the thought of Jenna leaving. "And I need lots of that right now."

Winter mewed at her. Beowulf sat at her feet, watching hopefully for crumbs.

"She's going to go," Wynn continued. "And I have to let her. But I sure am going to miss her." She swallowed against the tears that threatened. "It'll be hard without her."

But that didn't mean she needed anyone to take Jenna's place. Certainly not Beau—especially when she wasn't sure of him. Or herself.

Or anything.

She's gone. Dead and buried. But I'm still here.

It wasn't that Wynn expected him to forget, but he was...dark. *Grim.* And part of that undoubtedly came from his chronic pain, but the rest, that came from....

What happened to Marie was my fault, and I will never forgive myself for it.

And never was a long time.

Could she live with that? A shadow so long and dark they might never know light?

Because Wynn needed light.

She'd lived through years of darkness. Part of it had just been life: sickness and violence and death. Grief and uncertainty; pain. But the rest of it...that had been her.

All her.

Something she'd come to realize in the last few days. She was where she'd put herself—a choice she'd made, to wall herself off from everyone but those who needed her most. And while she might not have understood that at the time, she did now. The choice that left was clear:

Stay where she was, or move on.

Staying was tempting. She knew how to exist in that place; it was familiar, comforting. Without risk. Whereas, stepping out into the world and engaging, taking a chance on the chaos that was life...well, that was like flipping the bird at fate.

But she either stagnated or she grew. The farm had taught her what brought life.

And what led to death.

You poked the bear and woke him up—you did that, not her. And if you think I'm going to let you use her as an excuse to run, you have another thing coming.

She needed to decide. Because Beau wasn't going down without a fight.

Hard-headed, obstinate. *Bossy.*

But something had sparked to life inside of her with those words, something...hopeful.

Because she'd understood perfectly what he meant about sleepwalking through his life; about being woken from that state and never wanting to return.

He'd done that for her, too.

And now...now, she had to choose: wake up or stay asleep.

"What do you think?" She glanced down at Beowulf. "Should we leap?"

He grinned at her. *Thump, thump, thump.*

"Mew," added Winter.

And despite the uncertainty she felt, Wynn had to smile.

At least until a heavy knock on the front door sounded, one she didn't want to answer.

But no one else was home, and they were unlikely to just go away, so she sighed, set aside her dough, and went to see who it was.

CHAPTER 26

HE NEVER LEAVES ANYTHING.

"Not a goddamn trace," Beau growled.

He sat in his truck on Bald Bluff, which overlooked the town. He'd pulled over to talk to Cam about the ground search, which had restarted at the break of dawn. Like the night before, they'd found nothing, least of all Maddie Ripley. And even though procedure dictated they widen their grid and keep going, it felt like they were grasping at straws, and Beau couldn't shake the feeling he wasn't going to get there in time.

That they were being toyed with.

Fucking laughed at.

They'd found nothing to connect the Stick Man to Camp Blossom Hills, but they had found evidence of the trafficking ring Edward Duggar had been running, including half a dozen old shipping containers filled with weapons, drug paraphernalia, and a surprisingly state-of-the-art meth lab. Garrett and his team had gone back out that morning to widen the search and catalog what they'd found.

Garrett hadn't been kidding: he was going to annihilate Edward Duggar.

Beau envied him. At least his target had a name.

Frustration seethed within him; he hadn't slept, he'd hardly eaten, and his leg hurt like hell. He'd walked more miles in the last two days than he had in all the time since the explosion, and he was paying for it. But worse was the helplessness; forced to sit on his hands and wait while the evil played out.

It was a familiar feeling, and one he despised.

Been there, done that.

And he knew that was part of the fury simmering within him—to find himself in this position again, where all he could do was watch. If the Stick Man had wanted a perfect way to make Beau lose his shit, well, he'd hit his target.

The only pleasant part of his day had been driving out to Wynn's and delivering the present he'd bought her. She hadn't been home—which was probably just as well because he didn't have time to linger, but still, he was disappointed—but Ethel had promised she would deliver it.

Because, she said, she forgave him.

Which had, oddly, relieved him. When it shouldn't have even mattered. He didn't know her. Just because she'd taken personally his rescue of Clementine the Cat didn't make them...friends. But her abject terror and hysteria during Earl's arrest had infuriated him. He hadn't been happy about any of it—least of all the look of betrayal Wynn had watched him with—but Wynn was tough. She could handle Garrett. But Ethel...

Ethel was little more than a child, and for some mysterious reason, she trusted *him*. Beau hadn't thought that breaking that trust could affect him.

He'd been wrong.

About so many things.

And now here he sat, staring down at a town he hadn't wanted to return to—one for which he was now largely responsible—and contemplating a life he'd vowed never to live. One built on hope, which would have been laughable if he hadn't started wanting it so damn much.

Which is why it will probably all go to shit.

"Way to be positive," he muttered.

Christ, he needed to get back to work. Head down and check-in with Harry, who was leading several of the search teams, and Winston, who was manning the phones at the station until Beau returned.

Which may or may not have been a good idea.

But before he could start his truck, his cell phone rang.

Yet again.

"Mahoney texted me an hour ago," Garrett said without preamble. "It just came through. The ID on your pen is Ian Long—Bridget Long's twin brother."

Everything within Beau screeched to a halt. "Bridget Long, the first victim?"

"One and the same. Where the fuck did you get it?"

Beau's heart slapped his ribs. "Wynn's tenant, Sean Evers."

"Sean Evers is Ian Long."

Motherfucker.

Beau started his truck and threw it into gear. "Thanks."

"Goddamn it, *wait*—"

"He's there with her." The truck tore out onto the highway. "With all of them. Son of a bitch!"

"We don't know it's him," Garrett said sharply. "And if it is, the last thing we need is to tip him off."

Beau knew that. But his heart was suddenly threatening to explode, and all he could hear was the dizzying rush of his own blood. Adrenaline fountained through him.

Sean Evers was Bridget Long's twin. He was there when it happened.

And now he was here.

Claiming to be someone altogether different, living in Wynn's house, sleeping under her roof, eating her food—

"Don't fuck this up," Garrett told him. "We have to be smart—"

"I know how to do my goddamn job," Beau snarled.

"We're in the middle of this search; I'm at least half a mile from my car. There's no service out here, so I'm on the sat phone. I'll get to my vehicle and meet you at Wynn's. Don't do anything until I get there. Agreed?"

Beau hung up. His foot slammed the gas pedal to the floor. The truck lurched around a tight curve, tires squealing; he should have engaged his lights and siren, but didn't.

Couldn't. Not unless he wanted to give himself away.

Sean Evers was Ian Long.

Jesus Christ. No wonder the guy felt wrong; he was completely full of shit. His whole life had been lived inside of a false identity, one wholly unconnected to the death of his twin at the hands of the Stick Man.

Why?

A question Beau would ask. Among many, many others.

Provided he got the chance.

Fuck, fuck, fuck!

Panic was bleeding through him. Dread. *And sheer fucking terror.*

But Wynn was *smart*. And tough. And strong. She wouldn't be an easy target. She wouldn't—

His phone was ringing again. He wanted to ignore it, but couldn't. He punched the button on the steering wheel.

"Speak," he ordered and careened around another curve.

Goddamn narrow-ass back roads!

"This is Special Agent Grant Mahoney," intoned a flat voice. "Is this Sheriff Beau Greystone?"

Fucking perfect. "Yes."

"I am trying to reach Special Agent Garrett Morrison. Is Agent Morrison with you?"

"No," Beau said shortly. "He's at the camp."

"Camp Blossom Hills?"

"Yes."

"He is not answering his cell phone."

"There's no service out there," Beau told him curtly. "Try the sat phone. I have to go."

"Would you like the results of the testing conducted on the soil sample taken from beneath Emma Farley's index fingernail?"

Jesus Christ. Because this was the ideal time and place.

"I believe it is significant," Mahoney added, although his monotone disagreed.

"Fine. Go for it."

"As we discussed, the sample contained abnormally high concentrations of kaolinite, which contains one to one silicon—"

"I remember," Beau ground out. "What of it?"

"—to aluminum oxides and is not common to the area, the primary use of which is agricultural."

Beau growled softly. "Mahoney."

"I had the sample tested twice to ensure the results were both accurate and—"

"For fuck's sake man," Beau snapped. "Just tell me."

A moment of silence. Rain began to patter the windshield. Beau slid through a stop sign and around a corner.

"It is pottery clay," Mahoney said.

"Come again?"

"Pottery clay. The kind used to make cups, bowls, vases, urns and—"

"Figurines," Beau interrupted, his gaze locked on the tiny ceramic pig that sat on the dash.

From my mom, Harry had said. *For luck.*

"Yes," Mahoney said. "Will you let Special Agent Morrison know my findings?"

"Yes," Beau told him and hung up.

Then he stared at the figurine again. And he thought...*No.*

No. A lot of people made pottery. It had to be a coincidence.

Just coincidence.

But something within him had gone very, very quiet. And the dread spilling through him turned into a flood of fury.

He slammed on his brakes; the truck skidded to a stop beside the deep, narrow ditch that lined the road. He grabbed the pile of Blossom Hills Camp records from the passenger seat and tore through them.

His hands were shaking; he felt sick. All of the fear and panic and anger coalesced, chilling his blood, making his head pulse and his mouth water. And he didn't know what the fuck he was looking for—

There.

List of instructors for extracurricular paid community courses: Tony Holmes—Macramé. Kelly Little—Photography

101 and 102. George Hunt—Basket Weaving. Sandy Frome—Rug Making. Bethany Baker—

Pottery.

No, he thought again. But inside of him, the stillness had crystallized into cold, heavy stone.

He hit the call number for Harry's cell and waited. But it just rang. And rang.

And rang.

He dialed Cam; by the time Cam answered, adrenaline was pumping through Beau like a drug.

"Harry," he ground out.

"He's not here, Sheriff," Cam said in his easy way. "Can I help?"

"Where?" Beau demanded.

"He said he was going to get coffee. Probably got sidetracked—he's got a thing for that little blond waitress down at *Sally's*. He likes blondes."

Cam laughed, but Beau's blood turned to ice.

But still, he thought *no*.

Because...no. No. Not right there.

Right fucking beside him.

"Have him call me," Beau said and hung up.

For an odd, free-fall moment, he simply stared blankly out the windshield.

Was he jumping to conclusions? Had this bastard made him so crazy, he was seeing things that weren't there?

Had he finally snapped?

"Fuck," he said and called Velma.

She answered immediately. "Hello, dear, how is the search going?"

"Harry," he said, his throat thick, the word rough. "Tell me everything you know."

"Harry?"

"Everything."

"You don't think—"

"*Velma.*"

"Well, alright, dear, but you must...you must be mistaken." Her voice faltered. "I've known him his whole life."

"Tell me."

"Tell you what? He's a nice boy; he always has been. His mother Bethany is a local potter. She works down at the fabric store and volunteers at the animal shelter; she's in church every single Sunday."

"And his father?"

"Really, dear, is this necessary?"

"*Velma.*"

A weighty sigh. "Ferris Baker was a semi-famous lithograph artist; he was also a drunk and a brute. He died before Harry was born." She paused. "Why does any of this matter? What's going on?"

"Tell me what no one talks about."

"Conjecture and rumor aren't—"

"Tell me."

"But—"

"*Velma.*"

"Fine—but it's all hearsay." Another sigh. "Before Harry was born, Bethany would come to church black and blue with bruises; we all knew it was Ferris, but she wouldn't leave him. And then Jasper Hatfield returned from the war in Iraq, ran for Sheriff, and won. He and Bethany had been quite an item back in high school. He pursued her, but Bethany stood by Ferris, at least publically. And then one night, there was a call to the police. Ferris had beaten Bethany so badly, she was hospitalized. Two nights later, Ferris' studio burned to the ground with him inside."

"Hatfield," Beau said.

"No one could prove it. And then..."

"And then?"

"And then ten months later, Harry was born."

A moment of silence punctuated that statement.

"Baker wasn't his father," Beau realized.

"No." Velma paused. "Harry is Jasper Hatfield's son."

CHAPTER 27

"Deputy Baker." Wynn leaned against the doorframe. "To what do I owe this earthshattering pleasure?"

Harry stood on her front porch, clad in his fancy Sheriff Deputy duds, his hair wet from the misting rain. He didn't react to her sarcasm. Instead, he looked past her, into the house. "Can I come in?"

Wynn didn't move. "Why?"

"The Sheriff asked me to come by."

A ripple of unease traced her spine. "Is Beau okay?"

"Inside," he said and stared at her.

Apprehension washed over her. She stepped back reluctantly and let him in. "What's going on?"

"You alone?" he asked, moving into the hall.

She said nothing, watching him.

He halted, turned, and looked at her. "Jenna isn't here?"

"No." Her gaze narrowed. "Why?"

"Damn." He reached into the pocket of his coat and pulled out a pair of black leather gloves. "That's disappointing."

The unease spread, heavy and cold, making her skin

prickle. Wynn went still; she watched as he slid on the gloves. "Why's that?"

His dark brown gaze met hers. "She excites me."

Oh, fuck.

Realization slapped her like a brutal hand.

But then she thought—*no*.

No.

That was crazy. *Crazy.* Harry was...Harry. An unwavering fixture of Blossom Hills; the quintessential hometown son. Star quarterback, Prom King, class valedictorian.

He couldn't possibly be—

"She's the one I've been dreaming about," he continued conversationally. "But you keep a tight rein. If she's anything like your ma, I suppose you have to."

Wynn stared at him, stunned into silence. Beowulf chose that moment to exit the kitchen and hurl himself toward them, barking noisily. She scooped him up, opened the door to the coat closet, and put him inside.

She didn't even think about it; she just did it.

"Smart girl." Harry flexed his hands; the leather groaned. "Although I stopped killing dogs when I was twelve. They bleed out way too fast."

Wynn could only blink at him.

Harry Baker.

Stick Man.

"You son of a bitch," she snarled.

Fury surged through her.

She had a knife in the side pocket of her cargos and an entire lifetime of pain and rage welling in her chest. She thought about Emma and Jenna and all of the girls the Stick Man had murdered, and her blood turned molten.

"Careful," he tsked softly. "That's no way to talk to the man who's going to decide your fate."

Violence awoke within her, hungry from its long sleep.

"This can be hard," he continued. "Or it can be easy. That part's up to you."

She knew how to fight. Not properly—with fancy, practiced punches and deft footwork—but dirty, no holds barred brawling, where nothing was off-limits.

Nothing.

He would never know what hit him—

"What's it going to be, Wynn? Nice and easy, or painful and hard?"

She clenched her hands into fists. Her heart beat with heavy, dull thuds; adrenaline speared through her, so sharp and potent, she felt like she could fly.

He wasn't a big man, but he was a man—taller, stronger, heavier. If she—

"Oh, I recognize that look," he said softly. "We're gonna tussle, aren't we?"

A snarl worked in her throat.

"Alright," he said and shook his head, "but Maddie's gonna get upset if you're all bloody and unconscious when I drag you in. That girl's got a delicate constitution."

Wynn forced herself to breathe, in, out. In, out.

"Maddie is alive?" she asked calmly.

Harry smiled. "For now."

It would be so easy to launch herself at him. *So easy*. But—

Maddie was still alive.

Of course, Harry Baker was a serial killer; lying could hardly be put past him.

But it might be true. What he did to those girls took hours, if not days. He hadn't had Maddie long enough —had he?

She didn't know. But it didn't matter. There was no choice.

She had to go with him.

Because if Maddie was alive... Well, that's all there was to it.

So she had to put it away. All of it: the rage, the fear; the need to make him bleed.

Away. *Until it was time.*

Because the time would come.

Meanwhile...

"Fine," she said. "Let's go."

Now. Before Sean and Griff and Jenna returned.

Now, before she lost her nerve—or killed him.

Harry's brows rose. "Just like that?"

"Lead the way," she told him coldly.

He stepped back and motioned for her to precede him. "You first."

Wynn took a deep, uneven breath. Beowulf continued to bark from within the closet; outside, the rain began to fall in earnest. She looked around, but there was nothing she could do, no sign she could leave. No weapon but her knife and her wits.

She wished they could have a knock-down-drag-out. Break furniture and put holes in the wall.

Put holes in him.

But that wouldn't do. If Maddie Ripley was still alive, Wynn needed to get to her.

To save her.

Save them both.

So she squared her shoulders and walked out the door.

*****

Wynn's van was parked in the driveway.

Beau slid to a stop beside it and jumped out of his truck. He'd beaten both Garrett and Winston—who he'd called and asked to meet him—and he was still waiting to hear back from Harry, who had yet to return his call.

The fucker.

He could only hope it was because Harry was tied up doing his job—and not out carving Maddie Ripley into his next masterpiece.

Or disappearing into thin air.

"Calm the fuck down," he told himself.

Because there was nothing to say Harry knew the game was up. But the dread eating through Beau told a different story, one he recognized.

One of too little, too late, with disastrous consequences.

He should have gone straight to where his deputy sheriff was supposed to be—helping lead another fruitless search for Maddie Ripley—but he'd come here, first.

Instead.

He told himself it was for Ian Long—because Bridget Long's twin was a dark horse in this race, one Beau didn't trust—and because they'd all assumed the Stick Man was a lone wolf.

But what if he wasn't?

The internet had made it possible for all of the monsters to congregate; to get together and act like their twisted fuckery was *normal*.

What if Ian and Harry were accomplices?

What if it was Stick *Men*?

"Fuck," Beau snarled.

Because Ian Long was only part of the reason he was here. The other was far more visceral—stark and terrifying.

Wynn.

Even if there was no reason for Harry to take her. She wasn't his type. *She probably wasn't even on his radar.*

But something inside Beau was screaming.

He climbed up the steps, his leg pulsing with pain, and limped into the house—which he found cold and silent and empty. No warmth, no murmur of the TV, no baking bread or cooling pie.

No Ian Long. And no Wynn.

The dread turned into cold, heavy fear; it slid through his bones like ice water.

He dragged himself out to the barn—no Wynn. No Griff or Esme, either. No Eloise; no Ethel. No Ian Long, and no Jenna. Beau slogged on, making his way through the small orchard, past the planting beds, along the fence line of the pasture.

No one.

He stomped back to the house, which was still cold and gray and empty. He was soaking wet, his stomach was in knots, and terror was a knife lodged deep in his heart.

Where the fuck was she?

Where was anyone?

He slammed his hand against the kitchen wall, and howls erupted, followed by hysterical barking.

Beowulf.

His heart leaped; he followed the sound to a narrow door in the hallway, wrenched the door open, and the pup shot out and spun in circles, angry growls tearing from him.

"Hey, bud." Beau leaned down and rubbed the dog's head. "Where's Wynn?"

And why are you locked in a closet?

"Fuck," he said again, his heart sinking.

Because there was only one reason anyone would lock him away: to keep him safe.

Which meant...what?

An SUV pulled up and parked beside his truck, followed by a rusting, ancient yellow Ford Escort. Garrett and Winston. Beau stepped onto the front porch to greet them. Beowulf leaned heavily against his good leg, growls rumbling from him.

"What's going on?" Winston demanded as he climbed the steps. "You sounded like your pants were on fire."

"Is Long here?" Garrett asked from behind him.

"No." Beau shook his head. "But it might not be him. Or not just him."

"Not just him?" Garrett's gaze narrowed. "Who else are we talking about?"

"Harry Baker," Beau growled.

"What?" Garrett asked sharply.

Winston's eyes widened. "Holy shit."

Beau told them about the clay, about Bethany Baker, and about Harry being Jasper Hatfield's son.

"It's circumstantial," Garrett said. "It fits, but we need evidence."

"I know," Beau bit out.

"No wonder Hatfield covered it up," Winston said. "If I'd known Harry was his kid, I might have put it together."

The front door opened, and Jenna suddenly walked out onto the porch.

"What's going on?" She looked at Beau. "Where's Wynn?"

"You don't know?" The fear inside of him swelled. "Beowulf was locked in the hall closet when I got here."

Jenna's eyes narrowed. She turned and disappeared

back into the house. Griff materialized and stepped out onto the porch.

"Looks like the cavalry's arrived," he observed. "There a reason we need a cavalry?"

Beau hoped like hell not.

"Something's wrong." Jenna shot back through the door at a run. "There's no fire going, no food cooking, and the back door was unlocked. She never leaves it unlocked. Never."

Her pale grey gaze slammed into Beau's.

"Something's happened," she said.

He has her. Beau knew it such sudden, piercing certainty, he felt sick.

"We don't know that," Garrett replied shortly. "There's no evidence of that."

"The lack of evidence is the evidence, Ken," she retorted. "No fire, no food. Wynn would never leave the house cold, without dinner on the stove. Never. *Something is wrong.*"

"Wrong?" echoed another voice, and they looked up to see Sean Evers—also known as Ian Long—standing behind the screen door. "What's wrong?"

He has her.

Beau pulled open the door and dragged him out onto the porch.

"Hey," Jenna protested, but Garrett cut her off.

"What the hell is your problem?" Sean demanded. "Get your hands off me."

Beau slammed him against the wall of the house. "I know who the fuck you are. Where is she?"

Evers struggled in his hold. "Where is who?"

"Wynn."

"Wynn?" Jenna echoed. "Why would he know where

Wynn is? He's been with me and Griff all day. And what do you mean you know who he is?"

Beau looked at her sharply. "You're sure?"

"Yeah, since like one o'clock. Wynn was here when we left."

Beau's hands tightened; he wanted to smash Evers' face into pulp.

He fucking has her.

"Wynn's in trouble?" Sean abruptly stopped fighting. "You don't think..."

"We do think," Garrett put in. "Your sister was his first victim; you just happened to be here when he reappeared; and you're living under a bullshit alias."

"That bullshit alias was so I could have some kind of fucking normal life!" He looked at Beau. "You think he has Wynn, don't you?"

Beau only blinked at him, his heart beating so hard, his head was pulsing.

He needed to go. *Harry fucking had her*.

"Wynn?" Jenna repeated, her voice rising. "The Stick Man has Wynn?"

"You know who he is, don't you?" Sean gripped Beau's shirt. "You have to tell me."

Beau slammed him into the wall again, hard. *He needed to fucking go.* "I think you already know."

"If I knew, he'd be dead," Sean snarled. "I come back every summer, waiting for him. I spend every waking minute scouring this godforsaken valley, searching for any kind of fucking clue I can find. I've dedicated my life to hunting him. How long have you spent? A few days? I've spent *every minute since she died*."

Beau stared at him, his blood pumping furiously, his heart a panicked drum beat. Then he let Sean go.

"It's Harry Baker," he said. "My Deputy Sheriff."

"No fucking way," Jenna exclaimed.

"Language," he growled.

"It doesn't make sense that he would he take her," Garrett said flatly. "She doesn't fit his profile, and she's no threat to him."

"But I am." Beau started toward the steps. "Harry wants to fuck with me. To hurt me. I have to find her."

"Her and Maddie," Jenna said.

Beau glanced at her.

"We need to find both of them!" Angry tears shimmered in her pale gaze. "I'm coming with you."

"No." Griff stepped forward and put his hand on her shoulder. "You're going to say here and let these men do their jobs."

The look on her face was stricken. "But—"

"We'll find them," Beau told her. "I promise."

A hollow laugh broke from Sean. "Good luck with that. He's a fucking ghost."

"No," Winston said. "The Stick Man is a ghost. Harry Baker is alive and well."

A jolt went through Beau; he halted. Winston was right. They were after a man now, not an apparition shielded by anonymity.

"Maybe Hatfield left him property," Garrett said. "A house or—"

"A fishing hole." Winston slapped his forehead. "Goddamn, it can't be that easy."

"Explain," Beau ordered impatiently.

"Hatfield's got an old ice shanty. I saw it out on the ice last winter, but I didn't think anything of it, because I figured somebody was just making use of it."

"An ice shanty," Garrett repeated skeptically.

"It's perfect," Winston insisted. "Small, mobile, light. He could put it damn near anywhere and no one would question it." He paused. "In the summer, Hatfield would park it on a piece of property just north of White Pine Lake, some strip of land he inherited from his old man."

Beau stood frozen, his heart beating too hard, adrenaline a sickening rush inside of him. "Can you take us there?"

"Hell yes. Let's go get that fucker."

CHAPTER 28

She could smell the lake. Fishy, damp; the earthy musk of the woods.

By Wynn's estimation, they'd driven for almost twenty minutes, so she figured they were at either White Pine Lake or the River Falls Reservoir.

Not that it mattered. She was on her own.

Harry had tied her hands together with coarse rope and shoved a hood over her head; the drive had been made with her sprawled in the back seat of his truck. He hadn't bothered to check her for weapons—stupid and arrogant jackass that he was—and she was brutally aware of the knife in her pocket, but being unable to see, she hadn't wanted to chance trying to retrieve it.

She was going to have to be patient. *Not one of her strengths.*

But Maddie came first. She had to get to Maddie.

Then she would figure out how to get them both free.

Going to gut him like a fish.

Fortunately, Harry had tied her hands in front, so retrieving the knife—when she got the opportunity—might be possible. But deep down she knew she had to be prepared to take him on with or without a weapon.

Prepared to fight for her life, no matter what it took.

The sense of déjà vu washing over her wasn't welcome, but ironically, it helped keep her calm. Finding herself face to face with the same kind of terror she'd experienced as a child was unexpected, but not unfamiliar. And she found herself reacting now the same as she had then—with a plan.

Because some things really did never go away.

Like riding a stinking bike.

And for the first time, she was grateful for fucked up places her mother had dragged her; the crazy, dangerous assholes she'd had to fend off; the fear she'd been forced to turn into action.

Because—who knew? It just might save her.

The faint cry of birds serenaded them as they walked across what felt like an old cornfield—stubby stalks, long grass twisting around her ankles, round stones beneath her feet. The stifling darkness of the hood—and the inherent terror of being sightless—ate at the calm she was striving for, tempting her into reacting, but Wynn just grit her teeth and followed Harry without protest. He was dragging her behind him by her bound wrists—but worse, she thought, was the chatter.

Who knew a serial killer would be so verbose?

"I didn't plan to take you," he was saying conversationally as she stumbled along behind him. "You're not my type. Jenna's the one I wanted. But then I thought—why not? It's good to break out of your mold, spread your wings a little. Diversify. And you know, two birds, one stone. I get another canvas, and the Sheriff...that asshole gets what's coming to him."

Beau.

Who Wynn was trying really hard not to think about. Because she couldn't count on him to show up and save her bacon, and she wasn't the type to sit around and cry over spilled milk.

Nor had she ever expected anyone else to save her.

"Not a fan?" she asked sarcastically.

"He never should have won that election. If Velma hadn't stuck her damn nose into things, no one would have run, and the Town Council would have just given me the position."

Poor guy. "Why didn't you run against him?"

"I didn't want the scrutiny."

"Worried being a serial killer might be a detriment to your political career?" She snorted. "Have you looked around Washington?"

"You're funny, Wynn. I always thought that. I never had anything against you, you know."

"Wow, Harry, thanks. I feel so much better now."

"It's not personal," he told her. "Not really."

"Murder isn't personal?" She shook her head. "I don't think that's a thing."

He jerked her to a stop. The sound of something creaking—a door opening?—and then he shoved her forward—through a doorway, she thought—and she stumbled into something hard and wooden, nearly taking a header before she caught her balance.

The darkness of the hood condensed; the sounds of the birds became muted. And the coppery scent of blood was so strong, she nearly bent over and vomited.

"I brought you some company, Maddie girl," Harry said. "This is Wynn. She's my next project."

Hard hands closed on her shoulders, turned her around,

and pushed down; her butt hit the hard surface of a cold metal chair.

"I have some calls to make," he continued. "So you girls just relax, get to know each other. We're all going to be good friends before this is over."

The hood was ripped away. Wynn blinked in the semi-darkness, trying to swallow back the bile filling her throat. The smell of blood was overwhelming.

Harry bent down and tied her feet to the chair. Wynn looked down at his bent head, incredibly tempted to ram her knee into his face. To grab his hair and slam his head into the chair. To—

Down, girl. Not yet. Not yet.

She needed her hands free—and now her feet, too. She couldn't take him on while she was bound. She would need all of her limbs to fight.

Still, it was hard to argue with instinct. So hard, she trembled.

"Easy," Harry said softly. He wrapped a hand around her knee and squeezed. "Just breathe, Wynn."

Kick him in the face and stomp on his balls.

He patted her knee and stood. Wynn looked around; the space was small, only ten by ten. The walls were covered in old tin roofing; the floor was bare earth. Light speared in from the tiny space between the walls and the ground, narrow rays that barely lit the space. She could see a small table covered with some kind of tools, another chair, this one wooden—the one she'd hit—and a long, narrow cot, and—

Maddie.

Wynn froze, staring at her, trying to penetrate the darkness. Just a narrow shadow stretched out on the cot, her hands, and feet tied to the metal frame. She didn't move and made no noise.

"Why stick men?" Wynn asked softly. "What's your deal?"

Harry laughed softly. "Because it has to be meaningful."

Piece of stinking shit. "Isn't it?"

"I suppose," he said. He paused as if thinking about it. "They're a kind of tribute."

When he said nothing more, Wynn prodded, "A tribute to who?"

"My father," he said after a moment.

Wynn knew nothing about Harry's father. "Explain," she demanded.

"You sound just like him," Harry muttered. "Barking orders at me like I'm some kind of worthless grunt in boot camp. I fucking hate him."

Beau.

"Sorry," she said, not sorry at all. "He rubs off. Does your father know about this tribute?"

"My father is dead," Harry said flatly.

"Sorry," she said again, still not sorry.

"No, you aren't. You despised him."

The hair at Wynn's nape suddenly prickled. "I did?"

He leaned down; his gaze moved over her, remote and considering, as if she were a specimen he was considering dissecting.

Which she was.

"Hatfield was my father," he murmured.

Wynn blinked. "He was?"

"No one knew." Bitterness underscored the words. "My mother would never let her pristine image be sullied by admitting that truth. But I knew. He knew. And he did things, stuff he wouldn't have done for anyone else."

Her blood growing even colder, Wynn said, "Well, isn't that special."

"He always stood by me. Always. And he would have in public, too, if she'd let him."

"Why wouldn't she let him?"

"She was ashamed." Harry shook his head in disgust. "She's weak. Always has been; always will be. Not like him."

Wynn really didn't want to get into a discussion about Jasper Hatfield. "And the stick men...they're an homage to him?"

Harry shrugged. "He's the hangman."

For a moment, she just stared at him. "You mean...like in the game?"

"I knew you were smart. No one else has put it together."

Shocking.

"The stick figures are all of the bad people he put away. And the tool I use...it belongs to *her*. She has no idea I have it, or what I'm doing with it. Always so determined to be good and kind and better than everyone else. I've made her an accomplice to murder, and she doesn't even know it." He laughed again. "I'd give anything to see the look on her face if she knew."

Jesus. He was a psychopath.

Not that Wynn was surprised; anyone who committed the crimes he did wasn't right in the head. But to hear the words—to see that sick grin—made her skin crawl, and the terror she was doing her best to subdue struggled in her hold.

Because he was loco.

He straightened. "I have to go now, but don't worry, I'll

be back soon. Oh, and you can scream all you like. No one will hear."

The door opened, a flash of blinding sunlight, and then darkness again.

Wynn waited a minute. It felt like an eternity.

She blinked, willing her eyes to adjust. The smell of blood was thick and cloying and inescapable.

"Maddie," she whispered.

No response.

She reached for the side pocket of her cargos with her bound hands; her fingertips just brushed the opening. The awareness that Harry would be back—how long would a few calls take?—was like a hard hand wrapping her throat. Squeezing.

Tick-tock, she thought.

"Maddie," she said again, louder.

Nothing.

Wynn slid closer to the edge of the chair and turned, just a little; her fingers dipped into her pocket.

It was hot in the shack—shanty, she thought, for an ice hole—and humid. Sweat beaded on her lip. Her palms were damp. The beat of her heart was like a drum in her skull. The adrenaline that had been circling within her unfurled, making her veins hum, her skin pulse. She twisted her hips; her hands slid deeper into her pocket. Her fingertips brushed the cold steel end of the knife.

Tick-tock, tick-tock.

"Maddie," she repeated, her voice stern. "Answer me."

A small, responsive whimper.

Thank you, God.

Wynn twisted in the chair, her spine aching in protest; her fingertips grasped at the knife. Her eyes were finally adjusting to the darkness, and she could see Maddie; the girl was bare from the waist up, her entire torso covered in tiny, gruesome cuts and deep punctures. *Stick men.* Blood oozed from the wounds, pooling on the cot, dripping to the ground.

"Maddie," Wynn said again. "Can you hear me?"

The girl moaned. Tears slid from the corners of her eyes. Her head turned, and their eyes met; her face was battered and bruised.

"Help me," she whispered.

The sight of what had been done to her was like a hard, sharp blow. Wynn took an unsteady breath, then another, fighting to move past the shock of it. The smell of it.

The fucking horror of it all.

Tick-tock. Tick-tock.

"I will," she promised hoarsely. "Can you move?"

"No," Maddie said. She began to cry.

"No," Wynn said harshly. "No more tears. You can cry later. We're going to fight now. Do you hear me?"

"Can't fight," Maddie whispered. "He likes it if you fight."

He's going to die.

Wynn arched her back; her hands slid further into her pocket. Her fingertips pulled at the knife, carefully, slowly, until her hand could wrap around it. She pulled it out.

"When he comes back," Wynn said. "I'm going to take him down."

A wild laugh escaped Maddie. "Are you crazy? I'm crazy. It hurts so much. So much. Why doesn't he just kill me? *Why can't I just die already?*"

Tears burned Wynn's eyes. Of pain and grief, but mostly of fury. Her hands were shaking violently; she almost dropped the knife.

Tick tock. Tick tock.

She forced herself to stop. Take a deep breath. Wiped her damp palms on her pants and opened the knife.

"Please just kill me," Maddie begged.

"You're going home to your mom," Wynn said matter-of-factly. "And he's going into a grave."

She opened the knife and started cutting the rope that bound her hands; she managed to cut herself twice, and by the time the rope fell away, she was bleeding, too. She bent over and started on her feet.

"You are crazy," Maddie whispered.

"Like a fox," Wynn replied evenly.

She stood, and Maddie stared up at her, eyes glazed and wild.

"I'm going to cut you loose," Wynn told her. "But you can't move. You have to stay just like he left you." She bent over and began to cut the ropes that held Maddie to the cot. "When I go after him, then you run."

Another uneven laugh. "Crazy lady."

Tick-tock. Tick-tock.

"Listen to me," Wynn said sharply. She gripped the girl's chin. "Focus, Maddie. I know you're scared and you're hurt, but if you want to escape, you have to listen. Do you understand?"

Maddie blinked up at her; her mouth trembled, terror skittered through her gaze.

"Honey, you have to be strong," Wynn whispered. "I can't do it alone."

Maddie stared at her for a moment.

"Okay," she said and nodded.

Relief whispered through Wynn. She cut the last tie, freeing Maddie's legs. "I want you to go for his truck. If you can get inside, lock it. There's a radio in the truck; get on the radio and call for help."

"But what about you?"

"Don't worry about me." Wynn slid the knife into her pocket, picked up the metal chair, and folded it shut. Then she moved to stand beside the door. "When he goes down, you run."

Maddie only stared at her. Then she lifted her freed hands and stared at them.

"No," Wynn said sharply. "Put them down. Just like he left you."

She lifted the chair by the legs; it was heavy. It might not put him out, but it would put him down.

Maddie slowly lowered her arms. She stared at Wynn.

"What if it doesn't work?" she asked in a small voice.

"Then we try again," Wynn said.

Tick-tock, tick-tock.

"Who are you?" Maddie asked, blinking.

But Wynn didn't get the chance to answer, because, at that moment, the door was thrust open, and Harry Baker walked in.

She swung the chair and slammed it into his face; he fell back. She went through the door after him, lifted the chair again, and brought it down hard on top of him.

"Run," she bellowed at Maddie, but she didn't turn to look, to make sure Maddie listened, because Harry was wrenching the chair from her grip and tossing it aside.

"Goddamn you," he snarled. "I knew you were just like your bitch mother."

He grabbed her shirt, hauled her toward him, and slammed his fist into her face. Pain exploded in her skull, blood burst on her tongue. The ground rose to slap her in the back, and air burst from her lungs in a painful rush. Then he climbed on top of her, and his hands wrapped her throat.

"She was a pain in the ass, too," he grated. "Always poking her nose where it didn't belong. Seeing things she shouldn't see."

I saw you. I saw you! I know what you did.

For a breathless moment, everything stopped. Wynn heard her mother's terrified screams; saw the horror and certainty on Lara's face as she stared at Jasper Hatfield. Understanding flashed through her.

"She saw you!" Wynn bucked beneath his heavy weight; she fought to get her hand into her pocket. "That's why he killed her. To protect you."

A harsh laugh broke from Harry. "Not me, himself. He was cleaning up my mess when she saw him." The hands wrapping her throat tightened. His nails dug into her skin; Wynn grasped at the knife. "He had to put her down. Just like I have to put you down. Like mother, like daughter." He leaned close; squeezed her throat shut. "You're going to be my best work yet."

Her hand closed around the knife; she ripped it from her pocket and hit the switch that opened it. She struggled against him, gasping for breath. "You are some kind of crazy, Harry Baker."

"My work will go down in history," he snarled. "*I will live forever*. While you die alone and forgotten."

"Not today," Wynn told him and stabbed the knife into his side.

He squealed; the hands at her neck released, and he rolled off her. But she didn't let go of the knife, and she went with him.

She wanted that knife. Needed that knife.

"Fuck," he screamed, staggering to his feet, dragging her with him.

The knife was stuck.

Between his ribs. She twisted it, and he hit her again, a dizzying slap that nearly sent her back to the ground, but she held onto the knife—it was her only chance—

"I'm going to kill you for a long, *long* time." Harry grabbed her shirt and lifted her from the ground. She tried to knee him, but the angle was wrong. She wiggled and wormed; kicked his shin and twisted the knife deeper. Then she fisted her hand and drove it into his throat. He made a harsh, strangled sound and staggered. A second later, his elbow slammed into her temple. White lights burst behind her eyelids. He swung her around and—

Boom! Boom! Boom!

The sound of gunfire was deafening. Wynn jerked, but Harry had his hand wrapped in her shirt, and she was dangling above the ground, and she couldn't get away—he twisted her around. Her back slammed into his chest. One hand lifted to wrap her throat; the other arm lodged itself behind her head in a chokehold.

In front of them stood Beau, his weapon drawn, his face so cold and brutal that her wildly pounding heart skipped a beat.

"Let her go," he ordered.

The hand around her throat tightened. The pressure behind her head grew; Wynn had a sudden vision of her head popping off like a dandelion bloom. "How about I crack her like a walnut, instead?"

Her feet swung uselessly above the grass. But her hand somehow still gripped the knife.

And now she had leverage.

"Three." Beau's gaze didn't waver from Harry's face. "Two."

"No one is that fast," Harry murmured. "Not even you."

Wynn gripped the knife and pulled. It came free.

Harry screamed.

"This is for Emma," she told him and stabbed the knife back, deep into his belly.

"Fuck!" he roared and thrust her away from him.

Her hold on the knife broke. She stumbled forward and crashed into Beau; they went down hard in a tangle of flailing limbs.

"He shoots, he scores!" Harry wheezed. Blood spewed down his chin as he pulled her knife from his belly. "Fucking cripple."

He staggered toward them; a river of crimson oozed from his stomach. Wynn tried to untangle herself from Beau, to get to her feet, but she wasn't fast enough, and suddenly Harry was there, standing above them. One hand gripped her knife; the other held Beau's Glock.

He waved with gun and grinned. "Look what I found."

Beau snarled. He tensed, and Wynn realized he was going to launch himself at Harry.

Right into the line of fire.

She grabbed his arm. "No!"

"Yes," he growled and tried to shake her off.

"Don't worry," Harry smirked. "You both get to die."

He lifted the gun. Wynn's heart stopped.

And Beau tore from her grip and lurched to his feet.

"See you in hell," Harry whispered.

"Not today," said another voice.

And then—

Clang!

Something slammed into the side of Harry's head; his skull crunched, and his neck snapped like a branch breaking. He looked surprised as he fell to the ground.

Sean Evers stood there, shovel in hand. "I've been waiting a fucking lifetime to do that."

CHAPTER 29

"I can't believe I didn't know."

Cam stood beside Beau, staring at the semi-controlled chaos that had overtaken the Sheriff's office. The deputy was pale, his features strained. The smile that normally occupied his wide face was absent.

"How could I not know?" he continued. "We went for beers. Played baseball. Hell, he was part of my bowling league!"

Beau rubbed a hand down his face. His head hurt like hell, almost as much as his leg. Ever since he'd hit the ground that afternoon, it had been unsteady and weak, as if it was just waiting to give.

To send him crashing to the floor.

No less than he deserved, he thought.

"No one knew," he said. "Not me; not you. Not even his own mother. Don't take it personally."

"But it is personal," Cam insisted. "He was one of us."

"No." Beau shook his head. "He was never one of us. Baker played a roll, and he played it well. But to him, it was all just a game. Is that badge a game to you?"

Cam looked down at the badge pinned to his shirt. "No, sir."

"That's the difference."

Cam sighed. "I feel like I failed the whole town."

You and me both.

No matter that Wynn was—if bruised and battered—alive and well; that Maddie Ripley was safe in her mother's care at the local hospital.

That the monster who'd terrorized the town of Blossom Hills for nearly two decades was dead.

A success, Beau supposed.

But all it felt like was a loss.

"What do we do now?" Cam asked quietly.

"We move on," Beau told him.

His deputy nodded. Then he sighed again. "I need a drink."

Beau could relate. Not only did his entire body hurt, the epiphany he'd had as he stared down the barrel of his own gun made him want to crawl into a bottle and never surface.

My own goddamn weapon.

It was almost laughable.

Almost. If it hadn't been so fucking pathetic.

Taken out like a bowling pin. Jesus Christ.

He'd buckled in spectacular fashion when Baker had thrown Wynn into him; worse, he'd lost his Glock—which wouldn't have been a problem if he'd just been able to get to his damn feet. But his strength, his speed, his agility—

All gone.

And today, that fact had almost been the end of him. Which he could accept. But what he couldn't accept was that it had almost been the end of Wynn, too.

He'd known it was a danger—his pain, his injury, his *disability*.

But he'd thought—

Well, it didn't matter what he'd thought.

Fucking useless. Today left no doubt. If Sean Evers hadn't bashed Harry's skull in with a shovel—Harry's own shovel, no less, which was very karmic—both Beau and Wynn would be dead, two more victims of the Stick Man.

Along with Maddie Ripley.

The knowledge sickened him. Not just because of the harsh reality behind it, but because it meant everything he'd fooled himself into thinking could be his wasn't meant to be.

Would never be meant to be.

Not with Wynn; not with anyone.

It made him want to break something.

Or someone.

"Sheriff," said a voice from behind him.

Goddamn it. He didn't want to turn around. He wanted everyone to just go the hell home, so he could do the same. He didn't want to talk to people; not the FBI; not the locals. Not even poor disillusioned Cam.

And especially not Wynn.

Christ, he couldn't even look at her. With her black eye and her cut chin and her cheek with Baker's fucking handprint on it. Never mind that she was covered in blood—her blood, Baker's blood, Maddie Ripley's blood.

Beau wanted to crush her to him and never let her out of his sight again.

Ever.

Which he couldn't do.

Didn't have the right to do—not if he couldn't keep her fucking safe.

He sighed heavily, rubbed his throbbing leg, and carefully turned around.

Jack Farley stood there.

"Thank you," Jack said and stuck out his hand.

Beau looked down at it. "I should have figured it out sooner."

"You got him." Jack shook his head. "No one else ever came close."

"I had a lot of help." Beau accepted Jack's hand and shook it. "I didn't do it alone."

"You didn't give up," Jack said. "Me and the wife, we appreciate that."

Their gazes held; Jack nodded. Then he turned and walked away.

Beau watched him go, a swell of something heavy and painful in his chest.

This day was never going to fucking end.

He excused himself and left Cam to deal with everything. The plethora of FBI who'd shown up to catalog the Stick Man's lair and collect all the evidence they could; the shocked locals, who couldn't believe one of their own was guilty.

Wynn.

"You're a fucking coward," he told himself and closed his office door behind him.

But he needed to sit—before he fell. And he needed some goddamn peace and quiet.

Just for a minute.

His chair groaned as he sank into it. The phone continued to ring, unabated. Luckily, Betsy from dispatch had volunteered to deal with the calls and the questions, so Beau just ignored it. He closed his eyes; his head whirled.

And the cold stone in his stomach sat in relentless wait.

What the hell had made him think he could have something?

He knew better. He'd known it from the moment his life had blown up in his face.

But this place...this place had made him hopeful.

For one, brief, idiotic moment, he'd *believed*.

"Goddamn it," he snarled.

Because it hurt. To let that brief flicker of hope die. To let Wynn go...

Back into the darkness, away from the light.

Someone walked into his office.

"What's got your knickers in a twist?" Wynn demanded. "You're the man of the hour. Why are you hiding in here?"

God help him.

"Don't," he rasped, and the weight inside of him spread like cold, wet concrete.

"Don't what?" Wynn walked toward him. Bloody, bruised, belligerent. "Don't call you on your shit?"

"Man of the fucking hour," he said flatly. "Look at your goddamn face."

Fury and self-loathing filled him. The sight of her made his blood pulse in his skull. Her hair hung in a wild, dark red cloud around her; the shirt she wore was painted in crimson. And her eyes were storm grey, glittering with a wildness that made his hands clench into fists.

No one went through what she had at Baker's hands without it leaving a mark—no matter how tough she was. Beau had plenty of experience in processing blood and violence and sudden death; Wynn didn't.

And she needed him.

His entire body twitched at the thought. Instinctive and visceral, denying her—denying himself—hurt.

"I did this to myself," she scoffed. She halted in front of

his desk and put her hands on her hips. "I went with him. Freed his prisoner, smacked him with a chair, stuck him like a pig. That was all me."

"I'm sorry," he grated, his chest tight.

"Sorry for what? I'm alive; you're alive. Maddie Ripley is alive—and the Stick Man is dead." Her brows rose. "What more do you want?"

"We were two seconds from him spraying the ground with our brains."

"Maybe," she said and shrugged.

"No maybe about it," he growled. He met her gaze, sick with shame and disgust. "That was *my* fault."

"Is that what this is?" Her eyes narrowed. "A pity party?"

Beau shoved to his feet; rage licked at him. Pain stabbed down his leg. "You don't understand."

"Oh, I understand just fine." Wynn slapped her hands on his desk and leaned toward him. "You're mad because he used your weakness against you."

"My leg—"

"Not your leg," she said, her voice hard. "Me."

"I couldn't get up," he bit out. He leaned toward her. "And I dropped my fucking gun."

"Shit happens," she told him. "That's life."

"Not my life," he said.

Because that didn't sound stupid at all.

"Is that what you expect from yourself?" she asked curiously. "To be everywhere, all the time, prepared for any disaster?"

Beau looked away; *she'd come so fucking close to dying.* Did she even realize that?

How close they'd both come?

Because of him. Because he wasn't whole; he was less,

and vulnerable in a million different ways. Everything that had once defined him was nothing more than a memory.

The weight within him grew. "I can't do this."

"This," she repeated. "Define 'this.'"

"This," he snarled, his throat tight.

"Now who's running?" She cocked a brow. "That's it—you just quit?"

No. Yes. Fuck.

"I can't protect you," he grated.

She leaned closer until he could see the tiny flecks of blood that decorated her forehead. "I don't want your stinking protection."

But that was what he did. *Who he was.* And if he couldn't be that—

He couldn't be anything.

And she deserved someone who could protect her, who was capable of doing whatever it took to make sure she was always safe.

Someone who—

"You fucker," she said softly.

He stiffened. His gaze snapped to hers.

"This is all it took?" she demanded. "Some dickhead with a gun and a pottery fetish?" Tears suddenly glinted in her gaze, and Beau couldn't look away, the cold within him growing until it filled his throat and pressed against his skin. "Seriously?"

He flinched but said nothing.

"I almost believed in you," she whispered.

"I'm sorry," he said again, the words jagged and sharp in his throat.

She stared at him for a long, silent moment. Outside his office, people were watching. But Beau didn't care.

Not about any of them.

"You're a fucking coward," Wynn told him and walked out.

CHAPTER 30

"Are you sure you're okay?"

Wynn rubbed her pounding head. "I'm fine."

"No," Jenna argued, "you're not."

Wynn didn't respond. Because she wasn't fine.

Nothing was fine.

Her whole body ached; her face was a swollen mess. The residue left by the violence she'd both endured and perpetrated made her jittery and anxious and overly-emotional.

Wrung out hard and hung to dry in a cold, harsh wind.

Damn Beau Greystone to everlasting hell.

I can't do this. I can't protect you. I'm sorry.

"Fucker," she muttered.

"What was that?" Jenna demanded. She sat across from Wynn at the kitchen table, her face drawn, her eyes bright and hard. "Who's a fucker? The Stick Man?"

"Jenna," Esme admonished quietly.

"What? She said it first." Jenna leaned forward. "Who are you talking about?"

Wynn only shook her head. Esme was making tea, and

the sound of the older woman moving around the kitchen, humming softly, soothed Wynn. Something comforting and familiar and normal.

Something good.

All of the tenants had descended upon her as soon as she'd walked in the door—even Earl, who'd been released from custody that afternoon due to both the feds and the Dorchester National Bank Board of Directors dropping the armed robbery charges—and the cacophony of excited questions had just about done Wynn in. She'd been ridiculously grateful when Esme sent them all away—except for Jenna, who wasn't about to be sent anywhere.

"The entire male race," Wynn retorted.

First Sean, then Beau. Sean, she could forgive; Sean she understood. Even if it made her angry that he'd lied to them. But Beau...

Fucker.

And what made it worse was that while fighting for her life, she'd suddenly realized how badly she wanted to live.

To not just survive, but to *thrive*.

That no amount of fear was worth sacrificing possibility.

And now...Beau had let his fear decide for both of them.

I can't do this.

No, she thought, you won't do this. And it was like a blade carving her in two.

But the pain was nothing compared to her anger.

How dare he!

He'd been the one to stick his big, fat stupid face into her life. Into her business. Acting like he gave a damn—about Earl, about *her*. And now, just because he'd had a reality check—*welcome to life, buddy*—he was going to crawl back into the dark?

Well. Not much she could do about that, was there?

"Wynn!" Jenna snapped.

Wynn glared at her. "What?"

"Talk to me," her sister ordered.

"Jenna," Esme said again and set a cup of tea in front of Wynn. "Leave your sister alone. I think she's been through enough for one day, don't you?"

Color flushed Jenna's cheeks. "Something happened."

"A lot happened," Wynn said flatly.

"I mean with Beau. I can tell."

"Nothing happened."

"Bullshit."

Wynn put her head in her hands.

"Wynn," Jenna said again. "Tell me."

No. Don't make me. Please.

Tears she despised burned in her throat.

"He was really worried about you," Jenna continued doggedly. "If you could've seen his face when we realized where you were... He loves you, Wynn."

Wynn flinched. "No."

"He does. I saw it. I looked into his eyes, *and I saw it*."

The tears blurred her vision. "Jen, stop. Please."

"But he does. He really, truly does. What happened? What did he do?"

A tear escaped. "It's done," she said tightly.

"But why?"

Wynn looked at her sister's stricken face, and the ache in her chest spread like wildfire. "I don't want to talk about this."

"But—"

"Jenna," Esme said quietly. "Enough."

Jenna opened her mouth, then closed it again.

"I'm sorry," she said after a minute. "I love you."

"I love you, too," Wynn muttered, trying to stem the emotion bleeding through her. All of her defenses were gone, every tool she used to compartmentalize and process pain in total rubble. Between the violence and the blood and Beau's rejection, she had nothing left.

Nothing but tears.

Useless, she thought. But there was nothing to be done for it. They needed to be shed.

Then she could move on.

"Jenna, why don't you go check on the others?" Esme suggested.

"They're fine," Jenna said.

"Jenna."

Jenna stood with an annoyed huff. But she moved to Wynn and hugged her tightly, and Wynn felt the tremor that moved through her.

"It's okay," she said. *Another lie.* What was one more? "I'll be okay."

Her sister said nothing, just squeezed tighter, and more tears slid down Wynn's face.

Then Jenna left them.

"Drink your tea, dear," Esme said. "A good cup of Earl Grey makes everything better."

If only. But Wynn took an obedient drink. It slid down into her belly but did nothing to warm the cold that sat like lead in her veins.

Esme said nothing, and they sat in silence, drinking their tea, the sound of *Wheel of Fortune* murmuring in from the living room.

"If Sean hadn't shown up, we would be dead," Wynn said after a while.

"Ah." Esme set her cup down. "I take it Beau feels responsible for that?"

Wynn looked at her.

"No doubt he's very conscious of what he perceives as his weakness." Esme shrugged. "He's not the first man I've met whose disability handicapped him in more than one way."

"He was married, once. She died, and he blames himself. So today...I think it was like it happened all over again."

"I had no idea."

"I can't fix it," she said and hated the helplessness she felt.

"I'm sorry." Esme's hand covered hers and squeezed. "I know you care for him."

Yes. And today, Wynn had come to understand just how much. *The stupid fucker.*

"He was ashamed," she said, remembering the look in his eyes. "It made me angry. We survived. Why isn't that enough?"

"Perhaps his value has always been in shielding others. When you can no longer be that which you've always been, what's left?"

A pity party. But that wasn't fair. It wasn't just about pride.

It was about purpose, about self-worth.

I can't fix this.

"I want to punch him in the face," she said. "Smack some stinking sense into him."

"Well." Esme's brows rose. "There are other ways to breach a man's defenses."

Wynn snorted. "Like I'd know how to wage that kind of warfare."

"Dear, your weapons are written into your chromosomes. Trust me, it doesn't take much else."

Wynn only shook her head.

"Alright." Esme shrugged. "If you don't think you can do it."

"I'm not biting," Wynn told her.

"I understand." Another shrug. "Some things are simply *too* challenging."

Wynn glared at her. "Do you think I don't know you're manipulating me?"

"Is it working?"

Ethel walked into the kitchen, a long, narrow box with a bright red ribbon in hand.

"I'm sorry, Wynnie," she said. "I forgot."

Wynn stared blankly at the box. "Forgot what?"

"I forgot to give it to you."

"What is it?"

"A present from Sheriff Beau. He brought it for you."

He did? "When?"

"This morning. You was at the store." Ethel thrust the box at her. "I was gonna give it to you when you came home, but then me and Ellie went to church, and then the Stick Man took you and got killed, and I forgot all about it. But now I remembered. Here!"

A gift.

All of the chaos within Wynn coalesced as she stared at it.

"Well," Esme said, her gaze speculative.

"I don't want it," Wynn said.

"But you gotta!" Ethel insisted. She put the box down on the table in front of Wynn. "I told him I would give it to you."

The box was long and skinny. *Flowers*, Wynn thought dully.

"I don't want it," she repeated, and those stupid tears were suddenly closing her throat again.

"Please, Wynnie," Ethel murmured. Her sweet face scrunched into a frown. "I *promised*."

Wynn clenched her jaw and pulled the lid from the box. A brand new, bright red pipe wrench stared back at her.

"Crap," she said, and another tear traced her cheek.

"What's that?" Ethel demanded, clearly disappointed.

Esme began to laugh.

Wynn slammed the lid back down onto the box.

"Why'd he get you that?" Ethel wanted to know.

"Because he's a very smart man," Esme told her.

Wynn snorted, but the tears pressed against her chest and built in her throat, and she couldn't stop them from escaping.

Fucker.

"I don't understand," Ethel said.

"You don't have to," Esme replied, smiling. She looked at Wynn. "Well?"

"Well, what?" Wynn retorted, annoyed. She swiped at her eyes.

"Aren't you going to go and tell him what you think of his gift?"

She looked at the box, far too tempted.

I can't do this. I can't protect you. I'm sorry.

She'd make him sorry, all right.

No. Just...no.

But if she just gave up...well, that didn't make her any different than him, did it?

No, it didn't. And life was too stinking short—as they'd both been reminded today.

If she leaped and she fell...so what?

At least she would have tried.

She stared at the wrench. Her heart pounded hard in her chest.

"I might get arrested," she said grimly.

Esme picked up her tea and took another drink. "That's alright, dear. Sasha's still on retainer."

CHAPTER 31

YOU'RE A FUCKING COWARD.

The whiskey slid down Beau's throat and burned his belly, but it was nothing compared to the memory of Wynn's face when she'd thrown those words at him.

Words he couldn't argue with; his own words, so much worse when uttered by her.

This is all it took to send you running? Some dickhead with a gun and a pottery fetish?

I almost believed in you.

Goddamn her. She nailed him every fucking time. No beating around the bush; to hell with discretion.

Wynn Owens called it like she saw it.

It was one of the things he deeply appreciated about her.

One of the things he would miss.

You did the right thing, he told himself.

Even if he felt like dirt.

"Man of the hour," he muttered and took another swig.

Is that what this is? A pity party?

Always poking the bear. Making him own his shit.

Making him face it.

She made him better, he thought. Regardless of anything else, she wasn't afraid to call him out, and he needed that.

A kick in the ass.

He was worse for the loss. And it had taken everything he was to push her away.

He wasn't sure he could do it again.

Because after watching her today, he'd realized who Wynn was. *Really was*.

And she would never be anything like Marie.

Not that Marie had been weak. She hadn't. She'd been smart and strong in spirit and ridiculously willful; she'd stood unwavering beside him when he needed her most. But Wynn...today he'd watched Wynn punch Harry Baker in the throat and then stab him.

Wynn wouldn't expect him to save her. She would simply save herself.

As she'd always done.

I don't want your stinking protection.

She didn't need him to make the world safe. She'd be pissed if he tried. Ask him what the hell his problem was, and then shove the answer down his throat.

That, he realized, had always been part of her appeal.

Goddamn it.

"Stop," he told himself, annoyed. "Just fucking stop."

He'd walked out of his office shortly after she'd gone. He'd ignored the look Garrett gave him—as if the SOB knew exactly what he'd done—and avoided both Velma and the grateful citizens of Blossom Hills by escaping out the back door, only to find Winston leaning against his truck, smoking a cigarette.

Which had surprised Beau. He figured his new deputy

would be out tying one on in celebration, but Winston was sober as a church mouse. Maybe it was because, out of everyone, Winston seemed to understand Beau's discontent with the Stick Man's easy death.

Winston had wanted blood, too.

But in the end, he'd just clasped Beau on the shoulder and said, "Sometimes you gotta take the win, Chief," and walked away.

A win, everyone said. But Beau felt like he'd lost.

Pretty much everything.

Headlights washed across the cabin's front window, and irritation shot through him.

Jesus. One fucking night; couldn't they give him that?

One night of quiet, where he could lick his wounds in peace. Get his head straight and his shit together.

If that was even possible.

Well, damned if he was going to answer the door. They could just—

Wynn.

Beau froze. He watched as she parked, climbed out of the VW, and began to march toward his front door. She was carrying something; he couldn't tell what.

Damn her.

What the hell was she doing?

Didn't she know once was all he had in him?

All of his discipline, his pride, hell, even the cowardice she'd accused him of, none of it made a goddamn bit of difference when she was standing in front of him.

Fuck.

She pounded on his door. *Boom, boom, boom.*

Pissed, he thought, and anticipation surged through him. Excitement; adrenaline.

Joy.

"Fuck," he said and slammed the rest of his whiskey.

Then he limped to the door and swung it open.

Her hair was wet, her clothes damp from the rain. Her face was bruised; a long, slender cut traced her chin. She smelled like sunlight and apple pie, and for a moment, he just stood there, inhaling her.

"Here," she said and thrust something at him. "This is yours."

Beau tore his gaze from her face and looked down at it.

The pipe wrench.

He'd forgotten all about it.

Anger lit and caught flame. "That's a gift."

"I don't take gifts from strangers," she told him and shoved it into his hands.

"I'm not a goddamn stranger," he snarled.

"You are now," she said. "Fucking coward."

Then she turned to walk away.

Beau couldn't help himself; he reached out and gripped her arm.

"Don't," she hissed.

His hold tightened.

"You shouldn't have come here," he told her harshly.

She flinched. "Then let me leave."

She tugged against his hold, but he didn't let go.

Couldn't.

Didn't fucking want to.

"We almost died," he said, his voice raw. Reminding her. Reminding himself. Her battered face made him want to kill someone. "Because I'm fucking broken."

"We're all fucking broken," she retorted, her voice hard. "Get over it."

He stared at her, turmoil churning within him. Hunger;

need; despair. Hope. Such desperation and guilt, he felt sick with it.

So much fucking guilt.

"I'll never be who I was," he ground out. "That man is dead."

"Then you should let him rest in peace," she said coldly.

"I can't."

"You won't. Let me go, Beau."

His hand refused to release her. Thunder clapped; the rain grew harder, pounding the tin roof of the porch above them. The faint light from the cabin gilded her in gold; her eyes were dark, the bruises that colored her face angry in the warm light. Her wet shirt clung to her breasts, and her beautiful mouth was a grim line.

He couldn't look away from her. "I'm sorry."

"I don't want you to be sorry," she told him. "I want you to be brave."

The words stung. "You deserve better."

"You don't get to decide what I deserve." She tugged at his grip. "Let me go, damn it."

But his hand just flexed around her; his heart was beating too hard. He wanted...

Too much. The impossible.

"You don't get to run away just because I scare you," she mocked bitingly. "Do you think you're the only one with fear?" Her gaze seared into his. "Do you think I'm not scared?" A harsh laugh broke from her. "I'm scared of everything. Of Jenna leaving and never coming back. Of watching my tenants die, one by one, until the house is empty and cold with nothing left behind but grief. Of my land dying, and taking me along with it." She poked him in the chest. Hard. "But I put on my big-girl panties, and I deal. You want to crawl into a hole and bury yourself? Go for it. But don't pretend it's valor or sacrifice. It's fucking surrender. And you know it."

Blood roared in his ears. Beau let the pipe wrench fall; the box hit the wooden boards with a thud.

He stared at her, unable to respond.

She was right.

He was fucking terrified. He couldn't even begin to list everything he was afraid of; all the different ways he could fail. And it was driving him underground. Putting him to sleep.

Again.

"Life is hard," Wynn told him evenly, her voice quiet. "No promises; no guarantees; no forever. Just here and now. This moment. That's all we get. And we do the best with it that we can. End of story."

His heart beat like a hollow drum. Was it really that simple?

Just do the fucking best you can?

Because that...that was something he could do.

"Let me go, Beau. *Now.*"

He blinked at her, his gut churning.

Was he just hearing what he wanted to hear?

Was he just too fucking selfish to let her go?

Yes.

Yes, goddamn it, he was.

And he didn't give a shit. He'd tried to do what he thought was the right thing, but here she was, poking him, prodding him into living.

Giving him a kick in the ass.

Exactly what he needed.

So...*fuck it.*

He was going to keep her—and to hell with the consequences.

"If you don't take your hands off me," she told him, "I'm going to break your stinking hand."

All of the longing and need and relentless hunger that he'd tried to bury beneath his wounded pride poured through him, white-hot and ready to burn. He yanked her toward him. "I warned you not to threaten me."

She smacked into his chest. "Bring it on, tin man."

He leaned down and tossed her over his shoulder. His leg didn't like it, but he didn't fucking care.

"What are you doing?" she snarled.

"Being brave," he told her and carried her inside.

*****

Being brave.

Wynn's heart rattled in her chest; blood roared in her ears.

What in Hades had just happened?

She thumped her fist against the hard plane of Beau's back. "Put me down!"

"You're right," he said and kicked the door shut behind him.

"Of course I am!" She thumped him again. "About what?"

"I am a fucking coward. I'm terrified something will happen, and I won't be able to save you."

She opened her mouth.

"But you don't need saving, do you? Except from yourself. Getting on that goddamn roof." A hard hand swatted her rear end and made it sting. "That's not happening again."

Wynn hissed and rubbed her butt. "If you don't put me down, I'm going to—"

"Careful. I've had enough of your threats."

She wiggled furiously. "Put me down, damn it!"

"One minute at a time," he said. "I can do that. No more running. For either of us."

He leaned down and carefully set her on her feet. Then he stepped back and stared at her. "Deal?"

The look on his face made a rush of awareness wash over her.

"What the hell are you doing?" she demanded.

"I'm doing what you asked." His eyes stroked over her. "I'm being brave."

His gaze was as palpable as a touch. A tremor moved through her; heat licked across her skin.

"Don't," she warned.

Those brilliant green eyes met hers.

"This isn't a game," she told him, her throat tight. "I'm not playing."

"Neither am I," he said. "Once I'm inside you, there's no turning back."

Another, deeper tremor moved through her.

"I just came to return that stupid wrench," she said, her heart a wild drum. "That's all."

"No, you didn't." He stepped toward her. "You came to give me a swift kick in the ass. Thank you. I'm glad you're here."

She stood frozen. He was invading her personal space, his scent filling her senses, his heat washing across her skin. Suddenly everything she'd felt in the aftermath of their bloody afternoon came rushing back; the adrenaline, the chaos, the overpowering need to *live*.

To take everything she could, so she never looked back with regret.

"You don't get to quit when it gets hard," she said, still angry.

"I know." He stepped closer. "I'm sorry. It won't happen again."

She stared at him, terrified to believe.

"I promise to do the best I can," he told her quietly. "As long as you promise to do the same."

The pressure in her chest grew.

To wake up or stay asleep.

It didn't matter what he said; this was her risk to take.

That was why she'd come here, she realized.

Because some part of her had already decided.

No promises; no guarantees; no forever.

Just here and now.

"Okay," she heard herself whisper.

The tension in him seemed to ease, while hers just ratcheted up a notch.

"One minute at a time," he said again and reached up to tuck a strand of her hair behind her ear. "No rush. We can go nice and slow."

But Wynn shook her head.

She didn't want nice and slow.

She wanted him. *Them.*

Now. Because today, she'd almost died without ever having either one.

She kicked off her boots and let her coat slide to the floor.

"Wynn." Beau watched her with narrow, gleaming eyes. "Sweetheart, what are you doing?"

She reached down and pulled off her t-shirt.

His gaze raked over her, so hot she felt burned. Her breasts prickled inside of the lace bra she wore, and she stared at him, her blood a thick, hot rush that made her skin pulse.

"We don't have to do this," he rasped, but his eyes darkened, and he stared at her nipples where they peaked through the nap of the delicate lace.

She reached up and unhooked her bra.

His gaze crashed into hers. "Be very sure."

The warning in him made another tremor move through her.

In response, she shrugged off her bra and let it fall.

Her nipples were hard. The damp, hungry flesh between her legs began to throb.

His eyes grew hooded; they stroked over her. "You're beautiful."

Goosebumps washed across her skin.

"Take off the rest," he said, his voice rough. "I want to see you."

The intensity of his focus made her nerves prickle.

"No," she said. "Your turn."

That brilliant green gaze flew to hers.

"Your shirt," she told him.

For a breathless moment, he just looked at her. Then he reached up and pulled off the t-shirt he wore, revealing a chest carved with hard muscle, scarred and marked by time and war. A tattoo of a raven sitting in an oak tree covered his left shoulder, the tree lush with leaves, its bark rough and thick.

She wanted to touch it.

"Now you," he said, watching her.

Her breathing deepened; the drumbeat inside of her grew stronger. A molten river flowed through her veins.

She unbuttoned her jeans and pushed them down her

hips. Clad in just a skimpy pair of boy shorts and her socks, she stepped out of them.

The warmth of the fire from the woodstove burned against her overheated skin; outside the storm grew in intensity.

"Come here," Beau said.

She hesitated, perched on the precipice of the unknown. Not exactly afraid.

Just...

Awake.

He watched her, his gaze intent. "You have to be brave, too."

Yes.

She stepped toward him, acutely aware of her nudity.

Of the aching need inside her that went far beyond sex.

"We can wait," he said, his voice like sandpaper. "Today was intense. I need you to be sure."

A muscle ticked in the hard line of his jaw; the beat of his heart was wild in his throat.

He would stop, she realized. He might not like it, but he would do it if she asked.

Emotion swelled abruptly inside of her, and for a moment, she couldn't speak.

"Wynn," he grated.

She met his gaze. Trembled. "I'm sure."

"You tell me if you need to stop," he said.

She nodded mutely. There would be no stopping.

He lifted his hand and skimmed her nipple with his palm. She shuddered.

His gaze held hers. He did it again. "Do you like that?"

A violent tremor moved through her.

"Yes," she whispered.

He cupped her breast; his thumb rubbed her nipple. "And this?"

She arched toward him. "Yes."

He twisted gently, a bite of pleasure and pain that made a soft, low moan escape her. "And that?"

"More," she said and stepped closer.

"You aren't naked." His hand left her. "I want you naked."

She stared at him, her entire body throbbing.

"Now," he said.

"You first," she told him huskily.

"Poking the bear," he murmured, his eyes glinting.

She only waited.

His hand went to the button of his jeans, and everything within her tightened in anticipation. Then he hesitated.

"My leg's a fucking mess," he muttered. "I hate that you'll see it."

"Brave," she reminded him softly.

He growled but slowly stripped off his jeans. He wore a pair of soft black cotton boxers that did nothing to hide the hard line of his cock. And his leg…

His leg was a twist of bone and scar tissue that barely resembled a limb. The reconstruction of his knee left it too big and oddly shaped; a large chunk of muscle was missing from his thigh. His calf was slender, little more than tendon and bone, and the skin that covered him was mottled and scarred and thick.

Wynn stared at him, unable to fathom the pain.

"I can keep my pants on," he said, his gaze shuttered, every line of muscle that covered him taut.

She sank to her knees before him. The injury was

horrific, but she was no wilting flower. She put a gentle hand on the bony lump of his knee.

"Don't," he rasped but didn't move.

She ignored him, stroking carefully up the length of his thigh.

"Christ," he whispered.

"I'm sorry," she murmured.

His hand found her hair, tangled in it. "For what?"

"For your pain," she told him. "Inside and out."

The hand in her hair tightened. "Come here."

She leaned over and pressed a soft kiss to his calf.

A low, harsh sound rumbled from him.

She kissed his knee.

He hissed.

She rubbed her cheek against the inside of his thigh and nipped him.

"*Wynn.*" He trembled beneath her hands. "Come here, sweetheart."

Instead, she reached up and stroked her palm along the hard line of his cock.

"Goddamn it," he growled, and then he was pushing her back onto the sheepskin rug in front of the fire, and the sight of him coming down over her made a rush of wild, primal excitement surge through her. He stripped off her boy shorts, slid his hard hands up the inside of her thighs, and pushed them apart.

She inhaled sharply when he looked at the damp, slick heart of her, his eyes hooded and dark. When he licked his lips, a sound she couldn't stop broke from her.

His gaze clashed with hers.

"You're lovely." His voice was raw. "I want to taste you."

Another sharp spasm of heat and need pulsed through her.

"I should tell you something," she whispered.

He leaned down and flicked his tongue over her nipple.

Fire seared her veins. She made another breathless, hungry sound.

"That's nice," he murmured. "Let's hear it again."

He suckled her, his teeth sharp, that bite of pleasure and pain curling through her; she gripped the thick strands of his hair and tried to get closer.

"Seriously," she gasped. "You should probably know."

He slid his hand between her thighs and cupped her possessively; his thumb found the tender nub of her clit, and he stroked her with firm, steady strokes.

Wynn struggled to breathe.

"You're wet." Lust was vibrant in his voice. He tongued her nipple, and one of his fingers pushed inside of her, thick, foreign, too much and not enough. "Tight."

She fought to speak. "That's...because...I've never done this...before."

He froze. His gaze lifted to hers.

"Please don't stop," she whispered.

A harsh growl rumbled in his chest. The finger inside of her withdrew and then thrust again, slow and deep.

Pleasure splintered through her, and she gasped.

"Are you sure?" he asked in a low voice and thrust again. "I won't let you go."

Everything within her went tight and still, focused solely on the deep, slow, steady thrust of his finger.

"Wynn."

But she couldn't respond, lost to the wild, intense quickening inside of her. Instead, she gripped his hair and pulled him to her, kissing him the same way he kissed her. A deep, devouring kiss that was wild and wet and hungry. When he took control, it turned carnal, raw, consuming.

She wrapped her legs around him, surging against the hand working between her legs, the fingers that stroked her and thrust deep. Moans broke from her chest, spilling out into the air, but she didn't care. When his mouth tore from hers and his hand slid away, she made a sharp sound of protest.

"You aren't ready," he rasped, "you need to come first."

Hard, rough palms stroked her inner thighs and spread them wide. His tongue licked down her neck; he nibbled her collarbone. She hissed, and he slid down, finding her throbbing nipples, where he bit her gently, laving her with his tongue until she started to pant. Then he slid further, soft kisses on her belly, a nip of the tender flesh just above the patch of dark, wine red hair that covered her most vulnerable place. All the while, his hands stroked her, his skin rasping her sensitive inner thighs, his fingers trailing so close, but not close enough, to the place where she needed him most.

"You smell so fucking good," he murmured, and then his mouth was on her, his tongue stroking through her folds, deep, hungry sounds vibrating from his chest.

The sight of his dark head between her thighs made the pleasure spiraling through her go hard and tight; she climbed higher, trembling wildly, her cries turning desperate. He ate her hungrily, without mercy, pushing her higher, further, and when she bucked against him, one of his arms slid across her belly and held her down.

She made another sound of protest, but he only held her there, locked into place while he devoured her.

"You taste like wild honey and sunlight," he muttered.

He reached up and rubbed her nipple; Wynn moaned. Everything within her was taut, perched on a sharp edge of such intense pleasure, she was afraid to fall.

"So beautiful," he whispered. "I'm going to do this every day."

And then he pinched her nipple and suckled her clit with strong, heady pulls, and she splintered. A wrenching cry tore from her as she hurtled into orgasm, her body shuddering in release.

Beau rode it with her, his tongue stroking every last tremor from her. Then he looked up at her, his eyes like dark jewels, his mouth wet. Dark possession stamped his features, and she trembled because this was the man who'd survived hell. Who spoke so easily of death; who would die for her.

Kill for her.

Beau, at his most basic. And the sight of him made her want to come again.

"Now you're ready," he said.

Wynn reached for him, suddenly desperate to have inside her. Even as the fluttering of her orgasm faded, a new, stronger hunger was surging through her.

He slid up her body, the hair that covered him bristling her skin, the hard muscle that lined his frame pressing her deep into the sheepskin. When he settled between her thighs and his hard cock pressed against the entrance of her body, she arched against him, shaking all over again, perched once more on that steep edge.

"Look at me," he demanded. One of his hands held her thigh pressed wide beneath him. The other gripped her hip.

His eyes glittered wildly.

"More," she told him.

"And you say I'm bossy," he grated and leaned down and suckled her breast.

Then he thrust deep inside of her.

Pain seared through her. She arched with a sharp, startled cry, her nails tearing into his shoulders. The hand at her hip tightened.

"Easy, sweetheart." The hand on her thigh stroked down to the place where they were joined. He rubbed her clit with his thumb, spreading the slick moisture he found there, and a streak of intense pleasure seared through the ache inside of her. A soft moan broke from her.

"Sweet, beautiful girl," he murmured. "You're mine now."

Then he kissed her, deep, slow, leisurely, as if they had all the time in the world. And he stroked her: her clit, her nipples, the gentle swell of her belly.

It was too much and not enough; the discomfort was fading, and she could feel him, hot and hard and huge inside of her, throbbing intensely in the deepest part of her. She arched, her nails digging deep, needing him to—

"All mine," he whispered and pulled out of her slowly.

"Don't go," she protested, but then he thrust back in, hard, and pleasure burst through her like a rocket firing. "*Oh!*"

"Yes," he said and thrust again.

He stroked her clit; suckled her breast. Thrust again. And again. Harder, stronger, deeper.

Faster.

"*Oh*," she whispered, shuddering. "That's..."

"Yes." A harsh sound rumbled in his chest. She rose with him, meeting his next stroke, and the next, and the sharp, wild rise of sensation within her grew. She was climbing again, everything inside of her tight and intent on reaching the peak.

His strokes deepened, pounding harder, pushing her higher.

"More," she demanded.

"As you wish," he murmured and began to thrust with such sharp, hungry force, everything else faded. There was only him.

Them.

She was climbing higher, her nails deep in his skin as she held him. A soft wail broke from her; she found the hard curve of his shoulder and bit him. Hard.

"Fuck," he hissed.

"Please," she panted.

"Not yet."

His thrusts grew deeper, wilder, and Wynn moaned, caught in the maelstrom he wrought. Higher; tighter; so taut she thought she might break. And then another harsh, feral sound broke from him. His mouth touched her ear.

"Now," he said, and Wynn fractured.

Pleasure ripped through her, and she was lost. Her body convulsed in release, but he was still thrusting, harder, deeper, and she cried out soundlessly when another orgasm ripped through her belly. Beau threw back his head and growled as he came, his body trembling wildly as it thrust into hers. Then he collapsed on top of her, shuddering, and Wynn slid her hands into his hair and held him there.

Her heart was beating like the wings of a trapped bird; her breath shuddered in and out of her violently. But every muscle was lax, except for the residual tremors shivering through her.

Holy crap, she thought.

Beau rolled them over, still inside of her, and settled her on top of him. His arms wound tight around her; one of his hands traced her spine long, soothing strokes.

"I love you," he said, and her heart stopped.

Wynn levered herself up against his chest and stared at him.

"I just thought you should know," he said, his eyes stark with the raw honesty that echoed in his voice.

But there was no expectation there, only hope.

And Wynn knew then they were both crazy. Because they'd known each other all of a week. And yet—

"I love you, too," she told him seriously. "Have we lost our minds?"

"Maybe." He rubbed his thumb over her mouth. "But at least we'll go crazy together."

Yes.

"I'm keeping you," he told her roughly.

Her heart fluttered. "Promise?"

He rolled her back over. "Promise."

CHAPTER 32

Wynn had been fully prepared for a very nosy interrogation when Beau brought her home. Between Jenna and the tenants, she understood she was in for some intrusive questions and, knowing her little sister, probably a fair amount of snark as well.

The last thing she expected was the circus they pulled up to.

A news van, a catering truck, a Superior County Sheriff's truck, and half a dozen other vehicles parked haphazardly in her front yard.

"Crap," she muttered, frowning at the small crowd gathered at the side of the house. "So much for sneaking in."

"We're not sneaking anywhere," Beau told her darkly. "We have nothing to hide. Unless you're ashamed of me?"

She leaned over and pressed a lingering kiss to his mouth. "Prickly little pear."

"I'm the fucking *sheriff*." He wound his hand in her hair and kissed her back, hard and possessive.

Wynn broke away and sucked in a breath. She ran a

hand down the padded muscle of his chest, drunk on the freedom to touch him.

Hers, now.

He caught her hand, his green eyes serious.

"I claimed you," he said, and his tone made a shiver ripple down her spine. "There's no going back."

"Duly noted," she told him. "But you don't understand what we're in for."

Some of the tension eased out of him. "We beat a serial killer. I think we can handle a few meddlesome family members."

Wynn smiled slowly at him. She couldn't help it. That he understood her tenants *were* family made her forgive the scowl he wore. He'd been scowling since they'd climbed into the truck at his cabin.

Reality, she thought. *Back to the real world.* And no matter their deal, he was worried that she would suddenly freak out and run. Even though *he'd* been the one who'd tried to quit.

Silly man.

She wasn't going anywhere. Beau Greystone was the one she wanted, every snarly, brooding, moody inch of him.

God help her.

"If you say so," she murmured and kissed him again. "Tinman."

His response was instant and white-hot. The hold on her hair tightened; his tongue stroked into her mouth. Wet and open and hungry, as if he was still inside of her.

He'd woken her with a kiss like that. And then he'd woken the rest of her, his touch sly and deft and far too skilled. *Such intense focus.*

She didn't think she'd ever get enough.

"Think they'd notice if we just stay in the truck?" His

hand cupped her breast. "We can climb in the back. Plenty of room."

He rubbed her nipple, and Wynn hissed in a breath.

"If this truck starts a-rockin', they'll definitely come a-knockin'," she gasped and arched into his touch.

A ragged laugh escaped him, rough and deep; a sound so rare and captivating, her heart squeezed hard.

A handful of smiles. *A laugh*.

He was getting there.

"Goddamn it," he whispered and slid his hands away.

A pang echoed through her at the loss. But then he climbed from the truck, walked around, opened her door, and offered her his hand.

"Let's get this over with," he said, his eyes lidded, pure green fire. "We have sweet love to make."

She snickered. "Cornball."

"You won't say that when I'm inside you."

He pulled her from the truck. The rain had finally ceased, and the sun was warm and bright in the morning sky as they made their way to the front porch. Sean Evers stood next to the front door, talking to a sleek blond in a crisp lavender pantsuit and six-inch heels. He looked up as they approached.

"Sheriff," he said, his gaze on Beau. Then he looked at Wynn. Color rushed into his cheeks. "Wynn."

She eyed him darkly. They hadn't had a chance to talk after he'd bashed Harry Baker's brains in with a shovel, and it had been Winston Reynolds, Beau's new/old deputy who'd told her Sean was, in fact, Ian Long, the twin brother of the Stick Man's first victim, Bridget. The disclosure had annoyed the crap out of her.

Not because she didn't understand perfectly *why* he'd hunted the Stick Man. She would have tracked that bastard to the ends of the earth if he'd taken Jenna. It was the fact that Sean hadn't disclosed his true identity that annoyed her —an unnecessary lie, and worse, one perpetrated by someone with whom she was sharing her home. But then she'd imagined hunting her sister's killer, never resting until he was caught. How much sacrifice it must have taken; how much pain must have driven him.

And she'd let it go. Still, he was going to hear about it.

"You," she said, her eyes narrowing on him, "have some explaining to do."

He had the grace to flush. The blond he was talking to looked at Wynn in speculation.

"I know," he said quietly. "Can it wait?" He nodded at the blond. "Channel 8 wants to interview me."

Wynn arched a brow. Beau slid his arm around her and pulled her into his side.

"He did save our bacon," he murmured into her ear. "You should cut him some slack."

She leaned into his embrace. "I'm charging him double."

Velma burst unexpectedly through the front door; she skidded to a halt on the porch when she saw them. "Thank God you're here! They're out of control!"

And so it begins, Wynn thought. "What now?"

Velma pointed toward the house. "It's like watching a tornado tear apart a town! Hurry!"

"As sure as the sun sets in the west," Beau murmured.

"Told you so," Wynn replied silkily.

They climbed the porch steps and headed toward the front door.

"Hurry," Velma demanded again. She wore a billowing, bright blue tunic and silky pants; streaks of dark, emerald green had joined the pink highlights in her hair. She looked worried, her mouth tight, her hands wringing themselves together.

Wynn frowned. Velma rarely lost her cool. "Who's out of control?"

"Tristan and Sasha!"

Wynn halted and stared at her. "Tristan and Sasha?"

"I thought it would be fine!" Velma slapped her palm against her forehead. "I arranged for Tristan to interview Earl this morning, but apparently no one bothered to tell Sasha, and she was prepping him to talk with the lady from Channel 8 when Tristan arrived and..."

And all Hades broke loose.

"Crap," Wynn said.

"Quite," Velma agreed. She rubbed at her temples. "I thought perhaps they could get past whatever it was that happened, but...apparently not."

Wynn looked up at Beau. He stood beside her, his hand possessive on her hip, his warm, hard body pressed against hers.

"Do you know what happened?" she asked quietly.

"No." He shook his head. "Not the details."

Did no one know?

How bad could it be, if neither Sasha nor Tristan had never told anyone...not even family?

Wynn wasn't sure she wanted to know the answer to that question.

The sound of raised voices floated toward them. Velma sighed fatalistically and disappeared back into the house. They moved to follow, but Jenna surged through the door and planted herself in their path.

"You should get a load of *that*." She jabbed her thumb toward the door. "Holy sexual tension!"

Beau shook his head, a hint of a smile touching his mouth. "Jenna."

"Just saying," she said and shrugged. She looked at Wynn; then at Beau. A broad smile broke across her face. "Right *on*! I knew it!"

She threw her arms around Beau and hugged him. Surprise flitted across his face as he hesitantly hugged her back, and Wynn's throat suddenly tightened.

They needed each other.

Something she hadn't realized until that moment. That not only did she need Beau—Jenna did, too. An example of what a good, strong man should be. His advice; his protection; even his discipline. And Beau needed Jenna just as much: her youth, her resilience. That endless appetite for life.

"Yes!" Jenna crowed. She pulled back, grinning, her eyes glinting in the sunlight. "Earl owes me ten bucks."

Wynn blinked at her. "You made a bet?"

"I'm not freaking blind." Color touched her sister's cheeks. "It was a sure thing."

"You're giving me half," Wynn told her.

The voices inside the house suddenly grew louder.

"We'd better get in there," Beau muttered. The hand at her hip tightened.

"I wouldn't," offered another voice. They turned to see Garrett strolling across the porch toward them. "I'd let that fire burn out."

"At this rate, it's going to torch the whole house," Jenna retorted, rolling her eyes.

"Harpy," Garrett replied without heat.

"FBI Ken." She smiled sweetly. "Tell me, do you come with a gun and badge, or do they cost extra?"

Another rare laugh broke from Beau.

Two in one morning.

"Jenna," Wynn said. "Manners."

Her sister snorted. "This from you?"

Winston Reynolds suddenly rounded the corner of the house. He strode toward them, clad in a pair of ragged jeans and a *Def Leppard* shirt. "Hey, Chief. The Governor called this mornin'. Said he'll be in town on Wednesday and wants to meet with the team that took down the Stick Man. You got somethin' I can borrow to wear?"

Beau's brows lifted. "How do you feel about a tropical vibe?"

Something inside of Wynn went still. She leaned into him. "You don't have to."

She didn't expect him to give Marie away. Not his shirts or his watch, or anything else. First, she wasn't a wasteful person, and if it was useful, she kept it. Second, their relationship existed beyond and outside of what he'd had with Marie.

It was either strong enough to make it, or it wasn't.

Beau's hand squeezed her hip. His breath tickled her ear. "Don't worry, I'll keep the ugliest ones for myself."

Then he leaned down and kissed her, a hard, possessive stamp of reassurance.

"PDA alert," Jenna sang.

A crash sounded; the clamor within the house grew to rock concert proportions.

Beau nuzzled Wynn's temple. "Maybe they'll kiss and make up."

"And maybe they'll burn down my house," she retorted.

He sighed and stepped forward to open the door. He held it open for her—something that kept startling her, his penchant for opening doors. They stepped inside, and

Beowulf immediately charged toward them, barking noisily. Wynn leaned down and picked up him.

"Hi, sweetness," she murmured and kissed his head. "What's wrong with these crazy people?"

Beau rubbed the pup's ears, and the dog squirmed and grunted and tried to get closer. Sunlight slanted in through the door, turning Beau's eyes into dark, glinting emeralds. His mouth was relaxed, the lines that marked his face not so deep, and although he was limping slightly, the tension that normally clung to him was conspicuously absent.

"This is how it's going to be, you know," she said, studying him. "Barely controlled chaos with intermittent periods of anarchy."

He only snorted. "Sweetheart, I've been to war."

"I'm just saying: *anarchy*."

His gaze met hers. "As long as we're together."

Cornball. Still, a tremor moved through her. What she felt for this man scared the bejesus out of her.

"I'm holding you to that," she told him seriously.

"You'd better," he murmured. His eyes fell to her mouth.

A spike of sharp, piercing need stabbed through her. She gripped his shirt and pulled him toward her.

Velma appeared in the kitchen doorway. "There you are. What took you so long? You have to put an end to this!"

Beau growled softly. Wynn pressed a lingering kiss against his mouth and reluctantly let him go. Then she put Beowulf down and walked into the kitchen.

All of her tenants were seated at the table. Earl was freshly shaven and clad in a pair of new overalls and a pressed blue shirt; he looked excited. Esme sat beside him, sipping a cup of tea. Griff nibbled at a piece of toast on her other side, unconcerned with the chaos around him. Eloise had her hand wrapped around the wooden cross she wore, and Ethel, who sat beside her with a look of mystified fascination on her face, clutched the cape she was crocheting for Beau.

Velma leaned against the stove, rubbing her forehead. "Complete and utter *lunacy*."

Sasha stood at one end of the table, clad in a sharp black pantsuit, the picture of sleek professionalism. Her arms were crossed beneath her breasts, and her face was so red, Wynn was surprised she hadn't passed out.

Tristan James stood at the other end, his own handsome face hard and tight, a look of such intensity stamped across his features that Wynn hesitated.

They were glaring at each other with raw ferocity, seemingly oblivious to the people who sat avidly watching the train wreck of their reunion.

"Hi," she said into the brief moment of silence that had fallen upon her entrance.

She felt Beau come to a halt behind her. His hands found her hips. "Is there popcorn?"

Velma groaned.

Tristan glared at Beau, his eyes as black as night. "Did you know?"

His voice was harsh. Behind Wynn, Beau stilled.

"Not until a couple of days ago," he replied mildly.

"Because it matters?" Sasha mocked darkly.

Tristan looked at her, and something indecipherable crossed his face. "Because I would have come sooner."

A disbelieving laugh broke from her, and Earl raised a hand and patted her arm.

"It's gonna be okay," he told her in a conciliatory tone. "Tristan's gonna help."

A harsh snort. Tristan's face darkened.

"He's gonna interview me," Earl continued earnestly. "And I can get the word out about the new foundation, and how we're gonna help people."

Sasha stared at Earl without speaking. Wynn wanted to go to her friend and hug her. Sasha hadn't looked that devastated since the day both of her parents died in a drunk driving accident.

"I'm sorry," Velma said into Sasha's silence. "I didn't realize..."

"I just wish you'd warned me," Sasha muttered and rubbed her forehead. "We could have avoided all of this...unpleasantness."

"Unpleasantness?" Tristan echoed, a soft, dangerous rasp that made Wynn take an involuntary step toward them.

Beau's hold on her tightened.

"Let them work it out," he said into her ear.

"She's standing beside the knife block," Wynn pointed out.

A kiss pressed against her temple. "Let them be. It's long past time."

Well, that was true enough. Still—

"*You* should have told me," Tristan grated, his dark gaze hard on Sasha. "I would have—"

"Would have *what*?" she snarled. She shook her head sharply and snapped her mouth shut. "It doesn't matter."

"The hell it doesn't! If I had known—"

"It doesn't matter!" she snapped a second time.

"Oh, it fucking matters," Tristan growled.

"No, it doesn't!" she hissed. "Not then, not now. Not ever."

"It changes everything!"

"It changes nothing!"

They were yelling again, unmindful of those watching. Tears burned in Sasha's gaze; her cheeks were bright with angry color. She would be appalled at the loss of control. Her pride was all that had held her together for too long.

Seeing it crumble was painful.

Wynn turned and looked at Beau's cousin.

She only knew Tristan James from afar, having watched his and Sasha's relationship from the periphery, too busy taking care of Fran and Jenna and the farm to pay much attention. But now she studied him, taking in his dark, swarthy features and olive-toned skin. His hard mouth and onyx eyes, hair the color of inky black coal.

She could see Beau in him, in that strong profile and stubborn jaw. But his dark gray suit was hand made and custom-tailored, the fabric so exquisite Esme was undoubtedly drooling. His shoes were polished patent leather; the gleaming platinum timepiece on his wrist made Beau's Rolex look like a *Snoopy* watch.

He looked suave and elegant and expensive—except for the flinty, dark shadow cast over his features. That looked like Beau, too.

Experience and pain and death.

Which Sasha had born her fair share of, as well.

More than.

So Wynn cleared her throat and said, "Tristan, please go outside. Earl will be out in a minute."

He glowered at her, argument stamped across his face. She watched him glance over her shoulder at Beau and bite back the words.

"Fine," he bit out and stormed toward the back door. He halted before he went through, though, and sent Sasha a dark look of angry promise. "But this isn't over."

He disappeared before she could respond. The door slammed violently behind him.

"Well," Velma said into the silence that followed. "That was a fine mess."

Sasha looked around and blinked as if just noticing her audience. "Oh. That wasn't very professional of me, wasn't it?"

She looked like she'd been hit by a two-by-four.

"Talk to her," Beau murmured into Wynn's ear. "I'll get him."

She turned to meet that glinting green gaze.

"I really do love you," she told him.

"I know." He kissed her. "I love you, too." A sudden, devious smile curved his mouth. "I think we should make them our best man and maid of honor. They can duke it out at the alter."

She blinked.

Had he just suggested—

He kissed her again, hard, and walked out the back door after his cousin.

—a wedding?

"I need a drink," Sasha said.

A ring; a ceremony. *Vows.*

"Get in line," Wynn told her.

CHAPTER 33

Beau watched his cousin pace in front of the makeshift studio someone had set up in Wynn's orchard. Two plush, stuffed chairs sat beneath one of the apple trees, turned slightly toward each other—it looked cozy and personal as if people held intimate talks beneath fruit trees on a regular basis. Thick green leaves and branches heavy with fruit bobbed in the breeze above them, and Beau wondered what the odds were, that someone would be brained by a falling Braeburn before the day was through.

Probably pretty good.

The thought made him smile, something he caught himself doing more and more of.

But it was probably just the words Wynn had left him with.

I really do love you.

Solemn gray eyes, her tone unmistakably serious.

Beau hadn't intended to mention marriage—not yet. He was ready, but he had no idea how she felt about it. He'd been married; he understood what it meant. But she didn't.

And tying herself to a bad-tempered, disabled lawman might not be high on her list of priorities.

That didn't mean he was going to let her get away. But he'd planned to give her some time to grow accustomed to the idea, first.

So much for that.

He couldn't say he was sorry. Let her chew on it for a while.

Then he'd find her a ring.

"You're an asshole," Tristan muttered, stomping across the thick bed of clover that covered the orchard. His hands were fisted; a scowl twisted his mouth.

He looked like he wanted to beat someone bloody. Beau knew—because he'd been the recipient of that look less than six months ago.

"I didn't know she was here," Beau told him. "Not until two days ago. Scout's honor."

A dark look. "You should have called me."

"Sorry. I got distracted."

Tristan halted and looked shamefaced. "Christ. I'm an asshole, too."

Beau laughed, and Tristan stared at him.

"What?" Beau asked him.

"I thought I'd never hear that sound again," his cousin said.

Beau rubbed at the back of his neck and sighed. "I suppose I have you to thank for that."

"No. I might have beat your ass back into reality, but I can't take credit for anything else."

"All the same," Beau told him. "I appreciate what you did. I never did say thank you."

"No, you didn't. I believe the words you used were 'fuck off and die, you pussy piece of shit.'"

A flush touched Beau's cheeks. "That might be true."

Tristan shook his head, turned, and began again to pace. "I wasn't prepared for this."

Beau wasn't without sympathy. "We never are."

He adjusted his stance and rubbed his leg. People were gathered at the end of the house, Garrett, Winston, and several others he recognized. Another small group was a little closer, the Channel 8 crew getting ready to start filming. Overhead, the sun was hot; the scent of the sheep and the trees and lush green grass filled his nostrils.

Home, he thought. And the same piercing joy that had lit through him at the sight of Wynn on his front porch last night fired through him.

He wasn't certain what he'd done to deserve it. Nothing he could see. He'd managed to fuck up a good number of things over the last few years, so this...this just didn't make any damn sense.

But hell if he was going to argue.

"What's the problem?" he asked his cousin curiously. "You've loved her since you were a kid."

Tristan only continued to pace.

"Tris."

A sharp shake of his head.

"It's not that hard," Beau told him, and then thought of how hard he'd made it—for himself, for Wynn—and amended, "You just need to get out of your own way."

Tristan halted. He looked up at the sky. "I thought it was fucking impossible."

His words were edged with disbelief; Beau could relate.

"I've come to realize nothing's impossible." He rubbed a hand down his face. "What happened to Marie, that was my fault." He held up a hand when Tristan would have argued. "I know where my responsibilities lie. But she's gone. And

I'm still here." He shrugged. "It's not that I think I deserve it; it's that I'm too goddamn selfish not to take it."

"You do deserve it," Tristan said harshly. "You've paid your dues."

Beau knew that wasn't true, but didn't argue. "And you? Are you done paying?"

"How? It's the only fucking thing I know."

Beau said nothing. When he'd left for boot camp, Tristan and Sasha had been thick as thieves. Then Velma had written that they were done, but she didn't know why, and when he'd reached out, his cousin had stonewalled him. So Beau let it go.

But it'd clearly been worse than he realized. Tristan was a master at concealing his thoughts and feelings; perception was something he'd always been skilled at manipulating, but the clash with Sasha had knocked him on his ass.

And it showed.

"What the hell happened between you two?" Beau asked him.

Tristan's mouth twisted. "We can't all find true love, brother."

Beau started when he realized his cousin was talking about *him*. And he understood in that instant how lucky he'd been. First with Marie; then with Wynn. He'd found love—real love—more than once.

And it had saved him both times.

The realization humbled him deeply. He looked around Wynn's happy, healthy farm and felt his heart beat with sudden, breath-stealing force.

Whatever power existed in the universe, it had given him a second chance.

And it was up to him what he did with it. He hadn't truly appreciated the choice he'd made: to stop running and hold firm, to stake a claim, make a home, and do everything he had to in order to hold on to it.

Not until that moment.

"I almost let her go," he said. "Convinced myself she'd be better off. But that's a load of horseshit. I wanted it to be easy, and it wasn't. I got scared."

Tristan looked at him sharply.

"Just like you're scared. I can see it. And there's no judgment here. I know exactly where you are. You just have to ask yourself what's worse: life with her, or life without her?"

Tristan said nothing.

A hawk cried out, followed by the soft bray of the donkeys. Inside the house, Beowulf was barking, and the wind chime that hung beside the back door sounded softly.

"You already know what life's like without her," Beau pointed out softly. "You really think it isn't worth trying to find out what it'd be like with her?"

His cousin shook his head sharply, his black gaze turbulent.

"Sometimes," Beau told him, "you just have to jump."

"Easy for you to say."

"No. Nothing about this has been easy. And most of that was my fault."

Wynn stepped out the back door and hovered on the porch, watching them.

Beau lifted a hand, astounded all over again at what he'd somehow ended up with. The ache in his chest grew when she sat down on the back step to wait for him.

"I don't even know where to start," his cousin muttered. "Everything is just so fucked up."

Beau reached out to clasp him on the shoulder. "Someone smart once told me there are no promises. No guarantees, no forever. Just here and now. I'd suggest you start there."

For a long, silent moment Tristan just stared at him.

"What if it doesn't work?" he wanted to know, and Beau heard everything he didn't say.

All of the same dark, fearful words that'd been hammering at him since the day he'd first laid eyes on Wynn Owens. The ones that nearly made him quit before he'd even left the gate.

"Then it doesn't," he said and shrugged. "But at least you tried."

A harsh laugh broke from his cousin. "Jesus. You sound like Old Man Time."

"Well, I *am* your elder."

"Two years doesn't count."

"It did when you wanted beer."

A reluctant smile. "Dickhead."

"Yeah, but I'm your dickhead."

"Jesus," Tristan repeated. "I'm so fucked."

Beau patted his shoulder consolingly. "Welcome to the club, brother." Then he turned again to look at Wynn, who smiled at him. "Are we done here?"

Tristan followed his gaze. "She's waiting for you."

"She is," he agreed, still more than a little stunned by that fact.

Tristan looked at him, his dark gaze unreadable. "You're happy."

"No one's more surprised than me," Beau told him quietly.

Silence stretched between them. The hawk cried again, a sweet, piercing sound that echoed through the trees.

"It gives me hope," his cousin said finally.

Which Beau found incredibly surreal. Him, giving anyone hope.

"Mr. James!" They glanced up to see the blond from Channel 8 making her way gingerly across the uneven ground in her stilettos. "Are you ready to begin?"

Tristan sighed wearily.

"Guess it's hard being somebody," Beau murmured. "Poor little fella."

Tristan punched him in the arm. "Don't you have somewhere else to be?"

"I do. Makin' sweet love to my woman."

"For fuck's sake." Tristan scowled at him. "You're ruined."

A laugh welled in Beau's chest and broke into the air just as the blond reached them.

"I hope so," he told his cousin.

Then he turned and walked away, toward his future.

The End

******

Thank you for reading! If you enjoyed *Hail Mary*, please consider leaving a review. Reviews are critical for the success of independently published works.

Keep reading for a Sneak Peek at *Evolution: Awakening*.

EVOLUTION AWAKENING
BOOK ONE OF THE EVOLUTION SERIES

When Ash Kyndal inherits her Uncle Charlie's Private Investigation firm, she wants nothing more than an out. Because how could anyone think putting her in charge of anything is a good idea?

But Charlie saved her once, and Ash owes him. Big time. So in spite of her reluctance—and the mysterious, taciturn Russian who's abruptly materialized on her doorstep, intent on repaying a debt to a dead man—Ash dives in.

Because seriously. How hard can it be?

Two missing clients, half a dozen men in black, and one crazy, utopian conspiracy designed to alter the very fabric of humanity later, Ash has her answer: crazy hard. And now that she's found herself on the front lines of an unexpected, vicious battle over the fate of the human race, she has a choice to make: stay and fight, or run like hell. Because the clock is ticking.

And war is coming.

A dark romantic suspense thriller with a splash of conspiracy and captivating characters you won't forget.

★★★★★

"A suspenseful tale I could NOT put down."

★★★★★

"Stayed up too late reading this! Can't wait for the rest!"

★★★★★

"Incredible world building."

EVOLUTION: AWAKENING
CHAPTER ONE

TUESDAY
Las Vegas, Nevada

"You tell me what I want to know...or she's *dead*."

The breath accompanying those words exuded an aroma of red onion, spicy brown mustard, and pastrami on rye, which somewhat diminished their menace.

Still, Ruslan thought the Glock 45 pressed against his lapel looked serviceable enough. And the woman whose image was reflected on the laptop across from him—a woman who'd been tied to a wooden chair with coarse, cheap rope—also had a 9mm SIG pointed at her head, so the threat, while rather pungent, was quite real.

"You hear me?"

The short, stocky bald man whose Glock was creasing Ruslan's suit stood less than three inches away, so Ruslan assumed the answer was obvious. He was not, after all, deaf, something he also presumed the man would know.

Should know. If he was competent.

But competence was a rare and vanishing skill. The

ability and willingness to pull a trigger had somehow eclipsed intelligence, ingenuity, and dedicated expertise. No one took any pride anymore.

"I *mean* it, man. Dead!"

A gloved hand shot out and backhanded the woman on the screen; her head snapped back, and the chair she sat on slid across the floor. Ruslan watched dispassionately, noting the blood that trickled from the corner of her mouth, the swelling that had begun to bloat the line of her cheekbone.

The murder that glinted in her eye.

Competence. Theirs was about to be tested.

"You tell me where the kid is," the bald man snarled, "and we'll let your girl go."

An empty promise. In addition to the bald man, there were two others, men with faces of stone and weapons beneath their coats. Any talk of walking away was fantasy. But no matter. There would be no "telling." No letting anyone go. The Firm had been hired to protect "the kid," and that's what Ruslan would do.

No matter the threat. Or the cost.

"*You tell me.*"

"You're a frickin' moron!" Butch heckled from where he sat beside Ruslan, his body slumped against the plastic ties that secured him to a metal chair. The scent of day-old vodka oozed from his pores. "Ash ain't nobody's *girl*!"

"Shut it," ordered the bald man. "Worthless piece of drunk shit."

Butch only chortled. He was not, Ruslan suspected, as drunk as he appeared. But in the few weeks he'd known Butch Masters, the man had been inebriated at least sixty percent of the time, so it was difficult to be certain. That Butch was part of this at all only highlighted the fact that the men they faced hadn't done their homework.

"You need more incentive?" The bald man glared at Ruslan; Ruslan stared impassively back. "We can do that."

A fist slammed into the woman's face; this time the front legs of the chair lifted into the air before slamming back down. She shook her head; blood poured from her nose. She turned and spat at someone Ruslan couldn't see.

"How many of those you think she can take?" The Glock dug into Ruslan's suit. "Should we find out?"

The bald man was looking for a visceral response, but Ruslan was unable to oblige him. He rarely felt fear or anger; he rarely felt anything at all. And he never responded to threats. That he sat tied to a chair, watching his current employer get the hell beat out of her did not change that unalterable fact.

You are broken. He knew; he'd been told. The emotion that contaminated the world around him left him wholly untouched. A slab of stone without fault; no pores, no cracks, no crevices. There had been nothing in his life to fracture the stone—not torture, not death, not even the gore and devastation of war. And so this—while unexpected and tiresome—had little chance of doing anything more than throwing a monkey wrench into his day.

Incompetent idiots.

They had chosen Butch, who wasn't trusted. And they'd chosen him, who was capable of anything.

They deserved what they were going to get.

"You're a cold bastard," the bald man muttered, eyeing him with the same dawning frustration people inevitably fell into when they realized he wasn't human. At least, not human like they were. "You don't give a shit about her, do you?"

Another ignorant assumption, that because he didn't

feel, he didn't care. Most days, Ruslan was glad he wasn't like the rest of them.

"You're just gonna sit there and watch them beat her to death, aren't you?"

Butch was side-eyeing him as if wondering the same thing, but Ruslan only arched a brow. "What makes you think I know where the child is?"

The bald man shot a look at Butch, who shifted in his seat, his cheeks filling with color.

"Ah," Ruslan said. "I see."

When he'd swum to consciousness and found himself tied to a chair in a vacant warehouse, his head throbbing, he wondered how he'd been so easily retrieved. He was a very careful man.

Apparently Butch wasn't as ineffectual as he appeared. At least, not when it came to saving his own skin.

"You know exactly where she is," the bald man insisted. "And you're gonna tell us—or your girl can die one blow at a time."

An ugly death and one Ruslan didn't care to witness. Contrary to the ignorance of the man before him—and the one beside him—he did happen to care whether Ashling Kyndal lived or died. Very much.

First, she was the niece of a man who'd once done him a life-altering kindness, the kind of favor one couldn't possibly repay; a man Ruslan had crossed three continents to help, only to arrive too late. That regrettable fact only served to make walking away from her—and his unpaid debt—an impossibility. Which meant that Ashling was, for the present time, Ruslan's responsibility. And Ruslan took his responsibilities very seriously.

Second, quite inexplicably, he'd grown to like her. She was...unique. Not like he was unique, but her differences intrigued him. Which was rare enough, and extraordinary enough, that he would do whatever necessary to protect it.

To protect her.

So he flexed his hands, which were banded together behind his back with thick plastic ties, and dislocated both of his thumbs.

"Fuck you!" Butch made a sad show of struggling against his restraints. "Asshole!"

"I can make them stop," the bald man offered in a reasonable tone. "All you gotta do is tell me where the kid is. Simple. Otherwise..."

"I do not know where the girl is being kept," Ruslan told him. "But I can convince Ashling to disclose the child's location."

His hands were almost free, and anticipation licked through him, a finite thread of adrenaline that wove through his nerve endings like the finest of live wires. A small thing; one of the few he ever felt.

Hungry. For blood, for violence. And only partially because a woman he'd come to know and appreciate was battered and bleeding and beyond his immediate reach. The darkness that lived within him needed little to whet its appetite. It was a feral, self-serving, and pitiless thing. Always yearning for more.

Keeping it leashed took constant vigilance. But sometimes, Ruslan set it free. Sometimes he let it feed.

Today would be such a day.

It was fortunate that the large, empty warehouse they sat in appeared to be abandoned. Graffiti covered the walls; broken pallets lay scattered atop a badly cracked and crumbling concrete floor. The windows were cloudy. Most were broken, revealing slender beams of sunlight that speared higher as the sun began to sink into the western sky. Occasionally the sound of sirens serenaded them.

Somewhere that was nowhere, and death would go unnoticed.

"Why would you do that?" the bald man wanted to know, clearly skeptical.

"I value my life," Ruslan replied flatly. "It is worth more to me than a child I do not know."

Butch made a sound of protest, but the bald man narrowed his gaze in consideration. "What makes you think she'll listen?"

"She trusts me."

Which was not entirely true. But the man he faced didn't know that. Butch, however, eyed him again. Dubiously.

"You're making this harder than it has to be." The Glock tapped his shoulder. "Just give up the kid, and this all ends."

Ruslan only waited. People, as a rule, lacked patience; he, however, had an infinite supply. It took approximately seven seconds for the bald man to swear, pull a smartphone from his pocket, and dial.

"It's me," he snarled into the expensive technology. He engaged the speakerphone and thrust it toward Ruslan. "Put her on."

The laptop reflected a gloved hand shoving a matching smartphone beneath Ash's nose. She bared her teeth and looked into the camera of the laptop, meeting Ruslan's gaze.

"You are being difficult," he said before she could speak.

"It's a special skill," she retorted. "What about you?"

"Indeed," he confirmed.

"Good." Her gaze touched Butch, who squirmed and blushed and fought his plastic ties. "And him?"

"I didn't tell them shit!" he yelled.

Ruslan only arched a brow.

"Do you have this?" Ash asked.

Her tone was calm, but where her hands were tied to the chair, they gripped the seat with knuckles pressed white against her skin. She wore only a thin black tank top and boy shorts; her white-blond hair hung in choppy waves just past her chin and was streaked crimson with blood. She wasn't in the warehouse that he and Butch occupied. A white couch sat behind her, a small wooden end table and lamp on one end, a tall, blooming begonia on the other. Behind her, a large framed print hung against a pale blue wall, and in its reflection, Ruslan could see three distinct shapes.

Men.

"Yes," he said.

"You're sure?" she pressed, and he watched as she tensed, which delineated the long, slender rope of muscle that lined her shoulders and arms. Her feet were planted against the floor, her thighs sleek and still. She was strong, he suddenly realized. Physically. Mentally. More so than he'd understood.

And she was preparing to act.

Another lash of adrenaline whipped through him. Her eyes were a startling, brilliant shade of bright blue-green, reminiscent of the Caribbean sea; they held his, unwavering and hard.

"Yes," he repeated. "You?"

"What the hell is this?" the bald man interjected furiously. "You said—"

"I'm fucking furious," she replied.

"You're gonna tell us where that goddamn kid is right now!" the bald man gritted. "Or we're gonna—"

He didn't get the chance to finish.

Ash leaped straight up, flipped sideways, and slammed into the floor, smashing the chair she'd been tied to into pieces.

She rolled, swept out her legs, and a large form crashed to the floor next to her. Then she jack-knifed to her feet and kicked the man squarely in the solar plexus; the sound of bone cracking over the speakerphone was like a bat knocking one out of the park.

Another dark shape swarmed toward her, and she slid out of reach, the movement so fluid, she almost blurred. Her heel shot out and connected with the side of his knee. He screamed and fell. A third man closed in, gun in hand.

Instead of running, she grinned, a gruesome, bloody slash, and rushed toward him. Ruslan absorbed her ferocity, impressed. And oddly aroused.

"Bitch!" the man swore, but before he could fire his weapon, she ran nimbly up his leg and smashed her forehead into his face. He stumbled back and hit the table that held the laptop, which tumbled sideways to the floor. Ruslan craned his head, but he couldn't see, and there was another shout and then—*boom!*—the gun firing—and then—

Darkness.

He stared at the screen; adrenaline fountained in his veins.

"Shit," Butch cried. "Shit!"

"Goddamn it," hissed the bald man.

And Ruslan erupted from his seat.

ALSO BY HOPE ANIKA

THE GETAWAY (Book One of The Getaway Series)
AEQUITAS (Book Two of The Getaway Series)
IN PLAIN SIGHT
evolution: AWAKENING (Book One of The Evolution Series)
THE BEQUEST (Book One of The Guardians Series)
BLINDSIDED (Book Two of The Guardians Series)
HALLOWED GROUND (Book Three of The Guardians Series)

ABOUT THE AUTHOR

A novelist who lives in the Greater Yellowstone area, Hope Anika writes romantic suspense novels with strong female heroines and intense male leads. Her books have been finalists for the Romance Writers of America's *Vivian Award* and the *Daphne du Maurier Award for Excellence in Mystery and Suspense.*

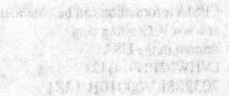

CPSIA information can be obtained
at www.ICGtesting.com
Printed in the USA
LVHW021040141121
703288LV00010B/1384

9 781736 255308